Fortune's Fool

PHAZE

Cincinnati, Ohio

Fortune's Fool

a collection of erotic romance by

BIANCA D'ARC
EVA GALE
CASSIDY KENT
SELAH MARCH

A Phaze Production

Cincinnati, Ohio

Phaze Books
6470A Glenway Avenue, #109
Cincinnati, OH 45211-5222
Phaze is an imprint of Mundania Press, LLC.
To order additional copies of this book, contact:

books@phaze.com
www.Phaze.com

Cover art © 2007,Jax Crane
Edited by Kathryn Lively

Trade Paperback ISBN-13: 978-1-59426-855-7
Trade Paperback ISBN-10: 1-59426-855-X

First Print Edition – December, 2007
Printed in the United States of America
10 9 8 7 6 5 4 3 2 1

Arcana: King of Swords

Bianca D'Arc

Also by Bianca D'Arc

Sons of Amber: Ezekiel
Sons of Amber: Michael

Dedication

To those who've taught me to think beyond. Most especially my Dad, who started me watching *Star Trek* when I was just a little kid and shares my love of science fiction to this day.

Prologue

The Rabbit Hole was well known on the civilian space station for its private booths and intimate atmosphere. The new owner of the small tavern was still, to some extent, an unknown quantity, but seemed a solid enough man according to local gossip. Ex-soldier, was the rumor. David knew Alex would be amused by what the grapevine had to say about him, though they didn't know the half of it.

Scoping the area out of habit, Dave noted the wide hall in front of the tavern was very near the mechanical parts of the station, which were off-limits to everyone but specialized workers. Alex must get a lot of traffic when the shifts changed, being on the edges of the civ area and right near the mech section. Good placement for a business like his.

Dave entered The Rabbit Hole and was immediately assaulted by dim light and the not-unpleasant scent of premium alcohol. It was the perfect atmosphere for a relaxing drink with friends. The bar was cozy and welcoming.

As his eyes quickly adjusted—a gift of his genetic Enhancement—Dave saw the man behind the bar. Alex spotted him and waved him over using the hand signals all soldiers knew. Several heads turned and Dave recognized the look of the men sitting around the bar, if not their individual faces. Soldiers. Like him.

For the first time in weeks, Dave felt at home.

Chapter One

Adele Senna re-read the address on the comm from her Aunt Della. The message had come from a small tavern near the mech section of the station, called The Rabbit Hole. Adele was new to Madhatter Station and had reserved living space on the other side of one of the giant rings. She hadn't ventured too close to the core yet, but was learning her way around as she sought out her beloved aunt.

The Rabbit Hole looked nice from the outside. Not upscale, but not a dive either, which was a relief. Aunt Della wasn't known for her judgment and was only a decade or so older than Adele, being her mother's youngest sister. With normal human lifespans now reaching well past the century mark, Aunt Della was still considered a bit flighty by the rest of her large family, but Adele loved her Bohemian ways.

A brilliant woman, gifted with a strong ability to see the future, her aunt failed to display much common sense. Or, at least, it seemed that way. Ultimately, her odd actions always had some purpose, but only in retrospect.

Adele wondered what Aunt Della was up to, setting up shop as a dealer and reader of cards for patrons of this middle-class tavern. She must have some reason, but Adele was hard-pressed to understand it, even though she had—at times—seen glimpses of the future, just like her aunt.

The psychic gift ran in the family. As far back as they could trace, the women of her family had been blessed—or perhaps cursed, depending on your outlook—with varying degrees of foresight. Aunt Della was truly gifted, but she insisted Adele hadn't yet grown fully into her power. Adele wasn't sure she wanted to. The few flashes of the future she'd received to date had scared the bejeezus out of her. She didn't know how her aunt dealt with it day to day.

Adele pushed through the portal and waited a moment for her eyes to adjust to the gloom inside. What she could see of the place was clean and well kept. The atmosphere was dark, quiet, and relaxing rather than sinister, as she'd half expected. She saw a couple of big men at the bar as her eyes adjusted slowly, scanning the room for her aunt. The place was set up with small private booths and one long bar area where the men were clustered. Soldiers, they had to be, though they were all in civ clothing. On leave or perhaps retirees, she guessed, and the bartender was built on the same grand scale. Soldiers were just bigger than regular human males. It had something to do with their diet and training, she knew, but other than that, she hadn't paid much attention.

Unlike many civilians, Adele had no real opinion of soldiers. Oh, she appreciated the sacrifices they made trying to keep the Milky Way Galaxy safe from the jit'suku threat, but she'd never really had any dealings with them on a personal basis. She knew many civ men discriminated against them—probably because they felt small by comparison.

She'd seen soldiers here and there throughout her travels, and they were all huge and rather intimidating. She supposed a civilian male would feel a little threatened by their towering height and imposing brawn, but she felt somehow comforted by their large, protective presence. Surely, if men such as these were fighting the jit'suku out on the rim, the rest of humanity would always be safe. They inspired that kind of confidence with their silent, somewhat menacing ways.

Adele swept the room once again but didn't see her aunt, so she decided to brave the quiet crowd at the bar to ask. She walked to an open space, feeling enclosed by the heat of the big men sitting on either side of her, but she refused to acknowledge the sort of tingly reaction that skittered through her body. It wasn't fear exactly, but it was definitely something that surprised her.

"Pardon me," she said in a voice that carried to the bartender. All eyes turned to her and she found herself the unexpected center of attention. "Can you tell me if Della Senna is here? I understand she's dealing here now."

The bartender slung a towel over his shoulder and walked toward her with a rolling gait that oozed sex appeal. She'd never been this close to a soldier, much less half a dozen of them, and each and every one solidly built, and handsome as sin. This bartender was perhaps the prettiest of the bunch, with perfectly chiseled features and a confident, friendly expression.

When he smiled, she felt the bottom fall out of her stomach. He was definitely what her old friend Mary would label DDG—Drop Dead Gorgeous.

"Della's on break, but she'll be back in about five minutes if you want to wait."

His deep voice sent little shivers down her spine. The man was sexy as hell and dangerous to boot. She could feel it crackling in the air around him as he stopped right in front of her on the other side of the bar. She was glad of the hard metal surface between them. His attention shifted to the man seated on her right. A slight nod and narrowing of his eyes was all that was needed to make the other man jump into action. A moment later, he'd drawn a barstool up behind her and politely assisted her to sit.

She shook her head. "Not important. You need to take the left hall when the time comes. Remember that, okay? The left hall. Not the right. Do you understand?"

He shook his head. "No, I don't, but I'll remember."

The bartender cleared his throat. "Better listen to her, Tim. Her aunt is the most gifted psychic I've ever met and she told me the gift runs in the family."

Chapter Two

"Dammit, Alex!" Della arrived behind the bar just in time to hear the last few words. "That's on a need to know basis."

"And these men need to know, Del," the bartender shot back, his smile for Della, though she pushed past him to reach for Adele's shaking hands.

"Sweetie, what happened? Was it a bad one?"

Adele nodded, drawing comfort from her aunt's presence. "The worst yet. Something's coming. Something bad, Aunt Del. Soon. We can't escape it."

"I know, sweetie. I've seen it, too. It's why we've been drawn here, I think."

"What's going on, Del?" The bartender crowded behind her aunt, demanding attention.

She whipped around to look up at the frowning man. "An attack. In the next few days, I believe. You all," she looked around the bar at the gathered men, "have a role to play."

All around her, Adele saw determination and a sort of excited fire ignite in the eyes of the soldiers. This is what they were born for. They had no fear, only strength in the face of an enemy as yet unknown.

"Will we win?" one of the men down the bar wanted to know as he raised his glass.

Aunt Della laughed. "You'd better or I'll haunt you, Perkins. Mark my words!"

Just like that, the dire mood was dispelled. Della came around the bar to Adele's side.

"I'm so glad to see you, sweetie!"

"Me too, Aunt Del." Adele was enveloped in her aunt's hug. When they broke apart, Timothy shifted over so Della could sit. She thanked him with a smile. "So, tell me what you're doing here? Dealing cards or reading them?"

"A little of both, actually." Della's curly hair sparkled in the low light as she shrugged. She produced a deck of old Earth playing cards from the pouch at her hip and began shuffling them expertly on the bar. Della was a bit of a card shark and had been employed as a dealer in some of the finest establishments in the Milky Way. Adele recognized the pattern Della was laying out on the shiny bar. This wasn't any sort of game. No, this was an ancient layout that could divine the future. Adele feared what the cards would reveal.

Della flipped the cards one by one, keeping her own council as to their meaning. Timothy took an interest and started asking questions as both Alex and David watched closely.

"What game is that?"

"Oh, it's not really a game. I'm just looking at the cards. See this one?" Della held up the King of Spades. "Old legends from Earth claim this card represented King David." She held the card up next to David's blond head and smiled. "This could be you, Colonel."

David took a swallow of his beer and shook his head. "I'm not a colonel anymore, ma'am."

Della lowered the card and looked hard at the man. "Our past never leaves us, Colonel," her expression lightened, "or should I say 'King'?" She passed the card to Adele and she noted the tingle of energy that came off the card as her aunt placed the deck to one side, pulling another deck of cards out of her pocket. Adele knew those cards. They were the tools of the prophesier. They were the tarot. Her aunt sorted through them until she pulled out two cards, placing them face up in front of her. The King of Swords and the King of Cups.

"This card," Della said, caressing the King of Swords with one fingertip, "corresponds to that King of Spades. See the resemblance now?" She held up the card depicting a blond man with startling blue eyes sitting on a throne and holding a gleaming sword.

He did indeed look like David. At least, superficially.

"And I suppose that one's me?" Alex asked, pointing to the other tarot card on the bar. The King of Cups had darker hair and blue eyes with a devilish smile in them, not unlike the bartender's. Adele marveled at the likeness.

"This one corresponds to the King of Clubs in the other deck. He was said to represent Alexander the Great." All the men listening either laughed or groaned.

"Don't give him any ideas, ma'am," one of the men down the bar called out. "He already has delusions of grandeur enough."

They all chuckled while Della continued to deal the cards, shaking her head.

"What is it, Aunt Del?"

"The King of Swords will play an important role, Adi. For you, personally, and in the coming conflict." A pensive look crossed her pretty face before she shrugged it off, clearing the bar of the cards and putting them back into her pockets. She turned to face Adele with a resigned air. "When the time comes, trust the King of Swords."

"Darnit, Aunt Del, I don't like this. Why am I here? All I see is destruction and danger. What in the world am I supposed to do here? I'm not a soldier."

Della laughed in her tinkling way. "You know fate bats us to and fro like so many ping pong balls, sweetie. It's your fate to be here at this time. Perhaps it's even more than fate. Did you ever think of that? You have a role to play, Adi, and it's an important one. When push comes to shove, shove back."

Adele hated the fatalistic tendencies of the women in her family, but guessed if you saw the future on a regular basis, it was probably unavoidable. She decided to stop fighting against it and just enjoy the moment of peace with her beloved aunt. It was, after all, the calm before the storm if their visions were to be believed.

"It's good to see you, Aunt Del. I've missed you."

The women hugged.

Chapter Three

David listened unabashedly to the odd conversation between the two women. Both were petite and lovely, but the girl at his side stirred something in him he'd never felt before. She lit a fire in his soul that made him yearn for more from his life. More from his expectations. More from *her*.

He'd only just met the woman, but already he wanted to be inside her. He wanted it more than he'd ever wanted anything, and once he got inside her he wanted to stay for a good long while. Maybe forever.

Yeah, getting into that exquisite young body would be as close to heaven as he might ever come. But if her premonitions were real—and Alex seemed to think they were—trouble was coming. He'd left the military behind, but not his training. Right now he was unarmed, but he'd remedy that shortly. He made an imperceptible hand signal to Alex and was relieved when the answer came back immediately from all around. The other men were armed and would protect the women should it prove necessary. Alex also signaled he had a cache of weapons behind the bar and that Dave was welcome to take his pick from among the stock.

Dave wouldn't leave the bar that night without at least some protection. Procuring further weapons would be his task for the next day. He wasn't sure if he really bought the ladies' supposed 'gifts', but he did believe in being prepared for every contingency. And being Enhanced, he knew there were such things as psychic abilities, though they were rare in the extreme. Still, he knew for a fact they existed, and Alex's endorsement of Della's powers was a strong point in her favor.

"Can we interest you in a game, Colonel?" The aunt's voice came to him over the increasing noise in the bar as shift change began. Workers were drifting in, looking tired and ready for a drink and some conversation.

Dave sat back and regarded the women. Della had the old deck in her hands again and was shuffling like a pro.

"What game, ladies, and who's playing?"

Adele chuckled and the sound rang through him, straight to his cock. Damn, the girl was pretty as a picture with those sparkling eyes and dancing smile.

"Poker? You look like a poker man to me," she teased.

"How'd you guess?" He stood and followed the ladies toward one of the larger booths opposite the bar.

"Aunt Della will deal for the house. I'm in for my own stake and Tim and Perkins are playing, too."

What followed was one of the most enjoyable evenings Dave had ever spent in or out of the military. A fast-moving game of cards proved the skill and cunning of both women. They were tough customers and didn't give an inch as they bet and played like pros.

Dave was used to the company of men and didn't normally know what to say to civ women, but he didn't feel any of the usual pressure with Adele and her aunt. The conversation flowed naturally, as did the beer and the credits. He won a few hands and lost a few, but everyone came away only a little poorer at the end of the game. Tim actually ended up the big winner, and he told them how he was saving up to bid for a homestead license, so the extra money would come in handy.

The boy had plans and Dave admired that. It made losing a few of his hard earned credits a little easier. From the gooey looks in their eyes, he got the sense the women felt the same. They asked questions and encouraged the young soldier to talk about his plans for the future.

Dave listened to the women talk, liking the way Adele and her aunt treated Timothy. He was shy, but the two ladies had him talking, laughing, and enjoying himself. It was a kind thing to do for a soldier. A boy that young had many years left in service and his odds weren't good for survival. Misunderstood by most of humanity, Dave knew first-hand this experience—this little impromptu poker game on a civ station in the middle of nowhere—was something the boy would remember for the rest of his life. However long that proved to be.

When the game broke up, Tim left the bar with a bounce in his step that hadn't been there before. Dave watched him go, feeling old and jaded. Had he ever been as young and easy to please? He couldn't recall.

"You're an awfully quiet man, David." Somehow Adele had managed to sneak up on him, though he wasn't alarmed. On some base level he'd been aware of her unique, ultra-feminine scent, though her presence hadn't registered on a conscious level. It was more innate. She was shrugging into the jacket she'd removed during their game, leaving her in a plain, deep green tunic that enhanced her eyes and showed off her curvy form to advantage. He was sorry to see her covering up, but it was getting late and he knew the bar would be closing shortly, in accordance with the rules of the station.

"I've spent a lot of time out on the rim, ma'am. The quiet out there grows on you."

She nodded slowly, though her eyes searched his. "I can't even imagine what it's like, living the kind of life you must have led."

He could read the honesty of her words in her beautiful eyes. The idea that a gently bred civ woman would be the least bit interested in his life on the rim surprised him.

Alex interrupted them as he removed the empty glasses from their table. "You be careful of this one, girl. Spec ops guys are rough customers." He winked in an exaggerated way, but the warning wasn't lost, even though she laughed.

"You ought to know, Alex." Dave shot back, outing his friend the way he'd just been outed. He turned back to Adele, expecting fear in her eyes. Spec ops warriors had the most brutal reputation and were often vilified in the galactic press, but she surprised him yet again. Her expression was questioning and totally non-judgmental.

"I've heard about you guys." Her gentle smile said it hadn't all been bad and David was relieved. "They say some of you go out on your own for weeks on end in single-man craft patrolling the rim. No wonder you don't talk much."

Dave shrugged. "You get used to silence."

"Then being here—on a civ station teeming with people and noise—must be quite a shock to your system."

He nodded tightly. "I'm still working on adjusting to civilian life."

She laughed softly and the sound enchanted him. "Me, too."

He wanted to ask what she meant, but she turned away, hugging her aunt and saying goodbye to the rest of the folks still at the bar. She reached right across the bar to kiss Alex's cheek.

The hot sting of jealousy startled Dave. He envied his friend for a peck on the cheek? Could he really be that petty? Or that desperate?

Adele turned back to him with a soft smile on her lovely face. He scrambled to get hold of the situation.

"It was a pleasure meeting you, David."

There was no way he was letting her walk the deserted halls of the station alone at this hour. She just didn't know it yet.

"If you don't mind the company, I'd be happy to see you home."

She seemed surprised for a moment, but not displeased by his suggestion. She looked back at her aunt and received a slight nod from Della, bless her heart.

"All right. If you're sure you don't mind. I just moved in over in Ring Four, Delta Section."

He nodded, glad he wouldn't have to lie. "It's on my way. I'm staying in Ring Five, Epsilon at the moment." The lower rent single rooms were in the farthest rings and sections. Hers was a better address, by far, though still in an area where a woman shouldn't be out walking alone during station night.

"Then I'd be glad to have your company." She smiled up at him and his heart nearly stopped. She was so damn beautiful it hurt.

Chapter Four

They left the bar together. Adele couldn't remember when she'd ever felt so safe in the presence of a man she'd just met. A soldier, for that matter. She spent a few moments wondering whether her instinctual trust of this giant of a man was merely because he was a soldier and therefore bigger and stronger than the average man, but dismissed the thought. She hadn't had the same gut reaction to any of the other men at the bar, though she had liked Alex and Timothy right off the bat. Some of the others gave her pause, though. Perkins, for one, downright frightened her. The man had killer's eyes and a ruthless set to his jaw that put her on edge. Yet, she hadn't sensed any malevolence from him—only the fact that he was capable of things best left to the shadows.

David made her feel things she hadn't felt in ages, if ever. She couldn't recall a more instantaneous attraction to any man. She wondered what he would be like in bed. Would he be rough or gentle, skilled or wild, thoughtful or selfish? Licking her lips in anticipation, she wondered if she dared find out.

It had been nearly a year since her last intimate encounter. She'd thought she was building towards a long-term relationship with Jeffrey, but he'd only been looking for a short fling with a convenient co-worker. When he'd been promoted away, their affair was over and he never looked back, while she was left disillusioned and disappointed.

She blamed herself. She should have been more careful about getting involved with a man who clearly cared more for his job, his rank, and himself, than he did about anyone else. He barely spoke to his family, having his secretary send gifts for important occasions with impersonal notes that he initialed. He had few friends, unless they were of higher rank and could further his career. He was a ruthless social climber and she should have seen the signs much sooner, but she'd been blinded by her desire to find love and acceptance. Instead all she'd found was heartache and hurt.

"Something wrong?"

David was all too observant. He watched her with an intense sort of alertness. It was disconcerting, but also endearing. He cared enough to study her expression and was sensitive to her mood. That wasn't something Jeffrey had ever done.

"Sorry. I was just thinking about the paths that led me here."

"Somehow I don't think you're talking about the transport tube." His lopsided smile touched her heart. He truly seemed interested.

Adele shrugged. "I was just thinking about how easy you are to talk to and how stupid I was to fear soldiers. You and the guys in the bar are the first I've ever talked to, you know. I mean, I didn't deliberately try to avoid them," she hastened to add. "It just never happened." She smiled up at him as they walked side by side down the deserted corridor toward one of the transport tubes. "I'm glad it did now."

He winked at her. "Me, too."

David gallantly motioned for her to precede him into the small transport car that would take them to the outer rings. She took a seat and he moved next to her in the small pod as the door slid shut, sealing them together. He was a big man and the two-person unit was cramped.

Adele's temperature rose when he stretched his arm around her shoulders. He tucked her next to his warm body in the cramped space.

"Do you mind?" A sexy smile hovered around his lips. "These things are too small for guys my size."

"Very convenient, though, huh?" She teased, looking up at him as she moved closer to give him a smidgen more room.

His eyes glowed as his head lowered. When he spoke, his lips were an inch away from hers, and his warm breath puffed over her chin.

"I'm not complaining. I'll take any advantage to get you into my arms, Adele."

Her abdomen rippled as his words hit home. The man was truly devastating and she wanted nothing more than to learn his taste and discover the answers to some of her questions. Would he kiss slow and easy or fast and wild? No time like the present to find out.

Leaning upward, she touched her lips to his, taking the initiative in a way she knew surprised him. His rumbled sigh of approval warmed her as he brought his other arm around and licked his tongue along her lips. One question was answered immediately. The man certainly knew how to kiss!

* * * *

David couldn't believe she was in his arms, and for a crazy moment he didn't think he would ever be able to let her go. Her taste was a homecoming, her gentle sigh as she relaxed into him, a welcome he would never forget. If he believed in such things, he'd think this was his woman. The only one in the universe meant just for him.

He'd heard rumors about the enemy jit'suku and the way they knew their mates by just one kiss. He'd wondered about it, scoffing at the idea of such instantaneous recognition. But now he thought he understood. This kiss was like no other he'd ever shared with a woman. This kiss was special. As was the woman.

He'd liked her from the moment he saw her walking with false bravado into that bar full of men. He liked her courage and her pluck, and he loved the way she looked. Petite and feminine, she brought out all his protective instincts, but he also admired her spirit. The way she squared her adorable shoulders had said this was a woman who could handle herself. As the night wore on, he'd come to realize it wasn't just an act.

She had a keen mind and quick wit. She also had a soft heart that showed itself in her dealings with the youngster, Timothy. Not every woman would take the time to make the shy soldier feel not only welcome, but as if he'd made a friend.

Friends among regular folk were few and far between for men like them. It meant a lot to Dave that she'd make the effort. It showed her true mettle and the depth of her compassion.

But her kiss sent him into another realm altogether.

This kiss spoke of fire and heat, passion and blazing arousal. He felt the impact of her little tongue tangling with his down to his soul. She was living flame in his arms and he wanted to burn with her. All night long.

Maybe forever.

The thought gave him pause as he drew back, just a bit, into himself. He tempered his assault on her lips, twining his hands into her hair. She was special and he needed to treat her that way. He had to show he was capable of more than just crude passion. He had to finesse her if he wanted to keep her interest.

When he leaned back, she followed as if she never wanted to let him go. Deep satisfaction filled him as she continued her subconscious pursuit. He let one hand trail down her petite frame to settle at her waist, before moving up her ribcage. When she made no protest, he cupped the tempting curve of her breast, squeezing lightly, seeking permission to go farther. She granted it with a gasping little moan that shot straight to his groin.

He surrounded her soft breast, loving the weight and shape of her. She was perfection. She was exactly what he'd always dreamed of in a woman. Enough to fill his hands and soft as a cloud. A feminine bundle with a beautiful heart.

Dave tweaked her nipple through the layers of thin fabric, pleased with her instant response. She practically climbed into his lap, so great was her excitement, and he relished every quick breath, every sexy little moan as he kissed her and kissed her, letting her know how desirable he found her.

And she desired him back. He could feel it in her response.

The thought humbled him. This perfect woman wanted him as much as he wanted her. If he had anything to say about it, they'd share this night and many more to come.

Just then an explosion rocked the station and the car they were in went dark, coasting to a stop in the transport tube.

Chapter Five

"Now?" Adele wiggled her way off his lap. Her voice was directed upward and Dave let out a laugh. Rather than fear, this incredible woman met the danger she'd foreseen with exasperation.

He could see the frustration on her face in the darkness of the pod. One gift of his Enhancement was incredible night vision. Swooping in, he placed a kiss on her surprised lips.

"You're one hell of a woman, Adele."

A breathless sigh was his answer as she gathered her wits. The kiss had rocked both their worlds.

But the station was under attack. Another dangerous rocking shook the tunnel and pod, and Dave knew it was time for action.

"Do you trust me?" He reached for her hand in the darkness. She couldn't see a thing, but to him the darkness was only a minor irritation.

"With my life." Her answer was immediate and gratifying.

"We've got to get out of here. The transport system will be the first thing they go for."

"So you think this is it, too? I mean, I know my visions have never been wrong, but…"

He placed a finger across her kiss-swollen lips. "If you believe it," he used one hand to release the emergency exit at the top of the pod, "*I* believe *you*." Climbing out, he lifted her up easily behind him, already scanning the long tunnel.

Brief flickers of light at the far end told him all he needed to know. He grabbed for the nearest handholds, clipping into the rail that ran the length of most of the main transport tubes. The station's gravity didn't extend to the transport system so the pods could slide along with relatively little effort. It made navigating in zero G difficult for most civilians when the tubes went down, but Dave was used to operating under much worse conditions, so he knew he could guide them to a safe portal with little difficulty. The hard part would be staying ahead of pursuit and avoiding any hostiles in whatever portal they chose.

He kept his voice low as he bent to her ear, spooning her in front of his larger body for the push off as he sent them sweeping down the tube, guided only by the utility clip on his belt, still attached to the rail.

"I'd like to try to make it back to Alex and the guys, if we can."

"Sounds good."

"We may encounter problems before we reach them though, so be ready for anything. I'm not sure how far away we were when we stopped." He chuckled wryly. "This little cutie was distracting me."

She punched his arm playfully and with little force, so as to avoid sending them tumbling in the zero G tube.

"There was this big brute distracting me, so I don't know either."

He leaned in and kissed her neck, shoving them a little further as they started to decelerate. It wasn't the fastest mode of transportation, but it was relatively quiet and would get them where they needed to go without detection. Hopefully.

Dave saw a few stopped pods, but the occupants were either still within or long gone. He raised his legs as they passed over the tops of the pods, Adele's body spooned inside his perfectly. She'd followed his lead very well so far and he was impressed. For a civilian, she knew how to work as part of a team and follow direction. That was something rare, he knew.

A light up ahead, just discernable to his eye had him reaching for the wall to slow their pace.

"We're one ring away from the bar," she said softly.

He nodded, not wanting to speak in case what he saw ahead really was trouble. Light flared as he stopped them fully. Definitely trouble. That flare held the unmistakable glow of rifle fire.

With a smooth motion, he stopped their progress near a side portal. The smaller portals usually led to service areas of the station in civilian designs, which was a good thing in this case. He wanted to avoid the populated areas and work his way to the more vulnerable parts of the station if at all possible, but he had to find a safe place to stash Adele first. Alex, and his predecessor before him, had undoubtedly created a network of hidey holes, but Dave had to find just one.

Unclipping from the rail, he muscled open the small portal and pushed Adele through. She was surprisingly good in zero G for a civilian and after his initial push, she managed to coast with little corrective motions off the walls, just a few feet in front of him.

He hadn't really intended to make her go first, but he had to close the portal manually so they'd leave no trail, and when he turned around, she was already ahead. There was no sign of trouble in this shorter tunnel and the soft glow of emergency lights allowed her to navigate safely enough, so he let her go. There were no occupied pods in this tube, though he saw a few empties in the various small stations they passed.

"Well, look what we have here."

A man's voice filled the tunnel, and a flare of blue light caught Adele by surprise. Her hand flew up to shield her eyes, but Dave's Enhanced vision had already compensated. He was moving before the other man had even lowered his hand from switching on the portable lantern. Dave used the zero G to his advantage, letting his momentum carry him into the smaller man and into the wall behind. His opponent had the wind knocked out of him while Dave appropriated the laser cutter he'd held in one hand. Dave shifted his grip and held the man by the throat, looking into his eyes with deadly intent.

"Holy shit! You're not one of them, are you?"

"One of who?" Adele had come up alongside and reached into the sleeve pocket of his coverall for his identichip.

"One of the jits, lady. They overran my section not ten minutes ago."

"Jit'suku? Are you sure?" Dave shook the man slightly to regain his attention.

"Sure as shootin', fella."

"Stanlay Kowliki, biosphere maintenance tech," Adele read from his card, then stuffed it back into the sleeve pocket. "You maintain the plantings, right? You're a gardener."

The man nodded as Dave let up on his collar a bit. "They came in through the biosphere hatch. Backed their ship right up to it and docked, though it wasn't made for such use. Usually only garbage chutes are attached to the hatch, leading out scows that haul waste organics away planetside."

"How did you get in here?"

"Service portal J-32." The man pointed behind him. "They hadn't found the service corridors yet on this side. Or maybe they bypassed 'em. Not much over this way, after all. I heard on the comms they were subduing the civilian areas first. Locking 'em down and gassing a few parts of the more heavily populated areas."

"Do you have a plan from here?" Dave asked.

Stanlay nodded. "I'm heading for my rooms. My wife is there with our son and I'd like to be with them should the worst happen."

Dave nodded and let the man go. Adele handed him his light that she'd retrieved. "Don't use the main tube. They're in there already. Use the side tubes and you should be okay for a while."

"I don't have to go far. Only the next ring." Stanlay assured them as he clipped in to the rail on the upper portion of the tube. Dave handed him the small laser.

"God speed."

"Thanks, mister. Sorry I surprised you, miss."

"I'm sorry I clobbered you." Dave shook his head and chuckled. Civilians. The man was eyeing him like he was a monster and seemed relieved to have escaped with his life.

"Good luck," Adele said as the man pushed off and shuttered the light.

"Will he make it?"

She nodded. "I think so. The question is, will we?" She smiled up at him and his breath caught. He leaned down and placed a quick, hard kiss on her lips.

"We will if I have anything to say about it."

Chapter Six

When the first explosion rocked the station, Alex hit the lockdown command on his bar and broke out the weapons. The men, bless their combat-ready hearts, were with him every step of the way. Luckily, aside from the vets and Della, the bar was empty. No civilians to worry about except Della, and she seemed more than willing to follow Alex's lead when he unveiled the secret passage he'd cut into the station's architecture over the past few months.

It led from behind the bar down into the lesser-used service conduits of the station, then into some hidden areas only a true professional would be able to find. It was there, in the bowels of the station, Alex had set up his lair.

He was more than just a simple barkeep, though the civilians running the station knew very little about why his 'former' bosses in the spec ops community had placed him there and set him up in business. The bar was a drop-off point and Alex was the conduit through which high-level intelligence was passed.

He had hidey holes all over the inner workings of this part of the station. They would definitely come in handy now. Leading his little group through the cramped passages, he was surprised at how well Della kept up.

"How are you doing, sweetheart?" Alex paused at yet another doorway to key in his special code on a well-hidden lock. Della panted softly beside him. She was a little out of breath from the quick-time pace they'd set through the conduits, but otherwise she looked all right.

"I'm good. Where are we going?"

"Someplace safe while we figure out the extent of the attack and what we can do about it."

Della reached out and touched his arm as he entered the last of the complex code. "What about my niece?"

Alex could see the worry in her beautiful eyes. "If I know Dave, he won't let your girl out of his sight and he's probably doing the exact same thing we are. He's looking for a safe place to assess the situation and make plans. If he's close enough, he'll probably rendezvous with us. Don't worry. He's a good man and an excellent strategist. He'll keep her safe."

"Colonel," Perkins sidled up next to them, "movement in the next tube over."

Alex nodded briefly and opened the hidden hatch. Relieved to see all was clear, he motioned them through, careful to close and lock the hatch behind.

They were in a small chamber. It was the first of his secret compartments and it led to several other escape routes, but for right now, they'd be safe enough to discuss preliminary plans. Plus, there was a secure computer hookup they could use to monitor what was happening on the station.

"Jake," he ordered quietly, "power up and jack into the system."

With a nod, the quiet man named Jake rolled back his sleeve and a flap of pseudo-skin that hid a small, state of the art interface. Along with Enhancement, Jake had undergone cybernetic implantation to augment his already incredibly sharp mind. Alex knew only a few very special brains could handle the implants and the kind of work Jake had become expert at during his time in service. Now officially "retired," Jake reported to

Alex while in the field. He was glad the man was here now. His expertise would come in very handy indeed.

Jake blinked a few times as he came out of download mode. "Bad news, Colonel. Jits have docked and infiltrated."

"How many?"

"At least one hundred, maybe one-twenty, judging by the ship they arrived in, and they've got control of environmental. I countermanded the order to flood all tubes with sleep gas, but it'll be overridden shortly."

"We should be safe enough in here," Alex reassured Della as she gasped. "There are secure scrubbers installed in all my compartments and the gas will be vented as soon as they think everyone's been dosed, so they can move around without cumbersome gear."

Jake nodded. "They already gassed the main shopping concourses on all civilian rings. Lots of sleeping people everywhere on the station, and others locked in their quarters. All the civ rings are in lockdown and the station cops have been locked into their garrison. I can't override from here."

"So they've got the run of the station already." Alex cursed under his breath. Grave expressions met his gaze as he looked around the room at his gathered troops. "Jake, were you able to get off an alert?"

"Affirmative, Colonel. It's on a subfrequency they'll probably never find. All your operatives on the station have been alerted. If they're awake, they got my sitrep through their direct comms and if they're sleeping, they'll get it when they wake up."

"Good man."

"Colonel," Jake straightened his expression grim. "The environmental system just overrode my bypass command. The tubes are flooding with gas, but it'll be a slow process because of the extent of the conduit network. Estimate at least six hours before they vent. The jits want to make damned sure everyone's asleep before they venture out."

Alex turned and punched a button. A bench slipped out from the wall and he sat heavily. "I guess all we can do for now is watch and wait. Without gear we can't move in the conduits until that stuff has vented and all my environmental gear is in the next compartment. Too far away to get to before the gas reaches us."

"Do we have anything useful in this compartment? Maybe something to eat?" Della asked.

Alex smiled up at her and patted the bench next to him. She sat at his side and his smile turned wolfish.

"We've got rations and something even better." He pushed a series of hidden switches on the irregular wall surface and a secret panel slid back to reveal an arsenal. "We've got enough firepower to take back the station—if we use it wisely."

Chapter Seven

Dave recognized one of Alex's more obscure signs just moments after the tubes started to flood with gas. Inputting his code on the hidden mechanism, Dave managed to get the hatch open before either he or Adele gave in to the pull of the gas, but it was a close thing.

Sealing the small compartment, the scrubbers inside the hidden chamber immediately went to work on the contaminated air he'd let in as they entered. He pulled a wide bench out from the wall and laid Adele on it. With her smaller frame, Adele had succumbed more easily to the effects of the gas and was the next thing to unconscious.

For a moment, uncustomary fear hit him. What if it wasn't just sleep gas? What if she'd been poisoned?

Dave tore through the supply cupboards to find a small med unit that would monitor Adele's heart and counteract most common poisons. He ripped apart the seals on her top, hesitating only briefly before slipping her sheer under-tunic down her arms, baring her breasts.

He attached the hand-sized unit over her heart, relieved when it glowed green with health. He had to lean in to read the findings and felt even better when the small unit registered sleep inducers only. He pushed a button to administer counteragents and the unit attached itself more firmly to her skin, sliding a small compartment open and jabbing her with a very fine needle.

Adele started coming around almost immediately. Her groggy eyes opened and Dave breathed a sigh of relief.

"What happened?" Her voice was still weak, but Dave was happy to hear it.

"You got a dose of sleep gas before we made it into this bolt hole."

"Why am I naked?" She leaned up and tried to gather the gaping cloth, but her arms were constricted by the under-tunic, still resting around her middle.

Dave flashed her a grin. "I may have overreacted a little." He gently pried the med unit off her skin, tracing the red marks left behind on her soft breast. "I was afraid the gas might've been more than just sleep inducers, so I dug up a med unit to check for poison."

"Was it?" Her voice had a breathless quality as his fingers continued to trace over her soft skin. "Poison, I mean." Her gaze shot to his as he brought his palm down over her breast, squeezing slightly.

Dave moved closer, tossing the med unit aside. "Just sleep gas, sweetheart. I administered a counteragent so you'd wake up." He moved closer as he felt her nipple harden to a sharp point against his palm.

"Thanks." The word whispered against his lips as he kissed her, slow at first, then with increasing urgency. She was beautifully made, a perfect fit for his big hands. He teased her nipples, rolling them between his fingers, pleased when she squirmed and moaned into his mouth. He had to taste her.

Breaking away from her lips was hard, but he needed the salt of her skin just as badly. He nibbled his way down her throat, pausing to suck her earlobe in a move that made her giggle. It was a hot sound, innocent and seductive all at the same time. He got harder just hearing her laugh. Hell, all he had to do was see her walk into that bar to make his cock stand up and take notice. She was that powerful. Like a drug to his senses.

Dave feathered his lips over her delicate skin, his hands moving lower to push the under-tunic away completely and slide the rest of her clothing down her long, luscious legs. He'd savor them. Later. But first he had a craving he needed to fulfill. Hers...and his.

"Do you feel it?" he asked, his lips sliding along her skin, skirting her nipple, waiting for the moment he would taste her. "Do you want me, Adele?"

"Oh, God, yes! Yes, David." Her whispered answer pleased him greatly.

"What—exactly—do you want, sweetheart? Tell me. In detail."

She hesitated long enough that he knew she'd never done this before. He looked up, meeting her eyes and saw fascination and a tiny bit of fear there. Fear of the unknown. But he also saw how the idea of speaking her desires out loud excited her. He decided to push a bit further.

"Do you want me to lick your nipples? Suck your luscious tits? Tell me, sweetheart. I won't do anything you don't ask for." He dared her, enjoying the way her heart sped under his hands, her panting breaths broadcasting her excitement. "Tell me, Adele. Tell me and I'll give you anything you want."

"I want—" She licked her lips and his cock twitched. "I want you to kiss me."

"Like this?" He teased her with little, almost chaste kisses going all around her nipples, but not touching the hard peaks that so obviously hungered for him.

"I want you to lick me, David." The words panted from her lips as she watched him. He could feel the soft stir of her breath against his head, making him hotter.

"Where?"

"My nipples, David. Please." The last word was lengthened into a little moan so sexy, he decided to give her what she wanted. What he wanted too. He zeroed in on one nipple, plying the other with his fingers while his tongue flicked and traced the hardened peak. Adele made the sexiest little sounds at the back of her throat as he moved closer, sucking her deep, meeting her eyes as he tongued her, drawing hard and testing her reactions.

She liked it a little rough, which surprised him, but pleasantly. It just so happened Dave liked it too. He could give her as much as she could take.

"David!"

Oh, he liked the sound of that breathless plea. He pulled at her, drawing on her skin with his teeth as she moaned then let go with a little sucking sound. He treated her other breast to a loving lick and a little nip that had her crying out in pleasure. Dave teased her soft flesh, raising her temperature.

All the while, his hands learned her. He'd pushed the cloth out of his way and now made short work of her panties, tossing them across the compartment. His hand settled into the apex of her thighs, his middle finger parting her folds and seeking within. She was slick and hot, wet and ready. He stroked over the little bud of her clit and she squirmed, then he slid his finger inside, testing her wet warmth.

She was tight. Her body stretched to admit his finger, but it was a gloriously snug fit. Used to professionals and women who sought out soldiers for a good time, David had never had such a tight pussy. He'd have to go slow and make certain she was ready because he wasn't a small man, but he'd make sure she loved every minute, every stroke, every spasm.

He fucked her with his finger, sliding through her fluids, ramming her tight hole, but slowly, with great care. She rode his hand. He liked her response.

Everything about her tantalized him. She was fresh and beautiful in a way he'd never had in real life. Oh, he'd dreamed of just such a woman, but he never thought one like her would actually come into his life, much less be panting under him.

When he judged she was ready, he added another finger. It was difficult at first, until her body stretched to accommodate him. One more finger and he knew she'd be ready for his cock. It couldn't be a minute too soon for Dave. He was about ready to come in his pants. The woman was that explosive.

"Take off my shirt," he ordered, placing nibbling kisses over her breasts and throat as she whimpered under the onslaught of his hand. "I want your hands on me, Adele."

Her head shot up, wide eyes meeting his. Eager little hands roved over his chest a moment later, searching out the fastenings of his military-style flight suit. After some searching, she found the latches and pushed the fabric aside. He had to leave her hot body for a moment to slide the sleeves over his hands, but when he went back to her wet pussy, he was able to introduce three fingers, stretching her even more. She fumbled with his clothing as he renewed his assault and cried out with a small completion, flooding his hand with welcome wetness.

"That's it, sweetheart. Just a bit more and then I'm going to fuck you so good, you'll be ruined for any other man."

She chuckled at that, her eyes misty with arousal. "I think I already am."

He took that as a challenge. "You ain't seen nothing yet, Adele." He maneuvered her into a prone position. "Lie back, sweetheart. The first time's gonna be quick and simple, but we've got a few hours 'til the gas vents. We can go slow next time." He shucked his clothes, throwing them across the compartment. "Woman, you set me on fire. I want to fuck you twenty different ways, but I think we'll have time for three. Maybe four."

Her mouth opened in shock and gave him ideas for next time. What he wouldn't give to slide his cock between those perfect lips.

"That many? I thought men had to, um, recover a bit in between."

"You've never been with a soldier though, have you? And you definitely have never been with me." He grinned at her as he knelt between her legs. Her eyes went immediately to his cock, making it even harder, if that were possible. The innocent, yet sultry way she watched him made him want to fuck her so bad, he doubted he could wait a moment longer.

Good thing he didn't have to. She was ready, he just wanted to bring her a little higher before he took the plunge because once he was inside her, he doubted he'd have enough control this first time to be certain of her pleasure.

It was a humbling thought. He'd never been so overcome by a woman before in his life. But Adele was special.

He spread her legs wide, one falling off the side of the bench as he settled between them. She had a pretty, pink, incredibly wet pussy. Leaning down, he couldn't resist a little taste.

She jumped when he licked her clit, but he held her steady, one hand on her small tummy. She was round and womanly, soft in all the right places and delicious. He licked her some more, sucking her clit into his mouth for a little tongue action. Like a shot, she came, harder this time, crying out as her abdomen rippled under his hand.

It was time.

Rising over her, he settled his cock between her luscious thighs as she continued to shudder beneath him. She was on a high and he aimed to keep her there. He hadn't been kidding. This first fuck was going to be fast and furious. He'd never been so hard or hot for a woman in his entire life. Just sinking into Adele was better than the best orgasm he'd ever had. Chances were, when he blew, he'd fly into orbit and might never return. But what a way to go.

He eased his way inside her tight hole with little pumps of his hips. He was careful not to hurt her, but she seemed oblivious. Her heels dug into his ass, pulling him deeper. He liked that.

"David!"

"Ssh, sweetheart. I don't want to hurt you."

"You're not hurting me! David, I want you now. Hard and fast!"

He swore and pushed home, loving the tight, hot depth of her. She cried out.

"Damn, woman, are you all right?"

"I'm fine, but if you don't start moving your ass right this minute, I'm going to kill you."

He leaned down to kiss her, grinning like a fool.

"Your wish is my command, darlin'."

He stroked deep, relishing the feel of her. Like warm, soft velvet against his most sensitive skin, she gloved him, giving him the ride of his life. Hard and fast, she'd said, and he took her at her word. He settled lower, stretching her thighs around him, seeking to bury his cock as deep as he could go into her heat.

Speeding his strokes, he neared the point of no return, but knew Adele was with him. Her keening cries were music to his ears as he jumped over the cliff with her, freefalling for a long time as his body jerked, his cum shooting into her womb with powerful force.

"David!"

He shouted her name at the last. Something he'd never done before. Nothing about this encounter had been familiar. It all felt fresh and new, and damn near mind-bending.

Could it be the woman who made the experience so special? He didn't know and frankly, didn't have the energy to analyze it as his body blew apart and reassembled into a satisfied, happy mass.

He'd rest a bit, then he'd fuck her again. And again. In as many varied ways as he could manage before reality intruded on their little hideaway.

Chapter Eight

Adele stretched like a kitten as she woke from a light doze some time later. Dave watched her with an indulgent grin. The woman just made him happy in a way no woman ever had before.

He leaned down and kissed her, enjoying her startled response that settled into warm encouragement within seconds. She was so responsive to him. It was a marvel.

"Mmm. What a nice way to wake up." She smiled as he pulled back. He loved the light in her eyes, the simple joy in her expression. She truly wanted to be there, in that dusty little compartment, with him. He could read it on her beautiful face.

No woman had ever wanted so badly to be with him that it showed plainly in her eyes. He wanted to see that expression again. And again. Perhaps for the rest of his life.

Whoa.

That thought gave him pause. It hit him like a punch to the gut, robbed him of air and made him wonder if he wasn't just a little crazy for even considering it. No way would a beautiful, cultured, educated and intelligent woman like this one want to settle down with a rough soldier. She could have anyone. Why in the world would she settle for him?

* * * *

A ring away, in the other hidden compartment, Alex kept his eyes on Della. She fascinated him. She'd done so since the moment she'd walked into his bar a few weeks ago. He'd never been so instantly attracted to a woman, but this woman was off limits.

Oh, he'd vowed to protect her with his last breath, and he flirted—as was his nature—but he'd never let it go any further. He'd wanted to pursue her when he'd first seen her, but then she'd stumbled into his arms, in the grip of a strong prophetic vision. When she recovered, she'd come clean with him about her psychic abilities, and that clinched it. She was way too special for the likes of him on a personal level, though he would take advantage of any precognitive words of wisdom she might want to share. He was a spy, after all.

"How much longer, do you think?" She sat next to him along one wall. The other men were cleaning their gear or servicing their weapons as they waited quietly for the gas to clear.

"A few hours." Alex watched her quiet nod. She hadn't even batted an eyelash when he'd uncovered the secret passageway. Most civilians would have been surprised, but Della took it all in stride. The idea unnerved him...and made him suspicious. "Why were you in my bar, Del?"

She turned her gorgeous, spooky eyes on him and he had to fight not to look away first. She saw too deeply with those almost mystical orbs.

"It was where I needed to be." She pulled that ancient, pictorial deck out of her pocket and fingered the card he'd seen before—the King of Cups. "I followed destiny to you, Alexander."

"I don't believe in fate. You'll have to do better than that."

"Oh, but it was fate. And I'll admit there was some practicality in there as well." She leaned close, and for a moment he thought she was going to kiss him, but she placed her soft lips on his ear instead, shocking him. "General Tierney sent me."

Alex felt a moment of shock, but recovered quickly. She'd spoken so softly even the Enhanced soldiers around them couldn't have heard. Still, Alex cast his eye over the group. A few were smiling and shaking their heads, probably believing Alex had made another conquest—as Della had probably intended. Oh, she was good. He turned his lips into her neck.

"Code?"

"Whiskey Delta Bravo."

She'd given him the right code and the right name. Damn him. Della was in the game, too, only she had an edge. There was no way she was faking those visions unless her niece was part of some much more elaborate scheme than Alex could credit. No, Della had true powers of prophecy. He'd seen it over the past weeks. That she was also a high-level spy made her actions of the past hours much more understandable.

Della patted his chest as she sat back, staring into his eyes. "I could see the questions in your eyes." Her fingers pressed a subtle message into his chest. "But I don't see anything of the immediate future right now. When I do, you'll be the first to know."

She moved away and Alex knew her last words were for the benefit of the watching men. The rest was a subtle message to him alone. She wanted him to know she was on the right side of this conflict and the code she'd supplied had gone a long way toward answering his most immediate questions about her. The rest could wait until after they took back the station.

He tugged on her hand as she moved away. "Thank you, Della."

* * * *

Adele felt fantastic. After the best sex of her life with an incredible man, she had no cause to complain. Except maybe for the fact the station was probably still under control of the enemy. The thought made her frown as she sat up, clutching the shirt David had covered her with.

"Do you think the corridors are clear yet? Have you heard any news on the comm?"

Dave started, clearly distracted. "Yeah, the tubes should be clear in another standard or so. I wouldn't want to chance it just yet, which means the jits probably won't be down this way looking for stragglers, either. But even if they were able to maneuver in the access tubes with full breathing gear, I'd be shocked if they could find their way into this compartment. It's fully shielded and hidden so well, even I had a hard time spotting it—and I knew what to look for."

Reassured, Adele began to shrug into her clothes. "So what do we have planned?"

"We?" Dave laughed once, and Adele knew immediately they were in for their first argument. "We don't have anything planned. *I*," he emphasized the word, "intend to go out as soon as the gas clears, rendezvous with Alex and company, then take back the station."

"And what have *you*," she sounded annoyed even to her own ears, "planned to do with me during all this?"

"Look, honey, I don't want to have to worry about you getting caught or killed by the jits." Apparently he realized he'd stepped in it, but he wasn't backing down, though he moderated his tone. "I...uh...care...about you." He seemed afraid to admit to any affection—perhaps afraid of her rejection. His hesitant words softened her anger. "I care too much to put you in danger. I'm trained for this kind of thing and have been dealing with situations like this most of my life. You're a civilian. I don't want you to get hurt."

She tugged on her boot and stood to face him. "I may be a civilian," she strode forward, standing toe to toe with the big man, not giving an inch, though her tone was gentle, "but up until a month ago, I was the Executive Officer of Lothlorien Station. I know my way around this station—hell, any civ station—probably better than you, Colonel. I've also had training. I'll admit, not as much as you, and I've never used it in a combat situation, but judging by the odds we're up against here, I'd say every body that can tote a rifle counts. I won't be left behind."

"Adele—" His tone held anguish, but she wouldn't be swayed.

"Let me help, David. I don't like seeing you in danger, either, but it can't be avoided. I can get us into the command center of this station faster than anybody. Let me help you."

"Damn." David's breath came out in a rush as he pulled her into his arms and just hugged her close. "I don't like this one bit. And why didn't you tell me you outranked me?"

She chuckled and sank into his muscular embrace. "Technically, my Civilian Station Service rank is colonel, just like you."

"Yeah, but you're command staff, not a field operative."

Adele shrugged. "I was command rank, but I got passed over for promotion, so I'm taking some time to figure out where my career—and my life—are going. I'm officially on extended leave, but all my codes are still active." She pulled back to look into his eyes. "I can get you anywhere you want to go on this station, David.

"Hell." He sighed hard, then bent to kiss her. She felt both regret and fear in the slight tremble of his warm lips against hers. He pulled back when she would have taken the kiss deeper. "I don't want you in any danger, but I could use CSS help on this. Military stations use different protocols and the intel I have on CSS codes is probably a bit out of date."

"I swore an oath, not unlike yours I suspect, to serve and protect the people who trust CSS to keep their stations safe and functioning. I can't abandon that. And I know I can help you."

* * * *

One standard later, Dave led Adele on a quick journey down one access tube and toward another. They'd eventually connect with the network of corridors leading to the command areas of the station. He didn't like having her in harm's way, but he couldn't deny her skill at navigating the crowded conduits and she'd already gotten them into two override-protected areas faster than he could have. She had current codes and since they were part of the CSS framework, they wouldn't alert any of the unfriendlies on the station.

What he'd been able to monitor on the public comms gave him pause. There were way more jit'suku than he expected crawling all over the station. They must've emptied the ship they'd docked at the biosphere hatch. Either that, or they had another ship attached somewhere else, though he couldn't find any mention of a second ship.

An audacious Plan B was forming in his mind, but he'd hold it in reserve until he was sure Plan A wasn't going to work. As it was, Plan A involved getting into the command section and regaining control of the station from there. If there really were as many jits as he feared, they'd learn soon enough if that plan were actually viable.

The compartment they'd holed up in hadn't had any comm gear. Dave hated that he didn't know what Alex and the men were up to, but if he had to guess, he'd lay odds they were in the thick of things. As soon as he could find a secure headset or some other means to contact them, he would. A coordinated attack would work better than a couple of groups acting on their own.

Rounding a curve in the access tube, Dave saw a flare of light ahead, and it didn't look friendly. He shot backward, looking for the access panel they'd just passed. There might just be enough room for both of them behind it, if they squeezed in really close.

Wordlessly, Adele followed his lead, not objecting when he stuffed her behind the thin panel first. It didn't shut completely, but he held it with one finger, hoping the jits—if that's who was coming down the tube—wouldn't notice. With one eye, he could just see through the sliver of space left by the open panel.

Sure enough, a few minutes later, a group of jits sauntered past, talking loud enough they couldn't hear Adele's ragged breathing or smell her fear, even with their superior senses. This particular group of pirates was rather disorderly, but they were only foot soldiers. Dave bet their commanders were a bit more on the ball if they'd been able to pull off a complete takeover of a well-protected civ station so quickly. After the patrol passed, they continued up the access tube, but Dave's recon of the control section showed way too many jits for them to get past.

Time for Plan B.

He headed into the main transport tube. It was back up and running, which meant coasting through the zero G barrel would be downright dangerous. If a pod came careening down the tube at them, they could be crushed against the walls. But Dave was counting on the jits limiting access to the transport system to their own people. After all, there weren't that many of them and the transport tube system was as vast as the station itself. The odds were good they could coast in the tube for the short distance they needed to go without getting hit by anything.

"Are you with me?" Dave saw Adele's raised eyebrows as he prepared to enter.

She nodded.

He loved the confidence he saw shining out of her eyes, even as she worried. In short, he loved her.

The thought startled him, but it felt warm and comfortable at the same time. His spirit soared and his heart expanded as he looked down at her. He bent and placed a quick kiss on her lips, wishing he had time to tell her how he felt, time to show her how much her faith in him meant.

Instead, he pushed off into zero G with her cocooned against him, just like before. They went the short distance to a biosphere side-portal and entered cautiously. Just as he suspected, the guards were minimal and they were able to use the cover of the shrubs, plants and trees in the biosphere to make their way to the chute that would take them to the jit ship.

He wasn't surprised to see the outline of the ship through the biosphere dome was of human design. The jits would never have made it this close to a civ station in one of their own ships. That would work in his favor.

"We're going to take the ship," Dave said quietly, pausing some distance from the jit guards.

"You've got brass ones, Colonel."

He heard the approval in her tone. "And when we're done, you can show me how much you like them again."

She surprised him by trailing one small hand down to his groin and cupping him through the thin material of his flight suit. "Anytime, Colonel."

He dipped to kiss her head. "Hold that thought, sweetheart. We've got some jits to down before I can show my...appreciation for your enthusiasm."

She gave him a final squeeze and stepped back. "Let's do it then, so I can get you back in bed."

"In bed," he mused quietly as he began to move toward the ship's dock, "against a bulkhead, on the bridge, anywhere, any time, sweetheart. You make me so hard, I hurt."

"Glad to know it's not just me." Her sexy little chuckle almost did him in. He had to do something before he dragged her to the floor and fucked her right here, right now, in front of the jits.

54

"Stay back here behind the tree. I'm going to take out the guards. When I give you the signal, join me on the ramp and we'll go in together."

"Yessir," she gave him a jaunty little salute and a grin. "And sir," she reached up and cupped his cheek, "be careful."

He turned his head and kissed her palm. "Always."

Chapter Nine

Adele watched through the foliage—or tried to. David was nearly invisible to the human eye and when he downed the guards, he moved faster than she could follow. His motion was smooth and soundless, poetry in motion, and she truly appreciated for the first time how skilled this man— this soldier—was.

As beautiful as his soul was inside, that's how deadly he was on the outside. It was a paradox she would enjoy studying. For the rest of her days, if he'd let her, but that was thinking too far ahead. For right now, she had to focus on the job at hand. Thousands of innocent lives were depending on them.

David disappeared up the ramp. Just when she began to worry, he reappeared, armed now with several rifles and other weapons, wearing a grin. He signaled her over and covered her path while she moved as swiftly and silently as she could. Of course, it was nothing like the swift silence David had managed.

Still, she made it to the ramp and they entered the ship together, heading for the bridge. David seemed at ease and she took her cues from him as he sealed them in and moved off at a fast pace.

"The ship's clean. I took care of the skeleton crew they'd left behind."

She'd seen the bodies of the guards. David had taken them down cleanly and efficiently. His matter of factness made her shiver, but she knew those jits would just as easily have killed them. They were a ruthless race, prone to kidnapping human women and selling them into sexual slavery, or worse.

"There were only six of them," he continued speaking as they entered the empty bridge. "Ship's sensors confirmed it, but I did a visual inspection of the areas I couldn't lock down."

She headed for the comm panel. She'd be the most use there for now.

"Sensors show four life signs in the aft bridge section." Her brows rose in alarm and she turned to look through the windows at the rear of the command deck. The Captain's lounge and map room was back there. She could see four humanoid forms huddled in chairs around the chart table.

"It's okay. That's where I stashed the prisoners. They're out cold and tied up besides. They won't be a problem. I thought it would be good to have a few to interrogate after this is all over."

So he hadn't killed everyone in sight. Somehow, that made her feel better. He was a killer, but he knew when to temper his deadly skills. She nodded, unable to put her thoughts into words and knowing this wasn't really the time or place.

"Strap in. I'm going to undock, but without a full compliment of crew, it could get bumpy."

She did as he ordered, but switched some of the command functions to her console.

"I can help with undocking. I've got tractors and locks on my console."

"Good thinking. I've got all the weapons, thrusters and directionals routed to mine. I was going to blast us out, but a gentler touch might be better. Release what you can."

"I'm on it. Just give me about thirty seconds." She paused, tapping commands. "Be prepared to fire steering thrusters in five, four, three, two, one, mark."

They worked smoothly together, undocking the ship and maneuvering around the dark side of the rings. Adele put her command codes to good use, tapping into sub-systems that would tell her whether or not she could gain control of the station remotely. Once she had all her ducks in a row, she turned to David, a smile of triumph lighting her face.

"I'm ready when you are, Captain."

* * * *

Timothy met up with the soldiers from the bar in an access tube and secured a weapon and comm gear from them. They seemed impressed that he'd hidden in an emergency med chamber when the sections started filling with sleep gas. He'd slept for a bit, but not from the gas. No, he'd decided to take a combat nap to conserve strength—as he'd been trained—until the gas cleared out and he could move around again. After that, he hit the access tubes, figuring the hostiles wouldn't be able to track him in the tight spaces.

He'd met the other soldiers briefly, then was separated from the group during a scuffle with some stray jits, Some of those old timers could move faster than the human eye could follow. Tim knew most of those guys from the bar were spec ops, while he was just a grunt. A young one at that. But these guys were like nothing he'd ever seen.

If he made it out of this alive, he'd have to ask them about it. Though he realized they'd probably tell him very little. Most of what those spec ops guys were up to was heavily classified, and if he wasn't mistaken, that bartender was definitely black ops. Even scarier shit than usual.

Tim exited the tubes and raced down a wide hall, coming to a fork. He hesitated only a moment as he remembered what the woman had said to him at the bar. The pretty little civ lady who'd smiled at him. What a sweetheart she was. But a little creepy, too. She'd told him to take the left hall when the time came and damned if that time hadn't just come.

Altering his steps slightly, he took the left hall without looking back, surprised when a few meters into the hall, a hand shot out from behind a locked gate. Tim just ducked in time to avoid the tactical baton across his path that would've decapitated him.

"Whoa, man. I'm human." Tim shouted as he rounded to face the gate. The sight that greeted him stopped him dead.

Behind that locked gate stood twenty or so uniformed police officers. They all looked madder than hell.

"Sorry, kid." The man wore the rank of captain and had the look of a military retiree. "Can you get us out of here? Damned jits locked us in."

"Why didn't they gas you like the rest of the station?" Tim moved cautiously forward.

"Can't. The garrison is protected with special scrubbers and overrides. The best they could do was lock us out of our weapons and keep us penned up."

Tim smiled cunningly, holding up his rifle. "Not for long. Stand back."

The cops smiled and cleared the gate, the captain turning to issue orders to his men while Tim cut them free using a special setting on his energy weapon. It was slow work, but within a half-standard, he had the gate hinges weak enough to pull apart with a little help from the inside.

"You're gonna get a medal for this, kid. If we live through it." The captain slapped him on the back as he left the garrison and his men streamed out behind him.

"Sir, you should know there's a small platoon of retired spec ops soldiers already working to take back the station. I was briefly part of the group, but got separated. I'm not fast enough to keep up with spec op guys." Tim felt embarrassed to admit it, but had to be truthful with this man, this fellow soldier.

"Few are, son." The captain patted him on the back. "There's no shame in that. Especially at your age. Do you have one of their comms?" Tim nodded and lifted the earpiece. "Good. Get on there and tell them they've got help. We'll be into the weapons lockers in another quarter standard, then we're good to go. We've got two hundred and twenty trained officers ready to coordinate with whatever those soldiers have planned."

"Do you want to tell them, sir?" Tim offered the headset to the higher ranked man.

"No, son, they know you. Introduce us first, then I'll get my own gear once we have the lockers open and talk to your friends."

* * * *

"Well, I'll be damned." Perkins actually grinned when Timothy gave his report. A short while later a gruff voice came on the line. Drill Sergeant Kenneth "Mac" MacGregor had retired, but was still quite a legend in the military community. Who knew he'd traded his soldiers for a group of civ cops on a perimeter station?

A few minutes after that, they got a second surprise when David and Adele patched into their comm from outside the station. Alex just laughed and started planning as the men listened in. David and Adele would lay low until the cops and Alex's team, were in place. Once they had the jits surrounded, Dave would contact the jit commander and demand surrender. A show of force might be necessary, which is where the cops and especially the spec ops soldiers came into play.

But it would take time to position everyone. Alex instructed David and Adele to orbit on the dark side for another half standard while they all double-timed it as stealthily as they could into key positions surrounding the command and control sectors of the station. Adele gave them some pointers on where and what, but Alex knew most of the layout. Still, the little lady surprised everyone who could hear with her knowledge of the station's inner workings.

Everyone except her aunt, who was listening quietly from one side of the room.

Della was content to be left behind during the actual fighting, but Alex had dragged her from compartment to compartment, hidey hole to hidey hole, barely letting the woman out of his sight. Perkins and all the men thought Alex was sweet on her, so they cut him some slack, but the woman was good in a tense situation, neither speaking too much nor bumbling enough to get them all in trouble with the jits. She was good people. For a civvie. At least that's what the men thought. Only Alex knew she was quite a bit more.

Chapter Ten

"Looks like we have about a half-standard to kill. Now, what," David leered at her and winked, "should we do with the time?"

Adele leapt into his lap and slid her little hands around his neck most satisfactorily. "I don't know, Captain, why don't you order me around and see if we can't come up with a way to entertain you?"

"Oh, I like the sound of that. For starters, why don't you take off your clothes?"

"Aye, aye, Captain." She stood and moved back until she was just in front of him, giving him a good view. Her fingers went to the fastenings of her shirt as she looked at him from under lowered lashes. The sex kitten had come out to play. She began a slow, deliberate striptease, holding his attention and drawing out the removal of her clothing, item by item.

Dave liked what he saw. He especially liked the sparkle of vivacious life in her beautiful eyes as she shrugged off her clothing in a slow, sexy striptease. The best whores in the galaxy had nothing on her, because this strip was special. This woman was special. He'd lay odds she'd never done this before in her life. That she'd do it so eagerly for him touched something deep inside.

"Come here." The words slipped out as she stood before him in just her panties. Luscious breasts swayed as she walked toward him, begging for his touch, his kiss. "I swear you're the sexiest woman alive."

She laughed and the light in her eyes turned to fire. She didn't believe his compliment, but he'd make sure by the end of this encounter she knew just how beautiful he thought she was. Sexy, alluring and the most luscious woman he'd ever seen.

"Take off your panties." His voice was scratchy. She stopped about a foot away, her eyes widening at his tone of command. "Do it, Adele. Show me your pussy." His gaze pinned her. Dared her.

A sly smile lifted one corner of her mouth as she rose to the challenge. Turning, she looked at him over one shoulder as she wriggled her panties down over the most luscious ass he'd ever seen. He wanted to reach out and grab her, but she turned before he gave into the impulse, dragging the scrap of white satin down her hips, revealing the little tuft of curly hair at the juncture of her thighs. She kept herself neat and he liked that, but she was ultra-feminine and just the tiniest bit shy.

He'd never had a shy woman in all his life. The fact that she wasn't a pro had a lot to do with her allure, but even more enticing was the idea that she wanted to be with him. *Him.* She was the first woman he'd ever had who hadn't either been paid for her services or had sought him out simply because he was a soldier. For those women, any soldier would do. They just wanted the thrill of the forbidden and he was glad to give it to them, but they didn't want him in particular.

Adele knew who he was, and still she wanted him. Dave knew in his heart, she wouldn't have bedded any of the other soldiers she met in Alex's pub. No, she was attracted to him. She gave herself to *Dave.* Not some nameless, faceless soldier, but to him and him alone.

"Climb up here." He patted the narrow space on either side of his legs as he sat in the command chair. There was just enough room in the big chair for her to kneel on his lap. Just where he wanted her to be. Hesitantly, she moved to comply, her tongue peeking uncertainly from the corner of her luscious lips as she maneuvered into place. He took her hand to steady her as she raised one knee, then the other, her pussy spread before him, wet and glistening. He licked his lips. Damn, the woman was hot!

He stroked her breast with one hand, catching the other nipple with his teeth. One hand moved down her hip, zeroing in on what he wanted most. His fingers delved gently at first into her dewy folds, sliding and slipping around the little bud as she gasped and strained against him.

"Easy, sweetheart. I've got you." He spoke against her skin as his mouth rose, seeking hers. He took her lips in a devastating kiss as his fingers breached her core, sliding deep. Her lithe body shuddered in his arms as she gasped. Breaking the kiss, he laid little nibbling kisses down her neck and back to her breasts. She was perfectly formed, big and round, just the way he liked and he didn't think he'd ever get enough of her.

"David!" She stiffened in alarm. He broke off, on alert, to see what had startled her. She stared behind the command chair, her eyes wide, her shoulders tense.

He didn't sense danger, but he did feel...

He swiveled the chair to the right.

...eyes on them.

Four sets of male jit'suku eyes, to be exact. The prisoners were awake and watching them from the windows of the captain's chart room. Dave looked to make certain their bonds were still secure and was satisfied they would not escape.

"They're no threat," he whispered as he returned his attention to Adele. She was creaming on his hand, though her eyes were still round with shock. Could it be his little hellion liked being watched? Dave nipped her breast, knowing the men could see them in profile and she squirmed even more than before. She did like it. He could tell. "Never did it in front of an audience before?"

Her innocent gaze pinned him as she shook her head in denial.

"But you like the idea, don't you?" His smile dared her.

* * * *

Adele could hardly believe the audacity of the man under her—or her own. There was something about those men watching her that set her on fire.

"You wouldn't—"

"Oh, but I would." Dave pumped his fingers inside her, rubbing right along her g-spot, making her insides clench.

"David!" Her protest was nothing more than a breathless whisper and she knew she was lost. She would do anything for this man. Anything.

He removed his fingers and settled his hands at her waist, pushing back slightly.

"Undo my pants." The sexy order made her breath catch. Oh, how she wanted him.

She freed his thick cock, cradling it with her hands, watching it. Wanting it. She licked her lips and he grabbed her wrists, demanding her attention. When their eyes met, fire leapt between them and it warmed her, body and soul.

"Next time, Adele. You can suck me next time, but I need to be inside you right now. I can't wait." He lifted her hips and positioned her. "Ride me, sweetheart. I need you now."

Daring greatly, she thought about the audience, but all that mattered was David. He was the center of her lust, her world, in that moment. The audience was just an added caress of eyes, of thoughts, but they weren't David. He was the most important ingredient in this little play.

Delicately, she took him into her body, sliding down bit by bit, holding his gaze the entire time. She smiled her joy and he groaned as she sheathed him, the expression on his face warming her. Could it be? The way he looked at her made her feel secure and...loved. But they'd only known each other a short time. Still, she felt her heart expand and thought she sensed something on his part as well, though he hadn't spoken words of love. Yet her heart pounded at the thought. She knew—crazy as it seemed—she had deep feelings for this man. She even...loved him.

Sinking down onto his thickness, she took him as deeply as she could. She loved him. In that moment, she knew the truth of it, and she'd do all in her power to help him, and cherish him for as long as he'd let her. She began to move on him, grateful for the urging and support of his strong hands. Starting here and now, she'd show him how much he meant to her. She'd give him everything she had. And then she'd give more.

"That's it, Adele," he ground out as they both neared an incredibly high, fast peak. He was ramming into her now, meeting her downward thrusts with forceful upward movements of his hips. He was in her deeply, body and soul, as she cried out.

"David!" She began to shudder and clench around him in the most intense orgasm of her entire life. Never before had she come so fast or so hard, but then, she'd never loved a man as deeply as she knew she loved David.

It didn't make any sense at all, but it felt more right than anything ever had.

She clenched again as he came with her, shooting hot jets of his cum into her eager body. She was wracked by ecstasy, wound tighter than she'd ever been and shot higher than ever before. She screamed his name as she peaked yet again, held taut on the edge of paradise for long moments.

She slumped against him as she came down, kissing his neck and nuzzling the stubble of his beard.

"You feel so good," she mumbled into his skin. "I love what you do to me, David. I love...you."

He stilled and every muscle in his body tensed. Not exactly a good omen. Regretfully, she straightened away from him, her hands on his shoulders as she looked into his stunned face. He looked like the fabled Earth deer caught in the headlights of an oncoming land vehicle. She smiled to put him at ease, though her heart took the blow silently.

"It's okay," she stroked his incredibly muscular shoulders. "I know it's too soon. It's crazy in fact." She shrugged and tried to smile, but he clutched her waist tightly.

"Not too soon, Adele. And not crazy." He paused as if searching for words. "Unless I'm crazy, too."

Hope lit within her heart. "You—" She realized in that moment, his cock was still inside her, his body still joined as intimately as he could be and now, it felt like their hearts were joining on some metaphysical plane as well. "You love me, too?"

Swallowing hard, he nodded. "I didn't think you'd want to know. I didn't want to insult you."

"Insult me?" She was outraged. "David, your love is a treasure. A precious gift. *You* are a precious gift. You could never insult me. Ever. I love you." She leaned down and rained happy kisses all over his face, pausing for a long, hot time at his mouth.

Somewhere in the distance a reminder tone pinged. She tried to ignore it. She really did. But David pushed back lightly, groaning as he did so.

"Honey, we've got to get ready. The team is counting on us."

Chapter Eleven

Shocked back to reality, she scrambled off his lap, giving one last, regretful look at his cock as she went.

"We'll finish this after we get the station back," she promised as she scrambled back into her clothes.

After that, the situation developed rapidly. Once everyone was in place, David maneuvered the large craft into position and manned the guns. It was a big job for one man, but David was more than able. All in all, he impressed Adele in every way. Damn, the man was capable. And hot. And he made love like something out of a dream. No, make that a fantasy. A very naughty fantasy.

She chuckled to herself as she got ready to interface with the jits on-station. Since she was the one with the codes—and the authority as a CSS officer—they'd decided she'd be the better voice of command and negotiation in this situation.

Once they were sure Alex and his men, as well as the station police forces were in position, she opened a channel directly to the command and control of the station. She hacked in through their backsystems to prove to them she meant business.

"This is Colonel Adele Senna of the Civilian Station Service. You have two minutes to surrender or suffer the consequences." She was able to bring up a visual of the command center and nearly chuckled at the scrambling jit'suku who couldn't figure how she'd hacked into their supposedly secure comms. "You should know that we've captured your ship and have taken prisoners."

That got their attention, she saw from her stolen vid feed. A moment later, the jit commander opened a channel to her, so they could see each other. The man was a hardened warrior with a stone face, but if she was any kind of judge, he looked more than a little agitated at the moment.

"You surprise me, woman."

"That's Colonel Senna, to you," she was quick to correct, politely, but firmly.

The jit commander inclined his head slightly, but never broke contact with her eyes.

"From where I sit, you are in no position to demand my surrender, *Colonel*," he emphasized the title with disdain. "In fact, I demand your immediate surrender and the release of my crewmembers."

Adele shook her head and laughed softly. "Nice try, but no deal. For one thing, we're targeting your mech section."

"You wouldn't disable the station. There are too many people here for you to risk it."

Her expression hardened. "Try me." They stared each other down for a moment. "But you should probably know you're totally outnumbered. Remember those station police you locked up?" She saw the man pale, just slightly. "Yeah, we found them. They've got you surrounded even as we speak. If you don't surrender in," she checked the chronometer, "twenty-six seconds, they'll open fire on your forces. I assure you, they are up to the task, and royally pissed off." One of the men behind the jit commander bent to whisper in his ear. "So what'll it be?"

The jit commander sat silent as rifle fire sounded on his side of the connection. She saw him dive out of the command chair as fighting broke out inside the command area. Adele watched the vid feed as Alex and his team stormed the control center, moving faster than the human eye could follow. Before she knew it, the jit commander faced her once more, this time with a laser rifle aimed at his head.

Dave touched her arm to get her attention. She muted her end of the channel so they could speak freely.

"Don't leave a record of Alex's involvement. Don't call him by name and don't record him or any of his men."

Slowly, she nodded. More was going on here than a couple of retirees helping a station in need.

"I understand, but after this is all over, you *are* going to tell me what's up with them. And you. Don't think I haven't noticed your superior abilities, David. You can do things no normal man can."

He lifted her hand to his lips and kissed it gallantly. "I'll tell you what I can, but there's a lot about me—and Alex and the guys—that's classified."

"Okay," she turned back to the screen, "I get it. I'll do what I can to keep their involvement off the record."

"Thanks, Adele. I wouldn't have asked if it wasn't important."

She met his gaze, sensing the seriousness of his words. She could do this. As a CSS officer, she understood need-to-know situations and secret ops. Thinking fast, she reopened the channel.

"I, Adele Senna, am hereby taking command of Madhatter Station under my authority as a colonel in the Civilian Station Service. Station police are hereby ordered to secure all hostile parties in the station brigs until such time as the rightful command chain can be reestablished and proper judicial due process reinstated." She recorded her side of the comm for the official record and patched it through to the station speaker system so everyone could hear it. Everyone who was awake, that is.

Many of the station inhabitants were still suffering from the effects of the sleep gas and would be out for another day or two without medical attention. She gave orders for medical personnel to be resuscitated first. They could organize waking the rest of the populace. In the meantime, station police were rapidly filling the brigs as small firefights erupted here and there throughout the infrastructure.

"I think that's about all I can do from here." Adele turned to David, who watched her with an admiring gleam in his eyes.

"If I haven't said it before, I'll say it now. You are one hell of a woman, Adele Senna." The very real appreciation she read in his devilish grin warmed her from within. "You handled that like a pro, sweetheart."

She shrugged. "Well, that's what I am." Throwing down the command stylus, she turned to face him fully. "Or at least, I was."

"So what happened? What brought you here?"

"I was passed over for promotion." She shrugged, trying to be nonchalant about one of the most hurtful episodes in her life to date. "Jeffrey was a co-worker, and my lover. Turned out while I was thinking long-term, he was all about the moment and climbing the promotion ladder—right over my foolish back. I still have the footprints on my ass to prove it." She tried not to be bitter, but it came out anyway.

"The bastard." David reached for her, dragging her out of the chair and onto his lap. "He didn't deserve you, Adele. You're a born leader. The command should have been yours. Not what's-his-name's. Forget him."

She chuckled, looping her hands around his neck. "I think I already have. The moment I laid eyes on you, colonel, I knew Jeff couldn't hold a candle to you."

David grinned. "I like the sound of that."

"Come to think of it," she tilted her head to the side, watching him closely, "few men could compete with your super-human abilities." She felt him tense under her. "Can you tell me about it, David? I've never seen anyone move the way you and those other soldiers can. It's definitely not normal."

He rested his forehead against hers. "I can't tell you much, but you've already seen some of what we can do. We were all spec ops—part of a special, even more secret program. We volunteered for...changes...to be made to us on a cellular level. It's given us some pretty amazing abilities, but it does have its drawbacks."

She felt him tense up even further. "What kind of drawbacks?"

"For one thing," he tried to shrug, but it was unconvincing, "it made me sterile. I didn't think it was such a big sacrifice at the time. I mean, I have brothers and sisters who are non-military. Some of them have kids already. I figured I didn't really need to worry about it, but now that I'm older, I realize my decision was potentially unfair to any woman I might get involved with."

"Well," she stroked the nape of his neck with her fingers, "speaking as a woman who you *got involved* with," she chuckled, "it doesn't make you less attractive on any level, David. Don't worry that some foolish woman will reject you over it. If one does, she's not worthy of you in the first place." Her own vehemence surprised her, as did the possessive feelings stirring in her heart.

She was afraid she'd revealed too much, but the light in David's eyes reassured her. He squeezed her waist, his lips covering hers for a tender salute.

"You're a wonder to me, Adele. I never thought I'd ever meet a woman like you and now suddenly, here you are."

"It's fate, David. Seeing things the way I do..." she hesitated, having never really talked about her abilities outside her own small family. "Well, it gives me an appreciation for the hand that fate plays in our lives. Of course, not everything is pre-destined. Human will plays a large part. But I know the path that led me to The Rabbit Hole—and to you—was my own good fortune." She stroked his spiky hair.

"So you're saying you're okay with the fact that I'm a little different?" He seemed to want to make sure of something, his eyes intensely studying her response.

"David, you don't mind about my gift. Do you?"

"How could I? It just saved our asses." He chuckled, then grew more serious. "It's part of who you are, Adele. I can see that. And I like you just the way you are."

She smiled broadly. "Then you have your answer." Leaning in, she kissed him with all the pent up desire in her heart, rubbing against his hard body in a way that made her breath catch in her throat. David's broad palms skimmed over her, shooting her temperature higher.

Then the comm chimed.

Time to go to work. They had a station to secure and a few thousand civilians depending on them to do it.

"We'll pick this up later," David promised as he helped her stand. Her knees were a little wobbly, but the promise in David's shining eyes steadied her...and made her impatient to get the work done. So she could play some more with her beloved soldier.

Chapter Twelve

Dave linked the four jit prisoners with force cuffs. Only their feet were left mobile so he could walk them off the ship and to the waiting station police. They cooperated since they knew there was no way to escape. There were two younger men who wore high quality gear and carried themselves a bit differently than your average jit pirate. The other two were older and had the look of personal guards. One of the younger men looked to be in his early twenties, and the other might've been in his late twenties or early thirties. The younger of the two stopped in front of David, curiosity on his angular face.

"Are all human women like yours?" His dark eyes glanced to Adele and back, curiosity written plainly in his expression as the other jits stood behind him, almost protectively.

"Many human women are courageous, intelligent and sexy as hell, but I will admit, my Adele is a cut above the rest."

"That is your heart talking," the oldest of the prisoners said with a hearty smile. "Though I admit I have seen few human females with this one's qualities. She is something else again."

"That she is." Dave knew he was smiling like a besotted fool when Adele finished her comm and came to stand next to him, but he couldn't help himself. Her eyes clouded for a moment and she swayed. Dave recognized the signs of a vision this time. He put out a hand to steady her.

She regained her balance and not a moment later, walked right up to the youngest jit prisoner and frowned at him.

"You should not be here, your majesty."

Gasps sounded from all the men as Dave's eyes narrowed.

"I go where I wish."

"You tempt fate, and she is not happy with you." Adele's beautiful face was stern, but a moment later she smiled. "Still, perhaps you've learned something from this adventure, but I recommend against such exploits from this point on. You'll one day have an entire galaxy depending on you."

"How do you know this?" One of the older men demanded.

"She has the ability to see the future." Dave stood behind her, his expression daring these men to try anything against his woman.

The jit prisoners surprised Dave by taking his words very seriously indeed. They looked at Adele with even greater respect and the older men bowed their heads, though their eyes never left her face—a mark of respect among jit'suku warriors.

"What do you see, Lady?" the young man asked in almost hushed tones.

Adele smiled. "You'd be surprised." She touched his shoulder, almost protectively. "I'll tell you this though. If you stay safe and continue on your present course, with no more adventures in our galaxy, you'll be the one to end the war. You'll be known as the Peacemaker, in the fullness of time. And your wife..." Her eyes seemed faraway as if she were looking at something only she could see. "Your empress will be a very special woman." Her gaze refocused on the young man. "She'll be human...but not. Pay attention to the man from the Pyramid when he crosses your path. He and his brothers will be the key."

"Lady, you speak in riddles."

Adele smiled. "When these things come to pass, you'll understand and hopefully note their significance. That's my purpose. To make you aware. But you must live your life and gain from your experiences. Just please don't take quite so many chances in future. The perils are great, and if you come back to this galaxy uninvited again, you'll pay the consequences."

"Then you won't turn me in this time?"

"Speaking for myself, I won't reveal your identity. In fact, because you didn't invade the station itself, but rather remained behind on the ship, chances are, there will be no charges levied against you four. They'll probably escort you to your side of the border and let you go."

"Is this true?" one of the older men demanded of Dave.

"Adele is a highly ranked CSS officer. She knows their procedures better than I do."

"And what about you, sir? Will you divulge my identity? Knowing it would probably spell my death?"

The young man's steadfast gaze impressed Dave. Here stood a man with deep honor and courage. And if Adele was to be believed, he would one day be the jit'suku emperor.

"You're just a kid," Dave said off-handedly. "I don't know who you are beyond that." Dave leaned down to look the younger man in the eye. "I trust Adele. If she says you're the one to bring peace between our people, then I'll give you every chance to do it."

"Yet you are a soldier."

Dave nodded. "I've been fighting on the rim for twenty years. I've had my fill of war. And we're too well matched. This'll go on forever if we don't come to a truce at some point. I'm hoping you'll be the man to do it. If so, God speed, Emperor."

The young man shifted uncomfortably. "I'm not emperor yet."

Adele smiled softly. "But you will be. I hope you'll remember us then. I hope you'll know there are many humans who would welcome peace with your people."

The boy looked skeptical, but held his tongue. After a moment, he bowed. "I thank you for your counsel. What are your names?"

Adele laughed, apparently caught by surprise. "I'm Adele Senna and this is Colonel David Hellerby."

The man nodded. "You have my thanks." They moved down the corridor to the ramp before he spoke again. "Are you not mates?"

David chuckled as they walked. "We only met yesterday, but I have every intention of keeping Adele with me for the rest of our lives. If she'll have me." She gasped and looked at him with an expression of joyous surprise that boded well for his chances.

The other men shook their heads and grinned. "It's easy to see you are destined mates," the oldest one said with a twinkle in his eye. "Congratulations."

* * * *

After they'd handed their prisoners over to station police, Adele and David reported to the command area to find the CSS officers had been revived and were quickly regaining control over all station systems. Adele signed off on the logs, turning command of the station back to its rightful leaders. They had things well in hand when Dave suggested he and Adele seek out The Rabbit Hole to check in with Alex and the men.

Aside from a short comm assuring Adele that her Aunt Della was fine, the spec ops warriors from the bar had faded away once order was restored. Only the young soldier, Timothy, stayed with the station cops, being lauded for his role in freeing the men who now processed the jit'suku prisoners for trial and most for eventual deportation.

Only the ringleaders, those who had killed or committed other crimes during the attack, and those with previous warrants would be detained, since there was little loss of life on the station. The rest of the crew would probably be sent back to their own galaxy after an initial holding period while the evidence was sorted.

Timothy was the hero of the action and both Dave and Adele were happy to see the pride on the young man's face as he was thanked and congratulated by the station commander. Officially, Adele, Dave and Timothy were going to be credited with assisting the station police in repulsing the jit invaders. Dave had cautioned Tim and Adele not to mention Alex or the other men and they seemed to understand that Alex and his team needed to remain secret.

When Dave and Adele walked into the bar, they were greeted with raised glasses and cheerful words. Adele's aunt rushed over and hugged them both.

"Thank you, David, for protecting my niece."

"My pleasure, ma'am. And she did more than her share. Without her command codes, the job would have been much more difficult." He couldn't help the pride that crept into his voice.

"Congratulations to you both," Della said with a tear in her eye. "You are going to be so happy on Earth, sweetie." She hugged her niece while Dave was caught a bit short.

"You saw us on Earth?"

Della nodded vigorously. "On a lovely parcel of land in the Middle of North America. With a beautiful family of your own."

"Family?" Dave croaked.

"Yes, my dear nephew." Della took his hand in both of hers and stroked the back comfortingly. Her voice dropped even lower as her next words floored him. "They were wrong when they said you could never be a father. You will be, David. Several times over. With my Adi." Tears filled the older woman's eyes when she looked up at him. Her smile was almost angelic.

"Earth?" Adele asked.

Dave focused on her, unable to deal with the revelation that he would be a father just yet.

"I was born on Earth. I've always wanted to go back and homestead near my siblings. I was working my way back slowly. Eventually, I want to live on the homeworld and..." he looked at Della who was beaming and nodding, "...raise a family. With you. If you'll have me."

"Oh, David!" Adele's reaction touched his heart. Her eyes reflected her joy—the same joy in his own heart. "I'll never let you go, you silly man. I love you!"

She hugged him, wrapping him tight in her arms as the men at the bar watched with envious smiles. Dave could see his comrades over the top of Adele's head. He was glad his brothers in arms were there to witness his happiness, but he knew he was home now. Truly. Adele was his home. Now and forever.

Epilogue

Adele and Dave were married quietly a few weeks later on Jupiter Prime Station, where she'd been born. A number of David's family came and they had an impromptu family reunion. Plans were made for David to apply for a homesteading license and by the following year they'd been granted permission to live on Earth.

A gift awaited them in their new home when they finally moved in. The message was oblique but they knew it had come from the young jit'suku man they'd let go. The future emperor.

He gave them a costly piece of crystal statuary from the jit galaxy that was worth a king's ransom on Earth. It also held a princely secret—a cache of gemstones and a seal of the Imperial House that identified Adele and David, and all their progeny, as those to whom the jit'suku emperor owed a personal debt. The multi-colored gemstones were a nest egg, the message said, to help get them started on their life together.

Adele knew they would come in handy one day, as would the Imperial seal...but not in any way the future emperor could have imagined. Fate, it seemed, was not done with them yet.

Hand of Fate

Eva Gale

Also by Eva Gale

101 Degrees Fahrenheit
Phaze Fantasies, Vol. IV
Desperate Measures

Dedication

To Selah, Ferfe, Ann and the Cage Critters. For four thousand dollar hand jobs and bending a few rules. Salute!

Chapter One

Boston, 1880

It was as if the carnival had come to town, and Abigail Drummond and her family were the penny freak show.

She scanned the handful of men gathered at the stone hearth, their drinks in hand. Every once in a while one of them would steal a covert glance her way, mutter something, and the group would break into muffled laughter. Too bad they were such nuisances because the instigator, well, he looked like the devil himself.

Even still, what she would give to crash their glasses over their heads. The muscles in her stomach burned from tension, her jaw ached, and to top it off a headache was starting to crawl up the back of her neck.

The only reason she attended this damnable thing was for her Aunt Judith, her godmother, even though it was all her mother's doing.

So she sat, being talked about and laughed at, while she did her best to read twittering women their palms. Same thing as always: the unmarried wanted to know whom they would marry, and married women wanted to know how many children they would have. How much money would they have or what the future held. The brave wanted to know if their husbands were having affairs.

Her mother sashayed into the parlor looking like a parrot amidst doves and clapped her hands. "Come! Come! Come!" She swung her arms wide and turned, the feather on her turban dancing in front of her face. "Sit! Sit!" She smiled at the handful of men, "Let my beautiful daughters tell you how to better your business!" Then she turned to the women, "My daughters will tell you if love comes your way!"

The few women cast hopeful glances at each other, and one sat down at her sister Camille's table. Her mother eyed her and she looked away, instead scanning the crowd, simultaneously hoping for and fearing her next customer. The Devil looked at her, his eyebrow arched, and she stared back , daring him.

Sometimes she wanted to leave Boston and start out where no one knew her family. Somewhere she could be Abigail Drummond, a twenty-seven-year-old who sometimes took in stray animals and sewed crazy quilts for the local mercantile. Anything but the palm-reading daughter of a Romany fortuneteller.

The gaggle of imbeciles roared out in laughter again, and she ground her teeth. Why they stayed there baffled her. They wouldn't sit for a reading, and they'd be better suited to the den where the bar was. If only they would go anywhere, rather than here.

There were five of them including Devil, who seemed to be at ease, but whose eyes were taking in every detail of his surroundings. It seemed his companions ceased to amuse.

He piqued her curiosity. Too bad a woman like herself would never be looked at as marriageable by his set. Even though she skirted polite society, she would be ruined for having an affair with him. Still, he was good looking, and he'd make the plummet from grace entertaining.

He caught her eye, raised his glass, and grinned. Just grand. Nothing like being caught staring. Her cheeks burned as she leaned down to pet Felicity, who purred and wove around her worn hem. Maybe some wilting female would think it her familiar. She could only hope.

Four more hours of this hell.

Aunt Judith had placed her table in the front parlor right off the foyer, a lovely tapestry cloth covering the heavy round oak top. Matching bronze candle sticks with crystal beaded bobeches were set in the center so that Abby could better see her clients' hands. If she got any clients. Even still, the candles lent a warm glow and the smell of beeswax soothed, even though they could have used the gas lamps. The fireplace crackled at her back, making her skin feel like it was on fire.

A glow of perspiration dewed her face and chest and she wished another guest would arrive so the cold January air would gust into the stifling room.

Instead, she stared at the arrogant one through her lashes. He stood a hair taller than his friends, and where they were average, he was solid. His jacket was cut generously through the shoulder and arms, perfectly tailored, but his unlacquered hair curled at his collar. All of the other gentlemen looked as if they wore shiny helmets. His clean hair looked…refreshing, like it would softly catch at her fingers.

The rasp of taffeta snapped her attention to her Aunt, who sat down across her. "Abby, darling. Here, let me be your first client."

Abby shook her head. "No, stop. You've done this too many times already."

"Once more won't hurt. And your mother always tells me our futures change every day based on the decisions we make. 'The way to determine your future is to act in your present'."

Abby closed her eyes and counted to ten. Aunt Judith chuckled and patted her hand. "All right then, how I can help?"

"You've done more than enough. Always more than enough. Just this alone is almost more help than I can bear."

Aunt Judith laughed out loud, and Abby cracked a smile. She was the only one who thought Abby's wry sense of humor funny.

The men laughed again as if they were part of the conversation, and Abby frowned. "Actually, you can help me." She leaned into the table. "Who are those men, and can you direct them to the bar?"

Judith's face lit up, and she put her hand over her mouth. "What will we do with you? Alright, they are Uncle Darren's acquaintances from business. The taller one is Mr. Dupree, President of the Boston Trust, and the others are owners of various other local businesses." She sighed. "They love to use occasions like this to ingratiate themselves to Mr. Dupree."

Well wasn't that wonderful. Not only was the devil Mr. Dupree, but also the Vice President of Boston Trust. Abigail always did set her sights high. Exercises in futility seemed to be a specialty.

If it weren't so sad it would be humorous how many times she was propositioned to by a man who thought her family's peculiarities meant she was a whore. She should have taken one or two up on their offers. She wasn't getting any for marriage, that was for sure. As soon as they showed interest Mother sat them down for a reading, and they would never come back. Maybe next time she would say, yes.

A wicked gleam came into Judith's eye, and she leaned into Abby. "I think I have an idea." She stood, shook her voluminous skirts, and walked over to the group. Abby smirked as they stood straighter when their hostess engaged them.

Abby was too far off to hear anything Judith said, but soon her aunt turned back, holding the elbow of the President of the Bank. Abby watched in horror, as they walked towards her. For all his taunting he was the most attractive man she'd ever seen.

As it was, she would never be able to hold her head up in public again, and now he was on his way to her table, a cat eating the canary grin on his face.

"Miss Abigail Drummond, may I introduce you to Mr. Caden Dupree." Judith turned to Mr. Dupree and motioned to the chair. "Why don't you sit down and see if Abby can tell you something interesting about yourself? Maybe even some insight to your business."

"Ahh, I...," he looked at Judith, then to Abby, and back to Judith again, whose face resembled a disappointed schoolmarm. He pulled out the chair and sat. Abby bit her lip and turned her face.

She looked down her nose at him and wondered if she should put on the 'I know everything about you' air, or if she should play the strange eccentric. Or maybe she could try and seduce him. If she were to take up any offers for an affair, she should at least have it be a respected man, such as the delectable Mr. Dupree.

Aunt Judith patted her back. "I'll leave you two. Please find me and tell me how your reading went when you're finished, Mr. Dupree."

"Yes, of course." He managed to say with a smile as he watched Judith's retreating back. He looked back at Abby, his eyes taking in every freckle of her face, and she sat straighter. His eyes gleamed.

"I don't believe one iota of this psychic bullshit. I'm here in respect to the hosts, who are faithful patrons and investors."

Abby stifled a yawn.

Well if that was how he was going to be, this had possibilities of fun. Perspective was everything.

Mr. Dupree leaned toward her, "Why don't I just give you five dollars and call it a night? We all know your family is Mrs. Anderson's charity case."

She tried to catch her breath. Five dollars might be nothing to a man like him, but for her family it was enough coal to last the Boston winter and more. It was shoes for her mother that didn't need yesterday's paper blocking the holes in the bottom. Was he that ignorant or had he meant to insult her, the insult growing with every dollar he offered? Certainly it was an insult, with the jab he had made about her family being a charity case. The only question really, was how she should react?

There were options. If she slapped him it would ruin the evening for everyone, and her mother would lose all her clients.

It took every ounce of self-control, but she studied him and didn't respond. And here she had thought him attractive. She might not be of his social standing, but she could play his game. Her tools were a bit more subtle, though.

A few months ago she pilfered one of her mother's special books. One off the shelf she and Camille were never supposed to read from. It was an old tome on sexual palmistry. Suddenly it seemed Providence that she studied it cover to cover and remembered it almost word for word. Well, let's see if he could take what he dished out like the big man that he was.

She gathered up every bit of artifice within her to soften her eyes when she put out her hand.

"Well Mr. Dupree, at least let me tell you something for such a generous amount."

* * * *

This whole night was turning into the biggest waste of time, and now it was a waste of money. Although he had to hand it to her, she didn't snivel when he called her family a charity case. He never did after the first time either.

He turned his hand palm side up and shoved it at her, and a sizzle of pleasure shot through him as she jerked back.

"So, tell me my future." He gave her his biggest smile. One that people in Boston signed on the dotted line for. "Earn your alms," he said under his breath.

She didn't say a word, just took his hand and cradled it in her small warm one, palm up, under the glow of the candles. He held a grudging respect for her when she didn't rise to his bait.

"This is your dominant hand?" She didn't look up to meet his eyes.

"Yes."

She nodded, and with her other hand circled his palm with her thumb. A shudder ran down his back. She ran her fingers over his, bringing his down from their curled position. Every finger she caressed and pulled down, one at a time, opening his palm and making his sense of touch more sensitive than ever. He wondered if she knew what she was doing, what action she emulated. His body did even if his brain didn't want him to.

As soon as she was done he could make his exit and head over to the brownstone he'd bought Beatrice, where she would be waiting for him. It'd been four weeks since he'd visited her. The relationship, for his part, had all gone south, but the tears, recriminations and guilt associated with disengaging from a long time mistress and friend kept him from ending it. And, tonight, with the way this girl so unknowingly enticed him, his body would have use of Beatrice, even if his heart didn't. The sooner he could leave and head over there, the better.

"Are you going to start anytime soon?" Impatience whipped his voice, and he wished he brought over his glass of brandy. Darren always made sure he had a few bottles when Caden came over. And Caden brought Darren good Cuban cigars that Judith prohibited from being smoked in her house. See, there was good that came out of these pitiful social obligations.

His hand relaxed into Miss Drummond's small one, and she smirked. It was just a little lift of the corner of her mouth. Maybe she did know what she was doing. He shifted in his seat.

"I don't have all night. I'm not here for your hoodoo, I'm here to socialize with business people."

She took his thumb and slid it between her fingers, bending it back and forth. His breath hitched in his throat. Then she turned his hand over and dragged the pad of her finger over the edge of his nail and studied the back of his hand. Maybe he should take his hand away and throw the money on the table.

"You're very loyal." She said it in a matter of fact way.

"So?"

She didn't even glance up.

"Very realistic and pragmatic. Assertive. But your hand is intricately lined. You've a complex personality."

He snorted.

"Your nails are square, your pad going past the tips, the moons are evident, and that shows me that you think substance and a person's character are more important than how they look. You're robust. Healthy. You're very strong. You persevere when others give up, and that's how you've become so successful." She met his eyes over the flames of the candles. "Despite your younger years."

He clamped his mouth shut, and he could feel his pulse in his temple.

She traced his middle finger all the way up with the barest of touches and circled the tip with her own. All of the blood that was pounding in his head flowed downward, and he put his legs out in front of him. Thankfully he was half under a heavy tablecloth.

"This is your Saturn finger. Your most powerful finger. It's thicker and heavier than the others, and see how your Jupiter finger bends towards it?" She traced up his pointer finger. He grunted. "This tells me you're sensible. Controlled, and you have unusual endurance. You are almost too disciplined, but it leads to your great achievement." She lifted his palm up to her eye level, then rested it back down onto the table. "Your Saturn mound is very high. You had a very troubled youth. Illness? There's loss of a parent? Separation from your family. Your heart was broken." Her eyes were warm like the color of whiskey and then she looked back down again. "But you've overcome all that. You've worked hard to do so."

He didn't need her pity.

"Enough, this is not what I came here for." He pulled his hand back, but her grip was firm. He rose up and looked around to see if anyone watched them.

"Stay, please. I'm not done yet."

He sat back down. "Make it quick." He lived his past, he didn't need any reminders of it.

"Maybe you would like to hear the interesting part?"

"Since I don't believe any of it, none of it is interesting."

"Well, maybe I can change your mind."

He looked at her, expectant, even though he was determined to discount everything she said. Her eyes held something closer, though, as if she were weighing her words.

"Your hands are thick, they move easily, but can't be manipulated. That means you have a lot of sexual energy, that you enjoy giving and receiving pleasure." She paused, "But, your Plain of Neptune is low, which warns me that although you are perceptive, you don't like personal involvement, you like being detached." She brushed her hand over the back of his. "Your skin is warm and not too soft, but yet not rough and calloused. That means that you're a responsive lover, but you like to assert yourself, too."

He reminded himself to breathe.

"Your fingers are thick. This means you love the sensual. Food, comfort, and large amounts of carnal pleasure."

"And what would you know about carnal pleasure?" His voice came out rough and scratchy like charcoal embers.

"Enough to know what I'm talking about." Her dulcet answer snapped his head back.

He rose to her challenge. "Would you like to show me how much?"

"Five dollars isn't enough."

"Well, what if I made it twenty?"

She patted his hand. "That's sure a lot of money to a charity case like myself, but I'm not a whore for any man, no matter my lack of finances."

He stood up reached into his pocket and pulled out a folded wad of bills, peeled five singles off, and threw it on the table.

"You know where to reach me if you need any more." He turned away from her and walked over to the hearth where his brandy waited. With one swallow he tossed it down and grabbing his coat off the tree, stalked out the door.

Chapter Two

The ice crackled under their feet as they walked up the steps. Abby gripped the wobbly railing and held on for dear life as her feet slipped out from under her. Her mother grabbed her by the elbow, hauling her up.

"I'll have to remember to put the ashes on the stairs." Her mother's voice was muffled from the scarf wrapped around the lower half of her face.

"If we had the coal in the first place." Abby was too mad to keep the scorn from her voice.

"We could go and cut some trees down." Camille held on to her other elbow and steadied her as she reached the porch.

Abby rolled her eyes. Of course Camille, the eternal optimist, still chipper even with what they'd been through. Chop wood. Right. Like any one of them could fell a tree.

Ever since her father's estate attorney paid a call to inform her mother that there were no funds left unless they sold the house, Abby became a cynic. Selling would turn them from poor to homeless. The money would be eaten up in rent. At least this way they had a roof over their heads. And her mother had something for her daughters, even if she had nothing for herself.

And there was the crux. For as much as strange and eccentric as her family was, and as angry as Abby got at the ostracism it caused, her mother was selfless in her motivations. For that, Abby stood as her staunchest ally. She would even go so far as to admit that growing up the way she did sculpted her character. You learned very fast when you are perceived as different not to judge others lest you be judged. Or, you were eaten with anger.

Her mother unlocked the door and shooed them all into the vestibule to hang their woolen coats and hats. Abby would have loved to keep hers on. Her breath was still coming out in puffs of white.

She stomped the floor shaking the clumps of snow off her feet and bent over to unlace her boots.

"Maybe we should all sleep in my room tonight. That way we can combine all the wood and make the room toasty?" Her mother looked at her so hopefully she couldn't say no. And she desperately wanted to. That odious man, Mr. Caden Dupree, infuriated her and she wanted to brood by herself. What she needed to do was berate herself for finding him even more attractive. What was wrong with her? He was angry, nasty, and callous without an iota of compassion.

But his hands said that wasn't the truth.

In his hands were strength, diligence, and sensuality. All of which made for a potent draw. One that she wanted to dwell on, in private, for as long as she could, but that didn't look like it would happen. At least, not tonight.

She sighed. "That would be fine." She gave her mother a hug. "I'll get dressed and bring over my blankets."

"What fun!" Camille clapped. "We can tell each other all about our clients. I had some interesting ones." She shucked her boots and headed up the stairs but turned back to look at Abby. "I saw the Vice President of Boston Trust at your table, Abby. You must tell us what happened with him." Her eyes lit up. "Maybe Mother can do a reading on you and see if he will ask for your hand!"

Abby turned to look at her mother, "Mother, please, no."

Her mother smiled and shook her head.

"Forevermore, Camille! Will you please stop trying to play the matchmaker?" Abby stomped up the stairs and wanted to smack the smirk off her sister. "Really. You would think I was stale cheese on the shelf the way you try to get rid of me."

Camille laughed. "Well, you are on the shelf, but you smell exquisite from all that bathing."

Mother chuckled and the sound made Abby smile, too. "Well, water is free but if we ever have to pay for it, I'll make a fine Limburger."

She slipped into her room before her sister could make another remark and started to undress. Wherever the conversations led tonight, she needed to keep them away from Mr. Dupree. If her mother ever found out how she'd taunted him she would refuse to let her read again. Not that Abby would mind never reading another palm, but she did break a code of conduct for her own personal gain. Even if it was just to torment. And she did gain. Five dollars worth.

She had slipped the money discreetly into the top of her boot, and now she stood undressed in the middle of her chilled room with it in her hand. If she gave it to her mother, which she wanted to do, she would have to answer questions which would lead to her lying. If there was one thing Abby knew about herself it was that she could not lie to her mother. Whether it was psychic ability, or the fact that she could read her daughter's face, her mother knew the moment Abby tried to lie. Too much had already gone wrong in their family for her to start heaping broken trust into the cauldron.

Maybe there would be some way she could buy something they needed with the money. Like coal, or food later on in the winter.

She looked at the bills on her bed and felt sick. What was even worse than taking it, was what she saw in his hand. Amongst all of that control were shadowed bits of his past, and his true character. His lines concurred with her intuitions, but for the most part she ignored what people's hands said. Even though she had been taught how to read palms as soon as she could comprehend the subtle differences, she never put all her faith in what she saw there.

It was enough to know that taking that money had been the worst thing she had done, and that for all his arrogance, he didn't deserve what she had done.

She picked the money up off her bed and tucked it into a bureau draw. Guilt was not a feeling she was accustomed to and it sat on her heavily.

There was a light knock on the door. "Abby, you ready?"

Her sister's voice came muffled through the heavy wood.

"I'll be right there, go on without me."

"May I come in?"

Abby heaved a sigh. This huge house left to three women and she still could never find a moment alone.

"Yes."

Camille slipped in, her mended wrap snug around her shoulders with her hair braided like a rope down her back.

She sat down on the edge of Abby's bed and stared at her.

Abby sighed, untied her stockings, and started to roll them down. "What would you like, Camille?"

Camille started to play with the hole in Abby's crazy quilt.

"Stop. Grandmother and I worked hard on that."

"I could embroider a ribbon rose here to cover the hole." Camille smoothed down the velvet nap.

"That would be nice." She stopped to fold up her stocking and looked at her sister. "Can you loosen my laces?"

Camille went around to her back and started pulling the strings out just enough.

"Ready?" Camille moved to the front and Abby took a deep breath and held it. Camille unbuttoned the busk and the whole corset came off in one piece.

Abby slowly let her breath out and took another, then rolled her shoulders. "Camille, what would you like?"

"I saw Mr. Dupree give you money."

* * * *

It just wouldn't happen.

He could feel it start, that lightning ball that crackled at the base of his spine and worked itself up to his scalp until his whole body tensed and fixated with it. Almost, just there, dangling out of reach, but then it dissipated.

What was her name? Abigail. Her hands. He focused on how her hands caressed his, how they mimicked the teasing of a high paid courtesan. He had no idea his palms could be so sensitive or that they were routed to his cock.

She'd taken him aback with her dark charred voice and her subtle sexuality. How she told him the kind of lover he was with complete understanding, but with the face of an ingénue.

He wanted her hands again. But on his cock, where they were meant to be, stroking him with that smile that made him hard.

Almost there, almost there. His eyes were slammed shut and Abigail told him how he loved the sensual, how he gave and received pleasure. He wanted to see her naked. What she looked like in climax.

There. There...now, yes, yes, yes...His scalp tingled and he grunted as spasms wracked him.

"Well, you took forever and a day tonight."

Funny, when had her voice begun to grate on him, sounding petulant and coquettish?

He should have told her not to speak under any circumstances, because it killed any relaxation he gained.

"Shut up, Beatrice." He pulled out of her and walked over to the wash basin, ignoring her staged moue.

"What was wrong tonight?" She rolled over onto her stomach and looked at him over her shoulder.

You. You were wrong. You *are* wrong.

"How long have we had this arrangement now? Five years?" He glanced at her as he washed himself off.

"Yes." A shadow crossed her face, but she reined it in.

He frowned. She was never a good actress.

No use for it, though. He'd been thinking about cutting out long before now. He liked her, but he wanted more. Whatever it would be, Beatrice was not the one he wanted it with. He felt bad because she'd been there while he worked himself up, and he made sure she got her share of that hard work. He was always fair, but feeling bad about decisions didn't get them done.

"Is there another woman?" Her voice was soft and broken.

She surprised him. He never thought she held that much emotion for their relationship. But that was a lie. Otherwise he would have cut it off weeks ago.

Remembering Abigail while he was here reinforced how stale his fling with Beatrice was. There was nothing of substance in his arrangement with Bea, so there was no use in maintaining it.

He found her when they were both poor and just barely off the streets. Only he had just started a good job at Boston Trust as an errand boy, running papers for the presidents and CEOs of the larger Boston businesses. He took care of her, always making sure she had food, and as soon as he could afford to, he bought her clothes and eventually the house. Not out of undying emotion, but a sort of one hand washing the other. Because, although he didn't love her, he didn't want to see her sick on the streets pimping herself to handfuls of diseased men.

Maybe he'd done more harm than good. But it was never his intent.

Somehow Abigail could tell. Maybe she knew even more than she told him. He'd worked until the smell of poverty no longer clung to him. And she brought it all up, innocently of course, but the truth of it was there again. He'd lashed out at her with the charity case remark, about how it wasn't so much about her being poor, it was her knowing the truth of him without him allowing her to.

Not that it mattered. Everyone knew how he worked himself up. He'd even started a program where lower income youths were given apprentice opportunities within some of the most prestigious Boston companies.

"No. But I think that may change."

"You won't marry me?" Her voice was whisper thin.

"What gave you that idea?" He pulled a towel off the stand, dried himself, and turned to face Beatrice. "No, I never had that intention and you know it." He combed his wet hair and checked in the mirror. "I would like you to leave within the week."

"For a vacation?"

"No. A permanent arrangement." He hated confrontations like this. He never did well with women.

She looked like a thunderstorm gathering power. All tumultuous and boiling anger. "How dare you." Her face contorted and she flew off the bed, coming at him with her nails bared. "You son of a bitch," she swiped at his face and he caught her wrists.

"Yes." He held her hands down with no effort and she started to kick him. With a twist he had her back to his chest and her arms pinned at her sides. She stilled for a moment, then started to rub herself against him.

"Your other woman won't fuck you like I do. You won't leave me...you like my pussy too much." She rubbed up and down and in circles against his flaccid cock. At that moment it dawned on him how cheap she was and how she repulsed him. He shoved her away and she turned to him, cupping her breasts in an offer.

"These are the best in town," she ran her tongue over her lips and pushed them up higher. Her teased hair and smudged eyes—a parody of a clown.

"You are pathetic when desperate." He turned and walked away to the armoire that held his clothes.

"You always were a callous bastard."

He opened it, slid a fresh shirt off its hanger, and pulled it on. "I'll be back next Friday to make sure you're gone." He pushed his onyx cufflink through and flicked the swiveled rod.

"What if I don't?" She inched herself behind the bed and picked up her clothes without breaking eye contact.

"Then I'll come throw your clothes in the street and have one of my men escort you to your new residence."

She stood straight. "My new residence?"

He scoffed. "Get that thought out of your head. There were no promises made in this agreement from the beginning." His arms slid into his coat and he straightened the collar. "You will certainly have something in place by Friday next for your living arrangements. I'll give you enough money to get a start. If you need a referral I'll write a letter." She still stood behind the bed, her face waxen, with a silk robe wrapped around her and held tightly in her fists. "Most of Boston knows who you are, and how long our arrangement has lasted. I'm quite certain there will be callers for you as soon as you make our dissolution known."

He walked out the bedroom door and paused. "The only things I expect to be taken from my alternate residence are any jewelry I've given you. Think of it as a parting gift. You could live off of it for years. And make sure all of your attire is gone. I want no remembrances. You don't want me to say unflattering things at the club."

Her sobs started as he walked down the stairs and carried through the house.

"I'll tell everyone the truth about you, how you were a dirt farmer and a street beggar!" she yelled out the top window.

He'd have to remember to have a cleaning service come in and freshen the place. The brass knob was cold and smooth in his hands as he pulled the door closed.

Chapter Three

"How may I help you, miss?" The bald man looked through his spectacles and down his nose at her.

"Miss Abigail Drummond to see Mr. Caden Dupree."

"And do you have an appointment?"

"No."

The man sniffed. "And what makes you think Mr. Dupree has a moment to see you if you've made no appointment?"

Abby resisted the need to pinch the bridge of her nose. She took a breath and broke out her most dazzling smile. The one that hurt her cheeks. "Mr...?"

"Frist."

"Mr. Frist." She smiled again, "That suit looks quite dashing on you, really." He looked at her pointedly and she rushed in, "I know that you are an extremely responsible employee of Mr. Dupree's, as I can tell from your diligent care of his appointments." He puffed up the smallest bit and she stole her opportunity, "So, even though I have not informed Mr. Dupree of my impending visit, I'm sure if you notify him of my arrival you'll see that he is most welcoming indeed."

Mr. Frist looked her up and down and nodded. "I'll see if he's in. One moment please."

He left his station to shuffle down an oak-paneled hall to knock on a door, and when he received an answer opened it up to poke his head inside.

Her heart started to thud like a tympani in her chest. Making the decision to come to the bank just near killed her. It was the right thing to do, she knew , but knowing never made the doing easy. And as angry as she had been, she still loved having his hand in hers. How he looked as she stroked his palm suggestively.

Her stroke of brilliance had worked in reverse, too. His skin had been warm and firm and she'd wondered how his hands would have felt caressing her, as she had him.

Later that night she'd gone back to her own bed, her desire was so potent. As she lay in bed she'd brought herself to climax fantasizing about his hands touching her. That it was his hands rubbing her. She squeezed her thighs together. His personality was so strong it sexually excited her, but he was harsh, and that made her feel guilty for wanting him. Both emotions together confused her. The enigma was how his hands told a different story. Maybe something she said provoked his reaction.

Although she'd been around palm reading all her life, and saw the many truths of it, she always gave people the benefit of choosing a different course, and so she'd done with him. He was strong, that was obvious, but he also had a depth to him that went far beyond the lines she'd seen in other hands. A large capacity for love and generosity, but hidden, so deep that it might as well, not have been not there.

She wanted to learn him. To explore why he made her feel the way she did. Especially since it was the fantasy of him that made her orgasm so furiously last night.

Now she had to stand in front of him and give his money back. Even though she knew he couldn't read her mind she was afraid he'd take one look at her and know what she'd done.

Moments later, Mr. Frist made his way back to stand in front of her.

"Mr. Dupree will see you, but he has an appointment now and another in a quarter hour so please make your meeting brief."

"Yes, sir. Thank you so much."

He led her down the same dark hall and gestured to a long heavy bench where she could sit and wait.

The trace of a baritone voice came through the inches of open door and her chest clenched. She would know the cadence of his voice at a theater intermission in a packed crowd.

He stopped speaking and a softer voice answered. A woman was doing her banking, nothing unusual, especially for a Monday. But then she heard a choked sob and she tapped her foot.

That bastard was probably in there treating that poor woman horribly. He had no heart. Look at the way he spoke to her at the party! She pursed her lips. She should have taken care of him right then. Huh, charity case. She had a mind to keep his damned money.

She heard Caden's voice again and the woman broke into a full cry.

Abby sprung off the bench and was about to yank the door open, but paused to peer into the room.

A woman in a worn black coat and once black boots stood enveloped in Caden's embrace. Abby bit back her gasp and knew she should sit down. Caden murmured something to her and she nodded into his jacket, sniffling.

Who could it be? His mistress? She knew he wasn't married. Would he be so crude as to have this woman at the bank during business hours?

Maybe she should knock and feign ignorance. No, it was none of her business and the woman was not being hurt. Abby had to admit, though, her curiosity was piqued. And a tinge of jealousy lurked there too. What about her made him loathsome towards her, but yet affectionate to this woman?

Just then Caden held the woman at arm's length and Abby stepped off to the side, but stayed where she could hear and see just a sliver.

"You'll be fine. I took care of the mortgage and I'll stop Smithson from speaking to you that way again."

"Thank you, Mr. Dupree."

"Caden, Rebekah. James was a friend of mine, too, and I would never allow his family to be homeless while I had the power to help."

"But it was so much money." She sniffled.

"It was a few hundred, and don't you worry about the boys, either. I set up accounts for them for when it's time to go to school. There should be enough in there by then for both of them to go to any university they choose."

The woman started to sob again. "But how can I repay you?" she said, barely intelligible.

Abby cringed, dreading his answer. Men never did anything so generous without expectations.

He patted Rebekah's back, "You love those boys and raise them right. Make sure they go to school and if they give you a problem send them to me."

"Thank you, Caden."

"Rebekah, James was my best friend. He believed in me when no one saw anything but a hustling scrapper." He swallowed hard. "I miss him too." He patted her back again. "So, you take care of those boys, that's how you thank me."

Abby blinked back tears and went to sit back down on the bench.

Frist came up the hall moments later, his clipped steps echoing.

Thankfully her gloves were on or she would have to wipe her hands on her dress, but she used them to dab at the corners of her eyes instead.

Frist rapped on the door. Caden's voice barked to enter and Mr. Frist opened the door for her and said, "Miss Drummond to see you, sir."

"Carry on, Frist."

Mr. Frist nodded at her and went back to his station in the foyer.

A moment later the woman appeared and as she walked past Abby she smiled sadly, her red rimmed eyes welling up.

"Sorry to keep you," she said, and disappeared down the hall and into the crowd.

She wished she'd never come, but she was also happy she did. It was just that now she was confused, whereas before she was very happily angry.

Now her heart softened, and all of those cutting things she planned to say evaporated with his generosity. The light he cast himself in was now more flattering, even if he didn't know her perception had changed. And her desire grew roots.

Abby took a deep breath and stepped into the room, the air hitching in her throat. She glanced at his hands that were folded in front of him.

Mr. Caden Dupree sat behind an enormous carved oak desk and got up to come around when he saw her. "Well my, my, isn't this a fortuitous day."

She thought she would have wanted to hug him for his gentle care of the woman, but instead, at the look in his eyes, the hairs on her neck stood on end as he escorted her into his lair.

He offered her a seat with a wave of his arm, and she wondered where the loving man who'd just comforted his best friend's widow was. Somewhere deep inside, she was sure, but right now she had to find out which side of this multifaceted man she now dealt with.

During the day at work he looked polished and the complete gentleman, far different than the Caden Dupree she'd seen the other night. Sitting at her table that night after she'd teased him with his sexual reading, he looked as if he were much less dangerous despite what she'd witnessed. Now she had the feeling she'd taunted a lion instead of a kitten.

As she sunk into the buttery leather of a chair he perched himself on the edge of his desk. Leather bound ledgers were set open and a filigree silver pen sat waiting by its side.

He studied her as she took in every detail. "To what to I owe this delightful visit?"

There was a knowing gleam in his eye, and she realized he thought she came to take him up on his offer. Her hands fisted in her lap. She didn't know whom she was angrier with, herself or him. Because as furious as she was with him for assuming such, she would have succumbed had he made an attempt to seduce her, although he had made his loathing of her profession very clear. Again, his conflicting facets. As curious as she was, apparently his assessment of her hadn't changed.

She stood up. "Mr. Frist told me you have a meeting shortly so I'll be quick," she opened her beaded reticule and took out the five dollars, handing it to him. "Here. I wanted to return this."

 Perverse satisfaction settled inside her at the shock on his face. Good, let him have to rethink his assumptions of her.

He didn't reach out to take it. "I gave that to you for your insightful reading."

"As well as that may be, I feel the need to return it."

"I refuse to accept."

She glared at him. "I'm a charity case if you remember." Her curiosity was quickly turning to anger. What infuriated her more was that, sparring with him didn't diminish her desire. If anything it heightened it.

"All the more reason for you to keep it."

Her mouth dropped open and she gasped. "I insist on returning it to you."

"No." He crossed his arms over his chest.

There was a sharp rap at the door.

"Yes!"

Mr. Frist's head appeared as if disembodied. "Your meeting, sir."

"I'm in negotiations, Frist."

"Yes, sir, but your appointment is here. I settled them in the-"

"In a moment, Frist."

"Yes, sir." He pulled his turtle head back and closed the door.

Mr. Dupree focused his burning glare on her and she thought for a moment she could still slip out the door after Frist, but he held her pinned with his gaze.

Why wouldn't he just let her do this? "Mr. Dupree—"

"You may call me Caden."

She sniffed. If vipers could grin, they would look like him.

"It's polite to return the invitation."

Her chin lifted. She knew he was playing her by insulting her manners but decided to see where he was leading. "You may call me Miss Drummond."

His eyes flared, and she stepped back. "The other night you had some interesting things to say about my life."

Her stomach flipped. Exactly the conversation she was hoping not to have. But she followed suit, didn't she? Thankfully she was prepared.

"And?" She folded her arms.

"And I would like to hear more about what you see in my palm. I'll pay you another five dollars, and you may tell your mother that you gave me a longer reading and earned the money."

That was not what she expected at all. She thought he would take his opportunity to take advantage of her spontaneous stupidity in teasing him inappropriately. She prepared herself to be yelled at. He might have ranted and raved, but him enticing her, asking for her to seduce him again...

Her heart sank , and she examined her dull black boots. Once he heard her reasoning he would never want to see her again anyway, which for some reason made her sad. She found him intriguing, not scary at all, although she did underestimate him. She took a deep breath. "I'm giving the money back because I took advantage of you."

He looked shocked. And she was sure that didn't occur often.

"How did you take advantage of me?"

This was absurd. The man was an arrogant and rude snob to make her explain. Why couldn't he just accept the money and her apology and be done with it? She wriggled like a worm on a hook, but in the end what she had done was unethical, and he deserved his answer. Anyway, she needed to be honest. Not for him, but for herself. For her mother, who though peculiar, had an ironclad morality pertaining to her and her daughter's abilities. It didn't mean that she had to like it, though.

"I used the reading to take advantage of you."

"I understand that. How did you take advantage of me?"

She blushed and swallowed feeling like she had sand in her throat. "Your sexual reading."

She peeked up from under the rim of her hat to see his eyes had darkened. His anger she could deal with. His desire was even more powerful. It provoked an even more elemental reaction in her. The one that made her masturbate last night. A reaction she didn't want him to see. "You made me mad when you called me a charity case. I used your hand to embarrass you. That was against my ethics as a reader. My mother doesn't know. My sister saw you give me the money.

"And what did your sister say?"

Abby shook her head. "She's young, she doesn't understand."

"Fine, I'll take your five dollars back. But I want you to give me another reading, right now." He walked behind his desk and swiveled the lamp towards her.

"But...you have an appointment."

"He can wait, believe me." He sat down and put his hand, palm up, under the light of the lamp.

It would be the end then. She would give him one more reading, and when she walked out her conscious would be clear. But her desire would become unbearable.

Not seeing him ever again would be a good thing, too, because he had set all of her senses on fire. For the past few days just the idea that he might be walking down the street and she would glimpse him made her heart pound faster.

And now, of all things he wanted her to do a reading for him.

A shiver ran through her knowing she would have his hand in hers again. It had never happened before, but when she read his hands her skin felt as if his touch were burning her like hot sugar. Stroking his palms made her want him to return the caresses and much more. Especially now that she knew under the gruffness there was a sterling heart.

She scooted forward and closed her eyes for a moment centering herself before reading. Her breathing calmed but as she reached out to take his hand her heart started to hammer.

It took a few moments, but when she finally thought she had herself under control she opened her eyes to see his green ones burning into her.

She'd made the wrong decision. She should have run out after Frist left.

* * * *

110

He couldn't believe she showed up and walked into his office. It was funny that she came to return the money. Anyone else would have kept it, no matter if they took advantage of him or not. People liked to assume that he used hundreds for handkerchiefs.

She took his hand into hers, and again all the blood in his body flowed south.

Her hair was different today. Looser. It pillowed her face, soft ringlets curling at her nape.

She tugged his fingers down and smoothed his palm. Each time she drew a finger down he got harder.

"Funny, you're a banker and your hand says that you're good with money." Her voice was rough and low, catching on words.

"That's good, then."

"You're very reliable. You love details." She dragged her fingertip down the length of his middle finger, and he shifted in his seat. "Your knuckles are wrinkled and apparent. You like to analyze things. You penetrate situations deeply with logic and thought. Each of your traits make you a good banker."

"I want the other reading."

She met his eyes over their hands, a question on her face.

"The other reading. Like the party. A sexual reading."

She broke their gaze and glanced behind her.

"If I do this, you'll never ask me to do another? You'll take your money back and never speak to anyone about this?"

"I promise."

She studied him and took a deep breath. "You have a long thumb. That means you have an abundance of sexual energy and a forceful personality."

"You told me that already. Tell me something I don't know."

She bent his fingers back towards her and studied his lines, tracing them with her fingers. "You have many whorls. That means you are an original thinker and that you don't like listening to rules. You're sexually adventurous."

He thought she would have left by now, that he would have scared her away, but she sat there knowing what he was doing, and her strength made him respect her. And want her more than he did before. But he wanted more out of her, he needed to know that she wouldn't back down from him. He wanted an equal partner in all things, in and out of the bedroom.

"Would you like to be sexually adventurous?"

"Mr. Dupree, I have to finish."

Could he tell her now that he wanted to hear her yell his name while she came? "I asked you to call me Caden."

"Mr. Dupree—"

"You're giving me a sexual hand reading and you're calling me Mr. Dupree?" Damn. He should have spoken less forcefully.

Her mouth hardened into a line then she huffed and rolled her eyes. "Caden..."

"See, that wasn't so hard."

She pulled his hand closer to her and dragged a finger down the outside of his palm, sending shudders through his stomach. "Your union line is broken and faint. You've had a relationship but it was not a lasting one, and it didn't mean that much to you."

He sat back in his chair but left his hand in hers. His friends knew about Beatrice, but with Abby not moving in his circles, she couldn't have known. Or could she?

She traced his pinky up and over the tip, back down to its web with a feather touch, and his erection strained his pants, "You have a long Mercury finger," her voice dropped lower, "and that coupled with your large Mount of Venus means that you are a good lover. Mercury is your communication finger and you can't be a good lover without communicating. Yours also curves toward your Apollo finger which can mean that you're seductive."

With that he pulled her hand to his mouth and kissed, his lips lingering against her warm skin, as he tasted her palm.

Chapter Four

Abby closed her eyes at his hot breath on her open hand. Passion rushed through her body, pooling between her legs and making his every breath a whisper stroke against her skin.

With his lips hovering over her, his tongue brushed her, and her breath caught in her throat. All at once his tongue was wet and dry, hot at first, then cool as his breath hit the moisture. A moan slipped out, and she looked at the back of his head over her hand, his soft hair with no lacquer.

He still held her hand as he walked around the desk, and pulled her up to him, pressing her against him. The heat in her sex grew to a tight pull, and she leaned in.

He ran his hands up her back and cradled her head as he brought his lips down on hers, sweeping his tongue into her shocked mouth, then teasing with nibbles and dips. Her stomach tightened and anticipation gathered.

Her body seemed as if it were on fire, sizzles jumping over her skin, and she slid her hands around his neck to draw him closer to her. She wanted him inside her, her reaction to his touch after her fantasy being too explosive to control. Even if she could, she didn't want to.

He kissed her again, his desire callous and raw. She arched her hips and met his erection with passion of her own, not believing the moment even as she did. He groaned into her mouth and let her head go, instead running his hands up her waist to the underside of her breasts, trying to cup them through her corset.

"So passionate," he murmured into her hair.

She couldn't think, her mind was flooded by his touch, by his tongue nipping and kissing her neck, under her ear. She wanted him, too, his skin under her hands and liquid, the way she felt.

"What can we do?" she said, hanging her head back so he could kiss it more.

"Whatever you want to do."

"I want my hands on you, on your skin."

He bumped his erection against her and groaned, then walked her backwards, never breaking contact, holding her steady, until they reached the door. He leaned her against the hard oak, with one hand caressing her, while he licked and sucked, and with the other he slid the bolt.

As the lock clicked she shivered. At being in the room alone with him, and with knowing what would happen while they were there. That she wanted it just as much as he did, and she had no care where they were.

She didn't know what brought her to this decision. Yes she did. The last man promised her marriage, but this time she didn't know what overwhelmed her senses, she wanted him with a matched intensity. And she knew he was different than he made himself out to be. Especially what she saw outside the office door. In his hands were her answers. Not many times before had she so truly believed in what she read. Even though his persona belied what she saw, his actions, his strength, his generosity—they were the truth of him, and that was the Caden she wanted.

There were other things in his hands that she didn't tell him about. Not that she believed all of it herself. But if it were to be fully realized, then his pain and his depth ran deeper than he showed. He'd overcome them, making his character stronger than most. She wanted to touch that part of him. She wanted to know the pain and hurt that shaped him. Not for pity, but for pride. He had his own morals, and they were chiseled in the trials of his life. She was willing to chance that this once, the truth lay in what she read.

She cupped her hands on either side of his face, kissed her desire and yielded, not just to him, but to the wanting within her. He pushed her harder against the door, pinning her with his body and hands. The mitered oak panels stiff behind her, holding her up.

With a low rumble he pulled away and, grabbing two handfuls of her chemise, petticoats and skirt, started to lift, bunching it at her sides and reaching underneath. He yanked, popping the buttons on her hips, and with a slight whisper her drawers fell. Cool air chilling her thighs was quickly replaced with warm fingers tracing the bits of skin left bare by her stockings. Her breath left her in pants as he stroked closer and closer, slowly reaching her patch of curls. Her heart pounded in her chest and the fire that burned between her legs spread over her body, radiating so that even his breath against her neck sent shots of pleasure skipping over her skin.

Never before had she ever felt both exposed and over clothed at the same time. She wanted her underpinnings, dress, and corset to disappear but closed her eyes at the eroticism of him taking her like this. With her bared legs and sex in his view, the perfume of her desire in her nose, while the rest of her was bound in cloth.

The strength of his body left her and she sagged forward, her eyes still closed. He chuckled and she heard the rustle of cloth hit the floor. When she opened her eyes he'd removed his jacket and collar and was taking out his cufflinks. He unbuttoned his shirt, but left it on and closed the space between them again.

"Your skin. At least as much as I can give you now."

She reached in under his shirt with her fingers splayed and ran them up his chest. The warm muscle firm and shuddering under her touch as she did.

He smelled like nothing she had ever referenced . Because he didn't use pomade his smell was unique, something spicy and of warm skin. She put her nose against his chest and inhaled, then touched her tongue to him, darting at his nipple. He groaned and rested his forehead against the door. She didn't intend to, it just happened, The taste of him combined with his smell was more of an aphrodisiac than she could withstand. She would have licked him all over had more skin been bared. In her mind she gave him long, dragging licks down his thighs and over his stomach with the tip of her tongue, making him shiver.

More skin, her skin and his touching head to toe, that's what she would like. She still ran her hands over his stomach and his chest, but paused over the nubs of his nipples. Back and forth she caressed them with her thumbs until his breath came in short bursts. She lifted his shirt and touched them with her tongue until his hips bumped hers rhythmically.

This was the man who minutes before tried to overshadow her with his personality. Now he was vulnerable to her mouth and touch, waiting for her to ease him.

He unbuttoned her shirtwaist, untied her corset cover, and reached into her chemise to lift her breasts out of her corset. He drew a nipple into his mouth with a long pull, and with his other hand he stroked the other. She arched up to him, wanting more, threading her fingers through his hair and drawing him down harder on her.

With a pop he released her nipple and she shivered at the cool air where his warm mouth had been. Then he drew the other in his mouth and ran his hand down to her thighs, curling around to the inner soft skin and teased her open with feathery strokes. He found her pearl and circled it until she pushed herself onto his fingers in frantic anticipation. Her fantasy met reality and the real was so much more powerful. He slipped one finger inside her and then two all the while still circling her nub with his thumb and pumping until she moaned into his neck and stroked his erection.

He took his hand away from the side of her head and unbuttoned his pants, then unbuttoned his drawers, letting his cock rest against her inner thigh. She looked down at it and drew her finger down its length, circling the head and back down to the nest of curls at its base. He was so warm and smooth under her fingers, and jerked into her hand. Her muscles clenched at the sight of the dew on the tip of his shaft, and her body hummed with tension.

She ran her tongue over her lips and when she looked up to his face his eyes were dark and hooded, his mouth strained.

Knowing that he wanted her, that she could arouse such passion in him, made her want him all the more. Even as his fingers glided effortlessly in and out of her, making her near delirious with need, the desire in his expression inflamed her more.

"Please," she whispered to him as she matched the movements of his fingers.

He reached down between them and guided himself along her opening and with one forceful push slipped into her.

The bliss, the fullness of him, the pleasure of his need overwhelmed her and she cried out. He covered her mouth with his and started to pump, so slowly, pushing her up against the door as he fully sheathed himself.

* * * *

It was all he could do to not come all over her dress when she licked her lips. He couldn't remember the last time sex made him so aroused as to lose control. With her particular kind of palm readings it felt as if he'd tolerated days of foreplay. His balls were already pulled tight.

He braced his hands on either side of her head and looked down where they joined, as he slid in and out of her, her wetness making his cock glisten.

When he looked back at her he realized she had been looking, too, and watching his reaction. The naked desire on her face almost shattered him again, and he stopped for a minute to catch his breath. He found her clitoris and started to tease it, running his fingers around her where they met and circling back up. Her muscles started to flutter around his cock and he pulled her legs open wider as she moaned into his ear.

With an upward thrust she pitched over, her cunt clenching on him, and he pinned her so that he could feel every tremble within her. As her orgasm ended he slid into her again, keeping her spread and open, both of them with their eyes glued to the sight of his shiny cock pumping.

She rested her head on his shoulder, "I never, ever thought it would be like this."

"Between us?" He eased her legs down, slipped out of her, and guided her over to the rug where he laid her down, a feast before him. He agreed. Not for one minute did he think it would be so tense, so explosive. Although she'd been true to character, even now. She never cowered, never accepted his posturing, but met him equally where she knew he was.

"Everything." She ran her hands down her breasts to her stomach, and back to her breasts to pull her nipples while she watched him.

He closed his eyes for a moment at the sight of her tempting him with her own hands. He's always had to coax Bea to do such things and he hated it. It was as if she held herself back from him when all he wanted was a full partner. Pleasure that was mutual.

"Touch yourself." He could barely get the words past his lips and his cock jerked at the anticipation of watching her.

Her face flamed in a blush that went down to her chest, but her embarrassment didn't stop her. He knew he was pushing her a bit, but she matched him, and he was proud of her. One hand left her erect nipple, skimmed the planes of her hips, and nestled her fingers through her sable hair.

He took his erection in hand and started to pump as she curved her finger into her cunt. Her face was still flushed from her orgasm and his desire inflamed at seeing her dress ruched around her hips, her breasts spilling above her corset. Her stockings were gartered and around her thighs, their paleness contrasting with her dark woman's hair.

She began to move her fingers in and out as he pumped to her rhythm on his knees at her feet.

Her eyes closed as she started to lift her hips, her arches becoming disjointed and jerky. He didn't want her to come again, not without him, and he was still so drunk with the look of her he needed more time to drench himself in her sensuality.

"Open your eyes," he said, his mouth tight with concentration.

When she did they were heavy and half-lidded.

"Lick me until it's slipping through my hand." She sat up and opened her mouth, her tongue pink and offering him the moisture he wanted. But with her new order she stopped fingering herself.

"Put your fingers back in your cunt." Her face burned at his words, but she did as he told her. When her small warm tongue kissed his cock with such luscious drags he pulled himself back again and inhaled as deeply as he could.

Her fingers were glossy as she circled her clit, still with her mouth enveloping him as he fisted the base of his erection.

"Let me suck your fingers."

She blushed again even darker, but brought her hand to his lips and placed her fingers, wet with her cream in his mouth. He slid his tongue over them and sucked as if they held the nectar of a ripe fruit and her eyes glazed.

He couldn't hold back much longer and the slight sizzle became a constant burn. Whatever made her like this, if it was just her latent sexuality, or their combined lust, he knew he wanted more. His mind was already imagining positions that his body couldn't perform because of the scant amount of control he had left.

He leaned back from her, disconnecting his cock from her mouth and nudged her back to lie down. Her taste was a luscious appetizer and he wanted to feel her shake underneath him.

The perfume of her filled his nose as he leaned down, spreading her knees open so that he could see all of her, so that she was completely open and aware of what he was doing to her. Or, more so, to himself. He looked down at his erection, still shiny with her saliva and the drip of liquid at its tip, and wiped it with his finger, placing it in her mouth. Ruby lips closed around it and sucked, letting it fall as she pulled her head back.

He groaned and levered himself down between her open thighs.

She tasted of musk and honey, and him. And that was the headiest of the three. It was almost feral of him, he knew, but it was arousing just the same.

Whispery mewls escaped her mouth as he darted his tongue deep within her, stabbing her as he held her down with his palm on her corset covered stomach.

With his other hand he tapped her clit until she groaned and rode his mouth, her cunt trembling and quaking against him.

He leaned back up, swathed the wetness from between her legs with his hand, and started to pump his cock again. She watched him with half open eyes, but then braced herself on her elbows as his hips started jerking with the smacking sounds of his fist.

He closed his eyes as the ball of fire sizzled down his spine and up to his cock. His balls tight against his base, he came, bursts of viscous cream shooting from him in long pulses, landing on the underside of her petticoats and disappearing within them.

When he finished he fell at her side, exhausted, wanting to undress her and curl her body into his so that they could sleep. And he wanted to wake up with her, still there, and start all over.

One thing was certain—he now knew what was lacking in his relationship with Bea. Equality. He wanted it from her, practically begged her for it for five years, taught her, and even went so far as to as to lay the blame of their lackluster relations on himself. He even had enough affection to take care of her. He didn't wish her harm, but he wasn't passionate about her either. And he'd more than had enough the last few months. Work held more appeal than Bea did by the time he let her go.

Abby perplexed him. He'd seen more of her character in their last two meetings than some friends he'd had for years.

She came here to give the money back.

It astounded him. She astounded him.

Most people thought he wiped his ass with twenties. He knew the five dollars he gave her, although paltry to him, was enough money to ease the bills for a few months. He knew what needing every penny was like, it was scored into his being.

After he got a job after school as an errand boy and worked himself into a better position he was eventually able to go to college with the help and support of those who believed in him. But he never forgot.

Chapter Five

To say she was confused would be a vast understatement. All she wanted to do was to give Caden his money back. Having it in her bureau all week sickened her with guilt, on top of her sister knowing about it. Of course she had to give it back after Camille said something, and she intended to. She just didn't intend to toss up her skirts in his office while she did.

Could generosity be seductive? Because it was when she overheard Caden's conversation with that woman that her chest squeezed and her sex got wet.

But she never planned on having sex with him in his office, let alone the first time they were alone.

Not that she felt guilty, not in the least. She wanted to skip home.

When she was younger there were stolen kisses at dances and parties. Some innocent ones under the holiday mistletoe, she'd even gone as far as a letting one admirer kiss her breasts that mounded above her décolletage. When she was twenty-five she gave up hope and slept with a male friend, someone she'd known throughout her younger years, whom she could trust because they were equal in keeping one another's secrets. They'd come to an unspoken agreement with their relationship and took advantage of its intimacy when the mood hit them. She was no prize in the marriage mart, and she never deluded herself that she was. She had no breeding to speak of, and no dowry to dangle as a worm on a hook. In some ways it was restricting, in others it was a freedom. Men were able to make careers for themselves, but she never would. So, she took what life gave her, and made the best she could out of it.

But this afternoon with Caden…no, she wasn't sorry for it at all. She was thrilled. Ecstatic.

She wanted to do it again. But he never said anything about their relationship.

She could offer herself as a mistress, but that wasn't what she wanted. If he ever married she would be right back to where she was now, her only gain being the years she aged. And the position of mistress didn't help her family, rather it would shame them. It was all too thick to think about just now.

What she would like was a bath. At least that way her mother and sister would give her some privacy. Camille teased her about being so clean, she didn't realize it was the only way Abby could escape them and just ponder things.

She went up the walkway and stepped onto the porch, where the door opened before she could even put her hand on the glass knob.

"Abigail, I'm so glad you're home. We were worried; you've never been so late." Her mother pulled her in and kissed her as Abby walked into the vestibule.

Mother took her hat and hung it up. "Hurry and get changed, we have to leave soon. Camille knows you like to freshen up before these things so she drew you water and got your bath ready."

Abby hung her coat on the hook, "Where are we going?" She had wanted a bath, but to take the time to ponder her new skin, not to be rushed out to mingle with people. Or worse, be stared at and pitied all evening.

"Judith got us invitations to the Preston's for Genevieve's birthday dinner, and Mrs. Preston would like us to give readings. I'll do Genevieve's; you and Camille can take anyone else who asks." She shooed

Abby up the stairs, "Hurry, we need to leave in two hours."

Abby slammed her hat onto the bench and stomped up the stairs and even harder when they creaked under her feet. Her mother sighed at the base, and Abby didn't even bother to turn around. She pulled her bedroom door shut with a satisfying thud and started to yank her clothes off.

As her petticoats fell in a circle around her the smell of Caden floated up to her and her stomach gave a flip. She closed her eyes and inhaled, savoring the reminder of her afternoon. Images of what they'd done flashed in her mind and just like that, she wanted him again.

She leaned down and picked up her petticoats, bringing them to her nose. It was overwhelming, how his scent made her giddy and sad all at once. She wanted to run her hands over him again, feeling him twitch and shudder.

What she did not want to do was to get all dressed up and go to a party where she had to pretend. She knew her talent enough that none of her readings were faked, but she just didn't want to make polite chatter. She wanted to savor her afternoon.

Caden had loosened her corset just enough for her to take a deep breath and open the busk. Her chemise was all askew and her corset cover had been torn a bit on the seams. They were all folded, and she stacked them into the bureau drawer and pulled a robe on. Then she folded her petticoats and placed them under her pillow.

She padded to the door and peeked out, making sure no one was there before she went into the bathroom. After she slipped in and dropped her robe, she went to stand in front of the full-length mirror.

Her neck was a little red from his rough chin, and her nipples were proud and chafed with circles where his mouth had been. She ran her hands down the soft plane of her stomach and over her mound. It still burned a bit and her thighs ached but it was a good feeling, making her happy and content. It reminded her how deeply he'd been inside her and how wide he spread her.

She turned away and stepped into the bath. She lowered herself an inch at a time, pausing as her sex met the steaming water, letting the hot licks of water envelop her as his mouth had. She wondered how she should go on from here. How, once your life had been irrevocably changed, did you pick up and move forward as if nothing had happened?

Seeing him again would be excruciating. How did women act when they met their lovers in passing or at events? If she ran into him at an event? He probably would go to any cost to avoid her. At least, if she kept telling herself that, she wouldn't be disappointed.

She begrudgingly washed him from her body, but she had her petticoats hidden under her pillow, so she could reminisce when she had some private time.

When she was done she got up, dried herself as fast as she could, pulled her robe back on and went to her room to dress.

* * * *

Caden lifted the knocker on the Prestons' house, and moments later Michael Preston ushered him into the oak paneled vestibule. A turned finial banister accented the spiral stairs, and dark green acanthus leaf wallpaper complimented the dark wood. Caden would have to acquire a decorator do something like this to his vacated brownstone. It reeked of old money, which is what the Prestons' were.

Going to their daughter's birthday party wasn't high on his list of evening entertainment's, but gossip told him that Abby would be here. He'd received the invitation weeks ago and hadn't planned on coming. Then again, he hadn't planned on having sex with her in his office, either. Spontaneity had its rewards.

Michael went off to get them both drinks and came back with two short ice filled glasses and by the color, a good Scotch. His hair was heavy with pomade and he still smelled like barbers' talc.

"Glad you came. I was hoping we could talk about a venture I've been considering." Michael led him into the parlor where, beside a blazing fire, Abby sat at a table. She looked even more beautiful than earlier in his office.

Her flushed face was intent on her client's hand as she traced the lines on the woman's palm. Her hair was up in a chignon with soft loops falling on her neck, where just hours before he had kissed.

When he looked back, he realized that Michael had been watching him.

"You don't want her, Caden." Michael gestured with his drink to Abby. "Her, right? I heard you'd given Beatrice the heave ho and by the look on your face I assumed you were thinking of taking on Abigail there."

For some reason the thought never occurred to him. He considered the idea for a moment, but then thought no, she wouldn't like that. For one, she would never leave her family when they depended on her so much. Secondly, she was too proud.

But that didn't mean that he couldn't do his best to convince her that it was the best route. Maybe if he helped with her family's needs she'd be more inclined to agree. He'd have to think up a proposition that was too good for her to pass up.

"Why not Miss Abigail Drummond, Michael?" He spoke low over the rim of his glass so that their conversation remained private.

"Her family, man. Not only would her mother not tolerate it, but everyone knows that they're …well…peculiar."

"Well, what about it?" For some reason Michael's statement rankled.

"I guess if you don't mind that kind of thing."

Caden stared at him pointedly. "That kind of thing?"

Michael had the wisdom to become flushed, but clapped Caden on the back anyway.

"Why don't we go into the library and talk about my new idea?" Michael nodded in the direction of the hallway.

"No, I think I'll wait for Miss Drummond to finish with her client, I'd like to get my palm read."

Michael jerked his head back, then gathered himself and raised his eyebrow. "For spiritual comfort?"

"I'm not after anything, Mr. Preston, I'm here to pay respects to your family for your daughter's birthday and socialize with your guests. If you want to pay a call to Frist at the bank I'll make sure he gives you an appointment. We can talk about your new venture then." Caden nodded and walked away from his host to stand behind Abigail's client.

He'd about had enough of Michael's grandstanding because of their friendship. He never hesitated to pull it out when he came upon the opportunity, and Caden hated that. Riding another man's shirttails never gained respect the way hard work and due diligence did.

He didn't come here to talk about business, he came to say hello to friends, mingle a little bit, and start a seduction. Of which, the said object looked to be avoiding him.

Caden gave a slight cough and waited for her to look up. Her brows knitted in concentration and she kept speaking with the puffy pink woman at the table.

He coughed again behind his fist and waited for her, as if he could will her gaze to him. This time she huffed but still kept her full attention on her client.

Fresh chit, not even giving him the time of day after she came in his mouth just a few hours ago. Then it dawned on him.

He was jealous of a pink, puffy frou-frou woman.

Even though he saw her in her naked splendor, right now, sitting at the table with her unfashionable dress and upswept hair, she was even more enthralling. The curve of her face was becoming familiar to him, and that knowledge was comforting. And equally horrifying.

She glanced up at him, her eyes flashing in genuine surprise and happiness, but when she looked around and realized her situation she looked guarded. Whatever those glances meant, he knew they weren't all good. Guilt or regret hopefully wasn't on the list, because he felt neither.

In the corner by a chinoisere screen was an unoccupied settee and wingchair, so he made his way past the few occupants of the room to sit down. He couldn't, and refused to take his eyes off of her. Not that she would disappear, but it was as if they were the only people in the room and he felt her, in some way, connected to him.

This time when she went back to her clients hands she kept peeking up at him, which for some reason he found endearing, even though the look on her face that followed was frustration and not happiness. If she gave him the chance he'd like to change that back to the happiness he first saw there.

He pulled out his timepiece and flipped open the lid. Dinner would be announced soon, and he refused to leave without speaking to her. Maybe a few nips and sucks would be in order, too.

Mrs. Drummond came through the French doors, and he watched as Abby's back became ramrod straight. Before she looked at him every few seconds, now she avoided any eye contact.

He waited a few minutes for her mother to leave, but she moved around to the guests standing nearby, making small talk. She was like a bad cold, lingering when you wanted it to leave.

And he needed her to leave. He could never get Abby alone with her mother standing guard. Abby would act all proper with her around, not like the lush wanton she was in his office earlier. That was the Abby he wanted, all pliant and willing.

Her five minutes were up. Enough was enough. He stood up, straightened his jacket, and walked over to Mrs. Drummond.

"Mrs. Drummond, have I told you how much I appreciated the excellent reading your daughter gave me the other evening?" He smiled as her face lit with recognition. "It was very inspiring."

"Thank you for telling me, Mr. Dupree. I've often wondered how she was received." Mrs. Drummond blushed at Caden's praise. She placed her gloved hand on his jacket sleeve, "Was she able to help you understand your purpose more clearly?"

"Why yes, I now have a crystal clear understanding."

"How delightful. If you need any other guidance, please stop by." She handed him her calling card and smiled as she turned to speak with another woman who had come up to her.

When he looked over at Abby she was staring at him, a look of abject horror on her face. He winked. Her blush was adorable.

"Miss Drummond, I've waited so patiently for a moment with you, but I find myself almost out of time. Would you care to walk me to the door?"

"Yes, please Abby. Mr. Dupree expressed some interest in your insightfulness and to perhaps have his hand read again?" Abby's mother offered from the circle of her other conversation. For some reason

Abby's mother using him like an advertisement didn't bother him half as much as Michael.

Caden offered her his arm. "Well, then I guess I'd better see you to the door," she said, as he led her out of the room.

He led her through the French doors into the empty vestibule, looked down the hall, and started up the spiral staircase.

She pulled her arm back. "We can't go up there!"

He yanked her to him and kissed her with all the frustration that filled him while he'd waited for her, sweeping his tongue into her mouth and pulling her head closer.

Abby melted into him for a moment then jerked herself away. He took advantage and yanked her up the stairs, and this time she followed.

Once Michael told him there were eighteen bedrooms, and he was certain he could find an empty one. He led her to the end of a long corridor and up another flight of stairs that looked less used. The floor was silent, and at the third door he paused and turned the amethyst knob as silently as he could. All he could hear was her breathing behind him. He poked his head in and seeing that the room was vacant, pulled her in.

Chapter Six

Abby knew it was wrong. She felt as though they were trespassing, that at the least it was indiscreet. But then, it would seem that Caden had a knack for trysts in indiscreet places, and the memory of what happened in his office made her wet, her wanting of him again, even now, overriding reason. Even though he locked the door behind them, someone could find them out at any time. Someone could have knocked, and her reputation would be destroyed. For some reason she didn't care as much as she knew she should. She only wanted to feel his hands run up her ribcage, and his breath on her neck, the weight of his body covering her.

Her mother was downstairs.

Was this how easy her lusting body ran to ruin? Falling right over the cliff of reason to the jagged boulders below?

"Caden, I have to get back down there, I can't do this. If anyone—"

His mouth silenced her last words as he began a sensual onslaught, and she slipped into the enchantment of his touch. His arms pulled her to him and his erection, even through four layers of cloth, branded her skin. She knew what it looked like, what it felt like, how he smelled and tasted, and she wanted it all over again. She snaked her arms up around his neck to kiss him back, nipping at the corners of his mouth and tongue, reveling in the tension between her legs.

He moaned when she did, exactly the response she hoped from him. She wanted to show him what she yearned to do. And the particulars of where, faded under the knowledge that he was grasping handfuls of dress up to get to her.

When the material slipped out of his hand he groaned and attacked the fabric fortress with both hands. He reached her bustle ties and rested his head on her collar, panting. Her heart pounded, seeming to reach its beat to her sex where she could feel the friction of her need.

"These fucking clothes will be the death of me."

She chuckled. "You're not the only one tempted to rip them to shreds."

"Just once I'd like you naked. Completely naked for the whole afternoon."

His words hit her like brandy, smooth and smoky with a hot burn. She would do just about anything to have that, too. But not here. She wanted the time to love and explore, and that couldn't be done in someone else's guestrooms.

He pushed his erection between her legs and rocked. "I want you. To feel your stomach quiver as I kiss down to where I know you're wet for me."

She inhaled, her eyes closing and rolling back into her head, his mouth hot on her collarbone.

She slipped her hands to his waist, opened her eyes, and started to unbutton his pants, then pulled the tie on his drawers, letting his erection spring free. The anticipation of his passion goading her further than she'd been before, she wanting him hot and in as much need as she was.

Just the sight of him, hard for her, made her close her eyes and swallow. If only they could be naked. She wanted him all over her, cupping her breasts, taunting her nipples with his tongue and fingers, pulling them until she shuddered and moaned in his mouth. Next she would take her time tasting him, licking the copper disks with her tongue, the planes and dips of his chest and hips under her palms, his erection in her mouth and his balls cradled in her hands.

It was as if when she was with him the rest of the world ceased to exist. Her senses were too full of him to be concerned, and even still she wanted more.

She sunk to her knees and nestled her nose into the skin of his stomach, his crisp hairs springing under her fingers as she spread her hands around the base of his penis. The scent of him filled her nostrils, marking her memory with her pleasure as she took him into her mouth, slipping her lips over his hard silken head. She looked up at him while he strained not to push himself further. He rested his hands above her head as if in benediction, and she wanted him to run his fingers through her hair, but even still she knew he couldn't. Not unless he wanted them to get caught. If she could have reached herself she would have, teasing her wet slit with her own fingers while he watched all of it from above. Or have him filling her and her mouth at once.

His eyes were burning charcoals, heavy with passion as he rested his hands on her shoulders, begging her for more with the small pushes of his hips. She kept her eyes on him as she sank another inch and ran her fingernails up the inside of his thighs to his sac, circling until he closed his eyes, his balls pulling upward. She drew one long nailed finger behind them and stroked, softly scratching the hidden pucker and smiled as his eyes flamed.

"Please." The single word came from gritted teeth.

She sucked in another inch then glided back up, around the flared rim, dipping into the tiny hole with a pointed tongue and going back down as he swelled in her mouth.

This time she bobbed, her lips swollen and wet, all the way down, as far as she could, taking him so deep that for a moment she closed her eyes and breathed through her nose.

She slid her fingers around to his firm ass and felt the shaking muscles underneath, the flexing that made him swell and throb with his checked need. Her tightened sex wanted him, swollen and slick as she kneeled, her arched back, and him slipping out of control with small thrusts.

She backed up and released him with a dip of her tongue and a pop. He reached down and eased her up by her elbow when she decided to push him down and back so that he lay cushioned on the thick, Oriental carpet.

She stood with a knee planted on either side of his hips and started to sink, her skirts bellowing out as she impaled herself on him. Her stocking feet curled up under his bum, pushing him in even further, bumping her womb and grinding into her hardened clit. The rasping friction of their joining made her fracture with shards of pleasure. She mewled and wanted to lean into him but for her corset, so she sat strait, her insides squeezing him as the rhythmic spasms eased.

His eyes rolled up and closed, his nostrils flaring in time with his lifting hips. "So good, you feel so good."

He palmed her face and brought his mouth up to her, kissing her as he moved for them. Bringing her with such sweet agony to a precipice without letting her fall off.

He ran his palms up her bodice and found between her corset and neck, a precious bit of flesh, which he kissed with scorching lips. Embers on her skin that burned a trail where they nipped and sucked, and she wanted them on her nipples, drawing them into his mouth.

Tension thrummed her body, her thighs trembling as she moved up and down, wanting to come, but unable to break free. She heard a rustle of crisp fabric and gasped as cool air hit her thighs. His searching fingers found their treasure, her hard clit, nestled in sensitive flesh which he caressed with long fluid strokes.

A frenzied snap of wires, white and hot, started her grasping and clenching, drawing him deeper if that were possible. Her breath came in short pants and she came, firing off in sparks.

Even as the last ebbs left her body he thrust up deep, evenly, pausing at her womb and, with her last pulse flexing, lifted her off onto his thighs as he slipped out and spent on her drawers.

Frustration flooded her as she watched the white fluid land on the material. She wanted him spent deep within her. She wanted to feel his seed fill her, to have it drip down her thighs as she walked home.

Was she greedy in wanting more? Wanting to not rush away, straightening clothes and making excuses to appease those who would look after her?

Was it wrong that she wanted days and nights? She needed laughter and quiet times, or an evening out with no one to answer to?

She'd gotten herself into a knot, but even still, she didn't regret it. Sadly, to her, these stolen moments were worth the deceit, if this was all she could have, or all that he might be able to offer. It was stupid and naive, but she wanted to hope. To hold that flicker close to her heart, that somehow they could make a way like her parents had done before her. But, she remembered her father gave up all, that he had to marry her mother. Although she knew in her heart that he never regretted one minute of it.

Caden wouldn't have to give up his money, but for them to have any sort of future would take at the least a chunk of his pride. The question was did he think she was worth the price?

* * * *

She still sat astride him with her head resting on his chest, trembling from her own orgasms. It was never enough. Never. He'd been with her twice now, and there were always pieces missing, that were held back because of their location.

Or perhaps because they'd never been naked. Only the important parts were bared for access.

That needed to be remedied. He would have to make a date with her and bring her to the brownstone. He could take her out, then back there.

No, not dinner. He couldn't be seen with her, not that way. She was still too much a part of society to be able to secret away with him like that. Not only was she still a part of society, but one of its non-desirables as well. He would have to take her out of town. Yes, that would do it. They would want to spend as much time together as possible so it would have to be somewhere close.

Hoping they would have that time together made him almost joyous, but having to plot and plan almost ruined it. Some men might like the games of liaisons, but he was finding it wearisome.

She got off him and started to ready herself— adjusting, tying, pushing her peaked nipples back into the corset. He did the same and they stood, needing to escape, but not wanting to leave.

He turned the knob and peered out the door, guiding her into the hall.

"Shhh." She slipped her hand into his and walked down the stairs behind him, so close that he could feel her breasts touching his jacket. He angled himself so that he protected her from any eyes that would spy them and sneaked down the back stairs. With the house having eighteen bedrooms, two sets of servant's stairs and two grand staircases, he doubted anyone would venture over to where they were, especially now that everyone would be removing to the dining room.

The dinner bell had rung moments ago, just as they came out of the guestroom, and he decided that they would split. She, her mother and sister were leaving now anyway and he would be gone by the time they walked out the door.

He tugged her ear and walked out the opposite way, slipping out the side door into the crisp winter night leaving her to wind her way to the parlor.

He stared at the brilliant stars in the sky. He hated sneaking about. It was for youths and their clandestine meetings, not for the likes of him. Whom was he kidding? Not five minutes before he was trying to figure out how to get her to spend the evening with him. Like in finances, everyone had their price, and he'd just found his. Still and all, she was a mystery to him. Maybe that was why he was so enthralled? Perhaps the newness of her coupled with learning her subtleties was a heady aphrodisiac. He wanted to know what made her so strong as to shoulder the labels people gave her, the loyalty she had for her family that made her take up the burden of being a pariah. And why she allowed him to break that loyalty.

Even with having just been buried deep inside her as she rode him, he would have her again, right now, and his cock agreed, but Michael's comments nagged at him even when he didn't believe the rumors.

Better then he should make some arrangement with her and set her up in the brownstone. He would be close, then at the main house, but not too far away that her couldn't hail a hansom and be there within ten minutes.

The Prestons lived in town not far from his main house on Knob Hill and he walked a few blocks more considering his circumstances. By the time he reached the club he hadn't come to any conclusions except for the fact that he wanted to sleep with her despite her profession, and he needed a cognac with a cigar. Not that those items would be a problem here, the cigars were on a silver platter on the welcoming table and the bar was open. He had his favorites available to him at all times.

He checked his coat and hat, lifted the top cigar off its pyramid and smiled as it was immediately clipped by the waiter.

The bar was long and of dark wood with an old brass railing and glasses hanging upside down like some queer chandelier. There were club chairs scattered about with cast iron scrolled reading lamps and side tables. Off in the back the card tables were filled, smoke coming up from them like chimneys.

He scanned the small crowd and found Charles Fernald and Robinson Fletcher playing poker with a few others.

He wove through the tables and pulled a chair out next to Fletch who glanced up at him and threw out a card.

"Slumming?" Fletcher asked, a cigar clenched between his teeth, his face shrouded in a blue-grey haze.

"Not hardly. Dinner at the Prestons, but I slipped out."

Charles ribbed Fletch in the ribs. "I thought you would be looking to replace Beatrice. Trolling the market district looking for a wayward milkmaid?"

"No, he's aiming for a palm reader." Michael walked up behind him.

All three men stared at him until Fletcher and Charles began to laugh so hard tears rolled down Fletcher's face.

Caden nodded at Michael. "Ditch your party?"

Michael shrugged.

Charles took a deep breath and calmed for a moment. "Did she see it in her future that she would be fucking the Vice President of Boston Trust?"

Fletch howled again and slapped Charles's shoulder.

Michael stood watching them and then turned to Caden, "See. I told you so."

"Which one, eh? Camille?" Fletch got back into the game and pushed out five chips.

"No, Abigail." Michael pulled out a chair and sat down.

"The old one? Man, the least you could do is take the younger one. The older one must not be a very good fortune teller if she hasn't found herself a benefactor by now." Charles counted his chips, "I see you and raise you two."

"Cheap tonight, Charles? Maybe I can loan you a few." Caden was as angry as the tip of his cigar was hot.

Fletch chuckled. "Put on the banker now, why don't you."

Caden decided he hated the three of them.

Michael snorted. "You didn't think she hasn't pulled this before have you? Why do you think her mother whores out her daughters to every party?"

Fletch shot back the last of his scotch and plunked the glass on the table. "Haven't you heard anything about their family?"

"No." He should have left already, but it was as if his feet were cemented in the floor. Dreading to hear what he would be told, but needing to hear it all the same.

Michael waved at the table with a flourish, "Sit while we tell you a few stories."

His hand rested on the back of the captain's chair as he looked at the three of them deciding if he would even entertain what they had to say, and how much he would allow himself to believe. Knowing that tales would be told whether he were there or not, he yanked the chair out and sat.

"So, we were saying that the mother whores out her daughters." Michael leaned back in the chair, his arms across his chest.

Not Abby, he wouldn't believe it for a minute.

"Not only does she whore them out, but she taught them all that psychic crap so they could rub around high as they could. Women love to spend their husband's money on that shit." Fletch threw down three cards and beckoned Charles, who was dealing, for more. "S'all lies, if you ask me."

So Caden had thought, too, until Abby had told him truths about himself that no one but him could have known.

"Sluts, all of 'em. Even the mother," Fletch continued. "'Specially now that the husband is dead. I've seen her at almost every party. She's always looking for those girls to match up with someone in our set." He nodded, pursing his lips over his cards.

It seemed as if Fletch tossed them back faster than usual tonight.

"Better watch yourself, Cade," Michael said. "Women like that are good for one thing only, and that's not being a wife." Michael poked Charles, "Anyway, those gypsy tricks are supposed to make you shoot your load faster than a scared skunk."

He could feel the sweat gather and the anger run through his body just like when he was about to get in a scrap in the old days. Maybe he should have stopped them before, but he knew anything he said would be wasted on them, and he didn't want them knowing what he was up to anyway. Pearls before swine and all that.

When he was young he had to prove himself with his fists. That was all he had. No longer, but even now he wanted to take Michael out back. But, he'd worked long and hard to groom himself to be better than that.

Still and all, looking at it logically, he knew nothing about her life. Nothing other than she shook when she climaxed and that she tried to give him his money back. Which in itself was admirable, but she could have done that so she could see him again, sacrificing the five dollars in hopes of making more.

He stood up and pushed the chair back. He didn't want to think that way about her, and he needed to clear his head. He planned on having her over to the house, and he still would, but maybe this time he wouldn't assume her honesty.

But when had she proved herself to be anything but truthful, even in sex? He knew the first time they were together she was embarrassed to do the things he asked, but even still she'd met him fully in his passion, even overwhelming him with her response. Beatrice on the other hand, with her it was always an act to get him to give her more, to make sure he kept up the house arrangement.

Caden regarded himself as a pretty good judge of character and although this time he allowed for being wrong on a few counts, he honestly didn't see that depth of guile in Abby.

"Are you going to stand there all night, Caden, or are you in?" Fletch shuffled the cards.

Michael sat forward, slipped out his cufflinks, and rolled up his sleeves.

"No, not this time. I have an early morning." He turned and walked off with his cigar still between his teeth. He took a paper off the bar, scribbled a note, addressed it, and gave it to the waiter.

* * * *

Abby pulled her scarf up over her nose and walked down the stairs from the mercantile with one dollar in her pocket from selling the quilt she'd made. The store never took any on order, so this would be the only money she got for a few months. It was never enough, but it was more than she had before she walked in.

Evening had arrived while inside she haggled for every nickel. It was the time of winter that lasted the longest. The sun went down around five in the evening and it seemed as if spring would never come. Everything looked gray, even though she knew spring would eventually come. She yanked her hat down around her ears and when she looked back up Mr. Preston was approaching with a beautiful blonde woman. Whom, she knew was not Mrs. Preston. Mr. Preston leaned down and whispered something in her ear and the woman leaned into him with a seductive smile. Abby kept walking, trying to pass, pretending she had no idea who he was, or that she ate his food the other night at his daughter's birthday party. And it looked as if he hadn't noticed her at all, which was a small miracle, because Abby was not good at urbane banter.

She snuggled into her coat and recoiled when the woman stopped right in front of her with a snide smile, Mr. Preston hanging back and going off to a storefront.

"So, I hear you're Caden's new slut."

"Excuse me?" Abby stepped back at the vicious tone, and her cheeks felt as if they'd both been slapped. She couldn't believe such nasty words were coming from a woman who looked as she did. Her hair was upswept in the latest style, her skin perfect bisque and her eyes riveting. She wore a dress Abby would have to save years to buy. Abby must have shown her thoughts because the woman's smile became superior.

"All this is what Caden bought me. He still loves me, and I know he'll come back. And you'd never fit in his circle anyway. So, why don't you scamper off like a good girl?"

Her vision swam a moment as she understood what the woman said, but she also realized that Caden broke off whatever relationship they had so it didn't matter. At least not to her. But the woman was obviously hurt by his actions, and Abby felt bad for her. She was enthralled with him and she'd barely known him.

And then she wondered if this was the relationship that she saw in Caden's hand. His lines showed that it was a long one, but it was also a shallow line, meaning it didn't mean much to Caden. Apparently the woman saw things differently. Abby wasn't surprised. After all, she was having a hard time defending her feelings for Caden, and she'd only known him a few days. But she saw his character, and his heart that lay in the lines of his hands.

Abby raised her eyebrow. "And you are?"

"Beatrice. Caden will know."

Even if the woman spent years with Caden, she obviously didn't know him. Once Caden made a decision it was final. And there would be no way that he would have the woman after she bedded his friend. Abby didn't know what to say to Caden about Michael, but she bet he already knew what kind of man Mr. Preston was.

"Not if I don't tell him. And anyway, I don't think he'd like Mr. Preston's leftovers." Abby gave Beatrice the once over. "Excuse me."

Abby heard Beatrice gasp and call her another name, but she kept on walking.

Thankfully her coat was long because Abby was sure anyone on the street could see her legs shaking. Her stomach trembled as she made her way around Beatrice to continue on her way home.

Would she tell Caden? Probably not. She didn't want to hear his explanations as to who Beatrice was, she already knew. And if she expected those answers from him, he might ask questions, too. Not that she was a light skirt, but he knew she was no virgin. Nothing good ever came of those conversations. Some things were better left unsaid.

But Beatrice was beautiful. She could see why Caden was attracted and why Michael Preston didn't care, if she was Caden's cast off. And Beatrice was right; she did fit in with Caden's friends better. Beatrice probably knew which forks to eat from, too. And if Caden had left her, how long did Abby think he'd want to be with her, when she knew none of those things, and could never be that person?

The inevitable would happen. Abby knew that, and she would be smart not to get anymore involved. But why was it that even to think of him made her anxious to see him again?

Abby walked up the stairs into her house and was greeted by the smell of her mother's chicken soup cooking and the warmth of the kitchen. She hung her coat on the tree and spied a note on the side table addressed to her and ripped it open.

Her mother poked her head into the foyer. "Oh good, you saw it. Dinner is in a few minutes. You have just enough time to wash up. Tell me what the note said over dinner?"

Abby nodded and climbed the stairs to her room, her heart as loud in her ears as her footsteps on the stairs. Caden asked her to come by the bank.

Chapter Seven

Frist had a bit of the sniffles when he brought her to Caden's door three days after the Prestons' party. So far, as he escorted her down the office hallway he'd sneezed three times and never took his kerchief from under his red nose.

Her mother thankfully hadn't insisted on seeing the note, Abby just told her, and Caden didn't incriminate. All it asked was that she meet him at the bank, Friday afternoon at five PM. It was a peculiar time to make an appointment, and it was all she could do to keep her anticipation from her mother and sister. She told them he might have a job for her.

A fine sheen broke out on her face as Frist rapped on the door, and she wished for a fan to cool herself even though it was winter.

"Come in." Caden's baritone voice boomed through the door.

Frist opened the door and there he sat, behind that massive block of oak with his feet crossed at its corner. He eased up, his movements lithe and slow, as if he knew who would be behind the door. She had the distinct feeling of being stalked by an animal much higher on the food chain.

A soft click told her Frist had removed himself to sniffle and wheeze back to his front desk, and now Caden stood before her, taking up all of her air.

A tiny gasp slipped from between her lips as he lowered his head to kiss her, the tension sizzling, her skin like water on a hot pan.

He pressed his lips to hers and broke off as quickly leaving her bereft. "Hello."

"Hello?"

His bemused smile teased a smile from her as well.

"I missed you," he said as he cupped her chin and traced the corner of her mouth with his thumb. The familiarity of his touch calmed her anxiety but heightened her ceaseless wanting of him.

She leaned her head into his palm. "I missed you, too. I'm so glad you sent the note. If you'd made me wait I would have been mad with despair wondering if I would ever see you again." She couldn't help the overdramatic teasing.

He smiled. "You could have always come here."

She shook her head. "No, if you sent no word, I would never have come."

"Then let me assure you, you are always welcome. I would hate to have you think otherwise." He kissed her again, a slight peck. "Wait right here."

He crossed the room, took his jacket off the back of his chair, and put it on, giving the short lapels a snap. Then he turned the knob on the paraffin lamp. The soft glow of the room faded leaving the lights from the town square as illumination, casting long shadows across the floor.

"I thought you wanted us to...to...meet in your office again." Her cheeks burned as she played with the buttons on the wrist of her gloves, thankful he couldn't see her clearly.

"Oh, no. Not that again."

She craned her neck to look at him as he offered her his elbow.

He caught her glance. "Not that it wasn't pleasant, but I've other things in mind for tonight."

"Other things?"

"Yes, like food, and conversation. And then I'd like to see you, completely unclothed, a feast of skin on my bed. I hope you made excuses for the next five hours."

"The next five hours?" Her voice wavered, her thoughts flipping like thrown cards trying to think up something to tell her mother.

"At least."

She had thought maybe two hours at the most. Her panic was followed by recriminations of getting involved and with the knowledge that her ilk had nothing in common with men like him. Nothing would come of this but a broken heart, but when she looked at him and her whole chest squeezed, how could he not be worth it? "Oh."

He opened the door, closing it behind him as he guided her out. "Did you?"

"Did I?"

He chuckled. "Make adequate excuses?"

"Oh, yes. I told my mother I was meeting you here first and that you would be interviewing me for a secretary position you had available, and then visiting a friend." She just didn't mention that it was what she would be telling her mother, not had told her mother. She didn't dwell on it. Frustration at her even having to make her whereabouts known only angered her. She was an adult, and still answering to others.

His laugh echoed through the vacant hallway. "Something like that."

Instead of taking her out the front doors he brought her the opposite way down the marble hall and after a few turns was at a door which opened to the alley behind the bank.

She questioned their exit for a moment, wondering why the front entrance was insufficient, but left it, deciding that he knew where they were going and therefore the best way to get there.

The night was dark and crisp with the promise of snow in the air. She hoped it didn't come tonight because it would make getting home atrocious and she hadn't thought to wear sturdy boots.

He hailed a hansom cab, which thrilled her. She would have walked with him, but the less time they wasted on getting wherever they were going, the more time she had to spend with him.

Alone together. Finally.

* * * *

After all this time he would bring her to Knob Hill, his home, not the brownstone. He hadn't realized when he started thinking on a more permanent basis, but he had. And he refused to analyze it. All he wanted to think about was the pleasure that lay ahead of them.

They would, for the very first time since they had been rendezvousing, be naked. That was an image that brought him to attention. He planned on having her sprawled across the bed for most of the night.

Because he'd sent the servants home early he would have to help redress her in all those damnable layers of corset and bustle, but playing the ladies' maid didn't bother him in the least. He was proud of his accomplishments in that particular area. He always thought that if purchased, he should know how to put it on a woman.

He opened the door of the hansom and took her hand as she stepped out, then led her up the stairs into the house.

She unbuttoned her coat without a word, and he hung it for her. He stopped a minute to let her take it all in, hoping that when he offered it all to her she would be unable to resist. The carpenters had just finished, and he was still admiring it himself. He had taken some ideas from the Prestons', but made specifications all his own.

She peered out from under her hat while she removed her pin. "It's quite lovely."

"Thank you, I've had it remodeled in the last few weeks. I'd hoped you would like it."

"You've succeeded, I do." She placed her hat on the bench and stood with her hands clasped in front of her.

He could see she was nervous, and more than anything he wanted her to be at ease. He could only think of one thing. What made him most comfortable.

"Take off your shoes," he said, as he sat on the edge of the bench and unlaced his boots.

She stood and stared at him, dumbfounded. "Pardon?"

"Take your shoes off. I hate wearing shoes while I'm at home. Unless entertaining, I never wear them ." He smiled. "Even when I play poker. I tell them it's my good luck charm." He settled his boots against the wall trim and wiggled his toes. "Come on," he patted the bench, "off they go."

She balked.

"Fine then, I insist. I just had my floors refinished and the water from your boots will ruin them. Off. Now."

She snickered. "Really?"

"I insist. Don't insult your host."

"I wouldn't think to insult my host." She perched on the corner and held out her foot to him. He laughed as he plopped her booted foot onto his lap and threw up her skirt. She gasped, then burst out laughing. Her smile lit up her face as he slipped the boot off, letting it clunk to the floor, moments later tossing its mate next to it.

He stood and kissed her then, taking her elbow to show her into the dining room where he had asked for a buffet to be set up. She walked next to him, her shoulder touching his, a grin on her face.

There were plates stacked on the sidebar and he took one and gave it to her, then took one himself. He'd asked for easy foods that they could eat all night, especially if they came back down for snacks.

He made sure she had at least a bit of food on her plate and he brought glasses and wine to the table, uncorking the bottle and poured a cabernet he liked.

It was strange sitting next to her at a table like this, informal and intimate. By far it was the nicest dinner in a long time, and the most anticipated. Not for the fucking afterwards either, but the whole of spending the evening with her. The only thing that he didn't like was that at some point it would have to end. He would prefer if he could go to bed, and wake up with her. To not have to pull out of her when he climaxed. Somehow before, he never felt the loss of that. Even more strange was not realizing his feelings about it had changed. All he knew was that he didn't want to start his day without seeing her over the breakfast table, and wanted to end it by holding her naked body to his.

"Would dinner qualify as payment for another palm reading?" He placed his fork and knife down onto the plate.

She pointed her fork at him and grinned. "It is delicious. I suppose I could tell your fortune for you."

She winked and he laughed. Her personality was so multifaceted, he could never tell which side she would show next, and each entranced him. She put her utensils down and held out her hand, beckoning him to give her his.

He slipped out his cufflinks and rolled up his shirtsleeve, offering her his palm.

"Last time though, alright?"

"Why?"

"Because I can't give you an accurate reading now, we've become too intimate and I can't be objective."

"That's a reason I can live with, and I'll be perpetuating."

She arched her brow, "Really?"

"Absolutely."

"I'll have to see how true that statement is."

She scooted forward and leaned in over his hand, spreading his fingers with hers, just like she had done every other time. And like every other time, the nerves in his hands acted as if there were an invisible string attached to his cock. At this rate he'd never be able to hold her hand without getting hard. He took a deep breath and concentrated on pacing himself.

"I want you to tell me about my love life."

She looked up at him, a shadow of concern crossing her face.

"What do you see?"

She blinked and looked back down, furrows creasing her brow. He would have to admit it wasn't the smartest thing he'd ever said to her. He'd soothe her fears soon enough.

Once he'd made the decision he went and bought an emerald cut sapphire set in a circle of diamonds, and it sat upstairs, in the bottom of a champagne glass.

Now all he had to do was get her up there.

Chapter Eight

Before when Caden asked her to read his palm it was a playful thing where he would seduce her. Never before had he asked like this. She knew she was setting her heart out to be trampled on, and apparently her time had come.

He needed to marry. She just never thought it in him to be so indelicate with it. She knew he didn't love her, but thought at least, he cared enough to not do this. Or maybe this is what people of his station did? Maybe she should know her position and expect to be asked such things?

"Come on, what do you see?"

She pulled her hand away, "I'm sorry, I can't. Not tonight."

"Why?"

His genuine puzzlement confused her and her heart squeezed. "I'm not objective, I said."

He looked down at her hand and brought it to his lips and gave it a feather light kiss. His sweetness made her throat knot, as if she was trying to swallow stale bread.

"I messed it up, didn't I?" He kissed her hand again.

"Messed what up?"

"I hoped you would see us in my hand, but somehow I have the feeling you didn't think that did you?"

Her heart started to beat wildly in her chest, part relief and still a portion of remorse. "No, I didn't think that's what you meant." She couldn't do this to herself anymore.

"You thought I meant to ask about another woman?"

She searched his face and realized that the thought never occurred to him. She traced the pattern on the tablecloth with her finger. "I know you need someone you can be proud of, that's in your social circle." She met his eyes. She tried to sound funny but it just came out sounding like cracked glass.

"I never planned on marrying any time soon. But if that's what you want?"

No. More than anything it was what she wanted, but there were many things she wanted and couldn't have. He didn't hold any respect for her gifting or her family's. Although it wasn't something she proclaimed from the rooftops, that didn't mean she didn't believe in it.

Even though he teased her all the time wanting readings, she knew it was a ploy he used to get closer to her. It would be different if he had to present her as his wife when she had already been to all of their houses as the entertainment. Abigail the fortuneteller now, as Mrs. Caden Dupree. Of course he'd say that it was all fine until one of the wives asked that Abby read her palm. Then all hell would break lose. He would never allow her to real palms the way she did now, and eventually it would distance her from her family and she would never slight her mother in such a callous way.

There was no middle ground between them.

It was the right thing to do, but why did it have to hurt so much.

She knew then that she needed to be strong enough to leave. And she would end it tonight, because her heart could not take the pain of seeing him one more day.

He stood up and threw his napkin onto the table, then pulled her up and to him. "I'm sorry, this has not gone like I planned. Let me make it up to you."

She gathered her pittance of courage and smiled. "Come into my parlor said the spider to the fly." Oh, her heart would be trampled tonight for sure. Maybe she should even leave now, because the fist squeezing her chest was almost unbearable.

His eyes gleamed wicked. "Yes, I would love to eat you."

Every shred of self-preservation she'd grasped onto scattered like ashes in the wind. Not that she had to be convinced or seduced into sleeping with him. All he had to do was crook his finger. It was emotional suicide how she danced to his tune, but she couldn't help it. After tonight he wouldn't be hers to tease and kiss, and greed? Greed was a powerful motivation.

"Lead the way into your parlor, *Monsieur* Spider."

He took her hand and led her up the stairs, her expectations fueling every step. If this were going to be her last night with him, she would make sure that it was a wonderful memory for them both.

The room glowed with firelight. He stood her at the bed's edge and started taking out her hairpins, letting them fall to the floor. He turned her around and unbuttoned her shirtwaist, peeling it off her arms and folding it then setting it on the bench at the end of the bed. All the way down to her corset he unwrapped her like a candy and started to kiss her neck. She shivered, leaning her head back so he could have more, relishing the feeling of sparks dancing on her skin. She'd been waiting all day for him to love her, and anticipation could be the most powerful of aphrodisiacs.

His lips trailed down to the hollow of her throat, leaving a burning trail on her skin and pooling heat in her sex. Tension coursed through her veins making every touch like an ominous rumble of thunder with the reverberations sounding in her heart.

Tonight would be their last night, and yet she wanted to hold herself back from the pain. But she couldn't. She couldn't give him less than all of her. If she held back she would always regret what could have been the most precious night of her life. And she would never let herself have another chance to make up for what might have been. Tonight was it, and she would make it all that she could, for him and herself.

So as he kissed her, trailing his tongue around the shell of her ear, she laid her heart down in an offering.

Pieces of clothing fell on the floor like cast off present wrappings and the cool air caressed her, making the heat from his hands that skimmed over every inch of flesh scorch.

Her heart cried for more, and surcease all at once, but his hands were on her, soothing her, drawing her under his spell. He bound her with silken cords of whispered words and kisses until she knew that when the evening ended she would be picking up pieces of herself, and leaving in shards.

He kneeled in front of her, holding her and pressing his lips into her stomach and sliding his cheek along its softness . She ran her fingers through his hair and tried to pull him up.

He growled and inhaled her scent, slipping his fingers in her wetness then kissing the hollow of her hip, making her thighs tremble.

Her heart burst with the words, but she smothered them with a moan as his tongue found the apex of her folds, teasing them apart until she was spread open before him.

She closed her eyes against the sight of him feasting on her and touching his shoulders, pulled him over her and sighed with his weight as he slid inside her, filling her almost until it hurt, her salty taste on his lips.

Her thighs gripped his hips, drawing him in, and wanting him deeper still, up to her heart.

Instead he took her legs and slung them over his shoulders, her heels bouncing on his back as he pounded into her. She pulled her legs down. That's not what she wanted tonight. She needed him parallel, hip to hip, feet to feet. To have as much of her touching him as possible. For their tongues to meet, and their breath to mingle. This was the last she'd have of him.

She hooked her ankles around his and gripped him with her thighs, pushing him in as far as she could. Then she pulled his shoulders down until he lay on top of her completely.

Tension hummed through him, the need to move under his straining muscles, but he lay there for her, still, until she lifted her hips up.

A rumble vibrated his chest and she lifted them up again, and this time he met her, but gently, almost as if he were unsure.

She tormented herself more than he with her need to be so close and filled. With his scent in her nose and body covering her, he had become so hard that her pussy squeezed in small spasms around him.

She lifted her hips once again. "Please."

His wet forehead rested on her shoulder and he took a shuddering breath, and on his exhale he impaled her starting a rhythmic drumming of wet skin slapping. She didn't want it to end, but with every drive he ground himself into her so deeply she came, her cunt squeezing on him to the point that she clenched her thighs, wailing in a low keen. Not a moment later she felt his own orgasm fill her, still pumping as he growled with his own release and not sorry at all that just once he left his seed deep inside her.

* * * *

"No." He asked her more times than she could bear, and now she was getting angry.

"What do you mean no?"

She opened her eyes to look at him. "I would never be accepted in your peer group. And I will not walk around proud of being your mistress. Moreso, I can't do that to my family. And what if I became pregnant?"

His heart stopped at the mention of children. He'd never even thought of that, and considering that he himself was once homeless he knew for certain that she was wrong. Money coupled with ambition washed all that away. Not the stink from your own nose, but it made you less offensive to others. A ball of fire swirled in his chest as he fumbled to get the last button through its hole.

"You're full of shit. You're just scared."

Her head snapped back. "Maybe I am. But you're not a woman in my position. I have nothing to offer other than what I am. Though that may sound like enough, we both know it's not. I can't reinvent myself for you so that I'm accepted by your peers, and because I'm not a man, they'll hold all of it against me."

He grabbed her shoulders and spun her to face him. "If you won't marry me then come live in the brownstone." Her eyes searched his face, looking for what, he didn't know. "I would be willing to take that if it was all you could give."

She took a deep breath. "I've said no, and I mean it. I won't. I can't hide away in alleys and be brought to secret assignations through darkened streets, and I won't live in your house."

He would take anything he could get and he would do anything she asked if it meant keeping her with him. "We could be circumspect."

She pressed the heels of her hands into her eyes, "No."

He scrubbed his hands through his hair and walked away. "You haven't given me a logical reason, and you can't think up many in favor of you marrying me. The least being that I could help your family to stop this charade of palmistry that they use to dupe people."

It was as if all the air were sucked out of the room and time stopped.

"I didn't mean that they way it sounded."

She walked over and glared at him. "There is the exact reason for me to not be your mistress or marry you. You never respected me to begin with. I've never lied to a person about their readings. It may not be logical like money and math, but it's not some snake charmer oil. Always the charity case, I was." She picked up her cloak. "Well, I never once fucked you for money, and I'll be damned if I marry a man who loathes my family so they can be taken care of. My mother would die of mortification that I lowered myself to your standards." She walked out the door and stopped. "And another thing." She came back in. "My father was very well respected within this town, and he adored my mother. His sadness as he died was that he wouldn't be able to protect her from the gossip anymore. He never would have escorted her through back doors." She looked him up, and down and shook her head. "I'll get home by hired carriage."

"Is there anything I can do to change your mind?"

"Goodbye, Caden."

At that she left and within moments he heard the front door slam, and the crunch of gravel on the drive. It was a grand finale for his perfect night. He poured himself a drink from the decanter and slung it back, then poured himself another, whiskey splashing over the rim onto the rug.

It was perfect for a few hours. He had mistreated her, and he was sorry. But being sorry now was too late.

He was good at strategizing at work, and he needed to bring that specific talent into this situation. He was looking at this wrong. This particular situation, was not a loss it was a negotiation. She just didn't realize it.

Unfortunately the perfect weapon for this problem would be harder on her because while he would know his intent, she would be left to wonder of his sincerity.

Patience.

Patience always won the siege. He knew she didn't feel indifferent toward him, and that was his ace.

He would have to plan carefully and keep watch on her so that he didn't wait too long.

* * * *

It was as if for the past thirteen weeks there was a solar eclipse. Not that he would have noticed. He had record gains this past quarter and was a cyclone of command that left some of his tellers crying over misplaced pennies. He felt a tinge of remorse, but didn't stop.

Spring would arrive soon and he'd not spoken to Abby since she left his home. He'd kept watch, making sure they had coal and food, and that she had taken no lovers. He couldn't blame her if she did, she didn't know his plans, but the dread of his weekly reports coming back with information on another man in her life was sometimes more than he could bear. In that respect, the agony of his plan lay squarely on him.

Not any more, though. He'd received word this morning that The Jennings' were having a Spring Festival. Complete with fortune telling. He cleared his calendar, and within ten minutes secured an invitation. Tomorrow night he would see her. He felt green, anticipation coursing through him.

But would she still want him? Would she accept those parts of him that he hadn't shown her yet? The ones he still hid? The parts of him that still dreamed of eating out of the garbage when he was nine, hiding behind the restaurants and being yelled at to get out of the alley while they threw bottles at him? How he yelled out in his sleep as he dreamt that they shattered above his head on the brick walls, shards of glass falling on his shoulders like sharp rain. When he had those nightmares would she look at him different in the morning? Or did she need him to be the Caden that everyone else saw all the time?

He'd be finding out soon enough.

Chapter Nine

Mrs. Jennings, their hostess, had gone all out in the spirit of the season. Bouquets of tulips and hyacinth bulbs in their forcing glasses were in every room. There was nowhere she could go to stop sneezing.

Other than allergies, spring was on its way and she, for one, was elated. She'd spent far too long in the house dwelling on her last conversation with Caden, and hoping every day that he would send her some word that he wanted to see her.

At first she thought it was lust, pure and simple, but nothing was ever, just lust. Something in the psyche drew people, even to satiate lust. Her mother told her that it was the recognition of the soul that brought two people together, even for short times. Never before had she entertained that there was truth in her mother's beliefs.

But it wasn't just that. She missed him. His smile, the way he smelled, and how he made her laugh. How she felt lying in his arms. The heavy thick contentment that seeped into her bones afterwards. The sense of perfection, that no matter what lay on the other side of the door, there, with him, she was safe and loved.

Maybe she was a fool for not running to him at his office and begging to be installed even as his mistress. Some days it was all she could do to just stand at the locked door with her hand on the knob forcing herself not to open it.

But she had withstood the temptation. She wanted him, but not scraps, and not his disrespect.

To love her was to love all of her, palm reading and strange mother included. He needed to be able to stand for her and with her. At least, that's what she wanted.

She set the vase of tulips off to the side so she could see the room to study the people milling about. It was a game she played trying to decide who would come sit for her readings. Her mother called that practice, but she just did it to occupy her time.

The party was exuberant and frothy, people milling about thankful, just like her that the sun decided to shine. Most of the women were dressed like petit fours and punch, and the men accordingly looked like they wanted to eat them.

Had she always been oblivious to those looks between lovers? That shared knowledge that made glances meaningful. Is that the way she and Caden looked at each other and was it as easy to tell by the longing on their faces?

She wanted to bang her head on the table. Could she go five minutes without thinking about him?

It had been thirteen weeks and there was not a day that she didn't think of him twenty times at least. She should be ashamed of herself. Really. It was time to move on.

She took a deep breath and looked across the room to where her mother and Camille were sitting with a few guests. Mother looked pretty, but tired. The stress of finances drained her and over the winter Abby started to notice that the purplish bags never left from under her eyes and what once were fine lines, now were engraved.

Camille sat, oblivious to her mother and completely twitterpated because a young man was paying attention to her.

"You look as if the weight of the world is on your shoulders."

Abby jolted and her hand flew to her mouth. "Caden?" She was too startled to stem the harsh tone in her voice.

"You don't sound too happy to see me."

Her heart caught in her throat as she drank him in. "I'm...you surprised me."

His gaze arrested her as he took in every detail, goosebumps rising on her skin where his eyes lingered. "I missed you."

Her cheeks burned under his examination.

"Would you like me to get you a drink?"

How was it fair that he looked more handsome than ever, his obsidian eyes haunting? Meanwhile she wore a mended gown from three seasons ago, updated with new lace and ribbon.

She patted her hair. "No thank you, I'm fine."

"Did you miss me?"

For a second she considered answering no. To hold him off and make him hurt as she had been, but it was futile to lie. She knew the truth was in her blush and her gaze and her decision had been her own.

"Yes."

She had nothing to be ashamed of, she just needed to be stronger than her emotions. She had lain naked next to him, sharing everything, and she refused to be ashamed of that now. Loving someone was not a flaw.

Still, she held her heart close, because it was so close to shattering as he eyes absorbed her.

He held out his hand. "Come walk with me."

"I can't." She shook her head.

"Why?"

"Don't ask such a stupid question."

He pulled out a chair and sat down. "Well then, read my palm."

She rolled her eyes and held out her hand for his.

She looked it over, "You will live a long life with much wealth," she said, in a thick Romanian accent.

"Can you be serious?"

"Can you be anything but?"

He huffed. "Can you answer my questions without asking another question?"

"If I do will you go away?"

He leaned in close, "You are so full of shit. You just said that you missed me."

She glared at him. "I missed you in my mind. You in the flesh is something I was wholly unprepared for."

"Yet here I sit."

"I answered in a declarative sentence. Two, exactly. Now go."

"Why are you being such a smartass?"

She groaned. "I told you, I wasn't ready to see you. I wanted to see you. I hoped to see you, but now, with you in front of me, I realize I was wrong. I need more time."

He sat back. "Time for what?"

"Time to get over you."

"I don't want you to get over me."

She tapped the table. "Could have fooled me."

He arched his brow.

"Did you ever send word? What was I supposed to think, that you were pining?"

"I asked you to marry me," His brows met making him look feral, "and you said no. What was I supposed to do, beg? Would that have proven my sincerity?" He jabbed his finger towards her. "You said no. I respected that. That is what you wanted, respect?"

"You twist my words! You did not ask me to marry you." She started to get up and jab the table but sat back down. "You agreed to get married, there were no questions asked. And if there were I would still say no."

Abby's mother swooshed over, the feathers in her hat following her. "Hello, Mr. Dupree. So nice to see you here." She looked at Abby, "Darling, you might want Mr. Dupree to go see the greenhouse. It's so lush and beautiful."

"Fine," she said under her breath as he held out his elbow. She placed her hand in the bend of his arm, and stiffened at the closeness and the heat of his body. If she were to have the strength to do this, she needed to keep from touching him. He led her though the doors into the lush humid room.

Abby inhaled the fresh green scent, and took the moment to calm down. After all, it had been her choice to leave him.

The greenhouse was lush with fig trees and ficus, pots of ivy and bulbs scattered about. Along one wall were orchids in various stages of bloom and candelabras set on tables making it seem as if the fae would appear any moment.

"How have you been?"

"Miserable." She turned to him and smiled wide and fake, "And you?"

So much for acting like an adult.

"Sarcasm does not look good on you."

"Well, it feels wonderful."

"Unleash your anger on me, I hope it makes you feel better."

Now she wanted to beat him with a tree branch. But he was right, she acted like a petulant child when it was her own doing.

She sighed. "Why are you here, Caden, haven't you broken me enough?"

"I missed you. I wanted to see you." He stopped and leaned down and placed a chaste kiss on her lips and her heart leapt, even though she didn't want it to. "I needed to see you."

"I believe I am in front of you." She steeled herself again, at the same time wanting him more than ever. He was here, in front of her and all she had to do was reach out and touch him. Her hand never left her side. Instead the pain in her chest made her take shallow breaths. It was as if she was trying to catch the pieces of an exploding star. And yet she would give everything to lean her head against his chest and have his arms around her.

He put his finger under her chin and tilted her head up to his and she closed her eyes. He stroked her cheek where a tear made its path down her face.

"Come live with me and be my Love,
And we will all the pleasures prove
That hills and valleys, dale and field,
And all the craggy mountains yield.

There we will sit upon the rocks
And see the shepherds feed their flocks,
By shallow rivers, to whose falls
Melodious birds sing madrigals.

There I will make thee beds of roses
And a thousand fragrant posies,
A cap of flowers, and a kirtle
Embroider'd all with leaves of myrtle."

The tears were flowing out the sides of her eyes now and he bent to kiss them.

"If these delights thy mind may move, Then live with me and be my love." His voice cracked out the last few lines.

She gathered up the tiny shards of her heart. "Posies are lovely, but I desire your respect more."

She sniffed and wiped her eyes with the hem of her sleeve.

She turned and walked out, and when she got to the door Mrs. Jennings awaited her.

"Isn't the greenhouse lovely this time of year? I forced the flowers for the party there. I had to start months ago, but the forsythia branches have only taken a few weeks." Pride of her accomplishment filled the older woman's face.

Abby nodded to Mrs. Jennings, and heard Caden come up behind her.

"Abby, I've seated your mother and sister in the kitchen for dinner," She looked behind Abby and smiled, "Ah, Mr. Dupree! I'm glad to see you saw the greenhouse. Just the man I was looking for." Her brilliant smile made her look a decade younger. "Would you escort me into the dining room for dinner?"

Caden stopped short, but recovered. Abby watched him and blanched, mortified at being laid so low.

"Yes, ma'am." He held his elbow out.

Abby escaped into the kitchen as they stepped out.

* * * *

She had walked out as quietly as she could, but he could feel shame radiate off her in waves. In that moment his failing of Abby became crystal clear. And even still he walked Mrs. Jennings into the dining room because he wasn't sure how to show Abby he understood what he'd done. Or that he was sorry for assuming her life was a sham because he didn't understand it.

And, it occurred to him that after tonight, he might never see her again.

So he walked beside Mrs. Jennings, nodding when appropriate, but running through probable solutions in his mind.

He placed his hostess at the head of the table, scooting her chair in when she sat and as he walked to his place setting, nodded to all the faces he'd always seen at every party. They were the standard of accepted civility in the city of Boston, and at some point in time he'd lost himself gaining their approval.

He'd prided himself on his lack of compromise so many times he never realized he wasn't watching close enough to how he gradually had become just as insular.

Mrs. Jennings thanked him as he pushed her chair in behind her and he nodded again, still consumed with the pain on Abby's face.

When he found his place card, he was seated next to the older single daughter of the Cranes, what was her name? Apparently he was now the next candidate for her marriage ticket as her parents cast hopeful glances from the other end of the table. He looked back at her and found that she caught where his gaze had held.

"Excuse them, I believe if I don't make a match soon they'll throw in some land and a horse to go with me. For the value."

He smiled, despite himself.

"Please forgive me, I've forgotten your name." Her eyes were twilight blue, and her hair dark blonde. But he preferred dark olive skin with wiry black hair.

"Sarah."

"Yes, we were introduced last fall, no?"

"I believe."

"Yes, yes, I remember now."

"You're off the hook now, I'll cover for you." She smiled but her eyes were sad.

"Excuse me?"

"You don't have to worry about me trying to wile my way into your favor. I can see your heart is taken already." She took a sip of wine. "And I saw the conversation at the greenhouse."

"Ah. Well, if that isn't embarrassing."

"Not really. I would hope one day someone looked at me the way you did her."

Her blatant honesty took him aback. Lots of things seemed to be taking him aback lately. As he snapped open his napkin and laid it on his lap the servant brought out two bowls of steaming soup and placed them down.

"Oh, here's the first course. Fiddlehead soup, of course. Spring and all that."

Her wry wit was refreshing, and he was thankful at not having to make small talk about inane subjects. Apparently she was going to let him brood in peace and try to think up a way to change Abby's mind.

He drank one glass of wine in three gulps, not even tasting it and ran though his options. Doing nothing was always an option. An ugly one, but one none the less. If anything though, he needed to apologize, or he wouldn't be able to look at himself to shave. He could send a note, but that would be crude. There was nothing else to do. He could not let her leave without seeing her. He stood up and nodded to Mrs. Jennings.

"If you'll excuse me." He started to walk out.

"Is everything alright, Mr. Dupree? The soup is not to your liking? I can have the cook make you something?" Anxiety tinged her voice, and she didn't deserve a scene.

"No, the food is superb. There's a lady in your kitchen to whom I need to apologize and convince to marry me." He got a thrill from the hush that fell over the table.

"In the kitchen?"

"Yes, Miss Abigail Drummond. You see, I've been asking and she's refused me quite often thinking that she would never fit in with our set." He looked at each guest, warning them. "I told her that she would never be set down by such a hospitable group. That you were all much more progressive than to hold her lack of finances, or her family's trade against her. After all, look how you accepted me."

Power did have its weight, and although he'd never used it in a personal way before, it felt good to brandish it now. They'd commit social suicide to snub him or Abby.

"It's been a long time since I first started at Boston Trust, and if you all remember I couldn't even read that well. Now I negotiate your interest rates. I may not convince her to marry me, but I expect you all to treat her with the utmost respect."

Mrs. Jennings flushed. "I'll have her and her family made settings at the table."

"No, no need. I'll go out there."

He left amidst a frozen silence and finding the kitchen, swung through the butler's doors into the room where he was greeted with a stunned quiet. The floor was tiled in black and white with stoves, ovens and cabinets edging the perimeter, and a huge French country table sat in the middle like a wooden island.

Abby, her mother, and sister looked up simultaneously. It took Abby a second to realize what it meant for him to be standing there, and he could tell when she did because her face became the exact shade of an India rubber ball.

"Abby." He nodded to her mother sitting next to her. "Mrs. Drummond, Camille."

The butler, who'd been standing watch for course changes came up beside him, "Mr. Dupree, would you like me to retrieve your plate? Or would you like a new one made?"

Caden scanned the plates on the table, noting that none were bowls of pale green soup. "If that's what I can have, I'll take it." The butler looked to the chef who smiled and scurried to make him a heaping plate of roasted chicken and potatoes. Thank God, this may have been the wiser decision for that alone.

It hadn't gotten past him that Mrs. Drummond had been observing him all the while. Caden expected to be insulted by her action, but rather he was happy for it. Things would be out in the open.

"Mr. Dupree, may I see your hand?" Mrs. Drummond asked.

He sat down, put the second napkin on his lap for the evening and gave his palm to her. Unlike Abby's readings, her hands were cool and firm and knowing. Like a doctor when he touched you with calm assurance. There was no arcing of sexual energy between them, and that factor alone told him more about him and Abby than anything.

"Hmmm."

Caden's brows gathered.

"Ahhh..." Mrs. Drummond nodded to herself.

Caden glanced at Camille and then Abby to see what they thought. Only Abby rolled here eyes at him.

"Well, well," she said this time.

Caden couldn't take it any longer.

"What? What do you see?"

Mrs. Drummond met his eyes over their hands. "You will be marrying soon."

Camille squealed, clapping her hands and Abby muttered, "Dear Lord," under her breath. "Mother, Caden doesn't believe any of this."

Mrs. Drummond met his eyes and let Caden take his hand back. "He doesn't have to, he just has to respect that I do. Now are you going to ask her?"

"I have been, ma'am. Just short of begging."

Abby sniffed.

"Abby, did you read that Caden would be marrying soon?" Mrs. Drummond asked.

"Yes, Mother."

Caden snapped his head around so fast everything blurred. "What? You never told me that."

Abby shrugged. "How was I to know it would be me? What if it were someone else?"

"There is no one else." Anger smacked him like bucket of cold water to the face, and it just as quickly left when he realized that she was justified in doubting him.

The servants and Camille's eyes were bouncing to the speakers like they were watching a cricket match, with none of them touching their food. He had to press his advantage now, before she regained this stupid notion that their classes were too far apart.

"I'll ask you one more time, Abby. Will you marry me?"

Now all the attention was focused on Abby, waiting for her answer.

"Yes," she said, into her plate.

The table cheered, and the wait staff congratulated each other until the butler gathered them all to go out and clear the bowls for the next course.

Caden squeezed Abby's hand and started to eat.

Chapter Ten

Caden's hands ran up her ribs and cupped her breasts, lifting them to his mouth, rolling one nipple between his fingers while he sucked the other, then switching. Abby moaned and hung her head back, her hair like a spider's web against the small of her back, feeling like silk against her skin. Every nerve in her body was alive and singing, not only for being with Caden, but the emotion of her love that washed over her like an incoming tide. How her heart hammered, how her senses rushed, firing underneath her skin, her ears and mouth.

He let go of her nipple with a pop and trailed his mouth down her ribs, past her stomach to the hollow of her hip. His breath teased her curls with his fingers following, spreading her open and letting the cool hit her, making her shiver with how naked she was. She tried to stay still on the bed, but the sheets were crushed in her hands as she clenched and unclenched them. He teased and nipped, licking and sucking until she rode an edge of pleasure that was sharp and frantic. As he darted his tongue in and around she lifted her hips to make him fill her more, until he splayed his hands pinning her as he pushed her off the edge, her pussy clenching on nothing and wanting more.

"Fill me." She meant it to be a request, but it came out a demand.

"Tsk, tsk. Say please, and I just might help you."

"Horrid man. Fuck me." She tried to pull him up but he was immoveable. "Please!"

"That wasn't so hard, was it?"

She nipped him on the shoulder as he slid in and arched his hips, lifting her, taunting back.

He rocked into her. "Are you happy?"

"What kind of question is that?"

He pulled out and rocked back in, taking her breath away and wiping the questions out of her mind. His questions, not hers. Hers still thrummed in her ears like a mosquito. Why her? Why did he love her, when he could have had any other woman out there?

His rocking became steadier , even and deep and he gripped her thighs, pulling her towards him and anchoring her there. She knew he was close, but he wasn't pulling out like he'd always done before.

Then as the realization dawned on her she looked at him, on his knees on the bed, now with her thighs held up around his hips. His face was set and he stared at her, her breasts bounced with every thrust and she knew he knew the same thing, the intensity of his eyes burning her with the knowledge. She could have said no, but an enormous wave of lust and love crashed over her taking her words away.

The tightly sprung coil flew and he was so deep that as he followed she felt the warm shots of liquid fill her with each spasm sending her into another shattering climax, like stars bursting inside her body.

He eased himself off to her side and wrapped a strand of hair around his finger.

"You didn't answer me."

She curled into him. "I'm happy."

"That sounds more like a question rather than a statement."

"I am happy." She kissed his chest, his hair crisp under her lips. She ran her fingers through the hair where her lips had just been and felt his heartbeat. Time seemed to stand still while they lay in the bed, even though shadows crept up the walls and the sun had gone down long ago. Hazy twilight and the down quilt they lay under cocooned them and kept the spring evening chill away. It was drowsy and safe there, lying in his arms and contentment seeped into her bones knowing that this was how every night for the rest of her life would be. She was very happy.

"I love you, you know. I wanted to tell you before, but it sounded trite for some reason."

When she remembered to breathe it was a gasp. The words filled her mouth but didn't leave it. Why, when this was what she wanted could she not just say them?

"It's fine if you can't say them back."

His words sounded flat to her though, and her heart pounded with having hurt him. It wasn't that she didn't love him. She did. What she couldn't understand was why he loved her.

He stopped playing with her hair and turned her around, pulling her into him.

"Do you think you could love me, eventually?" he said, into her hair.

How could this successful, handsome man think that she didn't love him? She loved him enough to leave him, hoping that he would find someone more suitable. What was remarkable was even with all his friends, and his money, he needed her love . Suddenly not saying the words seemed cruel.

"I love you," she said. "I love the way you help people without telling anyone. I love the way you're honest. How you never gave up hope for us. That, I love most of all."

He was so quiet she thought he'd fallen asleep.

"I love you for demanding that I respect you. I loved you before, but now it's so much more." He kissed the top of her head and pulled her to him. "I grew up very poor, you know."

"I read that in your hand. One of the first times I read your palm."

"I used to find my dinners in the alley garbage," he said, muffled into her hair.

A spear of pain shot through her, but she knew one thing he'd never want was her pity.

"But you never let that stop you," she whispered.

"No. But I still dream about it every now and then. Just in case I scare you."

"You won't scare me. Nothing can scare me, apart from me losing you."

"I yell sometimes when I dream that they're throwing things at me."

Her throat swelled and grew raw. "How old were you?"

"Eight and nine."

"Where were your parents?"

"My mother just left one day. I think she got tired of trying to feed me when she couldn't even feed herself. One day she just never came home."

She wanted to be angry with his mother, but she just felt sick that a little boy at eight had to grow up so fast. And here she thought that her childhood was hard by being her mother's daughter. At least there was food on the table and two parents who loved her. Being a misfit seemed nothing more than a minor inconvenience. At least she had parents who adored her. She was ashamed of herself for not realizing there were worse ways to suffer, and for dwelling on her perceived problems.

Abby could feel the tension run through his muscles, waiting for action.

"I understand if it disgusts you. If you want me to leave."

She rolled over and took his face in her hands. "That boy who fought to make his way is the man I love. All of that made you. Your relentlessness and hard work. Your ability to see a person's potential and not their station in life."

He touched her forehead with his. "You still want to get married?"

"Of course I do."

She pulled his hand to her and traced the lines on his palm with her fingertip. "You have a long lifeline and a major joining with a woman who loves you more than you understand. She doesn't love you despite your upbringing and flaws, she loves you because of them." She kissed his fingertips and he closed his eyes. "You will have a long marriage and three children."

"Four. I want four children."

Her heart skipped. "And you will have four children," she said back.

Flesh and Bone

Selah March

Also by Selah March

Moondance
To Have and Have Not
Phaze Fantasies, Vol. III

Chapter One

An artfully lit stage at the back of the club. A tall bench covered in padded leather. The scent of cologne. Fresh sweat. Old blood.

These things never change, no matter how often Leah dreams them.

She can feel the edge of the bench digging into her diaphragm, and the restraints around her wrists. The muscles in the backs of her legs strain to keep her balanced on her toes. To keep her shoulders down and her hips high, as she's been instructed. The blood rushes to her head. Pounds in her ears, drowning the murmurs of the gathered audience. She doesn't lift her eyes or turn her head to look at the people assembled to watch the performance. She'll have to face them soon enough. Next time, when it's her turn to handle the crop or the flogger. Them, or people very much like them.

A hand descends on the back of her naked thigh. The touch is quick, and so are the words that accompany it. "I'll make this as easy as I can."

Now she turns her head, trying to catch a glimpse of the owner of the voice. Male, deep and warm—unusual in this place of so many women. Men don't wield the implements here. The Madre is firm on that point. So, tonight there is a difference in the dream.

But it hardly matters who lifts the crop over her bare ass and thighs so long as he or she brings it down with enough force to bite. To leave a mark. To make her flinch, then push her hips higher still in anticipation of the next sharp strike. Because this is who she is—one who craves bliss shot through with pain, like veins of crimson in perfect white marble. Suffering underlined with the bold purple ink of pleasure. The shape of the dream and her desire never changes. Only the details.

Tonight the details include this man, who applies the crop with special attention, taking care not to strike over the same place twice. To make the sting electric, but not overwhelming, so that her whole body hums and tingles with sensation. Soon enough, she's fighting the need to grind herself into the horse's padded bolster, to relieve the pulsing ache in her cunt. But she won't because that's been forbidden, and even knowing none of this is real, she fears the consequences of disobedience in which the pain is not tempered with pleasure, but pushed to an extreme that would leave her broken in body and spirit.

The fortieth blow falls, and it's finished. She trembles, taut and panting, anticipating the finale. The touch returns to her thigh. Climbs higher. Skims over the raised welts ever so gently, making her moan. Her legs shake, the muscles spasm with the strain of holding her hips so high. The twisting agony merges with the thick, wet pulse in her pussy and the pounding in her brain.

"What do you want?" he whispers. It startles her, breaking the moment. It's not supposed to happen this way. She chooses to submit. After that, the choice is no longer hers. She becomes an empty vessel waiting to be filled with sensation for the entertainment of the patrons.

He moves around to stand near her head. She turns her face toward him, but he's too close and she can't twist her neck that way. She can only see his hands, holding the crop. Large and square, with long, blunt fingers. A scar on the back of the right one, shaped like a crescent moon. She closes her eyes and hears the sound of breaking glass. The shatter is muffled by distance and time.

"Do you want this? Tell me, Leah."

The crowd mutters, displeased. They'd come to see a show. To see a submissive pushed to her limits, made to plead and beg and cry. Maybe with a little humiliation and loss of dignity for an encore.

Any moment now, one of the acolytes would appear to drag them away—Leah and this unknown man—to face the consequences. The Madre would punish her for breaking her vows. Or force her and the mystery man to torture each other, until one of the two was no longer good for anything outside an ICU unit.

"What do you want, Leah?" His voice is so deep, she can feel it vibrate in her chest. He reaches out and snags a strand of her hair, where it's fallen loose from its braid, and weaves it between his fingers. "Tell me what you want. I'll do anything."

Anything? Who says that, and means it? That's just stupid. And she'd be twice as stupid to believe it.

What does she want, anyway?

The crowd's irritation is like a swarm of bees buzzing in her head, louder and louder...

She reached out and smacked the alarm clock. The audience, along with their noisy protest, evaporated. Then she stretched, groaning at the way the muscles in her legs cramped, and at the tense, frustrated ache between her thighs. In the silence of her bedroom, she heard the man's voice asking one more time...

"Leah, what do you want?"

She sighed and ran a hand over her face, scrubbing away the last traces of sleep. "Damned if I know."

Leah threw back the covers and crawled out of bed, leaving dreams and memories behind.

* * * *

"Today we'll be studying sexual perversion as depicted in literature."

Forty bodies sat up straight on uncomfortable chairs. The chatter echoing off the walls of the half-filled classroom died away. In the front row, a sophomore—the one with "virgin" written all over her preppy kilt and pearls—scrunched her face like she'd accidentally sucked a big old slurp off of a lemon.

Well, that got their attention.

Leah set her books on the desk and turned to write a name on the blackboard: Marquis de Sade. Beneath it, she scrawled the words, *father of sadism*, and underlined them twice. Then she turned to face her Basics of World Literature class. They stared at her, pens poised above notebooks. Even the uber-jocks in the back looked interested.

Crossing her arms over her chest and leaning one hip against the desk, she began, "The Marquis de Sade, otherwise known as Donatien Alphonse François. Can anyone tell me something about this man?"

Silence. Leah stifled a sigh. No challenge here. Nothing to make her think or try. Just the never-ending battle to make them—her summer term students, who didn't want to be here on a Friday afternoon in the dog days of August, and who could blame them?—think and try. The very definition of a losing battle.

"De Sade's philosophy was based on a single principle: perfect freedom. Freedom to do whatever struck a person's fancy, with no restrictions imposed by ethics, religion, or law."

The sound of pens scratching against rough paper was loud in her ears. She continued, "For de Sade and his followers, the pursuit of personal pleasure was the highest ideal."

The virgin sophomore—*I really should quit thinking of her that way, it's not fair*—raised her hand, and Leah nodded.

"When you say 'personal pleasure,' do you

mean...?" The girl's voice trailed off. She flushed a pretty pink against the white of her pearls.

"Yes. I mean sex." Leah uncrossed her arms and gestured toward the blackboard. "But not just regular, run-of-the-mill sex. We're talking about real perversion here. Taking pleasure in the suffering of others."

The good-looking blond junior at the opposite end of the row cleared his throat.

"Yes, Ray? You have a question?"

"More like an observation."

Of course. Ray Delacroix never asked questions when he could make comments, remarks, or observations. "Go ahead."

Ray shrugged and said, "You're way too uptight. There's nothing perverted about getting off on a little pain." He leveled a smirk at her and sat back in his chair, the muscles beneath his tight tee shirt rippling.

Leah felt her lips twist in distaste. She stepped away from the desk and went to stand directly in front of the boy. "Can I assume you have some experience in this area?"

Ray laughed. "You know it. Nothing like a little kink to spice things up, baby." He leered at her. "I'd be happy to give you some private instruction, if you're interested."

Several students gasped. A few tittered. A sharp bark of laughter rang out before it morphed into a coughing fit.

"I don't think that will be necessary. However, I'd like to try a little experiment. May I touch you?"

He rolled his eyes and grinned. "For sure, baby. Go for it."

With her right hand, she reached out and caressed Ray's left ear. He leaned into her touch, his suggestive smile deepening. When she was sure she had his trust, she closed her fingers around his ear and twisted. Not hard...just enough.

"Hey!" He jerked his head, but Leah held on, digging her nails into the flesh around his ear.

"I thought you liked pain, Ray. I thought it spiced things up."

"Let go, you crazy—"

"Hold still, and I won't hurt you."

He stopped struggling. "You wait 'til I see the dean about this, you nutty—"

"Listen to me," Leah said, keeping a firm grip on his ear. "Listen and consider. Imagine if, instead of your ear between my fingers, I was holding a different piece of your anatomy...say, your testicles?"

A groan erupted from one of the jocks in the back. Ray muttered an obscenity, his color deepening to an unattractive shade of magenta.

"Imagine if you were hanging in chains, and I continued applying pressure to said anatomy until the pain made you black out. Imagine if I then revived you by having you flogged."

The virgin sophomore made a gurgling sound, and Leah paused to glance at her. She'd gone as pale as her pearls.

"Okay, I get it," Ray said, his face nearly purple. "You made your point."

"I don't think so. I think you need to keep imagining...considering how it would feel to know I was 'getting off', as you put it, on your agony. Taking joy from your helplessness. Reveling in the knowledge that I could kill you slowly, and all for the sake of my own pleasure." Ray's gaze flickered to her face, and she smiled at him. "You still like the idea of pain?"

"That's not what I meant. You twisted it—"

She gave his ear a sharp pinch and let go. He flopped back in his seat. His face was bathed in sweat, and he was panting.

"I know what you meant. But de Sade wasn't about a little consensual spanking or a set of nipple clamps—he was the real deal. Inflicting torture for the sheer enjoyment of watching others suffer, more often than not against their wills." She wiped her fingers on her skirt, as if she'd dirtied them. "And he was imprisoned for over twenty-nine years for his writings on the subject."

Ray shot her a dirty look and mumbled something she didn't quite catch.

"What was that?"

He lifted his chin. "I called you a fascist."

Leah laughed. "You think I approve of locking people up because of what they write?"

"Sure sounds that way." His defiant stare didn't quite meet her eyes.

"Well, that makes an excellent topic for debate, doesn't it?" Leah turned toward the blackboard, intending to write something further about de Sade and his literature of perversion. She'd picked up the chalk and was reaching toward the board when a wave of scent drifted over her, strong and dark.

Latex? Why am I smelling...? And perfume. Chanel No. 5.

She looked over her shoulder, expecting to see one of the girls in the front row applying the scent to their wrists or neck. But no—they were all staring at her expectantly, waiting to see some other outrageous teaching technique that would likely get her ass hauled into the dean's office yet again.

Another whiff of Latex, and then a stronger one of perfume, and now she was hearing...

Oh no. Not here. Please-please-please not here.

But the guitar chords were unmistakable. *Hotel California,* by the Eagles, circa 1976. Playing in her head—a private performance, just for her. And getting louder.

She turned again and clutched the back of the chair that was pushed into the footwell of the desk. If she could hold on just a few minutes...long enough to get them out of the room...long enough to get home...

She took a breath and lifted her head. "A thousand words on the topic of free speech versus social responsibility, on my desk by Monday. Now scoot, all of you."

The chorus of groans that met her statement didn't come close to drowning out Don Henley singing about mirrors on the ceiling and pink champagne on ice. She stood at the desk as the room emptied, barely hearing the clumsy footfalls and excited, pre-weekend conversation. Only when the door banged shut behind the last student did she clamp her hands to her ears and squeeze her eyes shut.

Loud...so damned loud. The music and the voices, and the aroma of Latex and perfume, sharp enough to make her gag and sickeningly familiar. A surge of dizziness struck her. She wasn't going to make it—not even to her car, much less all the way home.

Just as her knees gave way, the door opened again. She felt the floor rushing up to smack her hard and heard someone shout her name, but all of it was muted by the sounds and smells in her head, and now...

Oh, God, now the pictures, too...

She saw a face peer out of the shadows. Sharp, almost devilish features, black hair, dark eyes, strong jaw covered in inky stubble. He was looking past her, at someone just beyond her, and he was saying...he was saying...

Chapter Two

He was saying, "Sure baby, whatever you want, I'm easy," and smiling at the redhead standing to his left. She'd just proposed a trade—a brief interview with her employer in exchange for his company, and maybe some fun and games later on. The scent of her perfume swirled around him, mixing with the medicinal odor that rose from her black Latex catsuit.

"You won't be sorry, lover," she whispered, barely audible over the clash of music and voices. The club was crowded. The ebb and surge of bodies filing past pressed them tight against the bar, leaving little room to breathe. Marcus reached up to loosen his tie, but the redhead beat him to it, yanking him down and latching onto his lower lip with her teeth. She bit hard enough to make him wince.

Kinky chick. And a little on the aggressive side for his taste, but beggars couldn't be choosers. He wanted that interview with the reclusive Madre Donnatella, though he didn't believe the woman had any information he could use. But, the trail was getting colder by the hour. If he didn't turn up something soon, he'd be shit out of luck, and Julian's murder would go unsolved.

He had to try. And if the freckle-faced cutie wanted him to spank her and tug on her nipple piercings to get what he needed, well...

Bonus. He smirked around the mouth of the beer bottle and glanced into the mirror behind the bar, surveying the Friday evening crowd at Hotel California, the area's premiere alternative hotspot.

Nothing like it in this part of the state outside the city limits of San Francisco.

From what he could see, the redhead wasn't anywhere near the kinkiest clubber in the room. He'd nominate the guy in the far corner for that prize—the one wearing nothing but a black rubber diaper and sucking on an adult-sized pacifier. Or maybe his date, who appeared to be taking considerable joy in whacking the backs of his thighs with an extra-large fly swatter.

Lucky for Diaper Boy that Hotel California continued to exist. Uptight, outraged citizens had tried to shut the place down more than once, but since nobody here was breaking the law...or, at least, nobody had ever been caught breaking the law...

The sign over the entrance read: "Safe, Sane, and Consensual. No public nudity or lewd acts. Follow the rules or leave the premises." The club had no record of citations, no nine-one-one calls, no marks on its liquor license—a clean shop, in other words. And likely another dead-end when it came to finding Julian's killer.

The redhead grabbed his chin, pivoted his face toward hers, and stretched up on tiptoe to nibble at his mouth again. Her breath tasted sour, but he didn't pull away. Couldn't afford to offend her. Out of the corner of his eye, he saw the tall, blonde barmaid take his nearly empty bottle and set another in its place.

"Hey, I didn't—"

"On the house, sir." The barmaid—also attractive and also wrapped in Latex, just like every other Hotel California employee—ran her tongue over her full, pink lips as she let her gaze wander all over him. Nice. Maybe he could talk her and the redhead into a threesome once he'd finished his interview.

"Let's go, lover," the redhead said. "My boss is waiting."

"Yeah? Is she as hot as you?"

She lowered her eyes in an obvious attempt to look coy. "I think you'll like her. And I know she'll like you."

He lifted his hand and caressed her face. "What's your name, sweetheart?"

"Clarice," she said. Her lips trembled. Nervous? That was kind of sweet. Maybe she wasn't quite the pro at this scene she pretended to be.

"Clarice," he repeated, running his thumb lightly back and forth over her quivering lower lip. "You remember our deal, right?"

She nodded, staring into his eyes as if mesmerized.

"Good girl." He winked at her, and she smiled in response. Then he reached for the bottle and tipped it back, taking one long swallow before the taste struck him funny. He turned the bottle in his hand to check the label. Definitely not his brand.

But Clarice was pulling at the sleeve of his leather coat, drawing him away from the bar. The music, which had been a background beat up until now, morphed into something heavier—something with monks chanting in Latin over drums and synthesized techno-funk. As they wove their way through the club, the air grew thicker with the musk of eager bodies.

"This way," she said, and guided him through a door. It opened to reveal the top of a staircase that led down into perfect darkness. "Come on, hurry up. She's waiting."

He pulled away from her grip on his sleeve and stopped to look at her. Even in the dim light, her agitation was obvious. Suddenly, something about this whole deal smelled wrong.

"Are you coming or not?" she said.

Two weeks since his partner's death and not a single break in the case. He couldn't blow this—couldn't let anything get in the way. Not even his better instincts.

Her hand fell on his sleeve again, tugging. He stared at her for another second. Then he said, "Lead on, sweetheart."

* * * *

"Are you sure you're all right?"

Leah lifted her head from where it was firmly lodged between her knees and tried to smile. Jeff Crandel, Associate Professor of Math and Good Samaritan, pressed the damp washcloth to the back of her neck and clucked like a chicken. The beads of sweat on his shiny pate and the way his hands trembled as he supported her back gave away his anxiety.

"Skipped lunch today. Stupid of me." She struggled to her feet, leaning heavily on Jeff's arm. The look of concern on his face made her smile. What a nice man. A good friend. "I'll be fine."

"Well, if you're sure..." He looked thoroughly unconvinced. "I could call over to the infirmary. Wouldn't take a second."

She shook her head. "What I need is a sandwich and a glass of milk."

No, what I need is a drink. Several drinks. That always helps.

Well, not really. Not if she were perfectly honest. But getting wasted on tequila would take the edge off and make her forget for a while. Maybe long enough for the music and the odors and that dark man's face to go away. And the memories they invoked. The memories...*God, they're the worst of it, by far.*

"I'm headed home for dinner and bed," she said. This time her smile was as genuine as she could make it while lying through her teeth.

Ten minutes later, she pulled into a parking space behind a plumbing truck and stepped out onto the sidewalk in front of her favorite escape. The Gringo was the kind of place that attracted working class stiffs—a rare thing in a college town brimming with academics and over-privileged students. Which made it perfect for Leah on this night or any other,she could lose herself in the stink of cheap beer and try to forget her dissatisfaction with her past, her future, her job and life in general.

She stopped at the bar on her way to a corner booth. "I'll take four shots of tequila, a salt-shaker, a lime and a knife. Put it on my tab."

A few minutes later she was well on her way to being pleasantly buzzed. Nothing like being a regular in a place where they didn't much care if you lost a finger while carving up your own fruit.

The unidentifiable noise blaring from the jukebox did nothing to smother the tune re-looping through her brain, like a calliope on crack. She'd always been a fan of the Eagles, but after this? *Hotel California* was off her playlist, permanently. At least the odors of Latex and perfume had dissolved. And the man's face. No more scary-handsome guy staring at her from inside her own head. Another thing she could do without on a permanent basis. Because of all the things that sucked in her life? These stupid, pointless visions were the absolute worst. She'd never forgive her grandmother for passing them on to her, along with the allergy to cats and the gene that attracted difficult, self-absorbed assholes. Why couldn't she have inherited the dimples? Or the long legs? No, she had to get the psychic ability. Whoop-de-fuckin'-do.

"Hey there, beautiful lady."

She snorted into the bottom of her fourth shot glass. She'd heard crappy lines before, but that one was the champ. "Attractive," and maybe even "pretty" in that bland, girl-next-door kind of way that really bit the big one when you were neither a girl nor had any interest in living next door...but beautiful?

"Can I join you?" Apparently the snorting hadn't dissuaded him. He slid into the seat across from her, and she took stock of his age (early-middle), his state of being (not nearly drunk enough to excuse the arrogant grin), and tried to come up with a polite way of saying buzz off, loser.

"No thanks. I want to be alone."

He squinted at her. "Huh?"

"I said..." She paused and cleared her throat, the better to shout over Joe Walsh's guitar solo as it bounced off the inside of her skull. "I said—"

Before she could finish the sentence, a husky feminine voice whispered in her ear, "Don't be shy, *caro*. Come in. It's not like you have a choice." And then deadly laughter, the kind that made every tiny hair on her body rise up and quiver. The Madre Donnatella's laughter, to be precise.

Oh, hell no. Not now. Not ever, ever again.

The man leaned back and stared at her. "Hey lady...you okay? You come over kinda gray all of a sudden."

"I..." Leah swallowed, her throat suddenly dry. "I need some air." She slid out of the booth and headed for the door. The man didn't try to stop her. So much for her compelling beauty.

Out on the sidewalk nothing was better. The music had finally stopped, but what had taken its place was much worse. Bring back the classic seventies rock, if this was the alternative.

The laughter had faded, replaced by the distant sound of the Madre's voice. Leah couldn't quite make out the words—just the whisper of heavily accented English, and then that low, amused tone that made her grind her teeth together.

I'm not nearly drunk enough to deal with this. She pressed her hands to her eyes, and there he was—the man, from before, the one in her head. Dark eyes peered out from under a shock of black hair, and his swarthy jaw clenched as tightly as her own.

She staggered on the sidewalk, then pulled her

hands away from her face. "That's it," she said. "That's all. You can stop any time now." Whom was she talking to? The Madre or the dark man? Or someone else altogether? Because she could hear two voices now, both of them female. One lighter and sweeter in tone, speaking in unaccented English. Pleading, in fact...saying over and over again, "Please...please, no. Don't."

When Leah concentrated, she caught the impression of red hair and freckles on pale skin, and the black, shiny surface of latex. Of course—that's what all the Madre's acolytes wore. And what else did she sense? Something less concrete, but no less real.

Oh, yeah. There it was, plain as the light of day, or at least as clear as the glow of the streetlight above her head. The emotion she always associated with her memories of the Madre.

Fear.

Chapter Three

The little redhead was scared.

He could tell from the sheen of sweat that covered her face, visible even in the murky light at the very end of the hallway that stretched from the bottom of the stairs, and by the way her body trembled so hard it seemed to vibrate. Her obvious fear should've made him nervous—should've put him on full alert. But mostly it made Marcus want to step between her and whatever was on the other side of the heavy oak door with the shuttered window. The door they were facing. The door upon which the redhead had knocked some thirty seconds before.

"Try again, sweetheart."

"Shh." She wrung her hands together and shifted her weight from one foot to the other. After another few seconds, she lifted her fist. Just before she made contact with the door, the shutter on the window slid open with a loud click.

Silence. Then a voice—feminine, but pitched deep and...was that an Italian accent? "*Sì?* What do you want?"

"It's me, Clarice," the redhead said. "The man is with me."

The man? Was he expected?

There was a pause and then the rattle and thunk of bolts being thrown back. The door opened slowly, like something out of an old horror movie. Clarice darted ahead into the room and disappeared somewhere to the left. Marcus stepped forward, but stopped just outside the doorway.

"Don't be shy, *caro*. Come in," the unseen

woman said. "It's not like you have a choice."

Still he hesitated. "Who are you?"

"Come inside and see," the voice said. Still deep and exotic, but now almost breathless.

He craned his neck to peer around the door, but only caught a glimpse of brick walls, a cement floor, and a massive fireplace. The space was lit by the flames burning there, as well as the dozens of candles arranged on the mantle and at various spots around the room. The flickering light made a warm, almost inviting atmosphere. He felt himself relax, if only a little.

The scent of Clarice's perfume mingled with wood-smoke as he stepped over the threshold. He expected the door to slam behind him like a special effect out of Dracula's castle, but it remained standing open. He turned to his right and—Christ almighty. He fell back a step out of sheer surprise. Was this the Madre Donnatella, reclusive owner of Hotel California?

Maybe forty years old, and tiny. Smaller than Clarice by four inches and a good thirty pounds. Black hair that fell straight to her waist, a maroon slash for a mouth, and a body arrayed entirely in a gauzy gown in the same shade of used blood. But it was her eyes that caught his attention, glowing in the dimly-lit room like a pair of moons. And then the woman tilted her face toward him, and he realized she was blind.

"*Buonosera*," she said. "I am Donnatella DeTagliera." Her accent made the name sound like a gyspy tune sung off-key. She smiled at him, and he half-expected to see fangs.

The music from the main room throbbed through the floor, the bass-line thumping hard in his chest and making it tough to breathe. When he closed his eyes, the cement under his feet shifted. He licked his lips and tasted the beer the barmaid had served him...and something else. Bitter. Vaguely medicinal.

Dammit. Fucking idiot. Something in that beer.

He'd been so wrapped up in getting that interview, he'd never seen it coming. They must've made him for a cop the second he'd walked through the door.

Whatever the barmaid had slipped in his beer made everything move at half-time. When he spoke, his tongue felt like a rusty anchor caught in his mouth. "My name is Marcus Colton."

"*Bravo*, Marcus Colton." Though her smile had faded, he got the impression Donnatella DeTagliera found something about him amusing.

He thought about identifying himself as a detective...but what if he was wrong? Maybe they didn't know he was a cop. Maybe the barmaid had drugged him all on her own, for her own reasons. He stopped to blink away the double vision, shaking his head to clear it. "Clarice tells me you might be able to answer some questions for me."

"*Sî?* Questions?"

"About the recent death of a friend of mine. Maybe you heard about it? His name was Julian Carlyle."

She made a gesture he read as vague encouragement for him to continue.

"Last seen alive a block from here. Body found on the other side of town. He'd been mutilated and beaten to death."

Clarice gasped. Marcus glanced at her and saw plain, outright terror in her eyes.

He pulled a Polaroid of Julian's post-autopsy face from the inner pocket of his jacket and passed it to the redhead, since giving it to the older woman would be pointless.

Clarice came to stand at his side and took the picture from his hand. "It's the blond one, Madre," she said, her voice trembling, her eyes cast down, abject fear in every line of her lovely body. "His cheeks are soft and white, like a child's. The bruises around his eyes are very pretty."

Pretty? What the fuck?

"Ah, *bravo*. The one with the little cry in his voice, so sweet?" Donnatella said, her accent growing thicker. "Of course."

Marcus stepped toward her, ignoring the growing tightness in his throat and the way his head felt heavy and stupid. "He was here?"

"*Si*, he was our guest." She lifted her hand and brushed her fingers against his chest, over the fabric of his shirt. He flinched, his gut tightening instinctively at her touch. "He was *molto* entertaining, was he not, Clarice?"

"Yes, Madre." The redhead's voice shook harder.

In the space of an instant, Donnatella dropped her hand from Marcus's chest and clutched his wrist, sliding her fingers beneath the leather of his coat and the fabric of his sleeve. Her long nails bit into the flesh. He knew it because he could see them pressing, leaving marks. But he couldn't feel it.

"How..." Fuck, his head was buzzing now, the sound muffling his own voice and hers. "How long was he here?"

Donnatella smiled, wide and shark-like. She licked her lips, and her tongue looked as red as the bricks surrounding the fireplace. "A day?" she said and shrugged. "Three days? A week?"

Marcus pulled his wrist away, feeling her nails make welts as they dragged on his skin. The buzzing grew louder, pressing in on his brain. He could feel himself swaying. The room...so fucking warm. Not enough air. He wanted out, but wanted answers more.

"What was he doing here?" He could barely force the words past his lips.

She laughed. The sound abraded the air, cutting through the noise in his head. Next to him Clarice wrapped her arms around herself and hunched as if in pain. Donnatella lifted her hand again and caressed his jaw, as if she had no doubt as to his shape or the amount of space he occupied. Almost as if she could see through the opaque film that covered her eyes.

"He was weeping, Marcus Colton. *Bellissimo,* the way he sobbed so sweet for me." She lifted her other hand so that she cradled Marcus' face. He tried to pull away and found himself frozen, his muscles locked and quivering. "This one's not so sweet, is he, Clarice? Tell me."

The redhead cleared her throat. Tears had left wet tracks on her cheeks. "He's taller, Madre, with black hair. His shoulders and chest are very broad. His eyes are dark and hard."

"Ah, *bravo,* not so sweet, I was right. But maybe he'll weep for me anyway? What do you think, Clarice?"

"Yes, Madre."

"I think so, too. *Sí,* I think I will drink his tears like champagne."

It was as if all of it was happening to someone else. Like he was watching a movie in which Clarice—at Donnatella's direction—stripped him of his jacket and shirt and jeans and everything else that served to protect his body. Because he couldn't move. Couldn't feel. Couldn't react, or even speak.

"A policeman? Like the other one, *sí?*" Donnatella said when Clarice told her about the nine millimeter she'd removed from his shoulder holster. "But no badge, I think. You work under the covers, as they say? How do they call this, Clarice?"

"A detective, Madre."

"*Sí,*" she said, "Detective."

He stared at her, willing words to force themselves over his paralyzed tongue. Willing movement—struggle. But he must've lost a few seconds, because then he was on his knees, sitting on his heels, with his back and shoulders pressed against the wall. The door had been closed. Had Clarice maneuvered him there, like a mannequin in a store window? How had he missed that?

The bricks were rough against his ass—his naked ass, for Christ's sake—what the fuck was he doing, letting it get this far? He summoned everything he had and took a swing at Clarice's face, where it bobbed in front of him like a freckled balloon. There was only the rattle of tempered-steel links against brick as his arm twitched. That's when he knew they'd chained him like a dog.

Donnatella approached him, holding something in her hand. A whip, long and thick and black, with a heavy handle. Crafted for doing serious damage. Its surface glowed like the skin of a cottonmouth.

"Now you are my guest, Detective Colton—*sí*, just like your friend. Will you entertain me as he did?" She passed the whip to the redhead, who held it as if it might bite her. "Let us see. Give him three, Clarice, across the chest. Be careful not to mar his face."

He watched as Clarice stepped back and raised her arm, lifting the whip over her shoulder. His eyes tracked the arc of its descent. He heard the crack as it struck his flesh, but he felt...nothing.

Again she raised the whip, and again he felt nothing, though he flinched this time because the blow fell higher, closer to his throat. And one last time, Clarice hefting the whip over her other shoulder and crossing the first two blows with a third, backhanded strike.

He struggled to drop his head to survey the damage. But Clarice was there before him, holding a mirror. The glass was surrounded by a wooden frame carved in an ornate pattern. On the surface were dark splotches of varying sizes. He thought he knew what they must be.

He focused on his reflection. His chest now sported three long, red welts. The third welled with blood where it crossed the other two. Still, he felt nothing. He lifted his gaze to Clarice's face. Her makeup was smudged beneath her eyes, and she was panting. Excitement? Terror? Hard to tell.

Donnatella appeared at her side. At some point during the festivities, they'd been joined by a third woman. Tall, with platinum blonde hair and a mischievous expression. The barmaid. Looked like he'd get his threesome after all, one way or another.

"*Caro*, you look disturbed," Donnatella said. "This is Shannon. She, like Clarice, is my acolyte. The drug she gave you dulls sensation. I could flay the flesh from your bones and you would feel nothing." She held out her hand and Clarice presented the whip.

Madre Donnatella, Priestess of Pain. Marcus had heard her called that by people in the lifestyle. As a priestess, of course she'd have acolytes.

"But where would be the fun in that?" She laughed, and the sound of it made the small muscles in his face twitch. "My eyes have failed me," she said. "I can no longer see the suffering of my chosen. I can only listen and feel. Taste and smell and touch."

She approached him, Clarice and Shannon at either elbow, guiding her steps. "How I adore to hear the cries of my chosen as I love them. The scent and flavor of their pain. The feel of hot, bruised flesh under my fingers. The falling tears, *sí*, and the flowing blood. *Bellissimo*. My favorite of all."

He wanted to spit in her face as she bent to breathe on him. His throat worked, but his mouth was dry. She reached out and ran a fingertip down the length of one welt, then flicked at the pad of her finger with her tongue. He felt none of it. Only rage and helplessness. And the first stirrings of fear.

"You will be *molto bellissimo* in your suffering, Detective. I tremble in anticipation of hearing you beg for your own death." She straightened and crossed her arms over her chest. "But first? First there are others who need attention. Is that not right, Clarice?"

Shannon moved quickly, stepping behind Donatella to grasp Clarice's arms and pull them behind her back. Then she forced the redhead to her knees.

"Madre, please—"

"Silence." Donnatella's lip curled as she turned to the redhead. "You have betrayed me with your foolish mistakes one time too many, *cara*. You swore the body would not be found, and yet here I have another policeman in my establishment, asking questions."

"I'm sorry, Madre. Please..." Clarice choked on a sob and lifted her tear-stained face, wrenching her neck to look behind her at Donnatella. "I am your supplicant. I beg you to punish me for my faults."

Donnatella smiled—a grin so evil Marcus felt his balls make a fair attempt at crawling back into his body cavity.

The next several moments moved at half-speed. He watched as Shannon stripped Clarice of her cat-suit, tearing the thin black Latex as if it had no worth. Her carelessness struck a sense of dread in Marcus's gut—this could go nowhere good.

Then the barmaid dragged the unresisting redhead over to where he was chained. "Cuddle up and grab on, Clarice. And if you let go—even once— I'll double the count."

Clarice draped herself on him, stretching out her hands to grasp his forearms where they hung in chains at either side of him. She pressed her naked breasts against his chest. He took no pleasure in it, nor in the fact that he'd been right about the nipple piercings. She rested her head on his shoulder, tucked her face into his neck and said, "I'm ready."

The first forty blows made his stomach churn. The sound of the leather striking her flesh seemed to get louder as time slowed down between each fall of the whip. Her body rocked against him with each blow, her hips grinding against his in a way that would've been a total turn-on if he could feel anything but the slightest shift of pressure. And if she weren't being beaten within an inch of her life. Because as much as he loved the kink, he had his limits, and this had crossed the line way, way back.

Clarice seemed to take it all better than he did, she began by sighing into his neck, and ended by keening quietly with every fall of the lash. He kept his eyes open 'til he made the mistake of looking down and seeing the mess Shannon was making of her back. Then it was all he could do to keep from throwing up over the poor girl's shoulder.

"Madre wants you to take the last ten from the cat o' nine," Shannon said, her voice breathy from exertion, she moved away to the other side of the room to a large, glass-fronted cabinet. Clarice groaned. The vibration traveled from his neck downward, making his stomach clench harder. The drug was wearing off.

Shannon returned, holding another dangerous-looking leather weapon. Each of its nine floggers was tipped with something sharp that glinted in the candlelight. Hooks? Shards of glass? He shuddered and looked away.

Clarice lost it halfway through the last ten, throwing her head back and howling like the damned. Blood splattered everywhere, landing in droplets on his cheeks and getting caught in his eyelashes. Then, finally, it was over.

"Don't let go," Shannon said and moved to put away the cat o' nine. Clarice sagged against him, still gripping his arms. He found that if he pushed forward with his hips, he could help support her weight. Yeah, the drug was definitely wearing off.

He turned his head slightly and saw Donnatella standing by the fireplace, where she'd stationed herself for the duration of the flogging. Her lips were stretched in a faint, pleased smile. Insane, murderous bitch. When he finally got out of this fucked up mess—

"What have we learned tonight, Clarice?" Shannon had returned and was kneeling behind the redhead. She buried her hand in Clarice's hair and pulled back on her head.

"To keep the Madre safe and protected at all times," Clarice whispered. "To think only of the Madre—her pleasure and her will. To serve the Madre in all things." She licked her lips, catching a rivulet of blood on her tongue.

"Good girl."

He didn't see where the knife came from. He only saw the gleam of the blade as it descended, and heard the sound it made as it sliced through Clarice's throat. And then the gurgling scream that rose from her lips, spraying more blood. A moment later he was drenched, covered in spurting, flowing crimson. He let his head fall back against the bricks, gritting his teeth and forcing a grunt of horror and pain past his lips.

He felt Clarice's still-twitching body being pulled away from his, and heard the thud as it fell to the floor in the center of the room. When he looked, Shannon was using a rag to wipe the blood from her hands and paying him no mind. Did they mean to leave the body there? Christ...she was staring at him. Glassy eyes and a second lurid, smile where her unblemished throat used to be.

From the other side of the room, Donnatella said, "Check his reflexes, *cara*."

He was ashamed at the way he flinched when Shannon stepped forward. But she only grabbed his left nipple between two fingers and twisted. He could feel the pressure, faraway and vaguely unpleasant. He didn't react.

"Nothing yet, Madre."

"*Bene*. We will leave him for a time."

Shannon crossed the room and allowed Donnatella to take her arm. Just before they reached the door, Donnatella turned her head in his direction and spoke, her every word like a bell tolling in his head. "I will return, Detective Colton, *sì?* And when I do, you will feel...everything."

* * * *

Leah sat hunched on her bed, cradling her head between her hands.

So much blood...

It ran in rivers down the walls of the room, splashed in puddles on the hardwood floor. And the Madre's voice, like the bass line of a funeral dirge set to techno-funk, rising and falling in her head. She couldn't make it stop. It was never going to stop. It was going to keep going, on and on, until she lost her mind and—

It stopped.

Perfect, sweet silence settled over her. After a few seconds, she lifted her head from her hands and glanced around. The blood was gone, too.

"Thank you," she said to no one in particular.

She'd managed to fall asleep with the help of one of those nifty yellow pills she kept for just such emergencies. On top of the tequila, it pretty much knocked her on her ass. She hadn't even bothered to undress—just sprawled on her bed and let the chemical relief stifle the voices and pictures in her head.

Eight hours later, she'd awakened to the sound of leather striking blood-dampened skin. Familiar, horribly so, along with the rancid scent of Chanel No. 5 mixed with fear and fresh sweat. It lasted ten minutes. She counted the strokes of the lash. Forty, then a woman's voice she didn't recognize saying something about a cat o' nine tails. And then howling, like an animal caught in a trap. The kind of sound she dreamt about even when she wasn't having visions. The kind she remembered. From before.

To dream like this two nights in a row—so not good for her mental health.

She waited for it to be over, knowing it wouldn't take long. The cat o' nine was never used in excess on a supplicant. The damage it inflicted was too great, and there was loss of blood and therefore loss of consciousness to consider.

"No fun to be had in beating a dead or dozing body," she whispered into the dark of her bedroom.

She heard the woman speak again. Another female voice answered her, hitching and quivering in pain, the words too muffled to make out. Then more silence. Leah let herself relax, believing it over.

Then the walls of her bedroom exploded with blood.

With this came the Madre's voice, laughing and murmuring. Repeating herself—something about how she would soon return, and then "you will feel...everything."

Twenty minutes on the clock. That's how long she'd been listening to the Madre's promise to return, and how long her walls had dripped crimson. She knew it wasn't real. Everything, all of it, just pictures and sounds in her head. Not much help in knowing it while the scent of the blood clogged the back of her throat, and the Madre's voice made her eyes water.

When it was over, she reached for the pill bottle on her bedside table, selecting two of the little yellow angels this time. The clock said quarter to four, but she had no classes on Saturdays. She could stand to sleep 'til noon, which is what two pills would do for her. She popped them into her mouth and swallowed them dry. Getting far too good at that.

Leaving her skirt, blouse and underwear in a pile at the foot of her bed, she padded into the bathroom and splashed warm water on her face. A bath? No, she might end up drowning herself when the pills kicked in. Something to eat? She closed her eyes and saw the dripping walls and nearly gagged.

All right then. Straight to bed it was.

She pulled on a white cotton nightshirt and slid between the sheets. The streetlight outside her window glowed against the ceiling. The red numbers on the clock marked the passing minutes. Good druggie dreams, that was what she was aiming for. Dark...soft...floating...

When she opened her eyes, she was standing barefooted on a cement floor in the corner of a room surrounded by brick walls. There was a low, heavy bench directly in front of her, and various pieces of furniture scattered about the room. The fireplace on the far wall was ablaze, and candles lit every corner of the space. Next to the fireplace, directly across from where she stood, was a section of wall covered with a long, black curtain. A mirror...the Madre's playrooms always had at least one big mirror...

She looked down and saw that she wore the same cotton nightshirt under which she was entirely naked.

Okay, another dream. Maybe even a good one—three times supposedly being the charm. Except...oh, God. What was that smell? She stepped forward and looked over the bench.

No...oh no...oh fuck.

The body of a redheaded woman lay curled on the floor in a pool of drying fluids. Her head was turned at an angle, so that her contorted face and the slash that ran from one ear to the other were fully exposed. Leah pressed a hand to her mouth to keep back the scream building fast in her throat. It wasn't going to be enough, though. She was going to make some sort of sound, and it would be loud, and whoever had killed the redhead would coming running and—

Except this was a dream, right? It wasn't really happening, so nobody could hurt her. The thought made the urge to scream go away, but it didn't make her feel any better about the dead woman.

Something grunted, and the sound echoed. She jumped back, stumbling over her own feet, and looked wildly around the room.

He was chained on his knees with his back against the bricks and his hands stretched to either side, a stack of neatly folded clothes—jeans and a leather jacket, from what she could see—lying just off to his left. His chest was marked with lash-stripes—she'd know the look of those welts anywhere. His head hung down, his face indistinct from her vantage point. But she could see the blood. All of it. Gallons, it looked like, though she knew that was impossible.

Had he been there all along? How had she missed him?

Dream, remember? Didn't have to make sense.

Right. Okay.

Voices outside the door. Women, two of them. Panic shot through her chest. Yeah, maybe none of this was real, but that didn't mean she wanted to meet the folks who'd butchered the girl. She whirled, searching for a hiding place. There, across the room, on the other side of that tall cabinet. Its doors were made of glass, but it protruded far enough from the wall that it might provide cover if she could get to the other side of it in time.

She dashed, skirting the body in the center of the room and...*oh, God.* The redhead's back was just flayed. Looked like the work of a cat o' nine. All at once, as Leah slipped past the cabinet and pressed herself against the wall, things began to fall into place. Yeah, maybe not a dream. Maybe another vision. And this time she had a starring role.

The door opened.

"Shit. Look at this mess," said the first woman, a slender brunette with long hair and thin features, dressed all in black Latex. "Shannon said it wasn't that bad."

"Shannon's idea of 'not that bad' is a little fucked," said the second woman, also a brunette, also attired in the customary ensemble of the Madre's acolytes, but wearing her hair in a pixie cut. They both laughed, standing on either side of the girl's body and looking down at her like she was a pile of trash left for them to clean up.

"Let me inject him first, and then we'll take care of this," said Skinny Brunette.

Pixie Cut nodded. "Whatever."

Dear God, please don't let the syringe be in the cabinet.

But the woman moved to the other side of the room, past the bench, where a small, round table stood. On it sat a wooden box. From there she removed what she needed and crossed to where the man kneeled against the wall.

Leah watched while she searched for a vein and injected his arm. The man never moved or made a sound. After, the woman grabbed a handful of his hair and lifted his head.

The man from her vision—the earlier one, back in the classroom. Of course it was. Who else would it be? And now he was in some serious trouble—as if being chained to a wall in the Madre's playroom weren't serious enough—because that injection... Leah had seen the results of that kind of thing before. Not pretty. Not after the Madre was finished with her fun and games, at least.

"You're gonna like this new drug, lover," Skinny Brunette said, leaning down and speaking directly into his face. "It's gonna make you feel goooooooood...until it makes you feel baaaaaaaaad." She laughed and let his head drop.

Pixie Cut joined her, and they stood looking at the man. "This one's hot. Do you know if the Madre plans on keeping him long?"

Skinny Brunette shrugged. "Hope so. We could

use the distraction." Then she returned the syringe to the box on the table, and she and Pixie Cut turned their attention to the girl's body. In twenty minutes' time, they'd wrapped it in plastic and managed to scrub away all traces of the blood, except for those still congealing on the skin of the man chained to the wall. Those they left alone, ignoring him completely. For his part, he never moved or gave any indication he saw or heard them.

"All right, let's get her the hell out of here. We've gotta get rid of this bundle and be back here in two hours," said Skinny Brunette and groaned as they lifted the body to their shoulders in preparation to remove it. "Clarice put on a little weight in the last few months. I'm surprised the Madre let her get away with it."

Pixie Cut shrugged. "She'll be bony again soon enough."

Again they laughed, and kept laughing all the way out the door.

Leah waited silently in her hiding place, counting the seconds, listening to their footsteps fade down the hallway. She held her breath, waiting...waiting...afraid to slip out into the open, because what would she do then? Where would she go? Not like she could follow those two ghouls—she'd be caught, dressed as she was. Hard to blend well in a white nightshirt. They'd take her to see the Madre, and... No. Not happening. She'd grab something lethal and off herself first.

This was bad. Maybe the worst possible situation she could imagine. She had to end this vision now. Wake herself up. Except...what about the guy chained to the wall? Didn't she have some responsibility to him? That's why this was happening to her in the first place, right? She was supposed to do something. To help in some way. Because shit like this was never random.

She closed her eyes, took a deep breath and held

it, working up her courage.

"You can come out now. They're gone."

The voice made her jump and knock her elbow against the corner of the cabinet. Sharp pain, proving beyond a shadow of a doubt that she was here. Real. A tangible, physical presence in this room and on this plane of existence. Truly a first for her. Her visions had never worked like this before— never moved her body from one space to another. The novelty of it almost made her wish she could enjoy the experience.

She stepped out from her hiding place and faced the man who kneeled against the bricks on the other side of the room. He lifted his head to look at her. When he spoke again, his voice sounded husky and raw, as if he were forcing it over a truckload of gravel in this throat.

"You the cavalry? Because if you are, I think I'm screwed."

Chapter Four

The girl...woman...whatever...walked toward him with a funny look on her face.

"So, you can see me? Then this is really...real." She ran her hand through her shoulder-length, light brown hair and frowned. "I guess I knew that."

He surprised himself by laughing. "Real as real can be, sweetheart. How did you get in here, anyway? Is there a trap door over there?" He gestured toward the far corner from where the woman had first seemed to materialize nearly thirty minutes before. He'd watched her, playing possum as she made her way across the room and hid herself in the corner between the wall and the glass-fronted cabinet. "Or maybe you're a magician, huh?"

She stopped directly in front of him and shook her head. "Definitely not, or I'd abracadabra myself right out again." She crossed her arms under her breasts. "We're both in serious trouble."

He couldn't hold back his snort of contempt. "What gave you your first clue? The dead body or the fact that I'm chained to the motherfucking wall?"

She winced. "Don't yell, unless you want those two harpies in here again."

"Right. Sorry." He cleared his throat. "What's your name? Where did you come from? And how're you getting us out of here?"

She opened her mouth as if to answer, then shook her head. "Where I came from is a long story, and you wouldn't believe me anyway. As for an escape plan—do you have a cell phone?"

Now why the hell hadn't he thought of that? The

mickey that the blonde barmaid had slipped him must've really fucked with his head. "In my jacket pocket." He gestured with his hand, making the steel links clank against the bricks.

The woman dove for the pile of clothes, giving him a nice glimpse of her ass as she bent to retrieve the phone. He watched her turn it on, holding his breath.

She frowned. "No reception. Can't say I'm surprised. They've probably done something to block the signal down here." She tossed the phone onto his jacket.

He shrugged and tried not to feel sick. "It was worth a try. So what did you say your name was?"

"Leah."

He nodded and shifted his knees, looking for a more comfortable position.

The woman—Leah—looked him over. "I suppose the Madre didn't leave the keys to those shackles lying around handy, huh?"

He growled in the negative. The spot where the dark-haired bitch had injected him had begun to itch and tingle, and the sensation was spreading up his arm. "That Madre lady needs to die. Like, yesterday."

Leah smiled, crooked and sour. "Better men than you have tried to kill her, believe me. I'll settle for getting out of here alive."

The tingly sensation had begun to move over his shoulder, down his back, and across his chest and belly. The feeling wasn't entirely unpleasant, but it made him want to move—to pull against the chains and rub himself against the wall. His skin felt hot and tight over his muscles, and now...oh, crap. No, not now, please. This was not the time for his dick to take an interest. He closed his eyes and willed the stiffening he felt below his waist to go away.

"Uh oh."

He opened his eyes. "What?"

"Looks like I was right about that injection." She was staring at his cock, which now stood out from his body at full attention. "This is bad."

He felt his face go red. "Not so bad. A little better than average, or so I've been told."

She rolled her eyes. "That's not what I meant, funny guy. The needle they stuck in your arm? Full of the Madre's special stimulant. Things are going to get...um...intense for a while."

She wasn't kidding. The surface of his body glowed with sensation. His muscles bunched and twisted beneath his skin involuntarily. And his dick...Christ, it felt like it wanted to turn itself inside out. He closed his eyes and breathed deep, trying to regain enough control to get some answers.

When he opened his eyes, she was chewing her bottom lip and looking anxious. The little line between her eyebrows had deepened.

"You seem to know an awful lot about how they do stuff around here," he said. "Why is that?"

She shrugged. "I used to work for the Madre, a long time ago. Ten years now."

He tensed, instinctively defensive. "You were one of them? These nutjobs?"

"Like I said, it was a long time ago, and I got out before..." She looked away, still worrying her full bottom lip with the edges of her straight, white teeth. She hugged herself tighter and paced back and forth in front of him. The way her bare legs moved beneath the short hem of her nightie...it was hard not to stare and wish he could touch her. Harder and harder, in fact—pun most definitely intended.

"Before what?"

She came to a halt right in front of him. He could've sworn he felt her body heat, even from three feet away. Every nerve in him screamed to reach out and touch. He leaned back against the wall and enjoyed the way the pitted surface dug into his shoulder blades. He shrugged his shoulders, letting the bricks abrade the skin. Ahh...yeah. More. Like that.

"Before I wised up." She narrowed her eyes at him, watching as he moved. "Hey, don't do that. You'll hurt yourself."

He was pressing harder into the wall and rubbing his back from side to side, as far as the short reach of his chains would allow. "Need to. Feels good."

She stepped nearer. "Seriously, you need to stop. You need to fight it. This is what they want."

"They want me to tear up my back on the bricks?"

"That's the whole point of the stuff in the injection. It makes you need...um..." She looked away again. Then she took a deep breath and continued. "It makes you crave sensation to the point where you're begging them to hurt you. Nothing they do will be enough, and you'll be crying for it. But then, when the drug wears off—"

"When it wears off, I'm fucked." All at once, what she was saying became all too clear. He remembered the condition of Julian's body when they pulled it from the Dumpster. The missing strips of skin, the burns. The deep bruising around the genitals. He shuddered, his gorge rising in his throat. And still his skin burned and ached for stimulation.

He hung his head, letting his shoulders slump, and took a few deep, slow breaths. A moment later, he felt a soft touch on his hair. Even that—the bare brush of her fingertips against the dead follicles— made his cock quiver and strain.

"What's your name?" she asked. Her voice was soft. She sounded sorry. Sympathetic. Like she cared. He wanted to believe it.

"Marcus Colton. I'm..." He stopped and swallowed. Could he trust her? Was she playing a game? What if she was really one of them?

Then again, what choice did he have? He sucked

in a deep breath, blew it out and said, "I'm a detective with the Santa Rosa Police Department, working undercover to solve a homicide—"

"Don't tell me any more. I don't want to know." She dropped her hand and backed away from him.

"But—"

"Really, it's better if I don't know. For both of us."

Frustration coursed through him, followed by helplessness. Both of them were chased by the certain knowledge that he'd screwed up royally and probably deserved what was about to happen to him. "Doesn't matter. I'm gonna die anyway, and you're probably not even real. Just some stupid hallucination brought on by the drug."

"Oh, I'm real." She pressed a finger to her chin, and he was suddenly reminded of a teacher for some reason. "I haven't quite got it figured out yet, but I think I teleported—"

"Teleported?" His laugh echoed like the bark of an angry dog against the bricks.

She shrugged. "You didn't see me come through the door, did you? There are no other entrances, and I didn't slide down the chimney like Santa, I promise."

"This is bullshit."

"Whatever, Detective. I don't understand it either. I've never been corporeal in a vision before."

He felt his face harden into a scowl. What the fuck was this dame babbling about? Visions? Teleportation? They were gonna torture him to death. That was real—as real as it got.

She sighed and said, "Corporeal? It means to take up space or be able to affect your physical surroundings."

"I know what corporeal means. I just can't believe I'm having this frigging conversation." He shifted his weight, keenly aware of every molecule of his own skin. The shackles on his wrists scraped, and it felt like a caress. The bricks gouged his back, and he wanted more. Even the cramps in his thighs and the sharp ache in his knees from his long-held position felt good, because it was something. Sensation. Stimulation of nerve endings. All of which was bad, because it meant that when the barmaid returned with her cat o' nine, he might be ready to beg her for it. Just the thought of it made him groan. In fear? In anticipation? Who the fuck knew?

"Listen, Detective," Leah said. "In about five or ten more minutes, you're going to be in a seriously bad way."

"It gets worse?" He lifted his head and looked at her. She'd bent down to talk to him, and her hair had fallen across her face. The nightshirt she wore gaped in the front, giving him a view of her goodies beneath. His dick jerked, and a sharp tug of want pulled at his balls. He groaned again.

"Yes, and then it lasts a good six hours without intervention." She looked around the room and dragged a hand through her hair. "I'd like to help you, but I can't take the chance of being caught here. If they can see me like you can...if they could touch me or chain me up—"

He nodded. "Don't sweat it. Just get the hell out and tell somebody where I am. Call the Santa Rosa P. D. and ask for Chief Gustavo Sanchez. He'll know what to do." *And God help me if the Chief chooses to be a little slow on the uptake.*

She crouched there, in front of him, chewing on her lip again. "I feel bad leaving you this way." Her gaze was on his cock. Or, at least, on something much further south than his face, and he couldn't imagine his bellybutton held that much fascination for her. "I could just take the edge off, you know? That might help. Give you some defense against the drug. So when they come back, you could hold out longer."

The way she talked about it...she made it sound so clinical. But his dick liked it, clinical or not. So much that it sat up and begged. Drooled a little, too. Marcus tried to keep his voice steady and even—the only part of himself still within his control. "What exactly did you have in mind?"

Instead of blushing, her face seemed to grow paler and resigned behind the fall of her hair. Hard to believe she'd once worked for the Madre. She seemed so...no, "innocent" was the wrong word. "Reserved," maybe. Or "self-contained."

"I think you know what I have in mind, and this is really no time for games, Detective. Believe me when I tell you that you don't want to be...like this," she gestured at his twitching, straining cock, "when the Madre gets back."

Julian's face—bloody, bruised and contorted in agony—flashed in his mind. "Yeah. I've seen the final product."

She nodded. "The Madre always said she found the male anatomy disgusting. I remember...I mean, someone told me, I never saw it myself or anything..." She took a breath and bit her lip.

He looked up at her. "What? You might as well tell me."

"The Madre likes to get men...aroused. Like this." She gestured toward his dick again. "And then punish them for it."

"Christ. What's her deal, anyway? I mean, what drives her to this, besides bugfuck insanity?"

Leah shrugged. "I don't know the whole story. Something to do with her father selling her to his friends when she was a girl. Which—if you think about—doing that to your own daughter? Enough to make anybody—"

"Yeah, my heart's bleeding cherry KoolAid over here." The muscles in his lower body cramped and twisted, making him jerk in pain. Except it felt good. Really good. He cleared his throat. "So if I let you...uh...help me out, won't she just inject me again?"

Leah stepped forward and pressed two fingers against the pulse-point in his neck. He drew in a breath, then a deeper one, savoring the scent of her skin borne on the heat of her body.

She pulled her fingers away and stepped back. "Your pulse is elevated. You feel it?"

Jesus, yes, he could feel it. His heart felt like it was trying to break down a cement wall. He nodded.

"The drug she gave you—which is essentially Viagra on steroids with a little extra kick—does bad things to your blood pressure and heart rhythm. It can't be administered more than once in a twenty-four hour period without risking a massive coronary event." She sounded more like a teacher than ever.

His turn to shrug, rattling the chains and using the opportunity to scrape his shoulders against the bricks one more time. "She's gonna kill me anyway."

"Yeah, but not yet. Believe me, if the Madre wanted you dead, you'd already be lying in a ditch somewhere." She looked at him appraisingly, which—for some reason—made his cock bob in the air like a Goddamn puppet on a string. "You're a good-looking guy. I'm betting she wants you for a toy, at least short-term."

"She can't even see me!"

"I guess after all these years she's developed a vivid imagination."

He looked up at her and felt the burn of frustrated rage once again. "You really do sound like you sympathize with that bitch. Are you sure you know which side you're on here?"

Her face changed then. Her lips compressed, and the line of her jaw hardened. She moved forward 'til she could splay her hand flat across his chest. The sweat from her palm stung on the welts from the whip. He sucked in a breath through his teeth—a noisy hiss. His cock pulsed, and his hips worked against nothing. Against the air, saturated with tension and the ghosts of agony and fear. He craned his neck back to look at her.

She said, "I know which side I'm on, Detective. Now let's cut to the chase. We have two hours— maybe less. Will you let me help you?"

His gut churned with helpless fury, but that didn't keep his dick from drooling silvery puddles onto the floor between his thighs.. Pain shot through him, catching him at odd angles and making him twitch. He craved more—like licking the serrated edge of a knife coated in honey. In another minute or two, he was going to lose it and start making noise. He couldn't let that happen.

It felt wrong—so wrong—to even think about getting off under these circumstances...but what were his options? He looked down at himself. His cock curved up against his abdomen, all ruddy purple. He could see the blood vessels beneath the thin skin. It'd never looked so angry before.

"Let me help you," she whispered again. "Let me give you some defense against these people. It's all I can do right for you now."

It was the broken note of pleading in her voice that did him in. He nodded once, closed his eyes and let his head rest against the bricks.

She let her hand slide down his chest. When her fingertips grazed his cock—like insect wings, maddening and barely there—his whole body jerked. Then she took him fully in her hand, and the sensation spiked high and vicious. Not pain, not pleasure—just feeling, intense and way past the edge of comfort. He bit the inside of his cheek and screwed his eyes so tightly shut he could see bursts of green light in the blackness.

She moved her hand, collecting the slippery moisture from the head. Her touch was hesitant, as if she feared hurting him. Every stroke seemed to take an hour as it traveled from base to tip. Torment...bliss...agony...like traffic lights, they flashed in his brain.

"Is this okay?"

Even the cadence of her voice made it worse. More sensory input on an already overloaded system.

"Yeah," he croaked. "Yeah, but...could you maybe..." He cleared his throat and tried again. "Faster?"

Her grip tightened, and her strokes quickened. Became swift and relentless, yet her touch remained strangely delicate. The contrast made him shiver and yank at the chains. In another thirty seconds, he'd lost track of everything but the urgent, fast-rising need to come that roiled in his balls. Each time she pulled upward, his hips jerked and stuttered. He held back his groans by sheer force of will and the strength of a tightly clenched jaw. He could see his goal. Taste it, smell it. His entire body screamed at him to let go.

But when he closed his eyes, the little redhead's face hung before him, accusing in its blank, dead stare. How could he let himself enjoy this? Not two hours after watching Clarice bleed out all over him?

"Shh," Leah whispered, as if she knew what he was thinking. "Pretend you're somewhere else."

He swallowed against the choking thickness in his throat. "I can't. It's too hard. I can't do this."

"You can because you have to." Her grip tightened again. "Tell me your favorite fantasy. What do you think about when you're...you know?"

"Jerking off?"

"Yeah." She sounded almost shy, and how funny was that, given the situation?

He sucked in a breath and tried to concentrate. "I like...uh..." He coughed. "Harem chicks."

"Harem chicks? You mean, like, veils and incense and belly dancing?"

Christ, he couldn't believe he'd just admitted that. To anyone, anywhere, much less to this woman under these circumstances. Did this drug have some kind of truth serum properties too? God, he was so fucked.

Leah sounded amused when she said, "Okay, I'll save the cultural and gender sensitivity lectures for another time and we'll just go with it. So...close your eyes and imagine I'm a..." she coughed, "harem chick."

He did as he was told.

She continued to speak, making her voice rise and fall as she wove the fantasy. "I'm here to serve you and only you. Your pleasure is my only thought, my only concern."

"Tell me how we meet." He sounded rough and desperate to his own ears, and he hated it, but he couldn't stop himself. "Tell me how you lure me back to your secret room."

Leah didn't miss a beat. "We meet in the marketplace. I help you buy some fruit from a vendor because you don't know the language, and then I invite you back to a place I know where we can be alone. A hidden door in a blue-tiled wall leads to a room draped in veils."

He saw the scene behind his closed eyes. The movement of her hand on his cock had slowed, but his pleasure at her touch was pure. No longer tainted by guilt and fear, if only for the moment. "Tell me what you're wearing."

"A sheer silk gown that looks like a running watercolor. Veils hide my face and hair, but when we're alone, I remove them. I remove everything, and I dance for you to the drumbeats from the marketplace. I kneel at your feet and anoint you with oil, and touch you like this."

Her strokes grew swift and sure once more. She added a twist of the wrist on each upward pull that yanked a grunt from him every time. He felt the slow build again, and he strained toward it.

"I touch you like this," she repeated, "and the drums beat faster. You see nothing but the soft veils, you hear nothing but the drums, you feel nothing but my touch."

All at once his ears were full of a low pounding. Was it bleeding from the dance floor above them? No...different...more exotic than even Hotel California's house music. The rhythm pulled at him, thrumming in his blood. The scent of sandalwood and patchouli drifted through his head. He opened his eyes. Before him, in place of the Madre's dungeon, was a blue veil rippling on a hot, dry breeze.

Leah's voice came in a husky murmur. "I use both hands on you, to drive you to the breaking point. Past the barrier of control. Feel it. Feel this."

His hips rocked forward, rutting and pumping in time with her working hands. His skin flushed hot and pebbled over with gooseflesh. The pressure at the base of his spine and behind his balls built, and still he fought it, because now he feared the whole idea of coming. What if he ruptured something?

Then her fingertips found the head of his cock where it was wet and slippery, and she pressed lightly into the slit. He wrenched his neck as he turned his face into his shoulder to muffle his shout. But even that flare of pain wasn't enough to dull the sharp bursts, one after another, that marked his release. He twisted in the chains, rising up on his knees, and spurted helplessly over Leah's hands, his own thighs, and the floor.

His shoulders shrieked at him as he sagged and hung limply, letting the shackles take his weight. Leah let him go, and he pulsed out the last of his orgasm untouched. He tried to lift his head. To look at her, to say something. But after another few seconds the only words in his brain were four letters long and crafted of still more frustration and anger and fear.

Because the drug-induced craving? The tingle and sting across his chest and belly that he'd been able to ignore while Leah had been stroking him? It had returned. And what was worse? His dick was rising from the dead right along with it.

Chapter Five

Leah wiped her hands on her nightshirt. They trembled, and her heart thudded erratically in her chest. She could taste adrenaline on the back of her tongue, as if she'd just snatched a child from the path of a speeding car. Or defused a bomb.

Yeah, that last analogy was pretty accurate, wasn't it?

But that wasn't all she was feeling, and she'd be a liar if she said it was, even if only to herself. Her nipples poked hard at the thin cotton of her shirt, and when she moved she could feel an achy swelling between her legs. His reaction to her touch—his tormented pleasure and painful satisfaction—had left her wet and wanting. Did that make her sick? Twisted? As bad as the Madre Donnatella and her acolytes?

She mentally dragged herself away from that line of thought. No time for that now.

She watched Colton carefully. After a few seconds, he lifted his head and coughed, not quite meeting her eyes. What did you say in a situation like this? She hoped he didn't try to thank her. Because seriously...awkward.

But when he opened his mouth, it was only to groan. She watched the muscles in his arms bunch and stretch, pull against the chains and then fall slack. She glanced down and saw that his cock had risen again, high and firm against his belly. Exactly what she'd been afraid of.

"It didn't work," he said. His voice was a gritty rasp.

"It's all right." She stepped forward and tried to catch his eye. Couldn't let him get too much into his head, or this wouldn't work. "I thought maybe it would take more than once."

"More than once?" He sounded more weary than surprised. "Can't do that again. It'll kill me."

"Don't be so dramatic. I'll tell you what will kill you, though—the Madre, and she'll take joy in doing it slowly if she comes back and you're still...all worked up."

He shook his head. "And you're so sure she won't kill me anyway. Why?"

"I'm not sure. But which way would you rather die, Detective? A quick slash to the throat, or..." She glanced over her shoulder at the glass-fronted cabinet in the corner. She knew what was likely inside. Bladed instruments crafted for flaying skin from muscle. Vises made to crush small extremities. She looked away and shuddered.

"Point taken."

She nodded. "And if we're lucky, she'll only beat you and leave you alive to play with tomorrow. That would buy us some time."

His smile was wry. "Yeah, that sounds like my kinda luck." He cleared his throat and shifted his knees on the floor. His cock bobbed with the movement. "I probably should've asked you this before, but...even if you could find a paperclip or something, you probably can't jimmy the locks on these, right?" He shook his wrists in the shackles.

"Sorry, Detective. I'm an English professor, not a cat burglar. I could quote you some Shakespeare, if you're bored."

He grinned. "Thought so."

"What?"

"Never mind." He sighed and rolled his shoulders. "All right, let's get on with it."

She saw the muscles in his abdomen quiver as she approached. She reached out her hand to touch him, and he said, "Wait."

"What?"

He inclined his head, looking every-so-slightly sheepish. "I feel like I should...I dunno...kiss you or something."

She felt her face open up into a smile—her first since she'd landed in this awful place. "That's not necessary. This isn't a date."

"No, but I'd feel better about it."

She stepped back again and considered him. "I'm going to say no, Detective. But I'll tell you what—if and when we get out of this alive, I'll let you buy me dinner. And if that goes well, I'll let you kiss me good night."

"Are you always this tough?"

She thought of Ray Delacroix's poor, twisted ear and smiled wider. "You have to catch me in the right mood. I'm going to touch you now."

His whole body looked rubbed raw. Flushed red and glowing with heat, as if from a bad sunburn. But his cock was the worst, and she almost feared to lay her hand on it. What if she hurt him? What if she hurt herself?

Okay, that's just stupid.

But he was stunning, with his black-stubbled jaw and the all-over blush and the slick sweatiness. And those nicely defined muscles—not too big, not too small. Not even the dried blood-spatters on his skin could make her think otherwise. Stunning and about to be slowly tortured to death for the Madre's amusement, if she didn't get down to business.

She reached out and took him in hand, listened to his rough groan, and noted again how his cock fit so well in her palm. Another part of him that wasn't too big or too small, like some fucked-up version of Goldilocks where the three bears preferred ball-gags and extra-large, studded butt plugs to porridge. And speaking of the three bears...Skinny Brunette and Pixie Cut had said they'd be back in two hours. It'd been at least forty-five minutes and probably closer to sixty. Time to get this show on the road.

She laid a steadying hand on his shoulder and collected some of the slippery moisture at the head of his erection to ease the way as she stroked. She'd need more finesse this time—a story about a subservient woman dropping her veils and a quick, two-fisted jerk wouldn't do it. Luckily, she'd been a pro at working men into a sexual frenzy once upon a time. Back then, she'd been fearless about searching out a man's hidden kinks and exploiting them 'til he was...well...porridge in her hands. She and Goldilocks had a lot more in common than the average guy on the street might guess.

She leaned in closer and murmured in his ear, "You know what I think, Detective? I think you like being chained. I think it turns you on, just a little."

The entire line of his body stiffened at her words. His mouth, which had fallen open just a bit, snapped shut. He turned his head to glare up at her, his pupils dilated with emotion—a brew of rage and lust she could almost taste. "You're full of shit, lady."

"Call me Leah. And you think so?" She tightened her grip and leaned still closer. "I think I'm right on the money. But let's see, shall we?"

She couldn't afford to be kind. Couldn't afford to avoid embarrassing him. He might not have been ready to admit how much he liked feeling helpless, but that was the least of his problems. She needed to find those kink buttons and press them, and she needed to do it fast.

Her gaze strayed to his hand, trapped inside the shackle. It flexed, the fingers stretching and curling in time to her strokes. If she took a step in that direction...bent over just a bit...she could keep her grip on his cock and touch her mouth to the first knuckle.

She made contact. He grunted. She ran the tip of her tongue up and down the crevice between his fingers. His whole hand convulsed, twisting in the shackle.

"Fuck." His hoarse voice cracked between them like a gunshot.

She pulled away, but not before noticing the scar, thick and pale and crescent-shaped, on the back of his hand. Identical to the mark on the man in her dream...was it last night? It seemed like weeks ago.

She shook her head. No time now to consider what it might mean—she'd think about it later. She moved to stand over him again. "Close your eyes. Listen carefully and let the story make a picture in your head."

She waited for acknowledgment. Finally, he jerked his head in what might've been agreement, reluctance in every strained line of his body.

It was enough. She leaned in close once more and whispered, "You're a member of the Sultan's household—a princeling or the son of a trusted advisor. You were caught committing a grave crime—spying on the Sultan's favorite concubine in her bath. You've been arrested and chained here to await execution."

He sucked in a noisy breath and swayed in the shackles. His head dropped back against the bricks. He said, "Go on."

She lowered her voice further and spoke

slowly, drawing out the words. Using formal

language to weave the fantasy. "I am the concubine.

I've slipped away from the harem to see you before

you're put to death. Your boldness has intrigued me,

and I want to know this man who would die for a

glimpse of me." She gripped his cock with her four fingers and let her thumb wander where it would, tracing the pulsing vein on the underside of his shaft. "When I see you bound and helpless, my mouth waters. I am powerless over any man, save you. With you, I can do anything I choose."

She felt a tremor work its way through him. Sweat saturated his hair and ran down his neck and chest. When he opened his eyes and looked at her, she saw defiance at war with surrender in his eyes. She knew what he saw—the concubine.

She ghosted her thumb over the head of his cock, the lightest touch she could manage. His breath caught, hitching in his chest. He jerked his hips back and away, trying to get free of her grasp. She held on and dug her fingernails into the shaft 'til he froze.

"I can give you pain," she murmured, directing her voice down the column of his neck. "Or I can give you pleasure."

There was a long pause. The air around them seemed to churn with emotion—fear, lust, anger, frustration.

Then he canted his hips forward and up, offering himself to her. It was all she needed to get the job done. She pulled and twisted, speaking low into his ear about all the ways the concubine would torment the doomed prisoner. Her hands. Her mouth. The length of her smooth, soft body rubbing against him like a cat in heat. Delight that never satisfied. Bliss that only prolonged his agony.

Without warning, Colton made a low, urgent sound and went taut from the ground up, his body a pained line of need. A beat...two beats...and then his cock spat a stream of white in a high arc that landed three feet away, over the place where the redhead bled out.

Leah didn't step back this time, or break physical contact as he jerked through the aftershocks. No time for niceties now. She gave him thirty seconds, then she slid her hand under his chin and wrenched his face up to look at her. His eyes were bloodshot and shadowed, but his skin was hot and buzzing with electricity beneath her fingertips. His cock never softened against her palm.

"Again," she said.

He flinched. Then he nodded and gritted his teeth, plainly preparing for imminent discomfort.

"Shh." She moved her hand from his chin to his brow and brushed back the salty-wet hair. "Shh...it's okay." Then she dropped into a low crouch before him.

This was going to be tricky. She hadn't been forced to contort herself in the service of sexual satisfaction in a decade, and it showed in the way the muscles in her back protested.

"You don't have to do that." His voice sounded creaky, like an unused garden gate. "Just use your hand again."

She looked up at him through her hair and said, "Won't work this time. You're over-stimulated."

"But—"

"Shh. I know what I'm doing. Just...kneel up."

He raised himself high on his knees with a grimace of obvious pain. The floor must've been killing him, but she couldn't do this alone—he'd have to meet her halfway. She licked her lips, preparing herself. It had been a long, long time, and this was different than a handjob. Less clinical, more intimate.

She let her hand drift over the cut of his hip, tracing the line of muscle and feeling the sweat that pooled in the curve. When she let her mouth follow in the shadow of her fingers, Colton groaned and rocked forward, as if he could already feel her lips on him where it mattered most. She shifted her grip on his cock, leaned in and ran her tongue over the leaking slit. Back and forth, lapping like that same cat in heat.

He jerked away with a muttered curse, leaving a smear of slippery-wet across her lips. She followed him with a gust of breath over his cock, then steadied it again within her fingers. When she spoke again, she let her lips brush the head. "You can't get away. Surrender is your only option."

She felt a jolt go through him as he let the back of his head fall against the bricks, once...twice...then a steady, reckless rhythm that spoke more of his frustration than any words. Literally pounding his head against a brick wall.

"Stop that." She flickered her tongue up and down the shaft, pausing to give special attention to that tender spot just under the crown, where all the nerves converged. "We don't have time for a tantrum."

He glared down at her. "Fair warning—if we get out of this alive, I'm gonna track you down and fuck you stupid."

"I bet you say that to all the girls."

She moved in for the kill, going at him with the flat of her tongue, long Popsicle licks and swirls. He muttered a string of curses, which she cut off mid-obscenity by catching him in her mouth, sucking him down to the halfway point. His hips flexed once, and then stilled on a shudder as if he'd exerted some supreme act of will over his own response.

She pulled off to whisper, "Go ahead. Do it."

He didn't seem to hear her. She glanced up and saw the rigid line of his jaw, and how his chest heaved with constrained gasps. Not good. He had to let go and let himself take what he needed, because this release had to count. Had to quell the craving. They didn't have time for another round of storytelling and happy endings. She leaned in and drew hard on the very tip of his cock to get his attention.

"I said, go ahead. Fuck my mouth."

She looked up again and he was staring at her. The expression on his face—desperation underlined by uncertainty and maybe a little hope—made her smile.

"Don't want to hurt you," he whispered.

"I'll let you know if you do anything I don't like." She used her teeth then, ever so lightly.

He seemed to get her point.

Then it was all she could do to keep up as he snapped his hips in a quick staccato, pushing past her lips for all he was worth. She relaxed her jaw and did her best to take it. Called on every trick she'd ever learned, and a few she made up on the spot. Closed her eyes and let instinct take over, tongue and teeth and hollow-cheeked sucking.

She glanced up when he made a ragged, broken sound. His face had gone a dark red that bled over his neck and chest. She could hear the low keening build in his throat. She grabbed his hip with her free hand and pushed back, letting him slide from her mouth just as the muscles in his thighs and belly bunched, and he came, warm and wet across her lips and chin. He held the arch in his spine another second or two, then fell forward, swinging in the chains.

She rubbed at his hip, as one might caress a horse that had won a hard race. With her other hand, she swiped at her chin. "Well done, Detective."

"I think that's my line. And for God's sake, call me Marcus." His voice was quiet and thready, as if he'd finally run out of steam. His gaze played over her face. "Christ, your mouth."

She licked at her lower lip and tasted blood

where it had split. "The hazards of friction. It'll be all right."

"Sorry."

"Don't be. I'm not." She pulled away and stood, stretching her back. She'd be sore in the morning, but not as sore as he'd be, so she didn't bother feeling sorry for herself. "You should try to sleep before—"

The sound of voices and footsteps beyond the door made her jump and stumble backward. Early...no way had it been two hours.

"They're coming. Get out of here," Marcus said, low and urgent.

"I can't just leave you—"

"Go, God damn it. Just remember to call Sanchez."

The voices came closer—near enough that she could make out the Madre's accent. The sound of it made her stomach curl in on itself with fear. She turned to look at Marcus, and all at once he seemed far away. Smaller too, as if she were looking at him through the wrong end of a telescope. Quickly she reached for the cell phone where she'd left it on the pile of clothes. She clutched it hard in her hand and looked once more over her shoulder at Marcus's slumped, exhausted form. The brick walls surrounding her warped and grew fuzzy, then began to fade into a black void that stretched...and echoed...and stretched...

Chapter Six

Marcus watched Leah grab his phone and turn back to look at him. He wanted to speak, to say "Thanks for trying, babe, you did your best," but he could barely muster the energy to lift his head, much less coordinate his brain with his mouth. And as he watched her dissolve into the thick, sex-soaked air—first growing translucent, then disappearing entirely—he had to wonder if she'd been real in the first place, or just another cruel, fucked up feature of the Madre's little game.

He let his head hang low and listened. He heard the door bang open, and the shuffle of feet on cement, then two voices—Shannon the barmaid, and the Madre Donnatella DeTagliera.

"Tell me, *cara*," Donnatella said, "how does our guest fare this evening?"

Through slitted eyes, Marcus watched Shannon's boot-encased feet approach. He fought to stay motionless as she pressed cold fingers into the pulse-point on his neck and said, "Someone's interfered with him, Madre. He's alive, but barely conscious."

"What else?" Donnatella's words were like a whip-crack over his head.

Shannon stepped back, as if to survey him. "Clarice's blood is smeared on his chest and face, as if someone has run their hands over him. And his..." She cleared her throat. "...his male member is limp and wet. There's evidence of recent release."

When the old woman spoke again, her voice

settled like frost over the room. "You will find the responsible parties and bring them to me for punishment, *sí?*"

"Yes, Madre. Belinda and Kathie were with him last."

"Then we shall begin with Belinda and Kathie." The hem of Donnatella's long red skirt hissed against the floor as she moved toward him. "But first, let us see if we cannot revive our guest. I hear his breathing, so shallow and quick. I suspect he's not as sleepy as he seems."

* * * *

Leah opened her eyes. The room was dim, but not dark. Cold. She took a breath and smelled fresh linen...her own perfume...the litter box in the bathroom, in need of a change. Familiar. Home.

She shifted on the mattress, lifting her hands to her face, and nearly screamed when the cell phone fell out of her open palm and onto her chest.

Real, then.

She turned her head and looked at the clock. It read six AM.

Real, and happening in real time.

She rolled over to face the window, stared out at the breaking light of dawn, and tried to reason her way through the situation. It didn't do her much good. Panic kept getting in the way of linear thought.

Get him out. Save him. Do it now, don't waste time, do something.

She reached for the cell phone, where it lay on the bedspread. Turned it on and played with it for a few seconds, figuring out how to scroll through the programmed numbers. There—Gus Sanchez. Thank God.

She dialed and waited. Somewhere in the small city of Santa Rosa, she knew another cell phone was ringing. Three times...four...

The voice that answered was deep and gruff

with sleep. "Sanchez here, and the fuckin' mayor better be dead if you're calling me at this hour, Colton."

Leah squeezed the phone tight in her hand and prayed her voice didn't squeak. "Uh, hello. This isn't Detective Colton, but he asked me to call you and—"

"Jesus Christ, did Colton leave his phone with one of his Goddamn groupies again? You tell that bastard he can—"

"Please listen, Chief Sanchez. Detective Colton's been kidnapped. He's being held..." Son of a bitch. She had no idea where he was being held. None. "He's in a basement, in a club owned by a woman named Donnatella DeTagliera. He asked me to call you—"

"Let me get this straight. Colton's been kidnapped, but you've got his cell phone? Why didn't he use it himself, if he could give it to you? And who the hell is this, anyway?"

"My name's not important. You just need to—"

"Listen, lady, this isn't funny. You can tell Colton that if he wants to talk to me, he can come to the Goddamn station tomorrow morning at nine. Until then, fuck the hell off. And don't call this number again, or I'll have the GPS on the phone traced and you'll be arrested for falsely reporting a crime."

"No, don't—"

But Chief Sanchez had departed with a final click in her ear. Leah turned off the phone and tossed it onto the bed. Then she slumped, letting her head rest in her hands. *Groupies? What the hell does that mean?*

Okay, time for Plan B. She glanced at the clock again. Six AM in California meant nine AM in Massachusetts. Plenty late enough. She reached for her own phone and dialed. It didn't ring on the other side—not even once—before a chipper, if decidedly elderly, feminine voice answered.

"And a very good morning to you, Leah."

"Hi, Gram. What's new?"

Her grandmother snorted into the phone. "Cut to the chase, dear. What's the trouble?"

Leah sighed. "Right. Well, there's this man—"

"I'm delighted to hear it. It's been far too long for you, and it's never good to go without. Oh my. He's a handsome one, isn't he? And so popular with the ladies. But..." Concern crept into her grandmother's tone. "Oh dear, he's got himself in a bit of a pickle, hasn't he? And you...oh, Leah. You cut it far too close there, at the end. You should be more careful."

This time, Leah's sigh was huge. And irritated. "If you already know what's going on, why did you bother to ask?"

"Forgive me, dear. I'm not as quick as I used to be. But why are you calling me? You know what you have to do."

"Well, I know I have to help him, but I'm not sure how. I don't really have a handle on this whole teleportation thing. Not sure I can make it work a second time, since I wasn't trying the first time."

"You know, Leah, if you'd ever taken even a little time to develop your gift, or study the underpinnings of some of the more basic mystical concepts, you might not have this problem. For example, did you know that accounts of teleportation occur in several major religious traditions, including Islam, Judaism, Buddhism and Christianity? It's really quite—"

"Gram, please." Leah sat up and swung her legs over the edge of the mattress. She looked down and saw where her knees were dusty from kneeling on the Madre's cement floor. When she licked her bottom lip, it felt swollen and tender against her tongue. "Can we save the lecture? I need actual solutions. Should I try the teleportation once more? Maybe take a weapon with me this time?"

There was silence at the other end of the line for several moments. When her grandmother spoke again, her voice was as somber as Leah had ever heard it. "You can't count on it working, Leah. Not with your lack of experience. You could end up anywhere—or nowhere. You could lie down for what turns out to be nothing more than a refreshing nap, and leave that poor man to suffer and die an agonizing, bloody death."

"Thanks for the imagery."

"Watch your mouth. I could be napping myself, instead of talking to you. I'm eighty-seven damn years old."

"Sorry." Leah scrubbed a hand over her face and caught the scent of male sweat and musk. It made her dizzy for a second. "I guess I could try the Chief again. Maybe if I'm lucky, he won't have me arrested."

Her grandmother made a skeptical noise. "We've never had much luck with the authorities."

Understatement. Eight years ago, Leah had been struck with a vision of a home invasion somewhere in one of the more upscale sections of San Francisco. When she'd reported what she'd seen to the police, they'd refused to take her seriously. Then, when the crime actually came to pass, she was hauled in for questioning and held on suspicion of being an accomplice to what had turned out to be a double-murder. She'd spent forty-eight hours in a holding cell before they released her for lack of evidence.

To say the experience left her profoundly mistrustful of anyone with a badge...yeah. Serious understatement.

"Isn't there anyone you can ask for help, Leah? Anyone you trust? Have you made no friends in that place?" Her grandmother sounded distressed. Sad. Disappointed in her. What else was new?

"I'll think of something, Gram. It'll be okay." She tried to sound confident. "Listen, I have to go. I'll call you later."

"See that you do." Her grandmother hung up in her ear, leaving an echo of an unspoken "*I love you and I'm worried about you and for Heaven's sake, be careful'* hanging between them.

Leah placed the phone in its cradle and pressed her hands to her face, trying to ignore what the trace fragrance of Marcus's skin did to her equilibrium. All right. If she couldn't teleport back into the Madre's playroom, and calling the police wasn't an option, then...what? Going there in person, so to speak? Walking right up to the front door, and...

Crap. She was back to the part where she didn't know where Marcus was being held. How the hell would she find him? She didn't have the first clue...except... She grabbed the phone book from the bedside table and started leafing through the Yellow Pages, under "nightclubs."

Yahtzee. Hotel California, downtown Santa Rosa. The ad said it opened at noon. Good. She'd need the time to prepare herself.

She sat and thought for a few minutes longer, then reached for the phone and dialed again. It rang four times, and then a sleepy, masculine voice answered.

"Hello?"

"Hi, Jeff? Jeff Crandel? It's Leah Benjamin. I know it's early, but I need to ask a favor."

"Leah?" He sounded a lot more alert all of a sudden. "What can I do for you?"

"This is going to sound crazy, Jeff, and I can't really explain it. I just need you to do it and not ask questions, okay?"

Jeff stuttered and stammered a bit before finally replying, "I'll do what I can, but...is it going to get me into trouble with the Dean, like last time? Because you know, that petition you passed around really stirred things up, and not in a good way. I'm not tenured, you know, and with my wife pregnant and all—"

"Jeff, listen to me. You're not going to get into any trouble. I just need you to go to a payphone at three-forty-five this afternoon and make a phone call for me. No one will ever know it was you, I promise."

There was silence at the other end of the line. Leah held her breath. This was it—there was no one else. If he turned her down...

"I wouldn't ask if I didn't really need your help, Jeff."

He sighed. "Who do I need to call?"

The muscles in Leah's neck and shoulders and back relaxed, and she exhaled as she let herself fall sideways on the bed. "Anybody ever tell you what a nice guy you are?"

* * * *

"Detective," the Madre said, her voice dripping venom, "you are such a very nice man, *sí*? Too nice, perhaps?"

The blonde bitch, Shannon, snaked her hand through his hair and yanked his head back. "Answer the Madre."

If he'd been able, he'd have spit in the barmaid's eye. But he had neither the strength nor the moisture left in his mouth to manage it. He settled for glaring at them both.

The Madre grinned at him, and it was ghastly. Her eyes, like two blank, pearly moons, seemed to stare right through his skin. "*Bene*, Detective, you are too nice and too honorable to tell us which of these wicked girls ruined my plans for you." She gestured in the general direction of the two women who'd disposed of Clarice's body—a thin brunette and another chick with short, wispy hair. They lay facedown on the cement, naked, their backs torn and bloody after an hour-long application of Shannon's whip. Their screams and cries for mercy echoed in his ears. Their protestations of innocence had gotten them nowhere, and left him feeling sick with guilt.

"But," the Madre continued, "as you can see, it

makes no difference. Your nice, honorable ways have not saved them from punishment. Nor have they saved you."

True enough. His chest sported ten new marks, and these were no mere welts. They were deep, open and bleeding. The pain overwhelmed him, but he reveled in it. Because it was pain, and he hated it. No craving for more. No desire to beg for further abuse. The woman...the quite possibly imaginary woman...

...Leah, her name is Leah...

...had been right about that much.

And still the Madre went on, her voice like the drone of a poisonous insect. "And now you will see how we deal with disobedience, Detective. Watch and learn."

No. They couldn't make him watch. He closed his eyes and wished he could do the same with his ears, praying for unconsciousness as Shannon did whatever she did to make the women lying on the floor gibber and shriek like banshees. Their palpable agony, and the wet, sloppy sounds of blood splattering this way and that, made his stomach clench and roll. He let his eyes drift open in time to see the pair of them drag themselves along the floor toward the door, with Shannon behind them, urging them on. At least they were still alive. More than he could hope for himself.

Then the world grayed out, not disappearing entirely, but receding enough that he could feel some relief, a brief cessation of pain and guilt.

It ended with a hard, loud slap to his jaw. "Wake up. Time for another drink. Gotta stay hydrated so you don't get sick."

Shannon laughed and shoved the mouth of a water bottle between his lips. He didn't bother to struggle, having learned through trial and error that the barmaid could force the issue if she wanted. At least she didn't seem interested in drugging him again.

He drank without opening his eyes. As he swallowed, she spoke to him, her voice low and angry. "This is all your fault, you know. What I had to do to Belinda and Kathie? They were my friends, and it's all your fault." She yanked the water away and slapped him again, landing the blow directly on his ear and making it ring. "I can't wait to see you really suffer. It won't be long now."

She left him. He opened his eyes and saw the long, crimson smudges on the floor in the center of the room. They complemented the stain left by Clarice's body. Highlighted it. Idly, he wondered how his blood would look mingled with theirs.

His thoughts drifted to the woman...imaginary? Real? Did it matter?

It had been hours. If she was real, she hadn't called Chief Sanchez. Or Sanchez hadn't listened to her—which was just as likely, because Sanchez was an asshole who'd never liked him anyway, and had never believed that his partner's death had been anything other than a random mugging gone bad. Only Marcus's stubborn determination—what Sanchez called his "bitching and moaning" about "bogeymen"—had kept the investigation open.

This reality of it was this—if some random chick really did phone Chief Sanchez at the ass-crack of dawn to tell him Marcus was chained in the basement of a sex club? He'd probably threatened her with arrest for making prank calls. And Sanchez was the only one in the department who knew Marcus was going undercover, and where, and why.

But none of that made any difference anyway, because the woman...Leah...wasn't real. No way. He didn't believe in magic, or psychic phenomena, or any of that New Age-y crap. Though she sure was nice to think about, with her watercolor veils, all see-through and soft.

Wait...no...that was the story she'd told him. The story had helped him. He couldn't deny it, any more than he could deny the evidence of it, where it had dried across his thighs and on the floor before Shannon had dragged those women into the room and...

No, not thinking about that. Thinking about Leah, who'd been there and gone away. Real? Not real? Didn't matter. He was screwed either way. The best thing he could hope for was a quick death, and it seemed like that wasn't in the cards. So he'd play the hand he was dealt. He was good at that—always had been. He'd go down fighting, one way or another.

The gray crept up on him again. He couldn't feel his arms or his legs, and he was cold. So cold. But the gray was his friend, and he fell into it, face-first. Leah was there waiting for him. She wore the watercolor veils, running all together, like they'd been left out in the rain. And she was smiling.

Chapter Seven

Leah stood on the sidewalk and watched as a tall blonde in a black Latex cat suit rolled out the green striped awning over the façade of the club. Then the blonde went inside, letting the front door slam behind her with a bang that traveled loud and clear over the sounds of noon-hour traffic. A few seconds later, the scrolled neon lettering that decorated the big front window sputtered to life. Hotel California was open for business.

Leah adjusted her skirt—tight red leather—and rubbed her palms together, grimacing at their clammy feel. Then she made her way down the block, watching her step in stilettos she hadn't worn in nearly a decade. At least she didn't wobble. An hour's practice in the hall outside her apartment had made sure of that.

She paused in front of the door and reached into her handbag, feeling for the small, hard lump secreted within the faux-silk lining. Her ace in the hole, so to speak. Then she gathered her courage and pulled open the door.

The inside of the club was gloomy compared to the sunlit street, but her eyes adjusted quickly. She caught sight of the blonde wiping down the bar. The woman glanced up and looked her over, plainly unimpressed with what she saw. Leah took a deep breath and started across the room, a fake smile stretched across her face and her gaze aimed low. Submissive. As she'd been trained, lo these many years ago.

"Good afternoon. I wonder if it would be

possible for me to see..." The sudden quaver in her voice betrayed her. She cleared her throat and began again. "I'm here to see the Madre Donnatella DeTagliera."

The blonde's eyes narrowed. "Who are you?"

"My name is Leah Benjamin. The Madre and I are acquainted. I used to work for her."

The blonde made a gruff sound of disbelief. "You don't look the type."

So much for the tight red leather and heels. "Just the same, I'd appreciate it if you'd let the Madre know I'm here. I believe she'd be interested in meeting with me."

"Oh you do, huh?"

Leah lifted her eyes and looked straight into the blonde's face for the first time. "Yes, I do. In fact, if she discovered I'd been turned away, I think the Madre might be very displeased."

The other woman held her gaze a long three seconds. Then she blinked. "Wait here." She crossed the room and disappeared through a door behind the stage, leaving Leah to check out the club.

Nice digs. Not as fancy as the brothel in San Francisco, but the Madre Donnatella apparently was no longer billing herself as the premiere Madam for the S-and-M set. She was a respectable club owner now, from everything Leah had been able to dig up in the five hours she'd spent preparing.

The door behind the stage opened, and the blonde reappeared. "The Madre will see you now," she said, her tone ungracious in the extreme. Leah had to bite her lip to keep from smiling as she followed the other woman down a long spiral staircase made of heavy wrought iron and then about halfway along a shadowed corridor, where they stopped before a wooden door. Leah looked further down the hallway. There was another door, there, in the recessed area at the very end. Marcus was behind it. She was almost sure.

The blonde knocked on the door. Leah heard the Madre's voice call out permission to enter and tried to control her instinctive recoil from the sound.

A moment later, she found herself standing before the woman who'd come to represent everything corrupt in her mind. The Madre Donnatella sat behind a huge, black-lacquered desk, her small white hands steepled before her. She was dressed in a billowing gown of rusty-red, just as Leah recalled from a decade ago. A computer monitor and keyboard rested to her right. A kitten—perhaps ten weeks old, perfectly white, with wide blue eyes—lay curled on the desktop to her left. The room around her was sparsely furnished, save for a gurgling fountain in the corner carved from black stone in some odd, complex shape that made Leah stare until the contorted angles and planes resolved themselves into three human bodies, twisted together in an agonized knot of torn flesh and broken bone. She closed her eyes and turned her face away.

She waited for the Madre to speak. She waited...and waited...knowing with certainty that the older woman could see nothing through her blank, white-filmed eyes, and still wondering what she perceived as she appeared to gaze at her. The seconds stretched into a full minute. Leah's breathing became shallow. Rapid. She hated herself for it, knowing this silent intimidation was only part of the game.

Finally, at the moment when she thought she would either scream or turn tail and run from the room, Donnatella spoke.

"The little sparrow returns to the nest," she said. And that was all.

Leah swallowed with difficulty. "Yes, Madre. I've returned to you." She could feel the blonde barmaid's eyes on her back from across the room. She straightened her shoulders. "I've come to ask your forgiveness, and to plead for the chance to make amends. And to receive whatever punishment you see fit, of course." It took some effort to force that last statement past her lips. She remembered punishment. What it meant, even for the willing. Remembered far too well.

The Madre smiled. Once, long ago, Leah had found that same smile charming. Beautiful, even. Then, it had represented safety. Acceptance. Understanding, and lack of judgment.

Now she saw it for what it was—a Death's Head grin. And she knew, without a doubt, that she'd stepped once again into the presence of evil.

* * * *

Marcus rolled his shoulders in their strained sockets, gathered what little strength he had left, and pulled against the chains for all he was worth. Not because he thought they'd break or yank loose from the wall, because he knew better. But what the hell else was he going to do? Kneel there, on legs that had long since gone completely numb, and wait for those lunatic females to come back and kill him?

Frustration burned him to the bone. A well-trained officer of the law with fifteen years on the force, and this was how he was going out? Chained to a wall by a bunch of crazy women? And maybe that wasn't the most enlightened way to look at it, but fuck enlightenment. He'd work on his sexism issues after he busted out of this loony bin and saw every one of these nutzoid bitches locked up.

He stopped pulling on the chains when he found himself panting from the useless exertion. No point in using up all his resources on something so hopeless. What he needed to do was think.

What time is it? His internal clock was screwed to hell, but he knew it was Saturday. At least, he thought he knew. Fuck, how he hated this waiting game. He needed to focus. Come up with a plan. He closed his eyes and concentrated on slowing his breathing...

...and heard voices approaching. Here they come. Round four, or was it five? He let himself go limp and listened as the door opened and...yes, that was the Madre Donnatella, and Shannon the barmaid. Who was the third? He waited to hear her speak.

"Shannon, please introduce Leah to our guest," the Madre said.

Leah? Shit.

Then Shannon's fingers were in his hair, yanking his head backward. He opened his eyes and saw the hostile sneer on the blonde's face. "Detective Marcus Colton, the weekend entertainment."

He looked past Shannon to where the other women stood. Yes, right there next to Donnatella— the woman from before. Except instead of short white nightshirt, she wore a black tube-top, a red leather skirt and stupidly high heels. Her light brown hair was pulled back in a loose bun, and her face was painted in lurid colors.

She didn't meet his gaze.

What the fuck?

He watched as the Madre curled one hand around Leah's arm, just above the elbow. "Detective Colton," she said, "this is our little sparrow, who has returned to the nest to ask our forgiveness, and do penance for her sins from long ago. She is lovely, *sí?*"

How was he supposed to respond to this? What the hell was going on? If Donnatella was willing to tell Leah his name, then she couldn't be planning on letting her go.

The Madre kept on talking. "Leah tells us her life is a misery, Detective. She tells us she wishes only to return to our service. To please herself by pleasing us. *Sí, cara?* Is that not so?"

Leah stared at the floor. "Yes, Madre."

"But we are not so trusting as we once were. We must challenge our sparrow. We must test her loyalty." She gave Leah a shove in Marcus's direction. "Leah, someone ruined our play last night by interfering with our guest. He was worthless to us."

Leah stumbled forward toward where Marcus knelt. As she righted herself, she peered at him for the first time from the very corner of her eye. In her face, he saw...what? Fear? Guilt? Shame?

He looked away.

She turned to face Donnatella and said, "Who would do such a thing? Your pleasure is our pleasure, always."

Her voice sounded different. The way she framed her words—it was formal. Stilted. It reminded him of something...some other time he'd heard her speak that way. The only other time— when she'd told him the story about the prisoner and the concubine.

A jolt of recognition shot through him. Of course—this was all an act. What she was doing now, pretending to fall in with the Madre's plans? A charade, a sham. She was here to help him, the little idiot. She'd walked right back into the lioness' den. For him.

Why did that make him so fucking enraged? Was it worse to be caught and held captive by a woman, or to be saved by one? Maybe...just maybe...he needed to tell his hypersensitive male ego to take a fucking hike.

"*Bene, cara*. We're so glad to hear you say that, but still you must prove it. You must show perfect submission...perfect, *bellissimo* submission." The Madre snapped her fingers, and Leah jumped as if startled. Then she lowered her head and stared at the floor. When she moved to kneel at the Madre's feet, it was with the practiced grace of much repetition. The older woman reached down and stroked her hair, as she might a cat's fur. Marcus tried not to stare, afraid to give away anything in his expression.

Donnatella inclined her head toward the

barmaid. "Shannon, please summon Yugiya."

Who the fuck was Yugiya? How many nutcases were in this joint, anyway?

Shannon left the room for maybe thirty seconds. When she returned, she was accompanied by a short but well-muscled young woman with black hair and blacker eyes, dressed in the Hotel California employee uniform of a black Latex cat-suit. In her right hand she held...Christ, was that a katana? It had to be. The slender, curved blade was hard to mistake. The young woman struck a pose of subservience, holding the weapon before her as if presenting it for a blessing.

The Madre, who'd been standing near the fireplace, smiled in her general direction. "Yugiya, so good of you to join us on your day off, *cara*."

Yugiya nodded, lifted the katana over her head and spun in a graceful circle, cleaving the thick, stale air in an intricate set of movements. Obviously some sort of martial art. Marcus appreciated the competent wielding of nice weaponry. Under other circumstances he might've liked the beauty in it, but all he could see in his mind's eye was his own blood and Leah's dripping off the blade.

Shannon asked, "Should I release him now, Madre?" and gestured in his direction. He stared at the blonde, not believing he'd heard her right. They were letting him go?

"*Sí, cara*, you may free him," the Madre replied. Then she turned her attention to Marcus, facing him with dead eyes that seemed to see right through him all the same. "Do you observe Yugiya and her lethal friend, Detective?" she asked. "I would consider most carefully before making foolish choices, if I were you. One wrong move and she'll take a limb, or perhaps some other part you may not care to live without."

"You're going to kill me anyway." The first words he'd offered in many hours. his voice sounded disgustingly weak in his own ears. He watched Shannon remove a key from a chain around her neck and move toward him, hating himself for flinching as she bent over him and reached for his wrist.

The Madre Donnatella shrugged, as if this were a foregone conclusion. "Then perhaps I'll choose to punish our little sparrow in your stead, *si?* Yugiya could hack her to bits in the blink of an eye. I feel sure you wouldn't want that, honorable man that you are."

Leah looked at him, just a quick flick of a glance, but he saw the warning in her eyes. Still, he couldn't quite manage to contain the single syllable that did a swan dive off his tongue...

"Cunt."

Shannon punched him hard in the gut. "We don't speak that way to the Madre," she said from between clenched jaws. As he struggled to suck in air, doubled over and grunting, she unlocked the second shackle. Then she grabbed him beneath his arms and hauled him to his feet. The bitch was strong. Even when he slumped against her, unable to support himself on his numb legs, she held him upright. And all the while, Leah remained kneeling at the Madre's feet, staring at the floor.

Pins and needles began to crawl down his legs and arms as the blood flow returned full force. Uncomfortable, but he was glad enough to have use of his limbs.

"Can he perform, Shannon?" The Madre asked.

The barmaid groped his dick, yanking on it with no finesse. "I think he needs more time, Madre."

"Shall we inject him again, *cara?* That would be entertaining, no?"

"It's not been twenty-four hours yet, Madre. Some of the drug may still be in his system. We could lose him."

"That would be a shame. I believe we can use

him further—perhaps two more days, if we are cautious, *sì*? He is so strong. So stubborn." Donnatella pressed a finger to her pointed chin, appearing to consider her options. "Tell me, Shannon, when Clarice approached him at the bar, how did she lure him? What did she promise him?"

"She asked him if he was into bondage games and spanking."

"And did the good Detective respond to her suggestions?"

Shannon gave him a shove. He stumbled against the wall, scraping his back. "He did, Madre."

"*Molto bene*. I believe I know how we shall proceed," said the Madre, her face beaming, her blank eyes darting around the room. "Prepare the tall bench, Shannon, and then make our little sparrow ready for her test."

Marcus watched as Shannon strode over to the corner and struggled to drag a large, obviously heavy piece of furniture to the center of the room. It appeared to be a tall, padded bench that looked like a pommel horse minus the handles. Leather restraints hung open at the bottom of each of its legs. He glanced at Leah, who never looked up from the floor. He could see the rising color in her face.

Finally, with the bench positioned to her liking, Shannon turned to Leah. "Strip. Now. But keep the shoes." There was a cruel twist to her smile when she glanced at Leah's pumps. "They amuse me."

Leah nodded, set her bag on the floor near the pile of Marcus's clothing, and did as she was told. Marcus tried to watch without watching. Couldn't deny he wanted to see...but couldn't help feeling bad about it. Chivalry was not dead. Only beaten into submission.

When she was naked, Shannon directed Leah to bend herself over the bench and prepare to be restrained. The barmaid closed the leather cuffs on Leah's wrists, From Marcus's vantage point, he could see how tightly she buckled them. Leah's fingers brushed the floor. Her light brown hair shook loose from its pins and fell in her face. Shannon left her legs free to angle down to the floor behind her, allowing her to rest her weight on her toes. The shiny black stilettos gleamed in the candlelight.

He tried not to let his gaze travel higher, to where her smooth, white skin was pressed into the leather. Or to where it was exposed to the warm, damp air of the room.

"She's ready, Madre."

"*Bene.* Fetch a ball-gag from the cabinet. A large one, please."

Leah made a sound, something like a stillborn whimper. Her eyes squeezed shut, and her lips moved in what Marcus assumed was a prayer. Why was she doing this? What could she possibly hope to gain by it? Now both of them were trapped, bound, and at the mercy of a sadistic, homicidal crazy person.

He stuffed down a groan of frustration as he watched Shannon grab Leah by the hair and lift her head.

"Open."

Leah said, "Wait, please, what time is it?"

"What difference does that make?"

"Just...please. What time is it?"

Shannon rolled her eyes and checked her watch. "Two-thirty. Now open the fuck up."

Leah shut her eyes and parted her lips. Marcus watched as Shannon stuffed the black leather ball inside her mouth and buckled the leather strap behind her head. Then he closed his own eyes, unable to stand the sight of it. Of her. Of everything.

"Is Detective Colton able to stand? Support his own weight?"

"Yes, Madre."

"*Bene.* Give him the special crop, please."

Shannon crossed to the glass-fronted cabinet,

opened it, and brought out the item the Madre had named. Then she brought it to him, holding it out in front of her as if it were some kind of ritualistic offering. Eighteen inches long, and made of black leather with a chrome handle it looked fairly harmless. But he knew nothing here was harmless. Its slender, flexible body was designed to leave marks. Cause pain. Pull muffled shrieks from its victims.

Shannon thrust it at him. "Take it. Use it on her." She pointed at Leah.

He knew he needed to be careful. Knew this could get very ugly real quick. That's what his brain was telling him when his mouth opened and "Fuck you" jumped out.

This time, when Shannon moved to punch him, he dodged her. But he'd forgotten about Yugiya. The smaller woman had the blade of her katana pressed just under his jaw before he could step forward to take the barmaid down.

Shannon's face was purple and twisted with rage. "Madre, he—"

"Silence, Shannon." Donnatella's voice was icy as she spoke to her acolyte, but warmed and became almost cajoling when she directed it at him. "Detective Colton, you do not seem to understand. We will accomplish a great thing today. A marvelous thing. Our little sparrow has returned to us to do penance. You've been offered a great honor."

He opened his mouth to speak, but Yugiya applied more pressure to the katana. He felt the skin break beneath the blade. Felt warm blood   seep down   his throat. If she wanted, she could kill him with a twist of her wrist.

The Madre continued speaking, her pale face creasing in a grin that chilled him straight through. "Such a great thing requires suffering. Down deep, where the soul abides, waiting to be set free. In the flesh, Detective. In the bone."

Chapter Eight

Marcus looked down into Yugiya's black gaze. Then he glanced at Shannon. The loathing in her face could've singed his eyebrows. "No," he said. "I won't do it. You can't make me."

"You think not?" Donnatella's grin widened. "Let me tell you, Detective, that in my cabinet of treasures I have tourniquets. It would take but a moment for Leah to lose her right hand, *si?* And to tie it off at the wrist so she does not die immediately. Such a horror that would be, *no?*"

For the first time in many minutes, Leah made a sound—a muffled exclamation behind her gag.

Fuck. They weren't getting out of this part of the program. He stared at Donnatella, trying to read her intent behind the opaque surface of her eyes.

"Yugiya?"

"Yes, Madre?"

"Give Detective Colton a...how do you say it...demonstration of what you can do, *cara*."

"Yes, Madre."

Before Marcus could protest, the small woman ducked and whirled, bringing the blade around low, near his legs. But it was the leg of the table she took out, dividing it cleanly in two. The table toppled to the floor. The drawer opened, spilling its contents— all the syringes and small bottles of go-juice—onto the cement. Some of them shattered.

Solid oak, that table-leg had been. He would have sworn to it. And not a fragile thing, but a good ten inches around. If the katana could do that—

"Fetch a tourniquet, Shannon. A small one, I

think—"

"No!" He stepped forward, and Yugiya was there, her weapon level with his chest. "Don't. I'll...do it."

"*Si*, I thought you might reconsider."

He closed his eyes, sucked in a deep breath and held it, forcing down the roar of hatred and rage that rolled and churned in his gut like an incoming tsunami. Then he opened his eyes, took the crop from Shannon and approached Leah, where she was stretched over the bench.

"Have you ever done this before?" Shannon asked him, her voice low and amused. Bitch. He'd show her amused.

He shook his head. She grabbed him by the elbow and dragged him to the side of the bench.

"Stand here, you'll get more power behind your swing. Lift the crop up and back, and bring it down hard. Don't try to cheat. If you do—"

"Yeah, I get it." He lifted his arm, and held it at the peak of the swing. Just as he was about to deliver the first blow, Shannon grabbed his other elbow again.

"Wait." She looked at Donnatella. "Madre, we forgot the mirror."

"Of course, *cara*. Uncover it so that Leah might observe her punishment."

Shannon crossed the room, passing Donnatella and moving toward a long, black curtain next to the fireplace. She reached behind the curtain and pulled a cord, and the black fabric parted, revealing a wide, full-length mirror. When Marcus looked into it, he saw his and Leah's reflections clearly. Leah only had to turn her head to see herself.

"Look, sweet sparrow," the Madre said, her voice almost a croon. "Look and see yourself. How helpless you are. Your suffering will be a thing of beauty."

Leah turned her head and looked. Marcus watched her face in the mirror. Saw her eyes widen and then blink, rapidly. He watched as the muscles in her shoulders tightened. The ripple moved up her back, over her ass and down her legs. She was preparing herself.

When he looked again at her face, she met his eyes in the glass. She nodded, once, short and quick. Giving permission. Permission to beat her? With a fucking crop, like a piece of livestock?

No, he couldn't do this. This wasn't happening, this was not who he was, God damn it—

She made a sound, low and urgent. He met her eyes again. She nodded once more, frowning and clenching her jaws on the black rubber ball-gag. She looked...determined. Demanding, almost.

All right then. Maybe she knew something he didn't. He sure as hell hoped so.

He returned her nod. Then he bent and made a show of flicking away a piece of broken glass from the floor near his foot. Before he stood, he brushed his hand against her leg and murmured, "I'll make this as easy as I can."

Then he straightened, swung the crop high and brought it down. The first blow fell in the space where the pale columns of her thighs bloomed softer and became the rising curve of her ass. She jerked hard against the restraints. He watched with fascination as the white stripe he left turned red and raised up into a welt.

"Again." Shannon said. "Give her forty. And make them good, or so help me—"

He turned and looked at the barmaid, and whatever she saw in his face in that moment shut her mouth.

He went to work, lifting the crop in an arc and bringing it down. He counted in his head, and tried to concentrate on the numbers. And on placing the blows in different spots, so that he'd avoid breaking the skin. He wasn't entirely successful, but he did his best.

By the time he counted fifteen he'd fallen into a grim rhythm. The sound of the crop striking Leah's flesh a counterpoint to her stifled cries. Somewhere around number twenty-five, he noticed how she flexed her hips, rocking her ass up into each blow. Now the sounds she made were more like moans. Longer in duration. Higher-pitched, with a rising and falling lilt.

He looked into the mirror and caught sight of her face. Her eyes were half-closed, and the flutter of her lashes against her pink cheek struck him as obscene somehow. Then she opened her eyes, and he couldn't mistake her expression. Even as he glanced away and tried to deny what he saw, he remembered her whisper in his ear, telling him to surrender. The wet burn of her mouth on him. No mercy for his strung out and screaming nerve endings. Relentless.

His cock remembered, too.

He let the fortieth blow fall in exactly the same spot as the first and watched as blood beaded in the welt. Tossing the crop away he stood there, panting. Sweating. Half-hard and disgusted with himself for it.

"He's finished, Madre," Shannon said. "He did a satisfactory job."

"*Bravo*, Detective." Donnatella moved a step nearer, stretching her hand out before her. The look on her face was almost one of...enchantment. Marcus tried not to stare, for fear he'd begin to heave the water Shannon had forced on him. "Feel her, Detective. *Sí*, push your fingers into her and see if she's ready for the next part of her penance."

"What the—? No!" He backed away, trying to avoid glancing at the juncture of Leah's red and swollen thighs. Failing. Funny how it was hard to miss the tell-tale rosy blush and glisten of moisture once you were looking for it, wasn't it? Damn. So twisted. All of them.

Including him, apparently. His cock agreed, but

didn't shrink away from the knowledge that he was one sick fuck.

Shannon grabbed his wrist. He fought her—of course he did. But there came Yugiya, prodding his back with the very tip of the katana, forcing him forward. Still, he struggled.

"He's resisting, Madre."

"Perhaps the good Detective doesn't like women? Such a pity."

He snickered. He couldn't help it. Her ploy was too damn cute. "That game won't work, Donnatella. I'm pretty secure in my heterosexuality."

Shannon and Yugiya gasped, hissing like leaky air-valves. Maybe because he'd laughed at their Madre, or maybe because he'd called her by name. Either way, the pair froze where they stood and stared at Donnatella as if waiting for her cue to butcher him on the spot.

But the Madre only inclined her head in his general direction, as if conceding his point. "*Bene*, Marcus. We are to use given names now, *si? Bene, molto bene.*" She steepled her hands before her and smiled at him, sweet as rat poison in a sugar bowl. "Perhaps you would prefer that Shannon have the honor of first penetration? We have some lovely toys in the cabinet..."

Shannon made a predatory sound in his ear, something like the grunt of a wild boar. "The studded one, Madre. Let me use the big studded one, please?"

He saw Leah's body stiffen, the backs of her calves bunching as if in protest. Her whole body must've been sore, stretched over that thing for so long, with all the blood running to her head...and now she had to fear that cunt, Shannon, raping her with some random torture device?

"No. I'll do it."

Shannon grunted again, in obvious disappointment.

"Is he prepared, *cara*? Can he perform?" There was a note of anticipation in Donnatella's tone that might've turned his stomach if he let it.

"He was, Madre, but he's faded a bit." Shannon made a grab for his dick. He dodged her, earning a poke in the ass from Yugiya's katana. Amazing how he kept forgetting she was there, what with the fact that she was the probably the one who would slice open his throat before the sun went down.

He bared his teeth at Shannon. "Just...give me a second, okay?"

"Whatever you say, Detective."

Before he died? He was going to rip Shannon's head off and shove it up her ass. That was the promise he made to himself as he approached Leah once more. Just as he was about to speak to Leah—to say something reassuring and tell her it was going to be okay—Donnatella piped up again.

"You should know, Marcus, that our little sparrow always had a special dislike of being penetrated while she was bound. *Si*, I believe it makes her feel too vulnerable." The Madre seemed to roll that word over her tongue just to enjoy its flavor. "Before she left us so suddenly, we were planning to break her of this silly fear. Is that not true, Leah?"

"She can't speak, Madre," Shannon reminded her. "But I can see her face in the mirror, and it's very red."

Donnatella's grin was blissful. "*Bellissimo.* Proceed, Marcus. Take our little sparrow, and teach her that she cannot dismiss us from her life as if we are nothing."

He swallowed, trying to dislodge the dry lump that had formed in his throat. This was wrong. It was a violation. Rape, even. Not even Leah's eyes on him in the mirror—not even the nod of her head that gave him permission to go ahead and fuck her—could change that. But he had to do it. No choice, yet again. He could feel the katana's kiss, just over his left kidney as Yugiya urged him forward. And now Shannon had produced a knife from somewhere, as well. There were stains on the blade. Clarice's blood, probably, though it didn't really matter. What mattered most, right at this second, was getting his cock hard enough to push inside of Leah before Donnatella lost her patience and gave the barmaid permission to haul out the studded dildos.

He closed his eyes and tried to center himself. Tried to conjure up the recollection of her touch on him in the dark, early hours of morning. He listened for the memory of her voice in his head, telling him a tale of a far-off land where women dressed in veils that ran and rippled like watercolors in the rain. He took a breath and smelled...patchouli. Incense. Felt a hot, dry wind on his face. Heard the beat of the drums, and over it...

"*When I see you bound and helpless, my mouth waters. I am powerless over any man, save you. With you, I can do anything I choose...You can't get away. Surrender is your only option.*"

He opened his eyes, stepped forward, and laid his hand gently on Leah's hip. Her skin glowed with the welts he'd raised with the crop. He traced one with his finger, then another. Leah shuddered and pressed herself into the padded leather of the bench. Trying to avoid his touch? Maybe, maybe not. He traced a third red line, where it ran diagonally from the top of her right hip over her ass to her left thigh. She groaned and rocked hard into the bench.

He reached lower and pressed the tip of his thumb into her slit. She jerked with enough force to make the bench wobble. He let his thumb glide along her slick crevice, then slipped it inside and made his other thumb join it. Then he spread her open, and she whined into the gag.

Hot. Wet. Deep pink, verging on purple. He

could see her clit, looking swollen and almost bruised. She wanted this...some part of her, anyway. Didn't she? Or was he telling himself that so he could live with himself later? He couldn't see her face in the mirror. Couldn't check her expression, or look for that quick, subtle nod. His position was wrong, the angle of reflection too far off.

He closed his eyes and pictured the words he couldn't say. The questions she couldn't answer—not out loud. Not expecting any reply. Not even bothering to hope.

Do you want this? Tell me, Leah.

She popped her hips up, tilting her pelvis, making herself available. Offering herself to him, as definite as any nod. And he was hard again—ready, willing and able. Good enough.

"Going to fuck you now, Leah. You ready?"

The height of the bench was perfect—Shannon was good for something after all. He slipped his cock along her blood-hot crease, all the way up to the place where her spine ended, and back down to kiss her clit. She whimpered, her whole body stiffening. He aligned himself and pushed, slow and steady. Her pussy opened around the head and seemed to suck him inside. Hungry. Greedy. He bit the inside of his cheek to keep from grunting and palmed the ripe curve of her abused ass.

Smooth constriction, and so damned hot he had to grit his teeth and count backwards by sevens to maintain control. He sure as hell wasn't lasting long like this. He would've liked to think it was the leftover effects of Donnatella's drug. He knew better.

He ground himself against her, his flesh hissing against hers with the sound of a burning match dropped into water. There was just enough room between the edge of the bench and her belly to slip a hand between and find her clit. He made circles with his fingertips, quick and light, and felt her shiver in response. It was all he could give her. Pretending this was a shared experience. Pretending this was about her pleasure and not her humiliation.

When he began to pump, the deep pull and slip-slide were like hits of pure sugar dumped straight into his bloodstream. He worked it, sliding all the way out and gliding back in slow. Deep. Eyes closed and telling himself it was just the two of them, no crazy murdering lunatics in the peanut gallery. Just them, and he was making love to her, not taking her over a bench while she tried not to choke on a rubber ball.

It was easier than he would've guessed because she was in his mind, whispering tales of harem chicks and fearsome warriors. Showing him pictures of what she'd do to him if she could. What she'd offer, what she'd allow him to take. What she'd take from him when he was too spent to move. It felt like sin and virtue, all tangled in hot, spitting wires. Like an addiction. Like fucking a dream. He didn't care if it was real. It was enough that he could believe for the three minutes it might take him to come.

She made a sound, high and helpless, and closed around him like she meant to keep him there forever. His whole body went tight. He grabbed her hips and arched, throwing his back into it, wanting every millimeter, every nanosecond he could get. Felt the sweet, hot zing spiral down his spine and burst, big and too bright behind his eyes and through his cock, and maybe he said Leah's name. Maybe he shouted it. Maybe it was just in his head.

He slumped against her, sliding his fingers away from beneath her. She shook under him. He could hear her breathing hard through her nose, and hoped she wouldn't choke on the gag.

"He's finished, Madre."

"So soon? How disappointing."

He ignored them in favor of rubbing his hand down Leah's back, over and over. Her skin was hot and dry.

"That's enough, big guy. Get off her." Shannon pulled at his arm and he stepped away. Leah yelped when his still half-hard cock slid out of her and slapped against the back of her thigh.

"Tell me, *cara*," Donnatella said, her face a study in sick fascination, "is our sparrow crying?"

Shannon left him in the center of the room to circle the bench and look. "Her face is very red, Madre, and yes. There are tears."

"*Bellissimo.* Unbind her and let her recover."

Shannon unbuckled the restraints at Leah's wrists and helped her to stand by yanking hard on her hair. When she was upright, the barmaid unbuckled the gag as well. Marcus watched as Leah brushed her hair from her eyes, worked her jaw, fought to regain her equilibrium. She didn't look at him. Shannon stood only three feet away, glaring. Yugiya kept to his right, katana at the ready.

Leah took a few rasping breaths. Then she licked her lips, cleared her throat, and said, "Madre, I request permission to thank you properly."

"Of course, my sparrow. Approach."

He watched as Leah wobbled in the Donnatella's direction, not altogether steady in her heels. The welts on her ass and the backs of her thighs seemed to accuse him out loud, as did the slow and painful way she lowered herself to kneel at the older woman's feet. He'd hurt her. With the crop and with his cock, he'd hurt her. He hadn't been given a choice, but he'd live with that a long time.

"Your pleasure is mine in all things, Madre." She said the words as if they were a catechism she'd learned by heart. Marcus couldn't help the disgust that twisted his gut. This shit was seriously fucked up.

And he'd begun to wonder...was he right in assuming Leah was here to help him? If so, this was an Academy Award-worthy performance.

"*Molto bene, cara.* But you know your test is not

yet complete. There is yet one more trial to prove your loyalty."

"Whatever you wish, Madre." Leah pulled herself off her knees with obvious difficulty and stood. "May I please use the ladies' room first?"

"*Sí, cara.*"

Shannon started forward. "But Madre—"

"You will accompany her, of course." Donnatella's voice was smug and careless at the same time, so certain she had nothing to fear. "Hurry back, my sparrow. Our games are just beginning."

Leah moved to the pile of her clothing and reached for her skirt.

"Wait," Shannon said, "you can't get dressed. Do you think we're idiots?"

"Shannon." Donnatella's tone held a warning.

Leah ignored the blonde and directed her words to the Madre. "May I please take my bag? I want to freshen my makeup."

The barmaid grabbed the bag from the top of the pile, unclasped it, and stuck her hand inside to search it. When she pulled out her hand, she held a cell phone—not Marcus's, and thank God Leah was at least that smart—and a wallet. She thrust the bag at Leah. "Wear those fancy shoes of yours, and try not to fall on your ass," she hissed, low and vicious.

They left the room together, Leah limping and Shannon trailing her. Before the door closed behind them, he heard Leah ask Shannon the time. He missed the barmaid's answer, but what difference did it make? Time was meaningless. All that mattered now was escape, and now he had his chance.

He turned, poised to make a move. If he could disable Yugiya—

"Tell me you would not be so foolish, Detective Colton. To die now? After only thirty minutes of freedom? Surely you'd rather wait and know the end-game, *sí?*"

As Donnatella spoke, Yugiya moved nearer, her stance threatening. She lifted the katana over her head. The moment stretched between the two of them, taut and endless. He watched the young woman's face, taking her measure. Would she really kill him? There was something there in her face...some uncertainty...

"Stand down, Detective, or I will tell her to take your right arm."

He saw Yugiya's grip tighten on the katana. Saw her arms tremble with tension. With a grunt of frustration, he stepped back and let his arms fall loose at his sides. Yugiya nodded in acknowledgment, and moved away.

He'd lost. Again. All he could do now was wait and see if Leah came through with whatever she was planning.

Donnatella's voice cut through his thoughts. "Do you wonder how I know what you are thinking, Marcus? When one has been without sight as long as I, one learns to know the scent of changing emotions. I smell your anger. Your fury. Your helpless rage." She let her head drop backward and made a great show of sniffing the air. "The perfume of your fear...best of all. *Magnifico.* But not so fine as the fragrance of your pain, I think."

The door opened, admitting Leah, all alone. She didn't give Marcus so much as a glance as she crossed the room to Donnatella's side.

"Madre? Something's wrong with Shannon. I think she's ill."

Donnatella frowned. "Shannon is never ill."

Leah looked at him then. Two bright red spots of color had formed high on her cheekbones. Her eyes sparked at him from across the room. He could practically taste the adrenaline coursing through her, and it sparked a rush of his own. Something was definitely up.

She turned back to the Madre and said, "I think

it's her stomach. She said she thought she'd eaten something bad."

Donnatella's frown deepened. "This is most inconvenient. I'll need to summon another acolyte."

"No need to bother, Madre." Leah leaned in close to the other woman, and softened her voice 'til Marcus could barely make out her words. "What do you require? I'm ready to serve."

He watched Donnatella's face for signs of suspicion. She appeared to consider Leah's suggestion. Finally, she smiled. "*Sí, cara.* I will choose to trust you."

Donnatella stretched up to whisper in Leah's ear. Marcus watched Leah's face as she listened. Her eyes widened, and she bit her lip. Then she nodded and turned away toward the cabinet. He glanced at Yugiya, who was also watching the action on the other side of the room. If he could just pivot quickly enough, he might be able to disarm her—or maybe grab the debris from the table and use it as a weapon—

"Detective?"

It was the first time Leah had addressed him since leaving him the previous morning. He turned to look at her. She was moving toward him, and he noticed her feet were bare. What'd happened to those stupid shoes? Then he saw what she had in her hands, and tried not to lose his shit entirely.

She held a tray. Arrayed upon it were several articles that shone and twinkled in the flickering candlelight, including a chrome-and-leather ball-gag—several sizes larger than the one Shannon had forced into Leah's mouth—two ivory-handled filleting knives of differing lengths, and the largest dildo he'd ever seen. The fact that this fake cock appeared to be made of stainless steel was only secondary to its massive girth. His entire body clenched as he stared at the tray, and then up into Leah's face, which wore a perfectly blank expression.

"Please arrange yourself on the bench so that I can fasten the restraints." She didn't quite meet his eyes as she said it.

"You're kidding, right?"

She looked straight into his face then. "What makes you think any of this is a joke, Detective?" A muscle in her jaw twitched. The tension radiating from her body was like a tangible force, pushing at him. "Do it, please."

"Hear how gracious is our little sparrow, Detective? How politely she speaks? She is preparing to conclude her test of loyalty. Her mission is to make you suffer for three hours, without respite. To free your soul from its prison within your flesh and bone." Donnatella's voice dropped, and she spoke as if she were savoring the words. "And then she will help you make the ultimate sacrifice, *sí?* And you will be ready. You will be grateful, as your friend was grateful. In the end, he could not even scream, so great was his gratitude, *sí?* It will be the same with you, I promise."

He glanced at Yugiya, who'd moved nearer again and stood at the ready.

Fuck. This was really going to happen. They were going to torture him to death.

"Please, Detective," Leah said. "Don't make me ask Yugiya to force you." Her eyes had filled with tears. He watched her blink them back, but she couldn't seem to do the same with her expression of pleading and desperation. She stared at him so hard he felt her gaze drill into his brain.

Trust me, Marcus. Just a little longer.

He almost nodded, then caught himself and glanced over his shoulder at Yugiya. She was watching them closely. He moved to the bench and bent over it, placing himself in exactly the same position Leah had occupied only half an hour earlier. He caught a whiff of her scent, musky and sharp, as he stretched himself over the leather.

"Do not forget to inject him, my sweet little Leah. We wish to let the good Detective have the...how do you say it? The full experience, *sî*?"

He started, every nerve in his body on red alert. No...not that fucking drug again.

Leah's voice came from somewhere behind him. "But, Madre, I thought Shannon said—"

"Shannon is overly cautious in her zeal to serve." Donnatella's voice had grown cold and hard in the space of a second. "Inject him."

He stood, pushing away from the leather. Yugiya was at his side, instantly, but she made no move to threaten him with her blade. He watched as Leah chose a syringe from the scattered group on the floor, and then an unbroken bottle of the drug. It glowed green and vicious-looking in the soft light.

He could see her fingers shake and fumble the job of filling the syringe. Could see how red her face had grown. She kept glancing at the door. As if she were expecting something...someone, maybe?

As if on cue, the door slammed open and Shannon charged in. There was blood on her face, running from a gash over her right eye. It looked deep, that gash. Deep and painful. Marcus loved that gash.

But his attention was instantly diverted by the rolling gray cloud that followed the bleeding barmaid into the room. Smoke. And a lot of it.

Shannon slammed the door behind her. "What did you do, you bitch?" She threw herself at Leah and wrapped her hands around her throat, forcing her to her knees. Marcus moved instinctively, and had nearly reached them when he felt Yugiya's blade at the back of his neck. He ducked and did a quick spin. She wasn't the only one who had studied the more violent arts.

He came up facing her. She held the katana before her defensively. In the girl's black eyes raged a battle between fear and resolve.

"You're not going to kill me," he told her. "Back off, run away, while you've got the chance."

Her eyelid flickered, just the twitch of a muscle. She didn't move. But behind her, on the other side of the room, Donnatella had finally caught a clue.

"What is happening? Shannon? I smell..." The Madre's mouth contorted, and her hands came up to curl into fists on either side of her face. "Is it smoke? Is it, Shannon?" The terror in her voice was almost as satisfying as seeing the barmaid bleed. A weakness. Finally. And a fatal one, if the amount of smoke flowing in from beneath the door was any indication.

"Shannon! Help me!" She took a step forward and stumbled over nothing, plainly caught out helpless by her own fear. Marcus watched as her perfectly smug and controlled manner crumbled into confusion and fear. He almost wished he could feel a little sympathy. It must've been horrifying to think of flames coming near when you couldn't see to run away.

He glanced at the pair to his right. The blonde's hands were still around Leah's throat, but she was looking at Donnatella, indecision plain on her face. Finally, she let go and allowed Leah to fall forward, face-first onto the cement. Shannon darted to the Madre and took her arm, steadying her. Then she turned to Yugiya.

"You stay here with them." She led Donnatella to the door and stopped to look at Marcus. "Don't get any fancy ideas, cop. I'll be back to finish the two of you."

Donnatella had begun to sob. She clung to Shannon's arm like a frightened child. "Please, *cara*. Take me out. Take me away from the fire."

The door slammed behind them. He turned to face Yugiya through the haze of smoke. "Don't listen to her. You can still run. You can get away. If you stay here—" The sound of sirens cut him off. "You hear that? They must be close—must be right outside if we can hear them down here." He took a step toward her, and she lifted the katana. But her face was unsure. Frightened. And very, very young. He stared at her, realizing for the first time that she couldn't be more than sixteen.

The Madre had much to answer for, including murder, but this? This was the worst.

Still Yugiya held fast, her blade aloft and ready. Marcus turned his head slightly, just enough to see Leah from the corner of his eye. She lay motionless on the floor, but he could hear her breathing quicken. He saw her hand twitch and curl into a fist.

And then she rolled, catching Yugiya by surprise. She took the girl out at her knees. Knocked her down. Kicked away the katana, all in one rapid movement. Even in the chaos of the moment, he had to be impressed.

He watched her crouch over the now-cringing girl, grab her by the hair, and look straight into her terrified face. "Run," she said, clean and sure and not even very loud.

She gave Yugiya a shove and the girl was on her feet, sprinting for the door. She opened it, and smoke billowed in. More of it than he'd expected. The room had begun to grow warm.

He took Leah's arm and pulled her to her feet. "Where's the fire?"

"First floor bathroom. I decorated it with paper towels and toilet paper, then set it on fire with this." She coughed into her fist and held up a lighter— tiny, pink and plastic. The kind you could buy at the grocery checkout. "When Shannon came in to see what was taking me long, I clocked her with the heel of my shoe."

The pounding of footsteps down the hall saved him from asking if that had been her scheme all along. Because if it had? He might've been forced to kill her. Both their lives at the mercy of those bugfuck crazy bitches, and she'd planned to save them with a lighter and a pair of heels?

As it was, he kissed her much harder than was strictly necessary.

Three firefighters appeared in the doorway, and the next little while was all about getting out of the building. Then they were sitting on the curb, watching Hotel California's soggy swan song, their matching nakedness covered by blankets. Marcus got the attention of a passing uniformed cop.

"Did they get everybody out?"

The cop shrugged. "They only found the two of you. If there was anybody else, they found their own way out."

Leah looked at him, her eyes wide. There was a smudge of soot on her cheek and another on the end of her nose. She opened her mouth to tell him something, but an EMT interrupted by insisting she join him in his ambulance for a quick exam.

"I'll be right back," she said.

He made sure he was gone before she could make good on her promise.

Chapter Nine

She knew he was on his way four days before he showed up at her door. Dreamed about him three nights running. Saw him standing there in the hall outside her apartment, with his hands shoved into the pockets of a brand new leather jacket and a smirk on his face. Looked like maybe he'd gotten a haircut, too.

That morning—a full two weeks after the fire that took out the entire back half of Hotel California and ended with the city demolishing the building— she woke early and made a pitcher of sangria. She bathed carefully, dressed herself in a blue silk kimono she found in the back of her closet, lit some incense, and sat down to wait. When he hadn't shown up by noon, she began to wonder if the dreams were wishful thinking.

She remembered what he'd said. "If we get out of this alive, I'm gonna track you down and fuck you stupid." Not the most romantic proposition she'd ever heard. And maybe the fact that he'd already fucked her negated it. But a girl could hope.

She got up off the sofa and poured another glass. The phone rang. She didn't bother to look at the caller ID.

"Hi, Gram."

"Is he there?" Her grandmother sounded excited. It was a little disturbing, to tell the truth.

"Is who where?"

"Don't be coy, Leah. It's unbecoming in a woman of your age."

Leah sighed. She'd been doing that a lot lately.

"No, he's not here. I don't think he's coming."

"Yes, he is. In fact...go fix your hair."

"What?" She set the glass on the counter and ran a hand over the loose bun at the nape of her neck. "Why?"

"He's on his way up. Be sure to call me after and tell me everything. And remember, Leah—destiny is all in the details."

What the hell did that mean? Leah didn't have time to ask, because her grandmother had hung up.

She stood in the kitchen and waited, knowing Marcus was in the elevator. Because Gram might be a pain in the ass, but she rarely got stuff like this wrong. Leah counted to ten...and then kept counting. Twenty. Thirty. Thirty-five and...

The sound of the bell made her jump. She set the sangria—which she'd managed to splash down the front of the kimono—on the counter and tried not to run to the door.

In her dreams, he hadn't brought flowers, but now he was holding a dozen blooms of the purest white.

"Innocence and truth? You really think so?" She stared at him over top of the bouquet he'd just handed her. Yeah, he'd definitely gotten a haircut. And now, minus the heavy stubble on his jaw, he looked a lot less dangerous. Funny how he didn't feel any less dangerous to her heightened senses.

He looked confused. "Huh?"

"White roses. They symbolize..." She shook her head. "Never mind."

"You don't like them? Here, let me—" He reached for the flowers and she stepped back, forcing him to move into the apartment.

"I like them fine. Come on into the kitchen."

He followed her. She could feel his gaze on her back and wondered what he was thinking. She didn't look at him again until the roses were safely stowed in a vase on the counter, and she'd poured him a drink.

"You weren't easy to find," he said, and drank half the glassful in one long swallow...which made her think he might be just a little nervous. So good to know she wasn't the only one. "All I had was your first name and the fact that you're an English professor."

She shrugged. "I would've given you my number if you hadn't...you know...disappeared."

"It wasn't anything personal. I had a lot to do."

She nodded. "Of course."

"Listen, I had to check in with the Chief and give a full report." He frowned , and his jaw was set in a tight line. "Then make sure there was an APB out on DeTagliera and Shannon—"

"You have nothing to justify, Detective. Frankly, I'm surprised you're here. It can't be easy..." She let her voice trail off and took another sip of sangria. All at once, she wished she hadn't answered the door. Or that she'd gone with straight tequila instead of this fruity red sludge. Then at least she'd be halfway numb by now.

"What can't be easy?"

Great. Now he sounded defensive to the tenth power.

She shook her head. "Nothing. I appreciate your visit. Is it official business?"

Maybe they had a lead on the Madre. Surely, after the hours Leah had spent giving a highly detailed statement and being examined by a police department-approved physician, someone would've called if they'd actually made an arrest. All that humiliation deserved a little consideration, didn't it?

"No," Marcus said, "it's not official business, and what did you mean when you said 'it can't be easy'?"

Leah turned away from him, dumped the rest of her drink into the sink and stared at the wall. "It can't be easy seeing me again after what you went through. What I helped put you through."

"Whoa." He came up behind her and put a hand on her arm. "What happened to me was in the line of duty. Besides, you saved my life."

She turned her head and looked at him. "And maybe that's part of the problem?"

His face changed. Hardened again for a second or two. Then he smiled. "I'm not that much of a jerk. A woman can save my ass anytime."

"And when you look at me, you don't...it doesn't..." She wasn't even sure where she was going with this. But it was difficult to believe he didn't associate her with some seriously traumatic shit.

He moved the hand that rested on her arm to her shoulder. "When I look at you, I feel grateful."

"Grateful." Lovely. Oh well. It was better than hating the sight of her.

"Yes, grateful. And I'm glad to see you again. I have questions."

"Ah, of course." She ran her hand down the front of the kimono, suddenly self-conscious. What must he think of her, greeting him dressed like a high-class prostitute? "Well, go on. Shoot."

He let his hand drop and stepped away from her. "First of all, I'm going to assume you knew DeTagliera's fire phobia from having worked for her before?"

Leah nodded. "It wasn't something anyone ever discussed, especially with someone like me. I was sort of...low on the totem pole. But I knew. I..." In point of fact, she'd dreamt about it, all those years ago. But she wasn't going to tell him that.

"But you were being groomed? To be an acolyte, like Shannon?" His voice had slipped into the cadence of interrogation. Clipped and careful.

"Yes."

"And why did you leave?"

She sighed. "What difference does it make?"

"I'd like to know."

"But I don't have to answer if I don't want to?"

He shook his head. "No. But I'm asking you to."

She turned away from him again. This was getting to be too much. Too painful. Maybe if she just said it out loud—told him about the visions and all the other special "gifts" she inherited from Gram—he'd go away and leave her alone. God knew enough men had. She said, "I had a vision. I saw the Madre order an acolyte to slit a man's throat. I didn't know...I mean, I knew things got a little rough in Donnatella's private rooms. I heard the screaming. But everybody always seemed to leave happy." She looked at him. "I left the day after I had the vision. You can believe me or not, I don't care."

"I believe you."

She stared at him, not sure. What if this was a game? What if the Santa Rosa P.D. had decided to hold her responsible in Donnatella's place?

"Why?" she asked him.

"Because you magically appeared and disappeared in the basement of Hotel California? Because I could hear you talking in my head? Because you saved my life?" He moved closer to her again. "I think we already covered this."

"I..." She felt tears gather in her eyes and fought them back. "I didn't think you remembered. I thought maybe the drug...and when I came back, you looked at me like you didn't know me."

"Never let it be said I can't work a poker face, baby. But I have perfect recall on the subject of you."

She laughed, and it kind of sounded like a sob. When he reached for her, she fell against him. The leather of his coat smelled raw and musky against her face. She let herself breathe and willed the tears away. "Any other questions, Detective?"

"Just one. Were you behind the anonymous call that sent the fire department to the club? The dispatcher said it had been phoned in by some guy. Very nervous."

She craned her head back to look up at him

without leaving the inner sanctum of his embrace. "Yes. But that's all I'm saying about that."

"Right." He pulled her tight against him once more.

"So now what?" She swallowed the ball of tension that had risen to the back of her throat. "Is this the part where you fuck me stupid?"

His laughter rumbled against her ear, way down deep in his chest. "Was hoping you'd forgotten that."

"Yeah, well. My recall isn't too shabby, either."

He worked a hand under her chin and lifted her face to look at him. "Leah, I need to know. What happened between us...what they made me do—"

"It's all right."

"It's not all right. It was rape."

"Then they raped both of us, didn't they?"

"But—"

"You said no, right? You did everything you could to avoid going through with it, up to letting them kill us."

There was a pause while his eyes searched her face. "You're sure? Because if you have even one doubt, I'll walk out of here and you'll never see me again."

"That sounds like a threat."

He didn't answer. Just looked at her and looked some more.

"Really, Marcus. It's okay." She pressed her face into his chest again to hide the red flush that was building in her cheeks. "Besides...I think you know I wanted you. How could you miss it?"

He cleared his throat. "I don't like to assume stuff like that."

"Right. Like there wasn't enough evidence to prove it."

They stood there, holding each other in her kitchen for another minute. Maybe two. He rubbed slow circles against her back, his hand feeling big and warm through the silk of the kimono.

Finally, he said, "Leah? Should I go, or—"

"No." Okay, that didn't sound overly eager or anything. "I mean, unless you want to."

"I'm more interested in what you want." He set her away from him and looked down at her, his eyes dilated and intense. "Tell me what you want, Leah. I'll do anything."

Whoa. An exact quote from her dream all those nights ago. Déjà vu didn't begin to cover it. She grabbed his hand. "How did you get this scar?" She ran her thumb over the crescent-shaped mark and heard the faraway sound of shattering glass one more time.

"I put my fist through a window when I was fourteen. Why?"

She shook her head. What had Gram said? Destiny is all in the details?

She glanced at him and then back at the scar. "Why did you do that? Break the window, I mean?"

"It was nothing. There was this woman. She was being...hurt. I could see through the window, the guy was beating the shit out of her. So..."

"So you saved her."

"I guess."

She turned his hand over and pressed a kiss to the center of his palm. "Take me to bed, Detective, before I jump you right here on the kitchen floor."

He peeled off his jacket and tossed it aside. They walked hand-in-hand to her room. He stopped her in the doorway and said, "Can I kiss you now? You said I could kiss you—"

"After you bought me dinner. It's not even lunchtime yet."

"But you'll make an exception."

"Awfully sure of yourself, aren't you?"

The feeling of his mouth on hers lit her up, burning down deep like she'd swallowed a mouthful of hot, spicy broth. Like heated lightning flashing in her veins. Like...like...like nothing that could be described with some lame, English 101 simile-slash-metaphor combination. Something inside her went soft and needy, and she clutched at him.

"Now," she said. "Right now."

"What do you want?" His voice was tight through his teeth, low and coarse and rubbing like sandpaper across every nerve in her body. "Tell me what you want. I need to hear you say it."

She backed toward the bed, pulling him along by his belt-buckle. "Want you to fuck me stupid, Detective. Just like you promised."

"I can do that."

"Yeah, I bet you can."

He pushed her down, knocking her back onto the bed. Then he rolled them so she lay on top, and held still as she worked open the buttons of his shirt and the buckle, button and zipper that held up his jeans. In another few seconds, he was naked under her. And then she felt shy. Like she hadn't been up close and personal with his body. In particular, his cock, which lay tight to his belly and twitched when the sleeve of her kimono brushed over the head. She watched his face as she took him in her hand. Closed her eyes and felt the blood-hot shaft. Remembered.

He groaned her name when she squeezed, and rolled them again—a half-turn this time. They landed on their sides, facing each other. He grabbed her knee and lifted so that it hooked over his hip. "I can't wait. Have to...next time—"

"Next time can be all about the gentle and romantic." She leaned over and licked across the corded muscle of his bicep. Then she sunk her teeth into his flesh, hard. He started, his hips thrusting forward against her. She reached between them and guided him home.

"There's gonna be payback for that, you know," he said, his breath hot on her face. "And I promise, it'll be a bitch." Then he was fucking her, the slick-rough press of his cock making her shake and bite back whimpers. He drew nearly all the way out, teasing her with the tip, dancing it over her clit and then sliding back down to push in. He grabbed her hips and angled her body so his mouth could reach her nipples. He took one in his mouth and raked it with his teeth—a threat that was more like a promise.

"Please," she said. "Please, ohgodplease." She didn't even know what she was asking for, unless it was more. He seemed to understand, because his strokes got longer. Harder. He ground against her in a slow circle at the height of every thrust until she buried her face in his neck and sobbed.

He rolled them a third time, then he was moving them up the bed with every thrust, rucking the blankets and sheets under them. Her shaking gave way to shuddering. The muscles in her belly and thighs tightened defensively. So good...so hard and so good, just like she needed it.

When she came, pleasure curled into every nerve ending, rolling out and back again, not letting her breathe or think or do anything but try to survive it. She felt him pull up tight against her, pulsing deep inside. In a choked voice, he whispered her name. She wrapped her arms around his neck and kissed his face. Fierce little pecks and nips that made him laugh when he finally finished coming.

It took ten minutes for her to find her voice again. They lay side-by-side staring at the ceiling. Not touching except for their intertwined fingers.

"They're still out there somewhere," she said. "Shannon and the Madre."

He turned his head to look at her. "Are you scared?"

"Are you?"

He cleared his throat and looked away. "I'm not happy about it, I'll say that much. Especially since they know you. They can find you if they try."

"What should I do about it? I'm not abandoning

my life for them."

"No. But you shouldn't be alone."

She lay there in silence for a few seconds. "Is that an offer?"

"Do you want it to be?"

She turned onto her side to study him. "I can take care of myself, you know. I'm not helpless."

"Yeah. So long as they keep making disposable lighters and stupid shoes, you're golden."

"Listen, you. I saved your ass."

"You did. And I told you, I'm okay with admitting that."

"You are? You're sure?"

"Yeah, if you're okay with admitting you could use a little in-house protection."

She stared at him some more. "We could try it. Temporarily. But if you change your mind—"

"That works both ways. You might hate having me around."

"You surprise me, Detective. I didn't expect you to be so...enlightened."

He snorted. "I'll check back with you in a week on that subject."

"You do that." She slipped her fingers from between his and lifted her hand to stroke his chest. "Now...about that payback? What exactly did you have in mind?"

He grinned at her. Naughty. Maybe even a little dangerous.

She'd never felt so safe in her life.

Miranda Writes

Cassidy Kent

Also by Cassidy Kent

Sunset Key
Raleigh in Rio
Dolce & Diana

Chapter One

She lit up his dull world like a firecracker on the Fourth of July. Ben knew that now as he leaned over her body.

Miss Julie's flaming red tresses splashed the warm hay with bright licks of color, the olive tone of her skin revealed as he pushed up her petticoats inch by inch. Her long, luscious legs spread slightly, even while her mouth played coy games with his mind.

"Do you really want me, Benjamin?" she asked, her lower lip quivering with apprehension and excitement.

Did he ever.

He woke up nights, sweating and dreaming over the ranch owner's daughter. She even haunted his days...

And now here she was, opening up for him like a sensual gift, allowing him to love her with his body as much as he did with his soul. Damned if he would pass up the chance.

He slipped an arm underneath her back, caring not for the needle-pricks of hay. All he could think about was his hand on her leg, sliding irreverently up the inside of her thigh. When he reached the gate of her pleasure, Ben took that moment to kiss her. Miss Julie's mouth opened gratefully, and when her silky, pink tongue slipped across Ben's, his erection pressed against her exposed flesh.

He tore the sleeve of her pretty rosebud ball gown and claimed her breast, groaning at the feel of her budding nipple against his palm.

"*Take me, Benjamin. Please,*" she begged.

"*I can't deny a lady her pleasure.*"

Her need for his sudden entry demonstrated itself when he palmed her sex. Lush, liquid desire covered his hand, and he knew he ought not make her wait. He removed—

BANG! BANG! BANG!

Miranda Franklin jumped out of her computer chair and gasped. Her two calico companions marched toward the sound, alternately hissing and mewling in defense of their owner against the perpetrator pounding on her door.

"It's okay, babies." She ushered the two kittens into the tiny bathroom of her one-bedroom apartment. "Be quiet now, Heckle and Jeckle. One wrong move and you'll get all three of us kicked out."

Miranda padded to the door in her writing attire: rubber flip-flops and a ratty green-and-white striped bathrobe. She pulled her dark, frizzy mass of hair into a ponytail in a futile effort to look presentable.

"Yes?" Expecting to see her landlord, Mr. Levinsky, she opened the door. She found herself talking to no one in particular, much to her relief. With a shrug, she almost closed the door, until she noticed the envelope taped to the frame. The outside had been boldly stamped *THIRD NOTICE.*

"Damnit," she muttered as she slumped down onto her futon.

Things had gone quite well for Miranda until just lately. Only six months ago, a mid-level agent had taken an interest in her romance novels and managed to garner her a two-book deal. At the time, a seven-thousand-dollar advance had sounded like a lot of money.

After a few rent checks and some major repair work to her Ford Fiesta, not much remained except a few measly dollars stashed in an old vase beneath her sink.

Not to mention, the same said agent had almost guaranteed her an outstanding advance if she could come up with a third book proposal within thirty days. "They're really looking for something different. Something vibrant and sexy that will knock their socks off," he had said. If she could hit on that, she could say goodbye to her unpleasant landlord and unreliable car.

Miranda knew an amazing cash-cow story was in her somewhere, but unpaid utilities and hungry cats proved to be quite distracting.

"Speaking of which..." She went to the pitiful shelving unit that she called a pantry in search of a can or two of cat food. After zeroing in on her prey, she peeled back the canisters and set them down on the kitchen floor.

After she let Heckle and Jeckle loose from the bathroom, Miranda decided she was somewhat famished, as well. A quick inventory of the fridge indicated she would find no help there. A bottle of vodka in the freezer and a long-neglected carton of Chinese takeout mocked her appetite and drove her to get dressed and face the world.

If the township of Elmhaven could be called "the world."

The little slice of Americana boasted one main street, surprisingly not *called* Main Street, but rather New Elm Street. A small park covered the expanse between the row of shops there and Miranda's apartment building. Although the skies were quite clear, she borrowed a five from her hoarded rainy day money and set off across the park.

The first leaves of October had just begun to fall, sprinkling the carpet of greenish grass with its autumnal decoration. Miranda sighed and wound her nubby orange scarf around her neck once more for good measure, her strides swooshing leaves in either direction. She absolutely loved this time of year, but the prospect of poverty and writer's block made it difficult to enjoy the simpler pleasures of life.

Some time ago, she had resolved to suck it up and get a part-time job. Miranda had adamantly hoped the advance would be enough to allow her to write for a day-job, but she wasn't too proud to admit defeat, if only for a little while. Problem was, none of the quaint little shops along New Elm Street *ever* seemed to be hiring. With such a small town, and therefore a small population, not much changed, including retail staff.

"No use dwelling on it," she said aloud, her thoughts moving to what she would buy with her cash. *A meatball sub from the café next to town hall, maybe?* "Mmm…"

Her path through the park passed several old wooden benches re-painted a brilliant cherry red. Miranda often stopped to idle awhile on one of them, sometimes bringing along a notebook to jot down plotlines that popped into her head. Today, there was no time for that, not with her stomach rumbling.

"Excuse me, miss…" A faint voice called to her from a bench by the sidewalk. Miranda came closer, curious about its owner.

"Here, dear, excuse me." An ancient old woman sat on the bench, surrounded by a multitude of old shopping bags. She leaned on a cane, a headscarf tied beneath her chin. Two blind, milk-pale blue eyes were set deep in her papery face. "Could you spare some change? I'm quite hungry."

Miranda almost left with a polite shake of her head. Then she thought about her own grandmother, an elderly lady just like this woman, except safe and sound in the attic room of Miranda's parents' house, rather than begging for quarters in a cold, New England park.

She slipped her hand into her pocket and pulled

out the five. Placing the bill in the old lady's outstretched palm, Miranda found her wrist suddenly grasped by the woman's other hand.

"Thank you, dear. I have only one thing to give you in return. Such a kindness, after all, deserves another." She patted the bench beside her, the smile on her lips somehow reaching her sightless eyes. "Sit beside me for a moment and I will read your fortune."

Miranda raised an eyebrow, but sat hastily. After all, this could prove to be excellent fodder for her next story. "You can read my palm?" she asked.

The old woman laughed. "I used to be able to read a great many other things—tea leaves, spheres, cards. Now I save my gift for very important purposes. But palms…palms I can still read."

Miranda flushed. "Forgive me, I didn't mean to doubt your abilities."

"No need to ask my forgiveness, child, your aura tells me your intentions are good." The woman looked up at the sky as she pulled Miranda's palm into her lap and fell silent for several minutes, the rustle of wind through the trees above the only audible sound. She ran her index finger over the tender skin of Miranda's palm, the various bumps and ridges, and the fingers one by one, until she stopped at the ring finger.

"Nope, still not married." Miranda rolled her eyes. "No matter how hard Mom pushes."

The woman dropped her empty gaze from the sky and down to Miranda. "You're a writer."

Miranda's mouth gaped open and she nodded. The old woman gave her a knowing smile. "You write wonderful stories of romance and adventure."

"If only you worked for Random House," Miranda quipped.

The woman fingered the crease at the top of Miranda's palm, lost in thought. "And yet, your heart line tells me you've never been in love."

Her pulse pounded at the statement's intimate nature. "Mom put you up to this, didn't she?" she deadpanned.

"Shh. Your fate is now. See this line?" The woman pointed to a long line down the center of her palm. "It shows when you make choices and when your fate chooses events for you." She began to hum softly, intermittently between pronouncements.

"A new opportunity finds you very soon. A tremendous adventure will sweep you up...and, just like in your stories, you will meet a man. He is not without power, but has lost something he needs to regain. You help him to find it." A smirk flickered across the old lady's face. "And he helps you in return."

* * * *

Moments later, Miranda was on her way again. She may have been five bucks lighter, but that loss caused an inexplicable buoyancy in her step.

My fate is now.

She ambled past the shops and restaurants of New Elm Street, a vague idea forming for her proposal. Then she saw the shop on the corner of New Elm and Oakhaven.

Farra's Fortunes, a newly painted sign read. *20% off all Cheiromancy, Cartomancy, and Crystallomancy services.*

It couldn't be just a coincidence, Miranda realized. She needed a job, she'd just had her fortune read, and this could be the beginning of the adventure that would kick-start her proposal. Although no *Help Wanted* sign hung in the window, she felt confident they might just need her.

A jingling doorbell announced Miranda's entrance into the shop, the stale warmth of the musty establishment providing some relief from the chill of the outdoors. The shop smelled odd. Mothballs, ink, and a strange, bleach scent. A faint whiff of incense floated above all of these odors in a fragrance that was only slightly more pleasing. She wrinkled her nose.

Patchouli, maybe?

Miranda took an unofficial tour of Farra's Fortunes, small as the place was. An old Tiffany lamp hung low over a small table in the corner. A decaying, midnight blue velvet cloth draped its surface, upon which sat a small black box. She noticed the figurines on the shelves and the display cases of various essential oils and incense holders, all covered in a layer of dust.

"Doesn't seem like this place gets much action," Miranda muttered. "Strange, in a location so close to Salem."

"I thought the same thing, myself." A petite, elderly woman emerged from behind a curtain covering the doorway to a back room. "I picked this spot myself, but we haven't gotten many visitors yet, I'm afraid."

The doleful expression on the woman's tiny face made Miranda light up with compassion. She looked like a kindly grandmother whose batch of chocolate chip cookies had just burned. "There probably aren't too many people in Elmhaven who know what cheiromancy is," she said, indicating the sign out front. "Maybe you just need a little help with promotions."

The woman giggled, pressing a hand to her mouth. "That's the last thing we need. We like to keep our clientele selective. Word of mouth, you know."

Miranda raised an eyebrow. "I guess. So, you're Farra?"

"Goodness, no!" The old woman smiled and looked about the store. "Farra was my grandmother. You can call me Edith."

"Pleasure to meet you, Edith." Miranda extended her hand for a shake, surprised to find the woman's shake was a hearty one despite her frail appearance.

"I came to inquire about a job."

Edith eyed Miranda from head to toe. "You have the gift, do you?"

Miranda's mouth twitched to the side, as was her habit when about to lie. "Yep. I sure do." After all, if the bag lady in the park could have it, why couldn't she?

Edith smiled sweetly. "I'm sorry, dear. You may have the gift, but you just don't have *the look*. People come here expecting the whole shebang, and you certainly don't look like any of *my* Gypsy ancestors."

Miranda thought about that for a moment. There had to be some way of convincing the woman. She whipped her scarf out and wrapped it around her head. When the fabric was tied at the back of her neck, Miranda made sure to display the gold hoops of her earrings. She closed her eyes and whirled her hands over an imaginary crystal ball, faking her best Gypsy accent.

"Though you have not yet experienced love, I sense that you will find it this year with a dark, handsome man." Miranda opened her eyes and searched Edith's face for a reaction.

She must have seen some merit in the performance, for the woman's skeptical expression warmed to a mischievous grin. "It appears you do have *the gift*. Let's see if we can hone it with a bit of on-the-job training."

Miranda smiled at the nice old lady's offer.

Completed book proposal, here I come.

* * * *

Matthew Archer lifted the binoculars to his eyes and zoomed in for a closer look at the brunette. He gasped, not expecting the powerful allure of her eyes, or that spark of fire he hadn't seen in a woman since who-knew-when. She wasn't a beauty by any means, but his groin automatically tightened in response to her brilliant smile. The way her long, curly mane bounced when she moved her head, the way her smooth milky skin led to a nice set of...

His imagination took off like a runaway horse and his mind filled with images of himself fingering those thick brown locks, then roughly fisting a handful, all the while losing himself in the blaze of desire flaming within the depths of her eyes.

Get a hold of yourself, Archer. Now's not the time to think with your dick.

He groaned in disgust at the momentary weakness and chalked it up to a non-existent love life since his break up with Carrie three months ago. Their relationship had subsisted on the mutual grounds of filling each other's physical needs. He'd been perfectly content until she'd told him he was too cold inside.

What the hell did that mean? *Too cold inside?* Okay, maybe his love life had fallen to second place in the race for his attention, but his work was his life. There could never be anything that beat the adrenaline rush of a good chase, or finding hidden clues to close a case.

Jeez, what was with women and their need for love? Carrie had thrown him for a loop. Archer's frown deepened and his irritation transferred to the woman on the other side of his binoculars. She had just induced a longing he had been damned good at repressing until now.

How could he find himself attracted to someone as mousy as her? He'd seen a lot of desperate types come through Farra's Fortunes, but this one beat all. Maybe if the woman wasn't bundled up in all that mess she might have a chance of landing a man. Instead, she was putting all her faith in a fraudulent fortuneteller who would blind her with promises of God-knows-what.

Archer reached for the coffee cup and took a long swallow, his eyes never leaving the scene unfolding before him. One minute the woman was speaking to the elderly shopkeeper and the next she had pulled the raggedy material from her neck and wrapped it around her head like a makeshift turban.

"Well, I'll be..." He nearly crushed the paper cup, slamming it back in its holder. "She's a member of the club." Archer frowned, disappointed to discover the brunette was involved in such shady dealings. She didn't look the part, but these days you never could tell.

Damn shame. Archer liked it better when he thought she was a patron, yet his odd attraction for her wasn't doused by the revelation. His interest was only further piqued, and he wanted to know what had led her to this criminal route.

Archer's jaw clenched in annoyance when he thought about the enjoyment the woman was having at ruining the lives of others. He could only imagine what schemes the two of them were cooking up in there. The way the brunette rehearsed her psychic mumbo-jumbo further incensed him. He knew the locals would no doubt buy the act with a sincere face like hers.

As long as Archer was back in town, he wasn't about to let some crooks take hard-earned money out of the hands of the good citizens of Elmhaven. Not if he could help it.

One thing was for sure, he couldn't believe his luck at stumbling across the counterfeiting operations in connection with the case his team had been trying to bust for months. Even more unbelievable was that the main players had been nestled in the sleepy town of Elmhaven, of all places. He just needed to pinpoint who the ringleader actually was.

Archer felt like letting out a howl of excitement. Christ, he was born and raised just two blocks from the main street and nothing like this had ever happened in Mayberry! The timing couldn't have been better. Maybe leaving Jersey after his suspension from the bureau wasn't a completely fucked up mess after all.

Now, if only he could get his hands on some shred of proof. This would be the proof he needed to hammer the last nail in the coffin and put this bitch to bed.

A smug smile of satisfaction formed on his lips.

He couldn't wait to see the captain's face when he forked over the evidence and single-handedly uncovered the mastermind of the counterfeiting ring. Archer would surely be reinstated and back on the streets doing what he did best in no time at all.

Bite me, Cap'n Jack!

Archer's adrenaline shot up, elated by the unofficial undercover work. The elation wore off as day turned to night and still they chatted away. Just when he thought the night might drag on forever, the two women broke from their deep discussion and exchanged information. He adjusted the lens, but couldn't get a good look at the paper handed to the brunette. A few minutes later the mousy broad left the shop.

His lips curled in disgust at the devious elation etched on her youthful face as she walked. Women were a conniving lot, and this one looked to be one he'd enjoy apprehending. Archer threw the binoculars on the passenger seat and turned the ignition on to follow her.

He knew it would be too risky to try to bust the operation alone, but he figured he'd gather enough evidence and then call in for backup. It wasn't like he was breaking any rules.

Archer's suspension was a damn joke, and everyone in the office knew it. The captain had a vendetta against him ever since he'd found out Archer had been sleeping with his daughter. In reality, did anyone really give a shit if he roughed up some drug dealer who didn't give a fuck who he hurt?

Sure, he followed rules, but he didn't see anything wrong in obtaining information his own way. Besides, the dealer had a reputation for seducing kids who'd been kicked around by the system. Some of the runners were often neglected latchkeys who craved love. Anyone paying them the least bit of attention had their loyalty.

Matt always had a soft spot for outcasts, and he made it his duty to help as many of these kids as possible to discover a better path than their current one. It was bad enough to hear the statistics on these youths robbed of their childhood. Hell, he'd seen his fair share of young victims face-to-face, so it wasn't tough to exact a bit of revenge on those deserving of it. Someone had to protect these kids and it might as well be him.

Matt slowed the car , and pulled into an empty parking space. The woman had sprinted across the path and he got out to follow her on foot. Somewhere along the way his eyes took notice of the sway of her hips and her long, lean legs as she walked through the streets at a hasty pace.

Focus, Archer. Matt wondered if it was the full moon playing tricks on him, because his sudden libido wasn't relenting. He tried his best to avoid admiring her backside and focused instead on the ugly battered shoes. The only problem was that his eyes managed to take an interest in her sexy ankles and the curve and slender shape of her calves in the sheer skirt.

He didn't know how long he shadowed her, but relief washed over him when she finally rounded a corner and took a short cut through a vacant alley. Matt hoped the night would end with more details than it began. Something tangible would make the last few weeks of excruciating boredom worthwhile.

The woman slowed her pace to glance over her shoulder, and Matt ducked into the shadows to avoid being discovered. The brunette stopped in front of a dilapidated apartment building, marred by cracked concrete and protected by bent metal bars over the windows. Not the finest section of town by any means, but he figured a woman with an unlawful background would want to hole up in a place like this.

Matt watched her unlock the aging gate and scurry in like a cat afraid of her own shadow. Her actions would have been endearing if she had been anybody else. The gate banged shut behind her and he let out a curse, knowing he wouldn't easily make it in that way. With a sigh, he considered waiting it out.

Over his dead body.

Matt's mind kicked into overdrive and he scanned the rows of windows, hoping to figure out which apartment was hers. Minutes ticked by before his gaze locked onto a shadow stumbling around in a darkened room before a flicker of light glowed within. A dim glow cascaded into several more and brought light to the darkness.

Why the hell wasn't she flipping on the lights?

Ah, candles.

Little Miss Gypsy intrigued him more each minute. After a bit of shuffling, her figure emerged and stopped in front of the open window. A smile touched his lips as he glimpsed the familiar mass of curls.

The soft cast of the moonlight made her a vision of loveliness. The ridiculous turban was gone and her silky hair spilled over her shoulders. Gone were all thoughts of his mission, the chase, and the discovery as she captivated him with her ethereal splendor.

His insides knotted up, mesmerized by her as she stood stoically, surrounded by the soft cloud of candlelight. She resembled a fairytale heroine, and he felt the coldness that had plagued his soul suddenly melt away as quickly as his senses.

Never in his life had Matt ached to hold someone, or hungered to possess another human being like he did at that moment. He tried to catch his breath and break the spell, and glanced up only to find the full moon laughing down at him.

Oh yeah, the cosmos were playing tricks on him and Matt Archer was in deep shit.

Chapter Two

Matt's eyes followed the dancing light shining off the candle as it created a visual path for the owner. Impatient for a closer look, he scanned the dirty alleyway for ideas to reach her window. His thoughts drifted to curiosity about her living space. How was it arranged? Did her possessions provide any clues about the woman?

His gaze skimmed the iron posts and metal scraps hanging off the aged building, and zeroed in on a fire escape that led up to her apartment. The stars must have aligned because this night had proved all too convenient. A strange superstition stirred within him, yet he couldn't fight his desire to see her up close.

After some maneuvering, Matt made it up to her floor and steadied himself on the platform as he peered inside. He felt guilty, a damn peeping Tom, but he coaxed himself into believing this was all for the sake of work.

Holy hell!

Matt almost went into cardiac arrest upon seeing her. He did a double, then a triple take, to make sure he wasn't imagining the scene playing out before him. The unexpected sexpot made his heart lurch and palms sweat from pure anticipation.

The woman stood barely clad before a mirror, staring at her own reflection as in a trance. She had shed the bulky clothing and was clad only in a transparent chemise and a thin, knee-length skirt. He watched her run her fingers through her hair, then pull it up into a French twist atop her head as she peered into the glass.

Matt couldn't pull his stare away from her. He held his breath, waiting anxiously for her next move. When he thought he couldn't stand the hesitation any longer, she touched those luscious lips and traced the shape with her fingertips, splaying lightly across them with a slow gentleness. Her hands continued onward, down her chin, lower to her throat and she closed her eyes, almost as if she imagined the caress of a lover.

Her nipples strained through the thin fabric and Matt had the urge to seize the hard pearls between his teeth. With a slow ease, the woman pushed the tiny straps off her shoulders, and the material swished to the floor at her feet. Her breasts bounced free from their restraints. The sight made him grow hard in response.

The multi-colored skirt followed the discarded chemise, pooling around her on the floor. One hand tenderly cupped a full globe while her free one caressed a path down her stomach until she reached the area just above her mound. Her hand skimmed across the lace panties, feeling the pattern sensually.

She inhaled deeply and her fingers continued the fiery path until she began her tender exploration. Archer's hand dropped to his crotch to adjust himself. In all his years he had never seen a woman more aware of her own body. This fascinated him and brought to light a fantasy that Archer would relish replaying in his head for years to come.

The torture continued when the woman slid off the underwear, now completely naked for him to enjoy. He drank in the sight of her milky flesh and shapely curves. His eyes dropped to her pussy and he knew without a doubt he was condemned to hell. He could easily eat that up all night long until she begged him to put her out of her misery.

The woman rubbed her breasts and savored the

feel of discovering herself. With a free hand, she soon dipped her fingers between the dusk of hairs and reached the spot she was searching for. Matt watched in utter fascination, as her hand teased her own flesh until her breathing visibly increased.

Her breath became labored, followed by soundless moans from the sensations of her self-love. He clenched his teeth as his cock swelled, his jeans cutting into his circulation. The woman squeezed her breast, her moans increasing with each stroke.

Matt's body hummed with awareness and lust as he devoured her erotic movements. He wanted to burst through the window and fuck her like she had obviously envisioned. He wanted to caress every inch of her with his tongue, to taste the sweetness of her body. How had he ever believed she was a mouse when she was clearly a vixen unleashing before his eyes?

His heart hammered against his chest as he imagined making love to her. He wanted to elicit the same reactions that her hand proved to provide for herself. He didn't believe much in potions and spells, yet she had cast a spell on him with every touch, every stroke, every flickering delight across her clit.

How could he be jealous of her fingers? Damn it, he wanted to give her those moments of orgasmic bliss! The torture built up inside him, layer by layer. His fingernails bit into his palm as he watched her take herself over the edge. He watched her head fling back in victory as she came, her body trembling until she was too weak to stand, and slid to the floor as gently as the clothes she discarded earlier.

Matt let out a heavy sigh, his breathing erratic from the sensual show that played on. His legs weaken and he propped a hand against the wall, trying to regain a steady breath. Guilt crept in and self-loathing spread through him for witnessing such a personal act.

Although he had wanted something tangible, he never would have thought he would be gifted with such a precious demonstration. He suddenly needed to escape, to get far away from this woman who seduced him in the most peculiar way. There was something strange and powerfully enthralling about her, something wonderful.

Something so bizarre, that it scared the shit out of him.

In his haste to get away, Archer stumbled during his downward descent. He slipped, losing his footing on the metal rungs of the ladder, and fell.

Falling, falling, falling.

In those few seconds when he felt helpless, his life flashed before him in perfect clarity. One minute he had nowhere and no one to hold onto, the next, his body landed in a solid bed of…trash?

Fuck.

He could only chuckle at the ironic analogy. Matt was no better than the endless piles of shit he had landed on.

Enlightenment coursed through him and he vowed he would have the mystery woman. He would reform her, show her how it really felt to be touched by a man of flesh and blood, not some fantasy that would leave her alone and empty.

After what he had observed tonight, Matt knew he would never be the same again.

* * * *

When Edith left the next afternoon, Miranda found herself in charge of Farra's Fortunes…and utterly panicked about her ability to do it.

Her new uniform gave her a bit of confidence. The white, off-the-shoulder peasant blouse made her feel exotic, and the swirling multi-colored skirt—combined with the headscarf of the same pattern—lent an air of authenticity. She desperately needed that right about now.

The inky, bleach smell of the shop was worse

than ever, so she decided to switch out the patchouli scent for something a little more to her liking. She had just selected Arabian Night, a refreshing blend of sandalwood and rose incense, when the jangling doorbell announced her first customer.

A man of imposing height ducked under the low frame of the front door. His very presence made her freeze as if he had caught her stealing from the cookie jar.

Oh, God, I can't do this, she thought. *He'll see right through me. How can I charge him for this?*

Miranda relaxed and relied upon the free first reading trick Edith had taught her. She couldn't feel bad about it if no money changed hands.

The customer slipped through the hanging beads of the foyer and moved onto the shop's main floor. He wore a fitted black leather jacket and casual, indigo jeans. A bit of white t-shirt peeked over the top of his zipper. The flames of the many candles she had lit bounced off of his light brown hair and his slightly tanned face.

Who has a tan like that in October?

Skin tone aside, his face also called for more than a second glance. She felt sure his placid expression hid something deeper, a subtle intelligence that would surface only when it was needed.

Miranda watched him covertly as he wandered the store, fingering merchandise with no apparent intent. His hazel eyes flickered over the various objects, the sensual lips of his full mouth moving not an inch from their motionless, straight line. Not to mention the five o'clock shadow.

Okay, maybe six or seven o'clock.

In other words, he was a heartbreaker. She would be surprised to learn that his story involved heartbreak of a different kind.

His own.

Miranda stealthily slipped behind the counter.

She couldn't say why, but she needed space between them.

"How much for a reading?" he suddenly asked.

She stopped herself from outwardly gasping and gave him a smooth smile, remembering her Gypsy accent.

"The introductory session has no cost. It is...priceless." She struck what she hoped was a seductive pose.

He acknowledged her offer, encouraging Miranda to begin the show. She took a seat at the table in the corner, lowering the lights through the sliding switch on the wall. He sat across from her and his sudden nearness caused her thoughts to scatter.

Stay cool, she told herself.

Miranda removed the top from the black box, displaying the crystal ball on its pedestal inside. The dim light from the lamp above shone down upon the orb, the imperfect bubbles within casting rays upon the handsome stranger's face.

"I see an initial," she said. "M."

He nodded. "That's my name. Matt. Everyone calls me Archer, though."

Bingo.

His gaze burned into her and she closed hers to avoid his glance. "Should I start by telling you why I'm here?" the man asked.

She took a deep breath and selected an opening line from Edith's cheat-sheet beneath the table. *Gain his trust.* "Err... No. I can *sense* that you are searching for something, Archer." Miranda's eyes snapped open. "True love."

An understated change flashed over his face, then disappeared. "Yes," came his simple answer.

Buoyed by her first "hit", as Edith had called it, she continued in the same vein. "You have not yet found that special person."

The man's heartfelt sigh touched Miranda's core.

"I thought I did. Then she disappeared."

"You were to be married," she guessed, wanting to know more about the love life of the man with sad eyes the color of deep, maple syrup.

"Yes..." A muscle twitched in his jaw. *He must be furious,* she thought. *But still wounded.* She truly wanted to make him feel better, even if only for a little while.

"Give me your hand." A wave of recognition passed through her as he did so. She wondered what in the hell it could have been, even as the flesh of her arms broke out into goosebumps.

Their eyes met over the sparkling sphere and Miranda saw that he had been as affected by their touch as she. His lips parted and she couldn't help imagining what it would be like to press her mouth to his, moan as his tongue slipped between her lips, pant when he began to touch her body. Maybe he would pull her onto his lap, work his hand up from her knee to her thigh, hike her Gypsy skirts around her waist.

She would beg him if she had to. Beg him to touch her breast, cup the curls of her mound, slip his long, thick fingers between the lips of her pussy and—

"Mmm, I see," she began again, running her index finger over his palm and ignoring the moisture between her legs. "You have long fingers and..." She took another glimpse of the cheat-sheet. "Large, square hands. You're obviously intelligent, Archer. You have no problem thinking clearly in a difficult situation. As for your girlfriend..."

"Fiancée," he corrected.

"Right." Miranda blushed. "Relationships are important to you, but your unfailing logic sometimes gets in the way of your feelings. You're very reliable and a bit of a perfectionist." She studied the long dark lashes that swept his cheek whenever he blinked. "You're a... *stimulating* companion." This reading was getting her more excited by the moment.

"And I can't think of why she would leave you," Miranda muttered beneath her breath.

"What was that?"

"Oh, just a spell for good luck in love," she covered. "Where was I?"

He smirked, heating her core yet again. "I think you left off at *stimulating*."

She could tell he wanted her. The comment said so. But, why then the unrequited love story? What was he hiding? She decided to give as good as she had gotten.

Might as well have some fun.

"You are a stimulating companion," Miranda continued, inspiration striking her. "And yet I sense the problem with your fiancée was a sexual one. You are both under a powerful curse, a dark spirit that hovers over your shoulders. You will need a spell for...*sex magick*."

It was one of the more costly psychic solutions Edith had taught her. She would have earned her extrasensory salt if she could get him to buy it. He deserved it for lying to her.

"Take off your shirt," she commanded. She selected an incense stick of the aphrodisiac variety. Lighting it, Miranda returned her attentions to Archer.

Surprisingly, he complied with her command, and the effect left her breathless. A scattering of dark, crisp hair covered the expanse of his solid chest, the rippling muscles of his arms and abdomen indicating he took care of himself, but wasn't vain. His facial tan continued down his neck and torso.

Miranda gulped, but continued on. "Generally, a sex magick spell requires both of you here, but in this case, I will be her stand-in spirit." She noticed her accent had slipped a bit and strived to regain it. "If you feel desire during the spell, do not attempt to crush it. It is what will reunite you and your lost lover."

She waved the incense around his partially nude body. When its ash had fallen into the holder, Miranda dipped her finger into it and gathered her courage. "You must be surrounded by sex magick in order to bring her back." She began to lightly dust his body with the ash on her index finger, swirling it in light patterns over his skin.

His nipples tightened and she pretended not to notice, dipping her fingers dangerously close to his belt buckle. She wished her tongue could replace her fingers, minus the ash, and not stop at the line of his pants.

Why did this man drive her to fantasy like no other had before?

Archer adjusted his weight and Miranda thought perhaps she had lingered too long. She grabbed a candle from a nearby shelf and began waving it around his body in circles. "This is the hot breath of your lover, destined to remind both of you of the heat you once shared."

Apparently, that one seemed to work , for his even breathing became heavier and more erratic as her movements increased. Miranda had just circled his body for the last time when the flame came a hair too close to his ribs. Archer seized her by the arm, startling her into dropping the candle.

Hot wax sprayed across his abdomen and he gasped, his face a contorted mixture of pleasure and pain. His eyes opened and Miranda saw the fiery desire in their depths. She backed away but he followed until she lay upon the velvet tablecloth with his body covering hers.

"This is me, not crushing my desire." He blew out the candle, leaving them in near-darkness. She realized he looked just as surprised by his actions as she was, as if he wasn't in control of his own mind and body. The evidence of his words pressed into the hollow between her thighs and she jerked away, shocked by the insistent throb of his cock. Her elbow connected with the crystal ball and sent it flying. It crashed into a thousand pieces on the hardwood floors.

"Oh, shit!" Miranda covered her mouth. She realized that she sounded more like a naughty teenager whose parents were out of town than a Gypsy fortune-teller out to seduce a client out of his money, but all she could think of was what Edith would say...or do.

"Um, okay, just...just wait here a minute." She slid out from beneath him and laughed awkwardly. "I guess I'm a real ball-breaker, huh?"

Edith had told her never to go into the private meditation room behind the curtain, but desperate times called for desperate measures and she had to find a replacement sphere.

Chapter Three

Matt watched Miss Gypsy scurry away, his cock still throbbing from the erotic ministrations of her so-called "sex magick." The hot candle wax had stirred a deep craving within him when it splashed across his flesh. Its quick burn, followed by the feel of hardened wax, added to his kinky thoughts. He might never have done that before, but he was all too willing to try new things.

Archer wasn't one to sit idle if the little criminal was up to no good. His training had prepared him for the unexpected, and if she had figured him out, he wasn't about to be conned by a con. He rose quickly and took a few seconds to adjust himself, cursing his inability to control his arousal.

Matt followed her into the back of the store and stopped at the open doorway. What he discovered was more than he had expected to find, and enough evidence to bring down the counterfeiters in one fell swoop.

The storeroom resembled something from a bad cop show, down to the single bulb swaying back and forth overhead from a wooden rafter. A bulky basin appeared overfilled with a pungent bleach concoction that permeated the room mixed with a fresh inky smell from a recent press run.

What caught his attention in the dimly lit room were the sturdy wires tightly stretched across one corner of the room to the other. The counterfeit bills were hung side-by-side to dry. The odor would have worked out his gag reflexes if not for the open door helping to air out the space.

Miss Gypsy turned to meet his gaze and a look of confusion flashed across her eyes. What a brilliant actress. He almost fell for her look of innocence.

Matt walked the expanse of the room, inspecting the various, tainted machinery's. Stained inkbottles and empty bleach containers lay around in a haphazard mess. Dark stains blotted the floor like a Jackson Pollack painting. He turned to the right side of the room and noticed the stacks of crisp white paper tightly shrink wrapped and piled high on industrial shelves along with additional supplies.

Matt whirled and gave her a suspicious stare. "I hope you've got one good alibi."

"This isn't what it looks like..." she sputtered defensively. "I'm not involved in...whatever this is," she said, gesturing helplessly to the evidence.

Matt looked her squarely in the eyes. "I thought that's what you'd say." He frowned at the tears brimming in her eyes. God, she was good. She made him feel guilty for what he was about to do.

Reaching behind his back, he pulled out the handcuffs tucked away in the waistband of his jeans, reached for her hand and held firmly to her wrist.

"I'm sorry about this," he said before flipping the cuff open and securing it around her wrist. "But you have the right to remain silent. Anything you say or do may be held against you..."

Miss Gypsy shrieked in alarm, "Wait. Who are you? What are you doing? I haven't done anything. There has to be something I can do to fix this."

"Lady, from the looks of things, you've done more than enough already."

"For your information, my name is Miranda. Not 'lady'! And I've never committed a criminal act in my life. Except for the time when I was five and stole a Tootsie Roll from Marvin's Short Stop and my dad made me go back and pay for it. Otherwise, you can do a background check on me and I swear it'll come up clean."

He reached for her other wrist and Miranda didn't try to resist when he pulled her hand in front of her before snapping the cuffs together. Matt couldn't believe she was cooperating with him. He had imagined she'd try her best to get away.

"I'm telling the truth! I just got this job. I know I'm not a real psychic..."

"You don't say..."

Miranda gushed, "But I needed the money! I needed the research for work or else my landlord was going to evict me."

"And what kind of con job are you researching here?"

"I'm a women's fiction author." He quirked a brow and she frowned. "All right, I write romance for a living. I spin tales of love and, and, and...adventure! And I needed to discover the inner workings of a psychic for material on my next novel."

He wasn't convinced in the least. "Grasping for straws, are we?"

Miranda blew away a loose tendril of hair that fell across her forehead and the frustration on her face made him bite back a smile.

"It's the truth. You can find my books on Amazon.com. *The Seaman's Concubine*, by Miranda Franklin! And *Wrangling the Rancher's Daughter* comes out this summer!"

Matt let out a rip-roaring laugh. "Somehow I don't think they'll be making it to my must read list." He quickly stifled his enjoyment at the spark of annoyance in her expression.

"I'll have you know *Concubine* has gotten a number of five star reviews."

"Impressive. I'd love to continue this idle chatter, but I actually have a job to do. I'd advise you to stay still for a few seconds."

Wanting to document the evidence before her back-up returned, Matt withdrew a palm-sized digital camera from his front jeans pocket and proceeded to snap pictures of all the faux loot. His eyes caught sight of several large trash bags hidden behind the door. He walked over and untied one of the bags and a slew of scrapped bills spilled onto the floor.

He bent down and scooped up a handful of the papers, tossing the misprinted bills aside after taking snapshots of the counterfeit proof.

Matt turned around and Miranda collided against his chest. "What the hell?" The nosy twit, she appeared to be just as eager to see what he had discovered.

"Do you mind, Miranda?" Her name rolled off his tongue all too easily and the slight tingling fired up again. His stomach squeezed at her nearness and he had the urge to kiss those lush lips.

Don't look at me like that!

Those big round eyes were begging for it. She licked her lips and his cock jolted to life. He gnashed his teeth together, not comprehending why his body flared up at the very sight of Miranda. There was something absolutely surreal about his lust for her and it puzzled him.

She wasn't his type. Or was she? A spark of memory captivated him. Miranda naked before the mirror, touching herself in all the places he ached to taste. Matt wanted to feast on those perfect breasts and explore every inch of this Gypsy who'd put a spell on him.

That's it. It had to be it. Shit! All that mumbo jumbo she did must have worked.

"You're in enough trouble as it is," he barked at her in frustration. "I'm going to have to ask you to step back."

Miranda didn't budge. Her sudden look of innocence took on a wicked gleam. She peered at him through thick, dark lashes. "What do I need to do to get out of this...*trouble?*"

Fuck.

It couldn't be. Miranda was trying to trade sexual favors to get out of this mess and he was salivating to take her up on the proposition.

Matt swallowed hard at the thick lump lodged in his throat.

Think, damn it, think.

He was on suspension, so *technically,* he wasn't on the clock. Which left him to consider his options. Was he fool enough to fuck her blind and deal with the consequences later? Or should he just turn her in and get her out of his hair once and for all?

Bad time for him to gain a conscience.

Matt had always chosen the right path, or at least not the dead-wrong one, so why did he suddenly find himself compelled to let his cock dictate his choice? And why in the name of hell did he find himself believing her far-fetched alibi?

God, she had begun running her mouth again while he deliberated with his conscience.

"...can't have my name blemished by an arrest. I can't ruin my reputation as a writer when I've worked so hard to promote myself."

"I suppose there may be one way..."

"Anything. I'll do anything! I swear I'm innocent of whatever you think I'm involved in," she pleaded with hope-filled eyes.

Was it just him or did the room suddenly grow warmer? Matt couldn't stop staring at her luscious lips as she spoke, her face filled with passion, the steady rise and fall of her chest. Perfect mounds he would quite enjoy feasting on.

"Anything?" He quirked a brow in interest.

"Anything."

Matt crossed his arms and heaved a deep sigh. "Well, perhaps there is something you can do." He dropped his arms and stepped in closer to Miranda.

He watched her ecstatic expression drop as a blush of alarm spread over her fair skin. She stammered and took a quick step back. "I...I didn't mean that kind of *anything.*"

He found this little game immensely entertaining. He took a step forward and trapped Miranda against the wall.

Leaning in close, Matt practically purred against her ear, "So which is it? Your freedom or your reputation up in flames?"

What? His mind screamed. *What the hell did I just say?*

He felt a warmth surround him, growing hot and fast as a light perspiration beaded across his forehead. What was going on? Matt couldn't explain his attraction to this woman. Miranda had a sexual hold over him and he didn't know what to think any more. Maybe the minx *had* put a spell over him. For fuck's sake, he was starting to fall for the mumbo jumbo. Even if she was a fraud.

He held his breath when she bit her lower lip, milling over the decision in her head. She flicked her tongue over her lips and his cock saluted in attention. When she finally spoke, his heart nearly lunged out of his chest.

"Yes. Yes, I'll do it."

* * * *

Miranda felt like a fool for believing that he wanted her to trade her body for freedom. Boy, was she wrong. She had been as bold as to close her eyes and lean in for a kiss that never came. *Moron!* All he wanted was for her to cooperate with him.

A part of her had been relieved, but the other half felt a deep disappointment. She had to admit the thought of hot, sweaty sex with this man was just the thing she needed to add to her novel. Sex with a stranger in a dark and forbidden place. It would have been perfect!

Instead, they were sprawled on the floor sifting through mounds of paperwork and comparing findings against the books. How lame was this? She blew out a frustrated breath. It seemed like hours. Every time he shifted, his thigh would brush up against her and she felt the world whirl on its axis. Once, he reached over and his arm connected to her breast. Her nipples had hardened to pebbled peaks and her thighs tingled from the contact.

He had unlocked one side of her cuffs to make it easier for her to review the papers, but she still felt the subliminal incarceration.

Miranda was beyond frustration. *Why don't you touch me already? Why don't you rip off my clothes and ravage me with kisses?*

She didn't realize she had been grumbling under her breath until he gave her a questioning look, his mouth quirked into a smile. "Something you wanted to say?"

Her brows drew together at the hint of laughter in his voice. "How would you feel if the roles were reversed? I don't think you'd enjoy being handcuffed like a common criminal."

His rich laugh added to her brewing anger. "Based on the evidence, *Miranda,* you are a criminal until proven otherwise."

She gripped a receipt in her hand and felt it crumple in her palm. "Ooh, I really don't like you."

"I don't need to be liked. Look, I want to find the evidence I'm searching for and wash my hands of you. I'm sure you want to be rid of me, too."

Miranda scoffed. "Oh, I want to be rid of you all right. I am *so* going to kill you off in my next novel. You'll be immortalized forever." The thought cheered her up.

"I will definitely expect an autographed copy, then." Archer's smugness only enhanced her growing disdain for him, but her rebellious body seemed to find him extremely attractive. Unhappy with her reaction to him, she realized her only course of action was to find the proof he wanted on Farra's Fortunes and get far, *far* away from him.

The sooner the better.

"I said I'd help you, but I never said I'd engage in conversation." Her perverse mind wouldn't leave those words alone. Thoughts popped to mind of *engagement* in several positions, with handcuffs intact. She felt her cheeks flush and hoped he didn't notice.

His face softened as he stared at her for a long while. "Hey, you all right? Are the fumes getting to you?"

She saw the genuine concern on his face. Miranda shook her head. "Everything's fine, although it's kind of hot in here." She only wished the floor would open up and swallow her. Never had she been so magnetically drawn to anyone as she was to Archer.

"All right, then. Let's go through these last set of ledgers." He grabbed several black, leather bound books and handed them to her.

His fingers brushed against hers and that familiar tingle worked its way through her body and stirred every nerve ending to arousal. Miranda made the mistake of looking at him and their eyes connected. In those brief moments, she fell victim to the fiery lust blazing within those intense hazel depths.

"Ma?" a husky, male voice called from the foyer. Archer froze, his hands wrist-deep in the filing cabinet.

"Oh, shit..." Miranda hissed. "I hope you're packing heat."

"Ma?" came the voice again. "You back there?"

"Oh, sh—"

"Quiet," Archer commanded. He wordlessly pointed to the small cabinet embedded in the wall.

Miranda knew he wanted her to hide there, to wait out the ensuing showdown between Ma Edith's dopey son and Sheriff Archer. He didn't even have the proof he needed and he had no plausible story for being there that would allow him to continue to collect evidence. If for some bizarre reason Archer didn't have a gun, he could wind up dead.

Or worse.

The sounds of the visitor's loping gait grew closer, moving in from the foyer to the main room. Seconds from the sound of the curtain swooshing aside, Miranda shoved Archer back against the wood paneling of the wall. She threw her arms around his neck and looked up into his shocked face.

"What are you—"

Miranda put a finger to his supple mouth. She didn't bother to deny to herself that she enjoyed the sensation. With a grin, she grabbed two fistfuls of his white t-shirt and hauled it over his head. She kicked off her shoes and threw a leg up around his waist, her skirt riding up her thighs.

"Quiet," she mimicked. Her mouth closed over his just as the curtain brushed aside.

A short, rotund man in his mid-thirties stood in the doorway. The dusk of night behind him outlined his face, the bare, hanging bulb of the backroom illuminating, yet harshly shadowing his features.

"What the hell is going on here?"

Miranda broke from Archer's embrace with heaving breath. She hoped her lipstick had smudged from the kiss and that her eyes slanted with passion. She hoped the man saw all of these things, earmarks of one hot night of clandestine ardor.

"What the hell do you two think you're doing?" the man asked.

"I—" Miranda blushed. "Christening my new work place?" She laughed, gesturing with Archer's t-shirt. "My boyfriend, Bobby, just got back into town and I guess we got a little excited.

Archer faked a bumbling hick persona. "We're real sorry. It's just that I'm on leave from the Army and me and my girl here wanted to make the most of our time together, if you know what I mean." He squeezed her against his side and Miranda nearly laughed at his goofy grin. The steel vise of a warning grip on her arm made her think twice.

Edith's son chuckled and folded his arms. "Didn't Ma just hire you? I doubt this was one of the job requirements."

"Yes, she did..." Her tone changed from guilty admission to pleading. "Please don't tell her. We're just having a little fun. I promise we'll get out of here." She gave him a wink and a naughty smile, sliding an arm up around Archer's neck again. "You know how it is."

The man gave her a slow, leering smile. The exchange felt a bit creepy, but mostly harmless. "Sure, lady. I know all about it." He nodded to Archer, who grinned again in mock embarrassment. "Just lock up when you two kids leave."

Cold air blasted into the shop as the doorbell jangled behind the man's exit. Miranda sighed in relief.

"You think that was pretty clever, do you?" Miranda felt his heart pound against the thin cotton of her peasant blouse. As if he had held himself in check during those crucial moments. "You could have just gotten us shot, you know that?"

She smiled and ran a finger down his naked chest, delighting in the feel of his sinuous muscles beneath her caress. "Relax, I just saved your investigation. Now you have a reason to be here."

Archer scoffed, his eyes narrowed slits of cool anger. "You think this is all some game, inspiration for that book you're supposedly writing."

Miranda knew it would irk him that she didn't appear sufficiently chastised. She loved it. "I thought you had to play games sometimes to catch a criminal. Didn't they teach you that in training, *Special Agent Archer*?"

He cinched his arms tightly around her waist. "Maybe you're the one who needs a lesson."

Ever the writer, Miranda had a good idea of what she was about to get into. They stared at each other, eye to defiant eye as she reviewed the past scripts of her sexual encounters.

Kiss mouth.

Fondle breast.

Fondle cock.

Oral (hopefully).

Fuck, fuck, fuck.

Done.

So far, this encounter had exceeded expectations. After all, she'd already been arrested *and* outwitted a criminal. Her fantasy life was always richer than her reality ever could be, which is why she took such pleasure in pleasing herself. Now that the handcuffs were on, all bets were off in terms of reality and the usual.

Besides the interesting details, there was something strange between them, something ethereal and predestined. This same sizzling connection made her feel as if she had little choice about the course of events. That each small movement was supposed to happen. Had to happen.

"This is some fantasy to you, isn't it? Something zany to put into a silly book?"

She blushed, genuinely this time, for it seemed he could read her thoughts. Sure, he had belittled her work, which she did not take lightly, but the idea that he could know her mind made her shiver. She wanted nothing more than to escape him now.

Good luck, what with your hands cuffed behind his neck.

He took the momentary fracture in her defenses as an opportunity to break her. Archer swung her around by the waist, pinning her against the wall. His unsmiling mouth came down hard upon hers, as if he was about to undergo the most serious of tasks.

The kiss was like a sigh of relief, a dam breaking after relentless pressure. It had been a while and

Miranda was hungry. Archer's mouth was firm and insistent as it closed over her upper lip. A warm gush of liquid heat wet her panties when his tongue slipped into her mouth to touch hers. He slid his tip over the side of hers and she relished the slow, sensuous stroke.

That pacing couldn't last for long, and the tempo quickly built to a frenzy as they battled for dominance over the heated kiss. With lips swollen and wet, they explored each other's mouths like uncharted territories. Miranda lost herself in the kiss until she heard a metallic click from behind Archer's head.

He had freed her hands. And she could only guess why.

His mouth left hers and she felt suddenly bereft without the connection, left with only the loud, throaty sound of her own gasping breath. He trailed kisses across her cheek and throat, following a slow, delightful path to her hairline. Archer then bit down on her earlobe, holding it firmly between his teeth as he tongued it back and forth. Unable to escape without pain, she silently endured the sweet torture.

"Fantasies are all right," he whispered into her ear, "in a lonely bedroom...in the darkness...but what if we made them real?"

The suggestion effectively knocked every coherent thought out of her head. He smelled like pure sex, a fragrance she had noted the moment she'd pulled his shirt over his head. The scent mocked her now, practically begging her to lick every exposed inch of his torso. The handcuffs still hanging from her wrist, Miranda slid her hand down between them and grasped his cock through thick denim. She outlined its tantalizing swell with her palm.

Archer groaned and Miranda wrapped her free hand around him, grabbing his tight ass to pull him against her. She spread her legs, rubbing herself all over his hardened length. His eyes widened in surprise, then narrowed, as if he had given himself over to the idea that she had pretty much lost her mind. Miranda agreed, but she could do nothing to help herself except ride the wave of lust to shore.

He kissed her passionately again, and her kiss was as bold as his, meeting him stroke for stroke, challenging him to outdo her.

"You think you can shock me, Archer?" Miranda asked, her tone designed to emasculate. "Go ahead and try."

He slid a hand up the inside of her thigh, causing a ripple of goosebumps in the cool air. He hooked a finger around the string of her thong and ripped off her underwear.

Here's something new, she thought.

His knuckle drifted down over her cleft and parted her sex. She moaned once. He swirled a finger between the lips of her pussy, gliding over the slick flesh, but never breaking their gaze until he brought his finger to his mouth to taste her moisture. Miranda was momentarily taken aback, and Archer looked smug, as if he'd bested her. No way would she let him think he'd won.

She smiled as he brought his hand forward and she captured his finger between her lips. Miranda had never tasted herself before and the idea of it drove her wild. With the saline taste of herself still on her lips, she went on to do him one better, unzipping his jeans and dropping to her knees.

Miranda prided herself on her ability to give a good blow job. She had nothing but contempt for women who gave a lackluster performance.

She yanked down his jeans and began with a long slow lick from base to tip, eliciting an approving groan from Archer. When her lips enveloped the head of his cock for the first time, Miranda taunted him by meeting his eyes and holding their locked gaze all the while she licked and sucked him off. After breathless minutes of pumping up and down over his hardened member, she tasted his pre-ejaculate. Her nipples tightened and tingled, excited by the prospect of tasting his come and winning their little battle.

Instead, he withdrew from her mouth and stripped down to nothing. Even in the garish light of the hanging bulb, the sight of his nude body floored Miranda. No desk job for this man. From the looks of his muscular thighs and rigid abdomen, Archer spent his time in the field, chasing down the bad guys or whatever it was he did.

Archer raised an eyebrow at her appreciative gaze, but then narrowed his eyes as if an idea had just occurred to him. He hauled her to her feet and held her by the elbow as he glanced around the room, seemingly looking for something. He must have found it, for he pulled her into the corner so fast that he accidentally booted the trash bags at his feet. Scrapped counterfeit bills spilled out at their feet, the botched leftovers of bleached dollars turned hundreds.

Miranda was so shocked that when he let go of her arm to shove her against the wall, she fell upon the pile of illegal tender. Although the move was disproportionately rough and violent when compared to their lovemaking, the aggression actually excited her more than anything. Miranda found that she loved to be on her hands and knees facing a corner. The bizarre thought of fucking a stranger on top of a mound of money in that same corner further encouraged her lust and excitement. It was decadent and outlandish.

She loved it.

Miranda lifted her skirt to the waist and spread her legs, exposing her pussy to him. He kneeled in the cash next to her, squeezing and kneading her ass.

"You smell like sex," he said.

She sighed. *Tell me about it.*

"You smell like sex," he repeated, "and I want to taste you again. I want to lick your flesh, to flick my tongue over your clit, to suck on the lips of your pussy. I'm going to fuck you with my tongue, Miranda."

Again, he tried to shock her with explicit words. Two could play at that game. She slipped off her top and unclipped the front closure of her white lace bra. Her tits brushed the counterfeit bills, positioned as she was with her weight resting on her elbows and her ass in the air. She swayed back and forth, her nipples caressed by the cotton papers.

She slipped her hand beneath her belly and between her legs, resting her head on her other arm.

"With your tongue, huh ?" She sighed dreamily, twirling a finger through the curls of her mound, watching him eye her every move. "I'll tell you how I want to be fucked, Fed." Right off the bat, she slipped two fingers inside herself in one quick motion.

"I don't want preliminaries. I don't want preparation. I want you to push right into me. I want to feel the head of your hard cock slip through my tight pussy." Miranda pulled her fingers out to lie on either side of her clit, squeezing them together until that little bud of excitement throbbed to be licked and owned.

She continued, calmly telling him how she wanted to be fucked, all the while watching his cock dip and rise at each word. "I want to *hear* you fuck me," she went on to say. "The wet, loud sound of your body slapping against mine should be the only thing I hear." The moment she had uttered the words, he growled, diving onto the pile of bills. Roughly digging his hands into her flesh, he grabbed her by the hips and put his mouth to her pussy.

Miranda cried out, more than ready to feel his tongue on her sex. He didn't disappoint her, starting out with one broad, flat stroke of his tongue on her engorged flesh. The heated liquid of his caress drove her to the brink of madness, forced her to rock back against his mouth, thoughtless of will or intention. Only pure need remained.

Archer cared nothing for her need or the insanity of her movements. He forced her to hold still beneath his ministrations, while he sucked her clit and labia. When she refused to conform, he hauled her legs over his shoulders and lay back against the bills, her breasts resting against his navel, her head on his thighs.

A perfect position for distraction from his passionate tonguing.

Without even a nod to gravity, his cock stood up straight, begging her to wrap her lips around its base, the coarse hairs there brushing against her face. Archer groaned and the sound vibrated against her vulva. Combined with the very thought of sucking his dick, that made her wetter than she had been before. She knew Archer could tell because he enthusiastically lapped up the excess flow of her juices.

Bless him.

As he lapped at her sex, she lifted up onto her elbows and studied his cock. It was nearly perfect, with just a slight curve to the right. His well-defined head was engorged with blood, fairly begging for her mouth. Miranda grasped him by the base of his dick as she closed her mouth over the head of his cock. She desperately tried to concentrate on him, rather than her own pleasure, pulling out every trick in her book.

Although it was difficult to focus through the multiple orgasms he gave her, Miranda managed to get him to the point that his thighs were shaking and his abdomen contracting against her breasts. She thrilled to know that he was about to orgasm and wrapped her arms around his thighs to ride it out. Archer uttered a warning groan even while he continued to flick his tongue across her clit.

With a wild roar, he spurted a powerful jet of come into her mouth. The taste and texture of his ejaculation along with the relentless tonguing of her clit battered her senses and forced her own jubilant climax.

They slowly descended from the heights of their wild and impassioned oral sex. Although they had brought each other to the brink of ecstasy, neither was satisfied.

Chapter Four

Matt was beyond words. He had been intent on satisfying her needs, yet this woman had unselfishly given him the same level of pleasure. Her actions were brazen, yet invigorating. He could not recall a time when a woman hadn't taken whatever she could from him without offering anything in return.

He couldn't put a finger on it, but their odd connection felt more real than any of his previous relationships. It was as if she alone had the ability to see through the wall he had built around himself. Needless to say, his reality appeared slightly off kilter lately. He wasn't complaining in the slightest, especially when Miranda felt so right in his arms.

Her chest pressed tightly against him and he couldn't resist kissing her delicate lips again. This time he wanted it to be gentle to make up for his earlier rough handling. Matt cupped her face in his callused palms and recaptured her lips, parting them with his tongue to further explore the sweetness within.

Their tongues danced to the rhythm of their beating hearts and she wrapped her arms around his neck, opening herself up to a deeper kiss. He encircled her waist with his hands and rolled around, taking her with him until he was on top. His body nestled between the vee of her thighs. When he finally tore his lips away, she let out a soft sigh of contentment. He smiled in satisfaction at her swollen lips and couldn't resist planting a quick kiss on the tip of her nose.

Matt Archer had done a lot of wild and crazy

things in his time, but never anything as spontaneous as rolling on a stack of freshly printed counterfeit bills with a luscious Gypsy.

His throaty laughter echoed through the dim room. "That was..."

"Illegal? Compromising?" Miranda suggested with a quirk of her brow.

"I was going to say intense."

"Intense, huh?" She smiled mysteriously. "I'll show you intense."

The feel of her swelling breasts against his chest hardened his cock. He was ready for her again and she knew it. Miranda lifted onto her knees and easily slid onto him with a sigh of perfect bliss. He sucked in his breath, surprised by her take-charge performance, but loving every ounce of it. Matt grabbed her ass, guiding her as she pumped up and down on his turgid shaft.

Matt loved the way her breasts bounced, adored the rapturous expression on her face as she rode him with enthusiasm. His body lit up like a torch. The heat consumed him, burning higher and higher, flames rising, and licked by Miranda's sensual yet provocative dance,he'd never had a woman spring alive during lovemaking like this. She captured him in a spell so profound he grew lost in the cocoon of her earthy charms.

Her movements increased, faster and faster until he almost believed his soul had descended his body. Their frantic lovemaking created a bizarre sensation that bonded her to him as if their separate heartbeats had merged as one. He could not explain the sudden unity, the feel of blood rushing through his veins as his cock stretched to the limit.

He knew they were on the verge and he wanted the feeling to last as long as he could hold out. With the pressure mounting, Miranda clenched her pussy tight around his shaft and all thoughts of control dissipated. His walls crumbled from the multitude of sensations she awakened in him. Matt allowed himself to let go, enjoying the wave after wave of ecstasy that washed through him until the storm subsided into a quiet lull. Matt trembled from the revelation that this sexual encounter resembled a dream. One he shared with a sex goddess who had brought the mystical light of the moon into this darkened room.

* * * *

The uncomfortable silence was killing him.

Matt Archer wasn't one to crave more than a one-night stand, but hell he wanted more of Miranda. Truth be told, a quick tumble based on mutual attraction wasn't going to satisfy him. Not with someone as insatiable and daring as Miss Gypsy.

He turned to glance over at her and his insides knotted up.

Her soft features radiated beneath the moonlight. Her silky strands flowed behind her back and spilled over her shoulders like a Botticelli painting. *The Birth of Venus* in all her magnificent glory. Emblazoned in his soul was the image of Miranda's nude radiance touching, kissing, and riding him to a fevered ecstasy. Looking at her now, this vision seemed to be in total contrast to the cold woman she had become moments after their heated lovemaking.

It was as if someone had flipped off a switch, transforming her into this matter-of-fact person who was quick to dress and even quicker to pretend that the whole sexual episode never happened. *As if the act is a trivial kind of research!*

Damn right it hurt his ego. He'd be lying if he thought otherwise. Matt let out a frustrated breath. Maybe the heavens were finally giving him a taste of his own medicine for all those years of having that love-'em-and-leave-'em attitude.

Served him right. How many rules had he broken tonight? He couldn't easily count them and the fact that he was willing to compromise his duties for sex put him in a terrible position. This behavior wasn't like him at all. He wasn't sure who or what was to blame for his temporary madness but he didn't like it one bit.

"Y...you want to come in?" The softness in Miranda's voice sliced through the silence.

A pang of guilt tugged at him and he determined it was best to make his escape while he had the ability to do it. "It's late and I want to fax the evidence to headquarters."

Her expression said it all. She had misinterpreted his words. Damn it, if he stuck around any longer he wouldn't be able to keep himself from making it up to her.

Get the hell outta there, Archer.

The proof was safely in his hands and she obviously had given him an easy way out, so why did the idea of leaving feel so wrong?

Aw, hell. Miranda was the most liberating lover he had been with in ages! She was as giving as she was eager to receive, and that was the biggest turn-on for him. Her lack of inhibitions had been exhilarating—a change from the quick and predictable relationships he'd had before.

The chilly evening walk to Miranda's front door had been awkward. He wasn't sure whether he should hold her hand or wrap his arms around her to keep her warm. His palm was sweaty during his indecision and he found himself feeling like an adolescent pining away for a secret crush.

"Well, I guess this is it, then." She stuck out her hand and he wanted to laugh at the absurdity. Hadn't they just had mind-blowing sex not more than an hour ago and here she acted as if they were virtual strangers.

Matt smirked but accepted her hand. "Fuck it," he muttered and pulled her to him. He planted a kiss on the lips he'd been craving since they left the store. If he were going to walk out of her life he'd be damn sure to get one good kiss.

He released Miranda and watched her sway unsteadily as she stepped back.

"I'll see you around," Matt mumbled gruffly. He turned to leave when she halted him with a question that ruined the *Casablanca* moment.

"Wait. What about Edith?"

Matt whipped around to glare at her. "Screw Edith. She's as guilty as her illegal counterparts."

Miranda's lips jutted out defiantly. "I think you're jumping the gun there, Archer. She's a sweet old lady who couldn't possibly be involved."

He frowned at her stubborn demeanor. "Don't get any ideas in that pretty little head of yours. It's my job to clean up the criminals around here so I don't want you back at that shop. You hear me?" He hoped his intimidating voice would get through to her.

"I hear you loud and clear, you arrogant ass!" she spat before whipping around, stepping into her apartment, and slamming the door in his face.

Matt Archer stared at the paint-chipped door and realized in that moment there was no better match for him than Miranda. After all, he loved a good challenge.

* * * *

"How dare he!" Miranda grumbled to herself as she stalked through the park on her way to work the next day. "'Screw Edith?' How about 'Screw you, Archer?'"

The parade of hardened criminals, con men, and tricksters must have done a number on his ability to trust people over the years. How could that kindly old grandmother possibly be in on the scam? No way. Sure, she might bilk the gullible out of a few bucks for her "psychic visions," but maybe she was actually psychic. And there was a world of difference between the *Psychic Friends Network* and a counterfeiting ring.

If she ever got it, Miranda would stake her next

advance on the guilt of Edith's sons. The old woman was just a victim in their shady dealings. And if Archer wouldn't be there for the people he had supposedly sworn to protect, well then, Miranda would.

Fidelity, bravery, and integrity, my ass!

The doorbell jangled as Miranda entered Farra's. She stomped out the cold on the mat just inside the door but stopped when she realized how eerily quiet it was. She shivered, giving herself a little pep talk. All she had to do was let Edith know what kind of shit her kids had gotten into, then jet.

And maybe join the Witness Protection Program.

"Miranda, dear? Is that you?" Edith called from the back room.

"Yep."

"Can you come here? I got a new shipment but I'm having trouble lifting it."

Miranda agreed wholeheartedly. *That back room is nothing but trouble.*

She sighed. "Let's get this over with."

Miranda pushed aside the curtain to the back room and took a breath to start her prepared speech. She managed to say, "Edith, I think you may be caught up in something pretty bad," before she saw stars and the world went black.

* * * *

When Miranda awoke, she groaned at the realization that her hands were once more bound together in the dank back room of Farra's Fortunes. This time, it wouldn't be sexy. It would be just plain scary.

"I'm so sorry, dear," Edith whispered. "They made me call you in here." Through a no-doubt concussive haze, Miranda saw that Edith was bound to a chair right beside her.

"Who?" she hissed. Better not to let on too much, especially at first.

"My good-for-nothing progeny. They're no sons

of mine anymore," Edith moaned dolefully.

"I was just coming to tell you that they—"

"Are counterfeiters?" Edith smiled wistfully. "I gathered that some time ago. I tried to get them to stop, but they wouldn't listen. And a mother doesn't turn her own sons over to the Feds. What was I to do?"

Miranda opened her mouth, but closed it again quickly. There was no polite response to that.

"And now they've caught one of those Feds snooping around here and they think it's my fault. And yours." Edith sighed and closed her eyes.

Miranda gasped. "Caught a Fed? Where?"

"He's tied up in the alley Dumpster right now." Edith shook her head at the depths to which her sons would sink.

"And if he makes a move, Rodney'll put a bullet in him." The man who had caught Archer and her last night didn't look so dopey anymore. "So if you don't start talking, Loverboy and Mama are gonna get it."

Edith narrowly eyed the man as if he was far beneath her, as if she despised her own flesh and blood.

I guess I would, too, if I was Mom to the Mob.

Miranda gave him a sullen face of her own and looked down, taking a moment to think out a strategy for the situation. Although she was not sure how many sons Edith had exactly, Miranda was fairly certain that only two of them were around at the moment. And if one was on Archer, she should be able to immobilize this guy long enough for it to distract Rodney.

If she could only untie herself.

* * * *

Matt woke up to a throbbing headache that felt like someone had slammed a sledgehammer against his skull. His face hurt like a sonofabitch, and a flood of memories came rushing back. After leaving Miranda's apartment he had gone straight home to fax the ledger pages to headquarters. He hadn't anticipated two goons jumping out at him like a couple of jack in the boxes. He had put up a good fight until one man clocked him across the face while the other used his body as a punching bag.

Matt tried to move now and discovered his hands and feet were bound. He lifted his head and was greeted with the end of a nine-millimeter barrel. A soft click warned him to stay comfortable on the lumpy bed of pungent garbage and scraps. Somehow, he wasn't surprised to find himself needing another hose-down when this was done and over with.

He cursed himself for allowing Miranda to cloud his judgment. The woman had him so wound up he had forgotten to keep his guard up in order to avoid incidents like this. Some agent he was! Never would he have found himself in this predicament if it weren't for Miss Gypsy.

He blinked a few times and the blurred image came into focus. The man pointing the gun at him looked like a contorted version of the guy who had caught him with Miranda in the back room the night before. Matt tried to formulate some escape plans when a piercing scream made his assailant turn away.

"I would say don't go anywhere, but it looks like you're all tied up." The big oaf chuckled as he walked away in the direction of the noise, giving a self-congratulatory clap over his own wit.

Matt waited until the footsteps faded before maneuvering his body into a sitting position. Only a minute's worth of struggle loosened the ropes. "Musta failed Seamanship 101. Fuckin' idiot can't even tie a basic hard knot."

After a bit more kicking and tugging, he managed to free himself from the restraints. Matt jumped out of the Dumpster and ran straight for the back door. He hoped to hell, Miranda hadn't gotten herself into any trouble.

Matt almost collided with the dopey goon in the alley doorway, but he had the presence of mind to kick the gun out of the man's hand. A solid right hook sent the criminal flying and Matt finished him off with the lid of a nearby trash can.

Matt figured the man would be out long enough for him to find Miranda and get her out of danger. When he made it inside he found the little vixen wielding a can of pepper spray like a deadly weapon. One of the goons lay on the floor yelping from the pain. A smile of relief spread across his lips at her bravery. He didn't know whether to kiss her or turn her over his knee and teach her a lesson for being so foolish.

Miranda squealed with delight upon seeing him and flung herself into his arms. Matt gave her a quick kiss on the lips.

"Now how'd you slip those ropes?"

She gave him a mischievous grin. "That was one of the few Girl Scout badges I did earn." Miranda planted a hard smack on his lips and he chuckled. Matt would have to discuss that trick with her later when he had her safely tucked away in his bed.

"We don't have much time, Miranda. We need to tie up this other buffoon and call for backup." He pried her away from his arms and she nodded in understanding.

The soft, familiar click of a cocked gun drew their gazes in Edith's direction.

"You won't be calling anyone," the woman growled. Her kind face had twisted menacingly, while her wild eyes flashed.

Miranda knit her eyebrows together in confusion. "I don't understand. You're involved?"

"I'm glad to hear you bought the Nana Edith routine. I've always said that criminals make the best actresses." The woman gave her a mocking smile.

Miranda's wounded expression increased Edith's delight. "Oh, honey. Don't look so sad. I'm sure death

won't be too bad. I'm actually looking forward to it."
The older woman raised the weapon and aimed at her
chest. "It's a pity, though. You had a lot of potential."

Matt stepped in front of Miranda to protect her
and Edith gave him a hard stare. "Let her go. It's me
you want."

"Too late for chivalry, my boy. Say goodbye."

"Wait." Miranda stepped out from behind
Archer. He gave her a look that could kill, wondering
what in the hell she was thinking. "You said I had
potential."

Edith raised a silver brow. "Yes, well…I thought
my sons had potential." She indicated the crumpled
figure on the floor with a nod of her head. "Look how
well that turned out."

Miranda swallowed and took a step toward
Edith. "You know I'm nothing like them. I'm smarter,
more reliable, more—"

"Yes, yes, I get it. You're the daughter I should
have had. Get on with it, I have a federal agent to
kill." Her cackle echoed through the room.

"We could be a team, Edith."

"What?" Matt bellowed.

"Don't you move," Edith commanded, eyeing her
Gypsy protégé.

Miranda continued, that smoky laugh of hers
turned to ice. "I'm just getting the hang of the art of
the con." She hooked a thumb back at Matt. "This one
half-believed I write *romance novels* for a living."

It was Edith's turn to laugh. The sound made
Matt's blood run cold and doubt began to set in. "So
you want in, eh?"

"I think I've proven my acting skills." Miranda
shrugged nonchalantly. "Maybe actresses make the
best criminals."

Matt's heartbeat ratcheted up another level.
Could Miranda really turn on him just like that?

Edith thought on this for a moment, her pale eyes
like quicksilver. "You're not blood. Why in the name

of hell should I trust you?"

Miranda smiled. "Because I'm going to kill you a Fed."

"Be my guest, dear. Before you dispatch our hero, however, please be advised that this gun will be trained on your every move. If you so much as think about crossing me, I will not hesitate to murder you."

Miranda shrugged. "Of course."

"And please. No Mexican stand-off. It's such a cliché." Edith sighed wearily. "Now pick the gun off my worthless heap of a son over there and do what you have to do."

She did as she was told and whirled around to face Archer. His mind's eye flashed with dozens of intense images of her. Naked in her candlelit room, covering his body with hot wax, rolling around on sheets of counterfeit. And now this final image. Her hazel eyes mocking him over the barrel of a gun.

"Now say goodbye," Edith instructed.

Miranda's eyes flicked over to Edith and then back to Archer. "Goodbye."

A shot rang out, whizzing past Matt's ear and ricocheting around the room until a groan rose up from the man on the floor.

"You little bitch!" she wailed. "You shot my idiot son!"

Matt smirked. *That's my girl.*

He jumped out at Edith and chopped at her gun hand directly above the wrist, moving her hand inward and forcing her to drop the gun. "I'm not going to give you the satisfaction of death," he said, looking into her cold, narrow eyes. "So look forward to this."

Matt whipped a pair of cuffs out of his pocket. "You have the right to remain silent. Anything you say or do may be used against you in a court of law. You have the right to an attorney. If you cannot afford an attorney, one will be provided for you at interrogation time and at court."

Miranda followed suit, tying up Edith's sons while Matt stood up and pulled out his cell phone to call for reinforcements. Neither one wanted to take more chances.

"Great," he said. "They put me on hold."

He eyed her movements with admiration while listening to the smooth jazz on the line. "That was some diversion, Miss Gypsy. Where'd you come up with that?"

Miranda shrugged, but glowed with his praise. "I've written a few Westerns in my day. She said no Mexican stand-off, so I went to the next best cliché I could think of."

Matt shook his head and roared out his appreciative laughter. "You are something else, Miranda Franklin. C'mere." He pulled her against him as they slid down into the corner.

Miranda laid her head on his shoulder while he trained the gun on Edith and her sons. "Oddly enough, there's no place I'd rather be right now than the dank backroom of a criminal's lair waiting for back-up."

Archer kissed her head and smiled. "I know the feeling."

* * * *

"The...freakin'...end!"

Miranda jumped up from her desk and did a victory dance in her bathrobe and flip-flops. Two weeks to the day from her exploits with Archer, she had finished the first draft of the manuscript for *Illegal Tender*. Never mind that she hadn't heard from Archer during that time. She could still use his moves to write one hell of a great sex scene between Agent Chad Hartner and his sexy psychic, Samantha.

Miranda sighed blissfully. All of her worries had melted away with three little words. *Three. Book. Deal.* Archer was a putz for disappearing like that, but she wouldn't let it get her down. She was a woman who could appreciate great sex and leave it at that. Even if their union had seemed somehow predestined.

Mystical.

"Enough with mysticism. Time for a hard, cold dose of reality." Miranda grabbed the waiting bag of trash from the kitchen and headed out the door. She gave her attire a rueful glance, but told herself no one would be hanging around the alley waiting for her to show up looking like a vagabond.

She reached the Dumpster and tossed in her trash, whirling around when she heard footsteps behind her.

"Does that Dumpster make you as misty-eyed as it does me?" Archer looked refreshed. Happy. Miranda tried to ignore her body's surge of remembrance at the sight of his tousled light brown hair and delightful, sarcastic brown eyes. *Well, good for him.* Meanwhile, her hair was frizzy and her bathrobe was ratty. *Great.*

Miranda narrowed her eyes. "Hardly."

"Well, I for one have fond memories of that tin box."

"I believe you're referring to the one behind New Elm Street. But I'm sure you'd fit well in either," she scoffed.

"I've spent some time in both," he replied.

Miranda raised an eyebrow. "I'm not even going to ask."

"That's a good thing for you *and* me." He cleared his throat. "Knowing you as I do, which is not very well..." he winked, "I figured you might want to know where I've been for the last two weeks. But you wouldn't ask me, would you, Miranda?"

"No, I wouldn't." She wrapped her bathrobe tighter around herself. "When a man says 'see you around,' I don't ask questions."

"I'm going to answer them, anyway." He took a deep breath. "When I arrested you...when I... *we* took down Edith's sons...I wasn't actually authorized to do it."

"Oh, God, I knew it. You're not even a Fed, are you?"

Archer's sensual lips curved into a triumphant smile. "Not anymore. I was on suspension during my investigation of Farra's Fortunes. When I brought those thugs in, they reinstated me, but I decided to give my two weeks notice."

"Why?" Miranda asked incredulously.

"I found that I much preferred to uncover the seedy underbelly of small towns like Elmhaven, rather than go for the gold with all of those competitive assholes up at headquarters. So I'm branching out on my own." He handed her a card.

Matthew Archer, Private Investigator.

Elmhaven, MA.

Miranda's heart skipped a beat.

"I'll be able to use a bit more of my, err…*unorthodox* methods as a P.I., anyway."

"Would those methods include seduction of your suspects?"

He hauled her over to him, bathrobe and all. "Only if they're very lucky."

Miranda gave him a pseudo-playful punch. "You're so damn full of yourself."

"So I am," he said. "How about you reform me over a dinner date?"

She wrinkled her nose in response. She wouldn't mind giving Archer another chance, but after all that excitement, dinner and a movie just seemed so…Elmhaven.

"Okay, then. I've got a stakeout tonight. You interested?"

Miranda flung her arms around his neck, grinning as she leaned in to whisper in his ear. "I'll bring the donuts."

About the Authors

A life-long martial arts enthusiast, **Bianca D'Arc** enjoys a number of hobbies and interests that keep her busy and entertained such as playing the guitar, shopping, painting, shopping, skiing, shopping, road trips, and did we say shopping? A bargain hunter through and through, Bianca loves the thrill of the hunt for that excellent price on quality items, though she's hardly a fashionista. She likes nothing better than curling up by the fire with a good book, or better yet, by the computer, writing a good book. Learn more about Bianca D'Arc and her books at biancadarc.com. Read Bianca's blog at: http://biancadarc.blogspot.com.

Always an artist, **Eva Gale** started writing to keep her sanity and instead found her life's passion. She loves thinking up characters and can get happily lost in endless hours of research. Along with other erotic romance stories, she is currently working on a full-length historical romance and paranormal romance. She enjoys reading, hunting for the perfect antique, art shows and gardening. Eva lives in the northeast with her husband and home teaches her 7 children.

Although she appears every inch the well-behaved wife and mother, in her heart **Selah March** is a hellion—contrary, hedonistic and, on occasion, more than a touch wicked. Her twin obsessions with eroticism and the supernatural have found a much-needed outlet in fiction. Through the characters in her stories, she gives free rein to a dark sensuality that might otherwise remain hidden away forever...and wouldn't that be a shame?

A former schoolteacher, Selah resides in the northeastern United States. She holds a B.A. plus graduate credits in English Literature, and is published in short fiction and nonfiction in local and regional magazines and newspapers. She enjoys solitude, long walks after nightfall, and the bracing rigors of a six-month-long winter. For more information, see www.SelahMarch.com.

As the daughter of an ambassador, **Cassidy Kent** is no stranger to overstuffed luggage and airport lounge cocktails. She has traveled the world in search of gorgeous men, scandalous situations, and beautiful backdrops and uses all of these as inspiration for the diverse story webs she weaves. Cassidy resides in the City of Angels for now. Her true identity is a mystery that only she and Thaddeus Brighton (her personal assistant extraordinaire) knows... To learn more about Cassidy Kent, please visit her online home at
http://www.cassidykent.com.

Printed in the United States
126700LV00001B/5/A